Sean Thomas

was born in 1963, in Devon. *Absent Fathers*, his first novel, was published in 1996. A full-time journalist, in recent years his work has appeared in *The Times*, *The Sunday Times* and *The Sunday Telegraph*. He lives in [illegible]

By the same author

ABSENT FATHERS

SEAN THOMAS

Kissing England

Flamingo
An Imprint of HarperCollins*Publishers*

Flamingo
An Imprint of HarperCollins*Publishers*
77–85 Fulham Palace Road,
Hammersmith, London W6 8JB

Flamingo® is a registered trade mark of
HarperCollins*Publishers* Ltd

www.fireandwater.com

Published by Flamingo 2001
9 8 7 6 5 4 3 2 1

First published in Great Britain by
Flamingo 2000

ISBN 0 00 651444 8

Typeset in Giovanni
by Palimpsest Book Production Limited,
Polmont, Stirlingshire

Printed and bound in Great Britain by
Clays Ltd, St Ives plc

For Sarah

Acknowledgements

I should like to thank Tim Cumming and David Crystal for their advice and support; my agents Gloria Ferris and Rivers Scott for the same; Andrew Roberts for a brief but very helpful correspondence; Ray Nichols likewise; and all the editors who have given me employ over the years: Paula Johnson, Nick Foulkes, Anna Maxted, Marcelle d'Argy Smith, Vanessa Raphaely, Mandi Norwood, Ian Belcher, Tom Loxley, Mike Soutar, Grub Smith *et al.*

Further Acknowledgements

The author is grateful to John Murray (Publishers) Ltd, for permission to quote from Peter Vansittart's *In Memory of England;* to David Higham Associates Ltd, for permission to quote from James Lees-Milne's *Prophesying Peace, Diaries 1944–5;* and to The McGraw-Hill Companies, for permission to quote from Eldridge Cleaver's *Soul on Ice* © 1968.

I have quoted the poem *Tip,* from *Slattern* by Kate Clanchy on page 258.

The quotes on pages 259 and 260 come from Craig Raine's *Collected Poems.*

Tom Mitford and I dined at Brooks's. I asked him point-blank if he still sympathised with the Nazis. He emphatically said Yes. That all the best Germans were Nazis. That if he were a German he would be one. That he was an imperialist. He considered that life without power and without might with which to strike fear into every other nation would not be worth living for an Englishman. I absolutely contradicted him.

James Lees-Milne, Prophesying Peace, Diaries 1944–5

That Hitler, he is a fidget.

Woman in a Tube Station, recorded live on BBC Radio, in October 1940, after a large German bomb had just exploded directly overhead.

1

liberty caps

Tony and Eddie and Alex were sitting on the bank, sitting on the grass of Lyonshall Common, by the river Arrow, in the October sun. The St Luke's Summer sun. They were waiting for the magic mushrooms to come on. Young, bright-eyed and twenty, Alex said

— Think I'm getting a rush

Tony nodded and laughed. The three of them had been arguing whether psilocybin semilanceata was superior to psilocybin coprophilia and whether in turn both these mushrooms were outranked for psychotropic properties by Fly Agaric; despite the fact that the last-named made you vomit for several hours. But now the argument seemed pointless. Assessing the smiles of his friends, Tony said

— I'm coming on too

And then they were all rushing, all tripping, all laughing. For hours they lay on the grass bank and counted the clouds and talked about the next year, the last year at college in London. Comparing the flies in the air to raisins in Garibaldi biscuits they talked about girls; comparing the willow twigs dragging in the Arrow to the trailed fingers of girls on Cambridge punts, they decided to walk to the nearest village, to Lyonshall village; to the pub.

Alex was holding a cane of willow with which he was swatting at Old Man's Beard and he was laughing and asking Eddie why he was named after a village.

Eddie replied that the village was named after him. They laughed. Eddie said: likewise the house. They laughed again. Eddie frowned, smiled, and the mushrooms made them all stop and stare at each other and laugh. At last Eddie said, you don't believe me, and he turned on the country road that led to Lyonshall village and he said, let me show you my house, it's across the river

Alex and Tony turned to look at the rushing sweetwater Arrow. At the parkland beyond. Eddie, taller, older, tripping the same as them, said

— Come on, I'll take you there

The afternoon and the mushrooms wore on, wore off; the three of them lay on the grass riverbank by the Arrow and laughed and watched the sunset and Eddie said

— Tony, skin up

The three of them walked lazily and schoolboyishly into town. They lay on Lyonshall Common and grinned. They sat in the village pub, The Love Pool, and drank 6X and swallowed more mushrooms; after that they pushed each other into the walls by the village church and talked about buses back to town. They lay on the riverbank watching the watercress; they watched the water hopscotching over rocks. Like silverheeled girls. The Love Pool. The Love Pool. They sucked and emptied their cans of beer and lying flat on the riverbank, Alex said

— It's getting cold

Eddie laughed and said

— Come on, a glass of hot purl! A dish of deer pie!

Alex looked at Tony in his brogues and old waistcoat, Tony looked at Alex in his rave-top and cap; the two of them shrugged, laughed and sprinted after their older college friend as he led them over the Arrow Bridge and up a lane and down another lane and up to a gateway with mouldering stone lions on its piers. Eddie said the gate led to Lyonshall Park.

Opening the old iron gate with a squeal of effort the three boys entered the park. It was quiet. The sun was setting serenely in the distance; they were walking past a wood.

— M'Ladies Wood

And after Eddie said this they walked up the crunching rubble of the Drover's Road. The warmth of the day was subsiding into autumnal dusks; into the pinks of guelder-rose berries, the reds of dogwood in the hedgerows.

Skirting the boundaries of Moortop Farm they came to the ford of Moortop Stream, where white cattle were knee deep: some cudding, some drinking. The cows regarded them shyly. The three of them forded the stream and walked on up the crest of a slope which gave onto: the view. In the hazy sunsetting distance, in the infinite regression of fading light, they could see turrets, balustrades, windows: the dark massing of a house as big as Lyonshall village. Lyonshall House. Alex looked at Tony who looked with Alex: at the old red bricks, at the raspberry-red walls of the smaller gardens. They saw the swans that sat placidly upon the lake. They saw the hamstone quoining, the black iron rainwater heads, the white tobacco plants under the windows.

They saw. They joked. They laughed. And Lyonshall House stood there in front of them in the half light with her lamplights coming on, a lady in a black dress necklacing herself with the family diamonds.

Striding in time they negotiated the kitchen gardens and walked through a rear door into a warm, brightly-lit dairy. Eddie pointed. Bottles of cordial glowed green in the candlelight behind pots of scoured copper; bowls of leadshot stood beside parades of leather pails. They passed through a final door.

The three of them were in a long room. It was ablaze with light:

with candelabra and chandeliers. As tall as he was young Eddie looked at his friends. His friends laughed at him. He laughed and said all three of them must stay there, at Lyonshall next summer, all summer, when college was over: and as he said this there was an opening of doors at the distant end and a girl walked in with her head held high and Eddie told them it was his sister Elizabeth, and Tony and Alex looked as one and her hair was the colour of yellow flag irises; in her cheeks was the colour of the Lancaster rose.

2

bunny mouths

— I feel like I've been wanked to death by a seven-handed gorilla
— You do look a bit . . . shite
— Thanks
— Take it you're on the gear again?
Eddie shakes his head
— Off it. *Actually*.
Tony:
— So what's the matter then? If you're not doing smack?
Eddie sighs:
— Really don't know. Maybe I should go back on – Demurring at any further questions Eddie looks around him: surveying the hubbub of the restaurant, the tables of people. Then he says
— Guess it's my age
— Thirty-three – Alex smiles – The perfect age for a man, isn't it? Wasn't James Bond thirty-three?
Tony
— And Jesus?
Eddie looks at the centre of the lunch table.
— *Thank you*. Now I feel better

— Can't all have an influential father

Tony says to Eddie

— I thought you were going on that programme, anyway. Where they knock you out for a couple of days and when you wake up you're cured?

— And after forty-eight hours the Lord did rise again

— Waiting for the appointment

— Yeah, right

— Where's our *food*, anyway? – Eddie has changed the subject. As one, the three of them rise, sniff, and scan:

— Here

Her largish breasts jouncing noticeably beneath her white shirt, the waitress leans across and sets a plate between Eddie's shiny cutlery: a plate with a central hump of pink gammon on the bone, islanded by a lake of small dark green peas.

The three of them look at the dish. Eddie sniffs

— What's *that?*

The waitress smiles, slightly nervous

— It's a knoll of gammon

– A knoll? – Eddie wonders – What's a bloody *knoll*?

Silence. Hand on white-aproned hip, the waitress stalls. Then, tucking a curl of dark hair behind her ear she does her best to explain:

— A knoll is . . . a traditional cut. One of our specialities. It's cooked for several hours on the bone to achieve that tenderness, you see, and . . .

And as she talks away Alex looks up at her and he thinks *I want to lift you up and sit you on the table and tear open your lovely white shirt so I can bite . . .*

When the waitress has retreated Eddie turns on Alex and says

— Why *did* you bring us here, Alex?

Alex looks at them, sighs, runs his fingers through his longish black hair:

— It's cool. They're cool as, these restaurants specialising in offal

– Glancing at his old college friend – And seeing as you live about five yards down the road I thought it might be the one place you would be able to find

Hmming, Eddie pokes a fork at the great bony hock of pink flesh sitting on his plate

— Hm

Sensing his old friend's unhappiness, Alex tries:

— Least you know it's fresh, man. That thing – Alex angles his knife like a finger at the thigh of gammon – That thing was probably rolling in shit this morning

— Mm*mmm*

Turning to the returning waitress Alex smiles and reassures:

— I'm sure it'll be lovely, thank you. Could I have another pint of Bass?

Her disappearing backside makes a noteworthy exit. Together Tony and Alex lean across the crisply white-clothed table, over the cutlery, the pint glasses, the small ceramic vase. They compare, they think, Alex says

— Great arse

Tony nods agreement, his wispy red hair lifting in a slight gust from the flapping kitchen door; his balding head shiny in the slants of Spring sunshine lancing down the narrow Smithfield restaurant. Now Tony says

— I had a dream last night

Eddie looks up from his barely touched food:

— Yah?

— About . . . arses

— Arses?

Tony uh-*huhs*, sitting back as the waitress sets a plate of pig's trotters before him. Trying not to start at the sight of the food, he elaborates:

— I had this dream I'd opened a shop called . . . Blokes' Arses

— M . . . ?

— The idea was blokes walked in and sat on the photocopier

machine and photocopied their arses. Then they wrote their phone number underneath the Xerox of their arse, and . . . left the photo in a file in the shop. Then if you wanted to . . . do some bloke up the arse you could come in the shop and look at all the photos of blokes' arses on file and if you liked the bloke's arse in question you could ring up the number underneath

Glass raised, Eddie toasts the room and his friends.

Alex:

— You don't think that could be . . . quite a significant dream?

Tony frowns; Alex says to Eddie

— I wonder what it means?

— Means he wants to fuck blokes up the arse

— Means he wants to open a shop. Imagine – Alex conjectures – Whole chain of them. Printabot

— Maybe – Says Tony – Maybe it just means I need a new woman

Resigned silence. Eddie oversees Tony's plate.

— What *are* you eating, anyway?

— Pig's trotter, I think

Turning to his other friend:

— And you?

— *Andouillettes* – Alex's bright, not-quite-thirty face lights up – *Andouillettes* – Giving his friend a slack-jawed impression – *That's a sausage full of tripe. Doh*

Leaning towards Alex's plate, Eddie pokes at the sausage with his fork, crushes a squidgy slice, and lifts the forked morsel to his mouth. Before it gets there he coughs, chokes, and dumps the slice of sausage back onto Alex's plate.

— The *smell*

— S'hardly surprising, is it? – Alex shakes his head – This is full of – Alex pokes at the slivers of greyish-white meat bursting out the sliced-open condom of translucent intestine – Pig's stomach. That's what pigs' stomachs smell like . . . I guess

— And I take it you are actually going to *consume* that? – Eddie turns to his side. Tony and Alex both stare at their old friend, as he mimes a dry-retch. Suddenly, Tony wonders:

— What did your mother used to call . . . your dick?

His head slightly aside, Alex considers the question

— I don't think she's referred to it directly, of late. 'How's your cock, Alex?' Might sound a bit weird

— I mean – Tony perseveres – What did she call it when you were a kid. When she was potty training?

— Ah.

Two girls walk out of the restaurant; one with hair the colour of cornfields in August, the other with lips that look as if they're always half open. Both of them take mulberry-coloured cashmere coats from the coat-rack. Alex dreams . . .

— Alex?

— . . . My dinky

— Your . . . *dinky*?

— Yeah

Gingerly slicing some pig's trotter into his mouth, Tony chews and swallows and turns to Eddie.

— Yours?

Eddie smiles

— Keith.

— Right.

— I'm afraid it's true

Tony shakes his head

— Your mum called your penis . . . *Keith?*

— Yup – Eddie opens his arms, explainingly – It was probably . . . This is my real mother, my bio-mum I'm talking about here . . . She somehow believed that penises were rather . . . she thought penises were terribly *common*. I mean, everybody's got one, haven't they? So she thought that made them rather vulgar and working class, and of course they do all the most dirty jobs, so she called them Keith. Because she believed that was a *quintessentially* plebeian name

— Keith – Alex laughs – Like it. Suck my Keith you horny bitch – Sinking the last of his pint Alex replaces the surf-bottomed glass on the sunlit tablecloth and chuckles some more; as he does so Eddie turns on the fattest of the three of them, on Tony.

— And you?

— Er?

— What did your mother call yours, anyway?

— . . . My widdler

— Your woodlow – Alex nods – Interesting

— Not my woodlow, my *widdler*

— Something to do with wood, getting good wood, sort of thing? I'm getting woodlow?

— *Not* woodlow. *Widdler*. **WIDDLER**!

The waitress, who has been waiting behind Tony for the last half minute, chooses this moment to cough and collect the plates. White blouse between them, she does a professional smile:

— Can I get you anything for pudding?

Eddie burps and smiles back:

— I'd like some tiramisu. A tump of tiramisu

She looks unsure; Tony says

— Give her a break, Ed

The waitress tells them she'll come back in a couple of minutes. Now Eddie shakes his head at Tony, at Tony's red Irish hair and his smartish tweed jacket and old unmatching stone-coloured strides.

— Terribly *sorry* Tone

— Well, it wasn't even funny. She's only doing her job

Eddie stares. Says

— And who are you to decide what's funny?

Tony stares back, sighs beer

— No-one, no-one . . .

— Irish fuckwit

— Oh great

— By the way have I ever told you how much I hate the Irish?
— Just a few times Ed
— God I hate the fucking *Irish* – Drinking more beer, spitting – The bloody *Oirish*. I mean. *Really*. Why can't you just fuck off home? Can't move for bog trotters in this country. We should have exterminated you properly when we had the chance. In the Famine.
— I'll have the rhubarb crumble – Tony says to the waitress; Eddie continues, giving Alex his let's-wind-up-Tony wink
— When the Scots first got to Ireland, you know what they found?
Alex, smiling
— Sod all?
— Nope – Eddie napkins his lips – They found the natives eating dung and worshipping the moon. Did you *know* that? They're just *abos*, the paddies. Neolithic *gippos* . . .
— And perhaps a coffee. Espresso
Alex returns a wink at Eddie.
— You know what gets *me*, man . . . 'bout the Irish
— No?
— Their stupid naff theme pubs. O'Shaughnessy's. O'Donahue's. Filthy McNasty's Old Whiskey Bollix – Alex leans forward – I reckon if they're going to be authentic they could at least do it properly. Find some *proper* Irish pub names
His taller, older, thinner friend grins
— Such as?
Alex, musing
— The Kneecapper's Arms . . .
Eddie, also musing
— The Ballot Box and Armalite
— The Intercepted Shipment Of Libyan Arms?
Tony sips his coffee, says:
— Yes yes – Wearily scooping some sugar from the jar into

his tiny cup – Just don't get on to Europe . . . Or blacks . . . or women . . . *Please*

Staring at the wood-panelled wall Eddie continues:

— Then again maybe they're niggers. The Irish. Celtic nig-nogs

Alex comes back, straightfaced:

— Mn. I reckon they're more . . . *chocos*. Like the Spanish, and the Italians . . . The Italians are even bigger niggers than . . . the Frogs

— The Frogs must be *niggras* – Eddie returns, sagaciously – Or maybe golliwogs?

— What about the Germans?

— Kikes. Because they eat smorgasbord. Like the Sweaties

— Yo – Alex laughs – *I'm* half-Scottish

Eddie nods:

— I know. But at least you're . . . half-English . . . ?

Alex shrugs:

— Half-Scottish. Quarter Scotch-Irish, quarter-English. Maybe a sixteenth Jap. I dunno – Alex grins, drinks more beer – What about the Japs, anyway?

— *Towelheads* – With an authoritative gesture, Eddie affirms – Definitely. Because they're cruel and heartless with tiny woodlows

Tony, from the end of the table:

— When you two are finished

Alex, ignoring:

— What about . . . Americans?

— That's easy – Eddie nods – Americans are slants. Cause they work so hard. Likewise the Czechs, the Maltese, the

— Cornish?

— Oh *Gaaaaaahd* – Eddie moans, rolling his eyes – How I loathe the *Cornish*. Short-arsed little hairy cunts always complaining about their fucking tin mines and smelling of haddock. *Fuck* the Cornish

— Women?
— Tsch – Eddie emphatically tosses his coffee spoon onto his saucer – Women are *gooks*.
— This is, by the way, hilarious – Tony says, as he folds his napkin and motions to the waitress for the bill. Across the table Alex is agreeing, sort of
— Well . . . I dunno . . . I reckon they're more . . . *dagos*. Women. Y'know? Vain witless braindead *dagos*. 'Where's Canada? Who's Poland? Why don't I ever read a proper newspaper?' – Balling his napkin Alex chucks it at the table – I mean, why *do* women always state the obvious as if it's a major insight? 'That Robert De Niro, he's a good actor. So that's where Canada is!' Jesus. *Birds*. What's wrong with them, why do they go on and on and on and on and
— nnn . . .

Silence descends. Tony, from experience, knows this signals the end of his friends' usual fantasy, their standard drunken rhapsody, their traditional attempt to inflame his soft-Left sensibility. As Alex and Eddie sit back, he brings their attention to the bill
— One hundred and twenty three pounds and eight pence

Eddie whistles.
— You'd have thought fecally-tainted viscera would be a *little* bit more reasonably priced, wouldn't you?
— You're paying for the ambience – Tony says, relieved, despite himself, to be able to rejoin the conversation – Or maybe the waitress's arse

Alex eyebrows him
— Yeah? And I thought you were a toffee-womble. Blokes' Arses, man, *I ask you* . . .

Together the three of them rise and sway beerily down the restaurant so as to collect their macs and coats from an old-fashioned curved coat-rack at the streetside window. As they do the sadness that comes at the end of a boozy lunch, the prospect of the hangover he can expect about six, softly snowfalls on Alex. Maybe he should carry on drinking?

Eddie has already decided

— See you around, chaps – He says, as they hit the cool fresh Spring afternoon air of St John Street. Taxis are cruising up and down; cars and courier bikers and secretaries in flared trousers.

Stood on the steps of the restaurant Alex looks at his taxi-hailing friend, sceptically:

— You're not going off to score, are you?

— Later

Together Alex and Tony watch Eddie crawl inside a cab, watching his too-thin backside disappear within

— Wouldn't get much business at Blokes Arses, would he?

— Mmm – Says Tony.

— Elsewhere?

— Well . . .

— C'mon man. One more pint?

— Why not

Inside the nearest pub, they head for the beer. The pub is noisy, full of after-lunch gaiety, a we've-decided-to-carry-on-drinking esprit. Leant over the littery wooden bar Alex orders a couple of Stellas; then he stands back and looks at his friend, waiting for his friend to say something.

Instead Tony studies his just-delivered pint, studies the tiny bubbles rising to disturb the disc of gold, and says nothing. Alex pays and drinks. The two of them drink and wait and then Tony says:

— Do you remember Gower Street?

— Uh no, I only lived there

— When we were both squatting?

— *Yes . . .*

— Well . . . You remember those hotels opposite the squat?

From a yard away Alex can smell the five pints on Tony's

breath; hear the five pints in his slurred voice. Alex says again yes; Tony says:
— I've . . . never told anyone this about this time . . . but there was this girl – Tony looks at Alex, Alex nods, Tony goes on – Well she was staying in the hotel in the first-floor room, directly opposite my room. She . . . kept on looking at me. We didn't have any curtains, and when she got up I would see her looking at me as I got dressed and she was . . . you know . . . very pretty – Tony drinks, sighs, goes on – Then one day I went to the door after I heard the bell and it was her, this girl, standing at my door, holding a bottle of champagne. Turned out she was American. About twenty. Lovely figure. Really . . .
  Alex grins
— And?
— Anyway she said. 'Can I come in, I've noticed you from the hotel over the road.' and I said, 'Sure.' and she came in and we went up to my room and we started drinking her champagne and we got pretty sozzled. Then I think I went out to . . . Apollo on Tottenham Court Road and bought a bottle of Scotch or something – Tony closes his eyes, concentrating – And when I took it back we just kept on drinking and drinking until she got up and came over to me and put her arm around me. Started kissing me. She was amazing, amazing breasts. I remember she smelled . . . I can still remember it now, right now. So anyway I kissed her back and we rolled on to my bed and . . . she . . . and . . .
— ?
— Threw up. All over. Everywhere
— So?
  Tony looks at his pint, again
— We didn't do it. She was sick for about two hours and finally she fell asleep and eventually I fell asleep next to her and when I woke up she'd gone and there was this note.

Saying sorry. And that was it. I went straight over to the hotel of course but she was out and when I went over again in the evening she'd checked out. Just gone. I didn't even know her name . . . Never even got her name

The pub is noisy, but strangely quiet. All around them is the buzz and the chatter and the sound of the fruit machine; but Alex doesn't hear it. He is looking at his old friend's face. Tony's eyes are shiny and his face is pink and Tony suddenly looks well-over-his-actual-twenty-nine: he looks middle-aged, fat, bald, and defeated, and when Alex says, quietly

— What is it?

His friend shakes his head again, looks down at the swirly carpet:

— Think Elizabeth is seeing someone else

3

good friday grass

just give me the gear just give me the gear ***just give me the gear***
— Everything OK then, Dee?

Brushing some rattish grey hair from her smackworn face Dee coughs, shrugs, and tremblingly reaches for her syringe; pulling away the duvet she momentarily shows her polio-thin legs and her scabby ankles and the yellow colour of all of her body. Eddie flinches, but remembers not to shut his eyes. Dee is searching for a vein in her hip. Or in her thigh. Anywhere.

— Fuck – She says. The needle has missed for the second time. Irritated, Dee stabs the rusty needle back into her thigh and digs around, inside. She twists and gearsticks the syringe, bending the needle into her body, searchingly. *Fuck* – she says again. She has missed, again. Clucking with annoyance Dee decides to go for the last option. She hitches up her left leg and leans her cheek on the knee and stares down at her genitals as this time she jabs the needle into the strip of hairy roadkill that lies between the ripped brown lips of her cunt and the old woman's pout of her arsehole. The needle sinks into the flesh and Dee nods, firms her lips and gazes down studiously as she pumps the blood and the plunger in, and out, and in, and out; like coitus.

Traffic noise. Traffic noise. Slowly Dee closes her eyes and glottal stops; then she moans; then she opens her eyes and looks vacantly at Eddie as if she can't remember who he is, then she falls back onto the bed menstruating blood onto the filthy sheets and she nearly passes out.

just give me the gear just give me

Gazing desperately away Eddie looks out the grimy windows at the trees and the drizzle of Tufnell Park, at the damp blossom on the sills, at the tops of buses occasionally slicing the view in half. Across the road there is an interior scene: of a first floor office where smart girls are selling airline tickets in a room with posters of golden temples in Thailand stuck on the wall.

— Mmnnnnn . . . nnnnnnn . . . – Says Dee, finally. She seems to have emerged from her dream; her dream of not being Dee; her dream of not being a forty-year-old heroin addict, heroin dealer, living in a filthy flat in Tufnell Park with only a criminal son for company . . .

Now Eddie shivers. He has not had heroin in twenty-four hours. His forehead is damp with sweat. He feels bad; he smells bad.

— So . . . *Dee* . . . could I get . . . a quarter?

— Sure – Says Dee, revived and more businesslike – No problem – Leaning over and under the bed, like an adolescent reaching for a pornmag, Dee rummages amongst the plates, knickers, and blooded swabs of cotton wool; as her duvet flaps and wafts Eddie catches a putrid and nauseating smell, of Dee.

He wants to puke; he tries to smile. Dee says:

— A quarter, wannit?

— Yes, Dee. Yes. A quarter

Any minute now? Please?

Trying not to stare, Eddie stares, transfixed, as Dee takes out her little hi-tech dealer's scales, with the small integral mirror and the tiny integral spoon. These scales, Dee's works, are the only thing in the room not crap: not grimed with blood, dried sweat, and dirt. The rest of the flat, in contrast, makes Eddie gag. The filth laps around his feet: discarded chip-wrappers and old vinegar bottles, burnt teaspoons and bowls half-full of congealed Rice Krispies, modest heaps of dog crap and copies of *The Mirror* that have been used as bloodswabs, and lots of pots and pans and plates and balls of fluff: coils of fluff: great piles of weird grey Hooverbag fluff that dustbowl along the floor whenever the door is opened.

— Shit – Says Dee, nodding slightly/slightly gouching. She has spilt a little spoonful of the delicate brown powder on the scales and has upset her delicate calculations.

— Havter start again, Ed. Sorry

— Don't worry – Says Eddie – No great hurry.

Fuck fuck fuck fuck fuck fuck fuck.

The sight of Dee beginning all over again makes Eddie want to cry. The cramp in his stomach is getting worse; the tenesmus in his colon. The urge to crap. *I have to crap.*

Croakily, Dee engages him

— So what've yer been doin then? 'Anging out at that place?

— *Sorry?* What *place?*

— That place. Wassit . . . – She nods, half-asleep for a second. Then perks – Ivy place. *Restaurant*?

Because Eddie is not obviously criminal underclass Dee appears to think he is therefore spending his time at the coolest premieres, the newest restaurants, the smartest book launches, the highest nightlife.

— Actually Dee, I've been sitting in my flat watching game shows. Watching *Countdown*. That's what I do

— Nah, don't believe it – Dee shakes her head, and then seems to expire. Without warning she splutters and croaks in a weird epiglottal explosion, a lethal-sounding throat-rattle that has Eddie thinking wildly about the police, and false names at hospitals, and excuses to nurses: until he realises that Dee is merely ... *laughing*. He has never heard her properly laugh before.

— Posh bastard like you ... – She rattles another laugh.

— I'm not so posh, Dee

— Sure – She makes a sceptical face – Woss your name again? ... Leeonsh ... Leeonshhhh ... Leee ...

— Lyonshall – Eddie gestures the words – *Lion's hall* ...

— Right. And that's not well pukka ... ?

Deciding to accept the compliment, Eddie goes back to studying Dee as she tweezers another quark of heroin from one side of the scales to another. From one side, to another; from one side to another. One side, another, one side ...

HURRY UP YOU OLD WITCH

— There – Says Dee – Hang on while I getyer wrap – Her hand talons across the carpet for a magazine, for any magazine that is not screwed up and thus probably concealing half a kilo of canine excrement.

Handing over a copy of some thin glossy magazine Eddie says – *Here* – Rather testily.

With a suddenly sour expression, Dee eyes him.

Shit, thinks Eddie. *Shit that was dim.* ***Never*** *show them how desperate you are.* ***Never show it.***

— So how's business then? – Eddie tries to change the subject. Dee looks up at a noise

— Oo's that?

A shout comes through from the hall.

— S'me. Dave. Who'd yer think?

— Dyer get the shopping en, nn?

Teen-wearily, the voice:

— *What?*

— Said, did you get the shoppin? I gave yer twenny quid?

Shuffling disinterestedly, Dee's son Dave enters the room, with a baseball cap, and a half-finished goatee, with oily jeans and nineteen years. His face is spotty, and stroppy. He does not acknowledge Eddie; nor does he acknowledge the fact that his mother is sitting half-naked in a bloodstained bed with a bag of brown heroin in her hand.

— 'Ere, 'ere's yer fucking shoppin – The son kicks the Tesco's bag halfway across the room.

Dee raises her voice, pathetically

— Don't you talk to me like that!

Sighing, Dave goes into the kitchen at the end of the room.

— Like what, you old whore?

— Like that! – Dee screams – I'm your mother!

— Yeah, right. So you keep saying

Eyes shut, Eddie rocks slightly, he gently rocks: *this isn't happening,* he thinks. *Don't let it happen.*

Forgetting the half-closed smackwrap in her hand Dee sits up; Eddie feels the inward despair as Dee yells across the flat:

— And you took my last rock, didn't you? You nonce! You took my last rock!

— Did I really?

— Yeah, yeah you did. What you take me for, a *cunt*?

Again Dave rejoins from the kitchen:

— So what if I did anyway? You were fucking out of it. And you owe me one

At this Dee rises and drags half the duvet off the bed, revealing too much of her yellow, unlookatable body.

— You shouldn't talk to me like that. I brought you up. I give you everything. Oo gives you all your rocks and all your smack then! Since you was knee high?

Returned from the kitchen, David stands framed by the door-jamb; munching on a piece of toast and Marmite he gazes flatly at his mother. And says:

— You are one fucking disgusting sight, d'you know that? Look at you. A spiteful old sack of pus. Call yourself a mother. You are a disgrace. You should be put down. They should put you to sleep. Like a dog, like an old *bitch.* All it would take is a simple injection. 'Cept you'd probably enjoy that, wouldn't you?

Heartbeat, heartbeat. Eddie tries not to look, sits waiting for the inevitable.

Then Dee jumps. Like a harpy Dee yells, screams and rockets across the room; through the crap, the filth and the dustballs she sprints until she reaches her son where she lunges at him. In turn he drops the toast and grabs her by the throat, rams her against the wall, and spits in her face:

— Cow

Knee raised she slaps his hand away and slaps his face, but this just makes Dave nastier: like a wrestler he arms her around the head, taking her head in his bicep he holds her steady as her face goes red and then, with a laugh he punches his mother full in the face, once, twice, until a sickening crunch makes them all pause. Eddie gazes about desperately wishing he wasn't here; madly deciding what to do: how to step in, *step out*. Blood and snot are belching from Dee's nose as Dee's son twists and slaps his mother across the face once again as she shrieks, as he says:

— Just give me the fucking money. Where is it? Where's the cash you old SLUT!

— Dive! Dive!!!

She is wailing, writhing, trying to break free; her bare feet kick against her son's shins but he has her firm as he tightens the neck-hold, enabling him to revolve his mother around and suddenly release her – For a second Eddie thinks that it is over, it is OK – But then Dee's son grabs his mother by the shoulders and begins to bang her head into the wall, lazily bouncing it against the wall like a basketball

— Gimme the cash!

— Diiiiiiiiiive! *Pleeeeeeze!*

Someone next door has heard; through the wall Eddie hears a shout. Someone is shouting through the wall. Images of police busting the door flood his mind and Eddie accedes to panic.

His stomach is hurting. He is half standing, half sitting, still panicked. Scanning the floor he sees the wrap that Dee let fall; the beige powder is falling out like powdered gold and this decides him: quickly Eddie fingers the powder back in the wrap and licking his finger he closes the wrap and tries not to listen to the neighbours shouting and Dave slapping his mother and saying:

— What did I do? To deserve a mother like you, *eh*?

— Dave!

— Filthy old Afghan like you, eh?? *Eh??*

Again Dave has thumped her; the neighbours are shouting and hammering; the wrap in his pocket Eddie crouches, stands, readies himself. Pausing not to look Eddie strides urgently across the flat and slips into the hall, then he runs to the door and unlatches it, takes the stairs three at a time; in the corner of his eye he gets a glimpse of neighbours gathered on the landing but he doesn't stay; taking the last five steps in one jump he skids to the front door and opens it and bursts out into the wet cold horrible sweet London air and he runs. Faster. In his trainers and his old leather jacket he runs fast down the street and up a sidestreet and he sees his rusty old car.

My car.

Without looking up or checking Eddie slaps the door open, falls inside the car and pulls the car door shut; in an ecstasy of fumbling he reaches for the glove compartment and takes out a prepared tube of foil; a flatter piece of foil; a lighter. Desperate, but desperately careful, he tilts the wrap and pours a trickle of the brown powder onto the foil; then he takes the lighter and chanks it alight. Next he runs the flame below the foil and uses the tube and inhales the smoke; the drugsmoke; the strange strange smoke; and as he inhales he starts to relax, to unwind, to lengthen, to relax, on the disappearing brown powder, this dessicated excrement, on this powdered evil, this dehydrated Satan, this quintessence of

4

snapdragon

Alex Laughland is sitting in the editor's office at *Cosmopolitan* Magazine for the weekly ideas meeting and he is fretting about his libido. His libido. What is he going to do about his libido? The sun is shining, it is a lovely May day, Alex is trying to concentrate on deputy editor Rachel Levy's important ad hoc presentation about the threat evinced in *Cosmo*'s latest ABC figures by the rise of the new wave of men's magazines with their

I WONDER WHAT HER NIPPLES ARE LIKE?

Oh, for Chri. What can he do? Why is his sex drive always there, always hanging around, embarrassing and crowding him, like a crap flatmate with no friends? Why can't he give it a rest? Why can't it stop?

Hand hung shamefully over an eye Alex enumerates the hours, days, weeks he's wasted entertaining this oik, this embarrassing slob, this crap hanger-on: the months and years spent peering up miniskirts, peeking down summer-blouses, checking out nuns, assessing friends' wives, dawdling by netball courts, staring at obviously underage schoolgirls in swimming pools, ogling sexy girl journos broadcasting from African famine zones, and . . .

Alex inwardly sighs at the very memory . . . flicking through medical textbooks to look at pictures of young women with polio who are also in the nude. Screwing up his eyes Alex attempts to look keen: to focus on the circulation figures that Rachel is breaking down; turning to Alex, Rachel asks
— So what do you think, Alex?
I want to see your buttocks
— Well, I think *Cosmo* has to adapt, without losing its essential *Cosmo*-ness.
Vanessa the editor nods, bouncing her pencil on its end.
— But in what way? Specifically?
Alex makes his special face, his special, concerned, I'm-a-valuable-addition-to-the-team face:
— If we want to liven things up, which we do, and if we want to win back all the readers who are buying *FHM* and *Maxim* and the rest, we could start with being a bit funnier. Bit raunchier. We could use a few more swearwords. All the new lad mags swear like buggery. I don't see why *Cosmo* should be so prudish
Shaking her dark-haired head, Rachel L intervenes, prim but petite in her pink and black-piping two-piece:
— Fuck is out. Company policy
A slight silence. Alex nods
— OK . . . but what about bollocks?
Vanessa hmms, turns to Holly the bubble-haired picture editor:
— Holly? What's our policy on bollocks?
Holly shrugs:
— Bollocks should be OK. Also arse, tit, maybe snatch. Shag is of course OK
— Of course
— There's no way we can use the c-word though
— Clit?
— The other one

— What about spunk, smeg, prick, vag, scrote, gash, wank, frig, wombats, hooters, funbags, knackers and jizz?

A pause. The sounds of the buskers in Carnaby Street waft through the open window, along with a mild, late Spring breeze.

Vanessa smiles, sternly:

— I'm not sure you're taking this entirely seriously, Alex. You are our resident unreconstituted male. *Cosmo*'s very own new lad. We need your input

Alex chuckles:

— I *am* being serious. Just trying to inject a bit of serious humour – An affable smile – I mean, I think that's what *Cosmo* . . . in fact I think that's what all the women's mags lack: a sense of humour. Some self-deprecation

Holly, the bubbly-haired picture ed, interjects:

— You don't think there's a fundamental difference between males and females when it comes to humour?

— Not really . . .

Holly, again:

— But what about that book. *Thingy*. You know . . . mmm . . . Thingy. Men Are From Mars, Women Are From . . . fffrom . . . from . . .

The Andromeda Cluster?

— No – Alex says, firmly – I really don't think that's true. I think *Cosmo* could easily afford to be a bit funnier, a bit more sardonic and self-aware. I mean it's ridiculous that we're not allowed to even hint that women might be in any way slightly imperfect. In my last piece I wrote a para about how women never read newspapers because they are, on the whole, less intelligent than heifers, and it was red-pencilled. The whole para

Rachel laughs:

— I cut that. Because on the whole it's not bloody true

— Yes, it is – Alex says – Women are like those subhuman tribes in New Guinea who can't count beyond two. You know?

The ones whose numbering system goes *one, two, ohh, a whole lot.* Women can only think about things immediately around them. They think *me, you, ohh, the rest of the world.* They're not interested in politics or economics or stuff like that because it doesn't happen within three yards of their person. I bet you don't know the relative size of the UK's GDP in world terms, do you, mm?

Sitting back, gazing at Alex, Rachel says:

— What on *earth* are you talking about?

— The relative size of the UK's economy. Do you have any idea where we stand in world terms? Do we have the tenth largest economy, or the fifteenth, or the fiftieth, mmm?

The buskers outside have stopped. Rachel looks at Vanessa, who looks at Holly, who smiles at Alex and says

— What do you mean by largest?

— By largest I mean . . . largest. *Largest.* When I say the largest economy I mean . . . The Largest Economy.

— Oh. OK. Sorry . . . how about twentieth?

Alex turns to Rachel:

— Rachel?

— God, I don't know. Twelfth? Fourteenth? A hundred and sixtieth?

— Fourth – Alex says – Britain has the fourth largest economy in the world. Just behind Germany, just ahead of France

From the other end of the sun-reflecting table Vanessa says:

— OK, so Britain's got a bigger one than France, but the Germans are better hung than us. Is that what you are trying to say? Why are men so obsessed with size, anyway?

Rachel laughs; Alex laughs:

— Fair enough, I just . . .

— I just want you to give me some ideas, Alex. This *is* meant to be an ideas meeting.

Detecting the tone in Vanessa's comments. Alex nods and obediently fishes out his pad, again.

— OK, yeah . . . um . . . I thought we could do a piece on Men Without Women. I heard an acronym the other day: WANKER. Wife Away, No Kids, Eats Rubbish. I thought we could do a piece on how men cope without women, or not, as the case may be

The three editors are scribbling away: a good sign. Alex goes on

— Also, I thought something on impotence might be interesting. For women to know what performance anxiety feels like . . . You could call it When Your Man's A Flop. A Visit To Softboy City. I don't know. Then you could do one on Why Men Like Underwear. And I think a piece on Why Men Like Porn might be good. And Why Men Do DIY. And Why Men Read Newspapers . . .

And thus the ideas meeting goes round the table, and round the table. And round the table. In between helpful remarks about men's fashion Alex shoots looks at Rachel who doesn't shoot looks back. Something about the slope of her neck, the ski-slope of her neck and shoulder, reminds him of someone, Elizabeth, maybe, maybe Kate, maybe Elizabeth; gazing at Rachel Alex wonders how Rachel would look in his bed: her white body in the dark of his bedroom, the curves of her white flesh looking like snow under moonlight, with its moguls and crevices, *her coldness his warmth, his excitement her love*. He thinks of her naked, he thinks of Elizabeth, he thinks of Lyonshall House, he thinks of Katy, his girlfriend: *her cunt, its cinnamon kiss.*

They are finished. As the ideas meeting ends the four of them file out of the door towards lunch and Alex thinks: why the hell not? And so as Rachel goes before he taps her on the shoulder; her vaguely surprised face faces about, and he asks:

— I don't suppose, you fancy . . . a bit of lunch?

The outer office is a bustle of girls at photocopiers, and

couriers delivering clear shrink-wrapped parcels of clothes for the fashion editor; Rachel turns above the clatter and smiles:
— Sure

Outside in the young sunshine Alex guides Rachel down Brewer Street, avoiding roadworks, avoiding parked taxis, avoiding a man noisily thumping metal beerkegs down a ramp into a cellar; slowly they thread through the stalled traffic of Broadwick to a little Japanese restaurant.

Inside the restaurant they drink water and snap into two their twinned balsa chopsticks; thereafter balancing the sticks on small china wedges. Now they chat; they order; the food comes. Mixing green mustard in soy; eating soft slices of raw fish; taking a sip of hot sake, Rachel says, demurely:
— You didn't seem very . . . happy, in there. In the ideas meet

Undoing the top button of his expensively English shirt, un-throttling his Italian tie, Alex relaxes:
— S'just boredom, Rache. I've been freelancing on *Cosmo* for five years now. There's only so many ways you can say Why Men Are Men, Why Women Are Women, Why The Heck Are You Buying This Stupid Magazine

Shaking her head, with indulgent disapproval, Rachel sips more sake from a china thimble:
— C'mon. It's not a bad mag. It's actually quite good in its genre – She smiles – Although . . . I do agree with what you were saying, about our being a bit funnier and all that. I've been trying to get them to take a few risks for ages. There's a certain amount of inertia at the top. But we still sell half a million copies a month

Salmon, soy, sake:
— Fair enough – Alex says – And you're right, *Cosmopolitan* isn't so terrible. It's just that. I dunno . . . It's like . . . freelancing is like having an endless series of one-night stands. It's immediately

gratifying, you get an immediate high, but in the end what have you got? Yesterday's papers. A lot of rubbish. Whereas . . . – He scratches his neck – if you wrote something . . . longer, that would be like having a serious relationship, it would be significant. And, you know, who knows, you might even leave something, might even make a difference

— You want to write a book?

— Nah, not any more – Vague gesture – But I wouldn't mind doing something other than magazine stuff. Maybe I could do something political. On a proper paper

Dipping her soft maroon slab of raw tuna in her saucer of brown ink, Rachel lifts it to her mouth, and chews, and chews, and her blue eyes sparkle, *sparkle*, and as she eyes Alex, she swallows, and says:

— I didn't know you were so serious. I always thought you were a beer and birds kind of guy

— Well, I'm not

Your tits, your arse, your cunt, your nipples, your pubes . . .

Alex goes on:

— Not totally, anyway. I have other interests, too – Rachel is making a sceptical, *such as*? face. Her lunch-partner elaborates:

— I think about politics all the time. I worry about it. I worry about my country, about her role and destiny – A slight pause, a hint of female incredulity. Alex continues – All that stuff, all that guff about Britain's relative GDP, that kind of thing keeps me awake at night. It's true – She laughs, he doesn't – OK OK perhaps it is just measuring dicks like Vanessa says, but I do worry about it. I worry what will happen if we join the single currency. I worry what will happen if we don't. Will Britain still keep her security council seat? Will we be excluded from the G7? That's the sort of crap that really angsts me out. I'm obsessed with nationality, with Europe, with history and freedom and . . . and

He has spoken too long. Rachel looks like she doesn't know

whether to be bored, or appalled; she is saying nothing. So Alex asks a question:

— I mean: are you patriotic?

— What?

— Do you feel – Alex punches his breastbone, to make the point – Do you feel something in here, in your heart, for your country. For England, for Britain?

— Nope

Mildly scandalised:

— Not at all?

— Not in the slightest – She shrugs, demurely – A country's just a country, isn't it? One country lane is much like another, people are pretty much the same wherever you go. My parents came from South Africa, I've lived here most of my life, but I could quite happily live somewhere else . . .

Exasperated, Alex looks to his side. Murmurs

— The love that dare not speak its name . . .

A longer pause. Alex wants nothing more than to go on, his heart is bursting: he wants to talk to Rachel, to someone, to a woman, to anyone: about his worries, his dissolving sense of identity, about how it is to be a Celt in England, an English Celt. How will he feel if Britain disappears? As the last Briton in England: will he feel like a stayer-on after the Raj, like an ageing memsahib in Simla? Maybe that's all he is *already*. A bit of driftwood left by the final great retreating tide of the British Empire

— Alex?

the Empire whose melancholy long withdrawing roar he seems to have been hearing all his adult life

— *Alex?*

contributing to the corrosive sense of defeat and retreat and decline that has accompanied his every conscious moment

— Alex?

— *Uh*

At last alerted, Alex looks across the saucers of fruit. He can tell by the opacity of Rachel's gaze that he has begun to lose her, in his reverie. This pains him: Alex doesn't want to lose Rachel. She reminds him too much of Elizabeth, or Katy . . .

They finish their plates of sliced orange, they put their hands around their hot china mugs of jade tea; and Alex reverts to type, to charm mode. With revived vigour he talks about his love life, his need for love, his respect for love: deftly, he gives her the vulnerable, emotional spiel; and salts it, too. Gambling on a hidden submissiveness in Rachel's body language, betting everything on a hunch that inside the career woman is a woman who wants nothing so much as to be thrown over a kitchen table and conquered, Alex gazes frankly and gallantly at Rachel as she looks back at him, as he says:

— I suppose what I really want is a woman who is my equal in every way, in every place, except in bed. In *bed* she must *submit*

And it works. As he says the word *bed,* and then the word *submit,* Alex detects the faintest shudder of her shoulders, the tiniest parting of her lipsticky lips. And as she does he knows she is at least hooked; he has gained her genetic attention. Which means, philanderingly speaking, he must end the lunch now.

Ordering the bill Alex signs the cheque with a flourish and swiftly they exit into the traffic and the sunshine, into the whirl of Soho. Standing on the corner of Poland Street and Broadwick Alex turns to Rachel as she looks at him with that shy, well-what-now? expression and again he thinks of Elizabeth, and/or Katy?, as he slaps down the ante:

— What are you doing Thursday night?

A taxi is wheezing on Regent Street; a lunchtime drunk tumbles precociously out of a pub. Rachel is smiling:

— Are you asking me out on a date?

— Don't know. Maybe. No. Yes. I don't know.

— *Right*

Alex makes a face; smiles:

— OK, Rache, I'll tell you what I'm doing. I'm wondering if you are the most beautiful woman in the EU. I'm wondering if you and I should start thinking about schools – Timing . . . – So, yeah: you could say I'm asking you out on a date.
— You've got a girlfriend, Alex
— I've got girl*friends*.

She tips her cheek to a finger, the gold buttons on her jacket catch the sun.

— I've been warned about you. They say you slept with the entire staff of *Harpers*
— Only features. And fashion
— Hm
— I've also snogged *Good Housekeeping*, and been on a blind date with *Woman's Weekly*. Does it matter? Please. I'm dying here. Throw me a line

Turning her head, showing a slope of neck

A slender throat, a white slender executable Anne Boleyn throat

Rachel starts up the road, strolling back to the office; for a second Alex stands there, forlorn, unbelieving, defeated; but then she turns:

— Ring me

5

chokers

— You're trying to tell me you've never bought a pornmag on your own?

Tony shrugs; Alex doesn't

— You're such a *wuss*

Another shrug. They are standing in the drizzle and the bustle of Putney High Street. Buses with high numbers slosh past; sad looking café awnings and gutterfulls of soggy litter and a faint smell of ammonia in the air add to the unappeal of their environs. Tony wipes the wet from his balding forehead and looks at Alex, imploringly

— Go on, please. Remember you in my will

— But I don't understand the problem

Tony spreads his hands

— Look, even if I had the guts to buy it I couldn't buy it here, this is where I get my *Independent* every morning. I don't want my newsagent thinking I'm some . . . appalling old pervert

Alex laughs

— All right, all right. And you definitely want that magazine? Only that one?

— Yes

— Right

Belling the door of the newsgents Alex goes up to the counter, approaches the middle-aged Pakistani in a cardigan, and says

— Excuse me, I was just wondering: do you have a copy of *Big Ones*? The Magazine for Lovers of Large Breasted Women?

The Pakistani looks across his stack of *Evening Standards*, slightly startled.

Alex gestures at Tony outside the shop, at a Tony who is loitering at the window and visoring his eyes and trying to see inside.

— It's for my friend out there, it's his favourite magazine

The shopkeeper double-takes, and then smiles

— Ah yes. Mr Rafferty. Yes?

— Yeah – Alex smiles – The publishing rep, lives at twenty-four. Takes the *Independent*

The shopkeeper gestures

— Of course. Top shelf, on the left

Going over to the top shelf Alex scans, and pulls down a copy of *Big Ones;* with sudden access of curiosity he then grabs a copy of another pornmag: *Forum*. Alex has never read *Forum* before. Paying the money Alex quits the newsagent to find Tony hopping agitatedly from brogue to brogue and whining:

— You didn't tell him it was for me did you? I saw him looking at me. You didn't tell him. What did you tell him?

— Calm down, calm down, I told him zip. Here's your mag you deviant.

Grabbing the proffered copy of *Big Ones*, Tony quickly and guiltily rolls it up, and stuffs it cylindrically in the pocket of his Barbour; they continue walking down the high street in the acid London rain and Alex says

— What time are you picking up Toby?

Nervously checking his watch, Tony says:

— Five. We'd better hurry up or Elizabeth will kill me

— What, because you haven't cooked the dinner and hoovered the house and done all the shopping and fixed the car and given your wife three hours of cunnilingus, what do you expect? This is the new millennium

Tony glances at Alex with such pain Alex wishes he hadn't said what he just said. Tony

— I still love her

— Even though she's having an affair?

— I don't know she's having an affair

— You said she was

— Well . . . Maybe . . . You know . . . it's weird . . . I had this dream last night

Alex rolls his eyes

— Oh Jesus

— It was strange

— Really

— Yes. Really. Really strange. It was very peculiar you see, I discovered you in bed with your mother, you were in bed with your mother in your old flat in Red Lion Square . . . I walked in on you doing it with your mum and I was going to ring the police but instead – Tony frowns, concentrating – Instead of ringing the police your mother invited me into the bed with you both and when I got in she got her breasts out, these huge great breasts, and she started squirting breast milk all over my face

Rush-hour traffic is piling up. Cars are hooting and taxis are doing U-turns; Alex decides to laugh

— You're totally fucking weird, aren't you?

Tony, mournfully, looking down at his damp green corduroys and his sodden brown brogues:

— I must be. Otherwise why should I still love Elizabeth

— Huh. Bitch on a stick

— Sorry?

— You said it. She *is* having an affair, isn't she?

Tony nods

— I think so. Don't know . . . but I think so

— So what are you going to do about it?

Tony flicks back his few forelocks of red hair and shrugs to say *what can I do* so Alex says
— Why don't you pay her back, have an affair yourself?
— I couldn't
— Why not, give her a taste
— No, I mean. I *couldn't*. I don't know how to. I've forgotten how to do it. How to chat up women. Where to take them. I've virtually forgotten how to make love
— What about that chick in Waterstone's in Hampstead, the one you said kept giving you the eye?
— I think she has a cataract
— Seriously, man – Alex sighs as they turn left into a nondescript street of redbrick semis – Just go up to her and say 'Would you like to go out with me one day', it's not hard

Over the collar of his Barbour Tony looks at his friend with incredulous apprehension, as if his friend is suggesting a particularly difficult route up K2
— But where on earth would I take her?
— Somewhere neutral – Alex smiles, reassuringly, professionally – Take her to . . . a gallery . . . the Hayward. That always impresses 'em. Makes you appear cultured and unpushy and yet also oddly romantic

Unsurely Tony nods and shakes his head but before Alex has time to continue his 'suasion they are walking up a short gravelly path, knocking on the door, and being ushered into a house full of children, one of whom is Tony's.
— Daddy daddy daddy daddy

Gathering his breathy excited ugly three-year-old son into his arms Tony breaks into a wide smile, and Alex notices this is the first genuine smile Tony has cracked all afternoon. As Alex looks on Tony chats with the childminder and gives her some money and all the time Tony upholds and squeezes his son who giggles and hugs his father's neck: causing Alex to experience the usual mix of sheer-relief and shameful-envy that his own childlessness affords him whenever he is confronted by his friends and their children. The childminder asks after Tony's daughter: Tony tells her that baby Polly is getting on fine and that she is staying with her grandparents for the week as she recuperates from a bug.

Outside Toby holds daddy's hand and yells

— Ice cream, ice cream, loppilop?

— Fucking terrorist cunt, look at him, IRA scumbag

Tony laughs

— He's only three

— I know, but still

Toby looks big-eyed up at Alex and says

— Canlhavenicecreem?

Alex has an urge to tousle his friend's son's corn-in-the-rain coloured hair but he says, instead

— No. You nonce

Tony shakes his head and half laughs at Alex

— You're just a big softy at heart, aren't you?

— You got it

Stopping at the corner of Tony's street, they both vaguely survey a row of rain-wet cars flashing in a watery new sun.

Tony:

— Quick beer?

— Why not

— She's due about seven

— Quick couple of beers then

Inside the house Tony goes to the fridge and collects a beer and hands it across; Alex ringpulls it open and sucks at the socket and jibes at the metallic taste. Tony says

— Make yourself at home, I've just got to feed Toby. But . . . – Tony looks sheepish – Erm, if you're going to smoke, do you mind blowing it out of the window or through the letter box or something?

— I've got to smoke through the letter box?

— Elizabeth notices the smell

— Elizabeth . . . *what*?
— Notices the smell
— But she smokes, doesn't she?
Tony, sheepish:
— Yes, but . . . you're virtually my only friend who still smokes. If she smells the fresh smoke she'll know you've been here and then she'll . . .
— She'll what? Stop having an affair? Stop denying you sex?
— She'll know *you*'ve been here
This pains Alex; he tries not to show it; as a diversion he laughs, flippantly
— Still hates me that much, eh?
— . . . I wouldn't . . . It's not that bad
Can in hand Alex points round the can with a forefinger, at his old college friend
— It is, Tony, it *is* that bad. Look at yourself. She's screwing your whole life up. She dominates you, totally
— Maybe . . . Toby, put that away!!
Tony is stooping to remove a sharp kitchen knife from his son's chubby little hand; Alex snorts:
— Where's your stereo, then?
— In . . . the bedroom . . .
— In the bedroom?
— Yes . . . In the . . . wardrobe
Alex tuts:
— You love music, Tony, why do you let her get away with it?
— She says it spoils the look of the sitting room
— Your guitar?
Knife in hand, Tony gazes ruefully at the fridge
— Sold it, so we could get a sofa
— Jesus. Christ. What are you like? You stupid . . . sofa buyer
— I still love her, Alex. S'not that easy
And the wet glint in his eye confirms that it isn't; confirms that Alex should lay off. Elizabeth is, as Alex knows, a touchy matter

between them at the best of times: for so many reasons . . . Right now she is virtually combustible. Explosive. Cursing himself for being so dim as to harp on the topic most likely to divide Tony and him, on one of the few occasions they get to drink together, Alex goes into the sitting room and pulls out a cigarette and cranks open a window, and blows his bluesmoke out of the window. Regretting. Wondering. Listening to his friend feed his son in the kitchen.

Alex shouts through:

— How often do you wank?

A shout back:

— What?

— *I said, how often do* you wank?

Alex has dropped the volume at the end of his sentence as Tony has come through, carrying his own end-of-the-day beer can. Stella up, Stella down, Tony tilts his balding head to one side and muses:

— Once a day. Sometimes twice . . .

Alex nods:

— Same as. Do you think that's a lot?

— Er, probably

— Where do you do it?

— Usually in the bathroom – Tony thinks – Sometimes in the kitchen, into the bin – A bashful, tipsy grin – Sometimes I use an electric toothbrush to . . . you know . . . Elizabeth's always wondering why the electric toothbrush keeps turning up in the kitchen – Another gulp of beer, discreet belch – And sometimes I do it in here, front of the telly

— Tissues?

— No. Not usually

Alex laughs

— Nor me. My flatmate caught me wanking over *Blue Peter* the other day, in the middle of the arvo, onto the carpet. There were all these girl gymnasts

Suddenly Tony stiffens to alertness as if he can hear his son crying in his bedroom; when Tony is reassured that his son is undistressed, he stretches his legs and relaxes once more, and then he and his old friend drink a couple of beers, and a couple more beers, talking the while, shooting, liming. Alex tells Tony he's got this new kink, this new thing he likes to do with his girlfriend, with his teenage girlfriend Katy: Nude Hoovering. Tony laughs, appreciatively. Deciding he's on a roll Alex tells Tony about another time, the other day, when Alex successfully persuaded Katy to clean his entire bathroom in a miniskirt and no knickers. Now they both laugh and Tony says 'Bottomless bath-scouring, excellent,' and Tony shakes his head and then they drink, and laugh, and drink, and talk: about the World Cup, and Brazilians, and girls' arses, and summer dresses, and the cricket, and the English class system, and Eddie Lyonshall, and drugs, and Steely Dan, and the disturbing size of most dildos.

Two hours later Elizabeth walks in the door and down the hall where Tony is on his own in the kitchen watching TV news. They exchange smiles, glances, nods. Elizabeth looks tired but still sexy. To Tony she looks intolerably chic and sexy in her cashmere jacket, her shortish skirt and slim black shoes. His desire for her pains him.

Setting herself down on the sofa in the corner of the big wooden kitchen Elizabeth crosses her legs, rubs her workweary face, tilts her already tilted nose, and lifts her azurite Lyonshall eyes to Tony and says:

— How are they?

Tony says their son is fine and asleep, their baby daughter better and coming home soon; but all the time he looks at his wife and just wonders if she really is having an affair, the affair, that affair that would explain why he feels so bad.

Ask her, ask her, ask her

— How was your day?

Elizabeth sighs and stretches, and quietly says

— All right. I had lunch with this guy from the Paris office. Nice chap, terrifically good manners. Why are the French so much more formal than the English? I've always thought it was meant to be the other way around

So it's him, Tony metaphorically slaps his forehead, *of course. Some smoothie French bastard. Should have known. Some rich Parisian stud, some well-hung besuited French bastard who makes you come until you cry out your father's name, who makes you scratch his back until the blood comes dripping like your tears*

— You look a bit tired – He makes a uxorious gesture – I've got supper ready – Pointing at the oven – Do you want some?

She looks at him, he sees the pity, the *pity.*

— Thanks . . . I've got to go out later on though . . . Some boring drinks thing . . .

— Of course

Tony wonders if he should hit his wife. He loves her. He hates her. She merely appears to have pity and contempt for him; he is trapped; he lays the supper on the kitchen table; uncorks the wine. Tony wonders how you can payback somebody who has nothing but pity and contempt for you. How can you hurt someone you love who doesn't love you? You can't.

Glugging the wine into a glass Tony coughs and looks at Elizabeth as she gets up and goes to the fridge and looks at the photos of baby Polly magnetised to the fridge door.

Ask her ask her ask her ask her ***ask her***

— Elizabeth . . .

Polite:

— Yes?

— I was just thinking . . .

— . . . Yes?
— Well. I was just thinking do you think we should have a dinner party? It's been a while . . .

Distracted by something Elizabeth says something: she mumbles, she equivocates. Tony repeats the question. She turns and shrugs her already slender shoulders:
— Why not. If you really want to. Who were you thinking of inviting?
— Just some friends . . . I thought, I thought – He breathes, breathes out; then he says it – I thought we could invite Eddie and Alex

A quietness. Then the predictable:
— Alex? You want to invite *Alex*?
— And Eddie
— You want to invite Alex and Eddie? – Not tired now, she is staring straight over, staring him out – Are you . . . – His wife is uncharacteristically flustered – You're wholly serious about this?

Is he serious about this? Tony quizzes himself. *Or is he just trying to hurt her, just trying to hurt her for something he's not even sure she's done?*
— They are my friends; Eddie *is* your brother
— Anthony, they are both idiots; Edward is a junkie

Silence fills the house, apart from the sound of Toby, waking, upstairs. The two of them stare across the scarred, baby food-stained, once-used-for-shagging, bleached pinewood kitchen table of their eight-year-old marriage; Elizabeth goes to speak. But stops. Tony can sense Elizabeth sizing things up. He wonders if she will accept; he wonders if she will respect him for insisting. Then he wonders whether, if she does accept, her acceptance will be predicated on the fact that she is having an affair and therefore feels guilty enough to allow him a dinner party she would otherwise forbid.

At last, Elizabeth makes a surrendering gesture; going through to the stairs to go up to their son's bedroom to sort their son she says nothing; then she just says, Parthianly, over her cashmered shoulder:

— You can do the cooking

6

mother of thousands

— A man should love his God, his country, and his parents. For only then can he love himself
— What an *utter* load of rubbish
Alex laughs:
— You think? I was gonna put it in an article
— For a start you despised your father
— May he rest in peace, the old git
— And you're at best agnostic
Alex:
— I'm not so sure about that . . .
— And you're completely schizophrenic about your identity
— Well at least I don't spend my time despising *me*
— *Que?*
— All your . . . atheism – Alex is speaking louder – It's just self-hatred. To hate God that much you must have hated your father, your fatherland. *The things that formed you.* Which is my point, y'know?
Eddie considers this, replies
— Britunculus
— Come again?

— *Brituncculus*, means Celtic pleb
— Right
— It's true
— No I believe you . . . *Suthangli cunt*
Eddie's turn to laugh
— Sorry?
— Suthangli. Means southern English twat . . . – Alex shrugs, verbally – Sort of

A silence. Eddie necks the receiver so he can light another cigarette, then returns to the conversation
— Anyway you missed out *school*, in your list
— Wassat?
— A man is surely made by his school. Formed by his schooldays as much as his parents or whatever. Surely?
— Mmmm . . . Ooooo . . . Jesus . . . ohhh . . . you . . .
— Uh?
— Fffwwwwww . . . wwwwwwww . . .

Mystified by Alex's latest phone-noises, Eddie grinds out his cigarette butt in a saucer, wanders over to the window of his bedroom, and stares across Smithfield roundabout as far as the TV cameras picketing the entrance to the Old Bailey. Eddie says, at last, interrupting the gabble:
— Alex? Hello?
— Sorry. Walking down Oxford Street. Birds everywhere.
— Of course
— It's not right, y'know
— Sorry?
— Girls, man, girls – Alex laughs, then stops laughing – Jesus. Look at her. Talk about hooters. Have you ever thought about it?
— Who? What?
— Women – Alex says – We've got nothing in common with them, they talk a load of pants, they're dull as fuck in the main, yet we're forced and I mean FORCED to spend time with them

just because they've got two bumps on their front and a different hip-to-waist ratio

— I see

— S'enough to make a man not believe in God, dirty *slut*!

— Is it?

Alex laughs:

— Nope. Yep. Dunno . . . What were you saying?

Watching the stethoscoped Bart's doctors as they move from Little Britain to Radiology, Eddie dredges the riverbed of the conversation:

— I was saying School must *surely* have as much of a determining influence on a man's make up as one's absent parents or a non-existent God

— Oh, Yeah . . . – Alex's voice goes indistinct again. Over the mobile-phone airwave Eddie can make out the noises of Oxford Street this bright afternoon: the chatter of schoolgirl shoppers, the BritPop blaring from clothes shops, the megaphoned shouts of hawkers in temporary warehouse-stores

— Sorry. 'Nother one. Jeezusss

— *Really*

— Really. Swear I could see the otter's pocket. I can! I can see her sodding monkey! Man. So is that why you're such a self-hating wanker, cause of that weirdo public school you went to?

Eddie smiles

— Perhaps . . . All my school was designed to do was churn out viceroys. And rear admirals. And governor-generals of Singapore

— Not a heck of a lot of use when Singaporeans are governing Singapore

They both go quiet. The phone dropped for a moment, Eddie flings up the sash bedroom window, thus to give his papal blessing to the sweet warm dieselly City air; then picks up the phone and goes on

— You know, I was *thinking* about this – He leans one hand on a window-frame – I worked out the other day virtually all of my peers are either doing drugs, or in the City. It was almost as if that was the *only* choice we had

— Half your peers *were* peers

— QED

— And you chose smack. Nice one, dude. You could be earning half a million pounds a year but instead you're wasting your Trust Fund on heroin

— Things could be worse . . .

— You could be dead. Fuck!

Eddie yawns, wearily

— Another girl?

— No, just remembered, features meeting . . . hold on, crossing the road

Eddie listens to Alex cross the road, listens to him saying:

— Look you bastard the lights are red so that means you have to stop just because you've got a big new cycling helmet for Christmas doesn't mean so are you going to Tony's dinner party?

— Yah, *probably*. I thought my sister had blackballed us for *ever*?

— She does. She has. I think she's letting him invite us to make up for the fact that she's having sex every day not with Tone

— Sweet

— Thought so too. Poor bastard – Alex sighs – OK, gotta go big guy. Keep off the beige

Alex's line clicks into quietness. Eddie shakes his head at his friend and wanders through into the living room of his flat and thinks

Trust Fund? If only.

Settling down at the coffee table, sweeping away straggly bits of tobacco, tiny mouse-droppings of hashish, burnt slips of tin foil, and six or seven rejected cardboard roaches, Eddie gets out his laptop, and his folder of false personae. As he does so he estimates, just as he does every time he does the books, exactly how much he has made through defrauding the Department of Social Security over the past seven years and when he comes up with the figure of *over a quarter of a million pounds* he smiles quietly to himself.

His attention on the thick file of documents, Eddie documents the progress of the various false identities he has stolen and/or concocted over the years.

Most of them are doing quite nicely, he decides: extracting half a dozen building society letters and other bank statements he notes how the welfare benefit-money has been paid directly into their respective accounts, as per, thus saving Eddie the unsavoury hassle of having to personally sign on, or personally cash any giro cheques. The reason Eddie doesn't have to sign on for his various false identities, and again Eddie smiles for the *n*th time with sincere satisfaction at the evidence hereby adduced as to his own cleverness, is that a number of gullible doctors have been convinced, by Eddie, that these false personae are schizophrenics or alcoholics or otherwise mentally disabled. As disabled people they do not have to attend any government offices in person; as disabled people they do not have to even be eligible for work; as disabled people their monies are paid directly into the various bank accounts that Eddie has set up for them.

So who needs a Trust Fund?

Unfortunately for Eddie, two of the false identities Eddie is using are causing him some concern, this afternoon. The first, Jimmy Robinson, a thirty-three-year-old unemployed actor allegedly living with his common-law wife and three children in a small maisonette on the Kentish Town Road, possesses the name and National Insurance number of the real Jimmy Robinson, one of Eddie's schoolmates who went to live in Hong Kong ten years previously. As Eddie well knows, as indeed Eddie learned from an intermediary just last week, Jimmy Robinson, the real Jimmy Robinson, is intending to return to England shortly. Given that the real Jimmy Robinson is more than likely to be taking up full-time employ in the UK (thus utilising his, Jimmy Robinson's, one and only genuine National Insurance number), Eddie knows it is imperative he *disappear* the fictitious Jimmy Robinson forthwith, lest the authorities get a sniff of fraud.

Pity, Eddie thinks, *just as the eldest Robinson child was about to get brain damage . . .*

Tapping into his laptop Eddie makes a note under the name Robinson, James: *Terminate Claim*. Then he turns to the second problematic ID: Mark Foster, thirty-one-year-old bachelor with a booze problem. At his basement flat in Poplar, in reality a windowless cellar for which Eddie pays a helpfully devious landlord twenty pounds a week to keep as an empty letterdrop, 'Mark Foster' has recently received a missive from the DSS, requesting further proof of his alcohol problem. If this proof isn't furnished, as Eddie knows, the DSS will soon cease pumping Foster's dole money straight into his bank account, and they will require Mark Foster to sign on in person.

Actually sign on? For all the warm air breezing in through the windows, Eddie shivers. He hates having to sign on: will go to great lengths to avoid having to sign on . . .

How to avoid signing on?

Sunk in thought, Eddie twiddles with the keys of his laptop. As he writes lpsfhgigkjghdabvbvbvngnng,g,ggkjgjgjhjjhltjktyuty across the top of the screen, he props a chin in the other hand, and muses. What to do with Mark Foster? To go to a doctor and actually fake serious alcoholism would be as difficult as it would be unpleasant. For a start he'd have to drink gallons of cider for a fortnight; and he'd have to feign delirium tremens, and he'd have to come off the heroin so he could act drunk rather than addicted. Yes, he'd have to come off the gear, come off the gear, come off . . .

Yes!

Erasing the gibberish from his laptop screen Eddie clicks into the file marked Foster, Mark, and makes a note:

Register As Heroin Addict At Private Clinic.

Eddie wonders why he hasn't thought of this before. By registering at a clinic he can score some methadone and Temazepam as well as get *Foster, Mark* off the hook: thus killing two birds with one extraordinarily handy stone. With a smug shake of his head Eddie leans across the table and takes his reward for being, once more, so incredibly smart: languidly Eddie locates his little wrap of heroin. After un-origami-ing the slip of paper Eddie tips enough powder onto a sheet of foil, takes a matchbox, puts a tinfoil tube in his mouth, sandpapers the match, takes the yellow flame to the foil: and inhales the resultant helix of browny-grey heroin fumes: slowly, lovingly, decadently, helplessly.

Kissing the syphilitic whore on the lips.

Later, how much later he doesn't know, Eddie wakes, stirs, wonders. It is night. Outside he can hear the first lorries arriving at Smithfield Market, the shouts of bummarees unloading the half-frozen pink-and-white pig carcasses from the chillwagons. From Cowcross Street come the whoops of drunken medics falling out of The Hope. Perhaps, Eddie muses, perhaps he should find another identity to keep up his income: if he's going to kill off Robinson, James. *Which he must.*

Unsteady on his feet, Eddie slouches across the pinhole-burnt carpet to a book-rack full of P.G. Wodehouse and Terry Pratchett. Between *Carry on Jeeves* and *Wyrd Sisters* Eddie finds his old school's most recent yearbook. Sprawling on the floor in front of the bookcase Eddie riffles through the yearbook's glossy pages, past the pleas for money, the sports reports, the gloating editorial announcing the arrival of an Arab Prince's son, until he reaches the 'Who's Doing What' section. Amongst the oldish old boys and newish old boys are a number of Eddie's school contemporaries; their rounder-than-he-recalls faces stare out at Eddie: reproachful, conspiratorial, tragicomical.

Stoned, Eddie looks at the names. Henderskelfe. Knollys. Cantalupe. Walrond-Drage. Entertained by the fine high ultra-pukka Englishness of the surnames, quite beautiful in their way, Eddie tries to put histories and outcomes to these his school-mates' ageing faces. Henderskelfe, Nenderskelfe, Schmenderskelfe. Used to be governor-general of Tanganyika. No. Not Him. His great grandfather that was. And where was Jamie Henderskelfe now? Earning £300,000 at Credit Suisse First Boston, sod him. And what about Justin Cantalupe? Great great uncle was Admiral of the Blue. So where was Justin Cantalupe now? Doing about five grams a week.

And so Eddie spends an hour:

> de Tollemache, Jonathan David, class of 1988, great great uncle accepted surrender of German authorities in Holland, £150K dealing Swiss Francs for Chemibank.
>
> Walrond-Drage, Ralph, class of 1987, great great great grandfather commanded British forces in victory over the Zulus at Ulundi, £500 on rocks.
>
> Slater, Simon Mark, class of 1988, father assisted in the devising of the Colossus decryption device at Bletchley Park, Yen/Dollar futures.
>
> Conyers, Henry Auberon Marcus, class of 1989, great grandfather VC'd at the 2nd Ypres, methadone.

At the bottom of the page, just as he is about to give up, Eddie lights upon a likely candidate. A *perfect* candidate:

> Caldicott, Matthew Jago Robert Broadwood.
>
> Since leaving School in 1986 Matthew has lived in

> Los Angeles where he has pursued a career in film and television. After appearing in several daytime TV dramas Matthew has decided to concentrate on the distribution of British films in the United States. Anyone wishing to contact Matthew can reach him on 001 212 333532...

Tongue-tip between lips, Eddie makes a careful note in his laptop. *Get Matthew Caldicott's National Insurance Number*. After that, as Eddie knows, it will be easy. Face blued by his laptop screen Eddie mentally runs through the rigmarole that will come thereafter: how after obtaining Caldicott's NI number from the dole office on the basis that he has been working abroad all his life until now, he will take a driving test in Caldicott's name, then get a licence in Caldicott's name, then open a bank account in Caldicott's name, then claim income support in Caldicott's name, then claim to be a paranoid schizophrenic in Caldicott's name by going to see a doctor and bellicosely accusing the doctor of sleeping with Caldicott's mother, and then, and then, and then . . . and then just sit back and let the money roll into the fictitious bank account of Caldicott, Matthew Jago Robert Broadwood.

Gear?

Foil in hand Eddie saunters back into the bedroom of his flat and stares out across the lamplit expanses of Smithfield roundabout. Lorries come, taxis go. Lighting, flaming, chasing, inhaling, Eddie holds his breath, exhales, reaches down to a shelf to give himself a final reward: a long fat Cuban Cohiba cigar. Guillotining the cigar end Eddie wonders whether anybody else has ever discovered the pleasure of combining heroin and Cohibas. It is, he considers, perhaps the ultimate cocktail of pleasures. Better than fellatio and ecstasy. Better than snobbery and cocaine. Better than fox-hunting on angel dust.

Torching the end of the cigar Eddie puffs, enjoying his last smoke of the day/the first before breakfast. Subsequent, quiescent, Eddie watches the meat-market juggernauts awkwardly negotiating the red-and-white plastic barriers in West Smithfield: installed so as to exclude IRA bombers from the Square Mile. Quiet and tranquil, Eddie reads the long white sides of the huge meat lorries: Rudland & Shorts; Hopkins and Sons; Roy Graham Refrigerated Containers. As the night wears on he listens to the whoops of the nurses getting drunk in the Robin Brooke Centre. As night turns around Eddie stands and surveys the great Victorian buildings of Smithfield Market; the great big copper-green cupola'd buildings so beautifully, so recently, so lovingly restored: and as Eddie looks at this he teeters, suddenly, he pulls up, he stops and looks down and sees the depths of freezing lethal blue water beneath the thin ice of his self-esteem and he is lost, he falls, he goes through the ice: and now he is thinking of his addiction, of his wasting life, of the cleverness he is squandering on a life defrauding the dole when he could be – what – anything – just anything – and instead here he is spending his time making up lies and smoking heroin and making up more lies and smoking more heroin and before he bursts into terrifying tears Eddie just manages to find his foil, flame up a dragon, inhale the smoke, and hold the analgesic smoke inside just long enough to save himself from the truth, to haul himself from the fatal water, to throw himself a lifeline of lies, to convince himself that everything is OK, that he's still got time, that he's still young, that one day he'll come off the drugs, that one day he'll do something, one thing, anything, that one day he'll do anything but this but for now he'll have just one, just one more, just one more

Blankly Eddie stares out the window.

Rudland & Shorts. Hopkins and Sons. Roy Graham Refrigerated Containers.

7

snow piercers

— OK, we've done nude hoovering. We've done knickerless ironing . . . What next?
— I'm trying to do my maths homework.
— So?

Alex is lounging on the bed in his eighteen-year-old girlfriend's bedroom, listening to her mother do the washing up in the kitchen downstairs, listening to her unemployed brother play the guitar in the bedroom next door. It cannot be denied, Alex thinks, he may be prematurely balding and a bit of a weirdo but Katy's brother plays the guitar extremely well. Even as Alex is thinking this a soaringly Clapton-like guitar lick comes carolling through the thin dividing wall in this small house in outer London: and it occurs to Alex that the sweet sassiness of a Fender Strat riff, the raffish parabola, is much like the place where Katy's small-waisted back casually curves and swings out to her succulent arse

— I know – Alex suggests – Topless Homework

She gives him that look, that dangerous smile: she pushes back her longish black hair: gives him her smart, hostile expression
— You want me to do my homework with no top on?

— Er, yeah . . .
— You're not weird at all, are you? I mean, is this NORMAL? You're the first really old bloke I've been out with

Alex chucks a pillow at her; she punches it away, says:
— If you give me sixty quid I'll do it, topless. But only one question
— Sod that. I'll buy you a drink
— Don't WANT a drink. I don't want anything from you. I don't want your money. Pay for my driving lessons then

Again she laughs, again he looks at the smallness and the sharpness of her teeth; her cat-like teeth, her white skin; her dark eyebrows sceptically raised . . .

For one of those swaying, highwind moments Alex feels and fears, as he always feels and fears when he is with Katy, that he might be falling, falling in love with her. That he might already be in love with her. Manfully he pushes this concept of the inconceivable out of his head. Elizabeth was the only woman he had ever loved, could ever love, would ever love: surely. He had built his whole adult life around that idea, he had laid wreaths every month on that necessary idea, he had predicated and blamed all his last ten cynical years on the somehow just and righteous bleakness of his Elizabethlessness – so it was impossible that Alex could love another; absolutely and utterly impossible; particularly if that other was a difficult, moody, fierce, strange, inexplicable, annoying, devious, monosyllabic *eighteen-year-old.*

For the third time in half an hour Alex looks around the schoolgirl bedroom: at the accoutrements of immaturity: the poster of a hunk holding a baby, the pop concert tickets thumbtacked to the wall, the pink fluffy pig by her pillow, the surfboy magazine, the small jelly dragon on a shelf, the school assembly photos of the Lower Sixth (which Alex surreptitiously ogles when Katy isn't looking). His survey over, Alex despairs of himself. *I have nothing in common with this girl,* he decides. *I actually don't like this girl. I maybe even hate this stupid girl.*

— So you want me to take my top off?
— Gnnnmm . . .

Autistic, Alex nods. Katy laughs. Evincing that bogus coyness, that playful reluctance which always delights and infuriates, Katy openly laughs at Alex's helpless masculinity as she says

— OK but only if you turn around

Obediently Alex turns his face to the wall.

Once revolved, Alex sees, however, that he is still able to see: Katy in the mirror; breathless he spectates, gripped he watches her peel away the top over her head, over the topknot of her tumbling hair. His breath gets locked in his mouth as he gazes and mutely adores as she reaches around and squeezes to unhook the back of her bra, as the bra comes away and the effortless breasts spring out and go

Up . . .

Immediate on seeing this Alex's stomach and heart fill with cold liquid metal, with pain. Shuddered, he closes his eyes and tries not to think: on the fact that he will not always be here with his girlfriend to see her semi-naked, will not be here with his lovely adolescent mate, will not always be annoyed by her immaturity, her silence, her arrogance, her quickness, her wit, her eyes, her hair, her youth, her breasts.

— OK saddo. You can look now

Turning away from the mirror Alex looks: Katy is, indeed, doing her homework with no top on. She has a big ring binder on her lap; a calculator on her knee; she is writing something on some blue feint A4.

Alex is particularly enraptured by the way her breasts jiggle forward, slightly, with each jerking scribble of her chewed-to-bits pencil.

Later he is taking her jeans off and wondering why she never wears stockings:

— Why don't you ever wear stockings?
— Because you want me to wear stockings.
— Katy, would you ever say that you are in any way a tad fucking contrary?
— No. I just do things to ANNOY you
— Katy . . .

She squirms, delightfully, in his arms, like a rare jungle cat, a civet, a serval; this thrills him, the rare felinity of her, the precious animality. Holding Katy, Alex sometimes thinks of the cruel wound she could inflict with just a word, a scowl, an insult, an outright refusal to undress for him; often when he gropes and manhandles her Alex feels like he is playing with a particularly sexy man-eating leopard-cub . . .

Up on the ells of his arms Alex looks down into Katy's uplooking eyes, and tries again to describe to himself the colour: the colours of her extraordinary eyes. Whereas the rest of her, of Katy, could be taken for a dark-haired, white-skinned, only slightly off-race English girl: her truly remarkably mixed-race background is forever revealed, exposed, mineralised in the blue-grey-brown-green of her extraordinary irises: the flecks of Portuguese gold and Pakistani golden-brown, the misty Northern blue and grey: it is all there, forever, precious stones set in the gold of his memory, Fabergé'd by his memory.

— Here, let me

Helpfully Katy unsilverstuds the top of her jeans; assisted Alex pops the rest of the fly buttons; working as a team they lift her up and pull the jeans down her soft white legs and with rising panic Alex unlaces her small Doc Marten boots.

— Why don't you ever wear girly shoes?
— Why don't you ever wear HATS?

Peeling the boots off one by one he strips her socks and kisses the instep of her small feet, kissing along her calves he feels the prickle of her unshaved legs, the prickle like when he used to kiss his father when he was a child. Further up her thighs Alex inhales her teenage skin and then between her legs he nuzzles for her place, the place, the place where God knifed her; he is hungrily licking her thick pubic hair and he is reminded how she never shaves her pubic hair: as he loses himself in the soft sabled Romanov princess of her beautiful cunt he still can't help wishing she would occasionally trim her pubic hair.

How can he tell her? How can he hint to a teenage girl that she should do her bikini line? Many times Alex has wondered this in the six months he and Katy have been stepping out, have been fucking. How can he tell her? Shouldn't her mother tell her? Why doesn't she realise herself, or do girls have to be taught that? Perhaps he *should* hint?

— Oh whim oh way oh whim oh way . . . in the **jungle** the silent **jungle** the lion sleeps tonight . . .

From about a yard above him he hears a girlish laugh, and an incredulous:

— What the FUCK are you doing?

Laying off his tongue and lips, he gazes up over the parapet of her mons pubis, at her distant face:

— Women should only swear in bed, sweetheart

— OK, what the frigging sodding hell are you singing for?

— Oh, nothing . . .

Perhaps, Alex muses, as he rededicates himself to the task, as he descends once again to the shop floor, perhaps next time he goes down on his strange wierd fierce etcetera girlfriend he should wear a pith helmet. Perhaps he should mention his sightings of mad and harrowed GIs, Missing in Action. Perhaps, perhaps . . .

But now to find the clitoris. But how to find the clitoris? All the time Alex has been with Katy he has found it almost impossible to find her clitoris. So difficult is it to find Katy's clitoris Alex has taken to nicknaming her clitoris Lord Lucan. Occasionally there was the odd uncomfirmed sighting, but basically he wondered if he would ever really track down . . .

Ah. Is this it? Parting some tender pink that-must-hurt flesh he tries his tongue; she squirms above him; she starts to get wet. Licking further, laboriously, Labradorily, Alex tongues her and juices her up; makes her wet. But is she wet enough? Putting two fingers inside Alex wonders and frets if she is . . .

Wet for me?

For a moment he fears he might have to artificially moisten her again, that he might have to nip down to the kitchen and get the Utterly Butterly or the I Can't Believe It's Not Vaginal Lubricant but, no, suddenly she does, suddenly she is wet, slick-wet, and this time she is wetter than she has been in a long time and consequently Alex is big and stiff: arrogantly he lifts himself over her and gazes out of the faraway windows of his own soul into the soft wet scintillance of her bright, melting eyes, at her sweet, combative, helpless, determined, submissive, leopardesslike, yes-I-am-your-little-girl smile.

Later they lie in bed together and she says

— You better go soon. My mum will be up in a minute to kick you out. I've got college tomorrow

— You mean school

Under the duvet she kicks him, and giggles:

— You know I'm going to SCREAM and my brother will come in and find us and they'll put you in prison and somebody will kill you

— Thanks

— Molester. Rapist. Pervert – She leans over and kisses him – *Kiddie-fiddler* . . .

Picking up the paper Alex flicks through. Reads, coughs, flicks.

Eventually annoyed by the lack of attention, Katy wonders at him from, the other end of the pillow

— Why do men always read the paper?

— Why don't girls ever read the paper?
— Because it's BORING. What does it matter if there's a war in Croatia or Wales or wherever it is it doesn't exactly affect you?
— It's inherently interesting – Turning another page Alex gazes across and looks at Katy lying there, intimately naked, smoking her fiftieth cigarette, showing her nipples above the duvet line, looking happy, looking at him, looking at him as he expounds:
— It's good to keep informed about current affairs, y'know? It's your responsibility as an intelligent human being to know what's going on. It's
— Dull?
— Yeah, OK – Idly rifling the Arts pages Alex scans and skims, and stops at an article:
— Look at this, they're giving the Orange Prize for Fiction again

Katy yawns, without needing to
— What's that?
— It's a prize for the novel written by a woman. It's a fiction prize only for women
— And that's interesting?
— Yep – Alex nods – I think it's a really good idea. In fact they should extend it. There should be special Nobel prizes for women. The Nobel Prize For Chemistry That Actually Isn't Very Good But It's By A Bird. The Nobel Prize For Economics By Some Helpless Bint. The Pulitzer Prize For Stupid Ar
— Time to GO
— Time to go?

Again Katy kicks him under the duvet
— Yep. Time – Grinning – Unless you want my mum to walk in and find us in bed together and call the cops and have you arrested

Sitting up and reaching for his socks
— OK, but, before I go, say . . . fuck me

— Nope
— Cunt?
— Nope
— How about: I'm your little girl stick your big fat cock in me Daddy?
— Mmmm . . .

Alex looks at her excitedly, Katy completes:

— Nope
— Why won't you ever talk dirty? It's boring. Why won't you talk dirty you filthy little bitch?
— Because you want me to, now get the fuck off me
— OK OK, but I told you
— Women should only swear in bed yes I know but I am in bed now GO!

Getting into his trousers Alex hops around and finds his boots, pulling on his expensive shirt and even more expensive jacket, he stiffens to button; but by the time he's done, by the time he's leaning to kiss the warm forehead of his teenage girlfriend, she is already as far under the duvet as it is possible to be without suffering hypoxia and all he can do is tap her on the top of her head and say

— Gonna miss you
— Sure – She lifts a small white hand from under the covers – Bye bye, weirdo, and DON'T forget to pull the front door HARD . . .

And all the way home on the Tube Alex can smell his teenage girlfriend on him, can sense her perfume around him, her persona. And as they rattle through Finchley and Golders Green and Camden, through Euston, King's Cross and Old Street, Alex stares out at the pictureless black Tube windows, and he wonders why he is so sad and unhappy about the fact she makes him so unsad, so happy.

8

hurts

— So you're heartbroken?
— Yes. Really
Alex, exasperated:
— Just cause your wife is shagging all of your friends?
— Thank you
— Well, get a grip. I mean. *Death* is a bummer. *Terminal cancer* is a downer. Your wife *possibly* being shelfed by some geezer . . . that's just

The sudden silence indicates Alex has moved from the phone, presumably to attend to something in his office. Stood by his kitchen window in Putney Tony gazes out at the glory of the plane trees coming into full-summer green; then he hears Alex pick up the phone again and explain

— Sorry. Just playing cricket with the boss. Not that Jews can *play* cricket . . .

Sipping from an earthenware mug of tea Tony hears Alex again turn aside from the phone and turn to the editor of his magazine, and say

— You throw it. You don't *sell* it

Scuffles, whoops, swearwords: from this end of the line Tony can hear all the usual background laddish banter that makes Tony feel, as always, a little envious of the relaxed liberality of Alex's job: or at least that part of Alex's freelancer's job that sees him in the offices of the lad magazine, *FHM*.

At length, above the general badinage, Tony hears Alex yelling *Zyklon B! Zyklon B!*

A pause. Tony continues holding, expecting to hear Alex being sacked. Instead he catches Alex's editor:

— Zyklon B? You don't think that's a little bit tasteless?

Alex:

— And odourless

The sound of another pretend fight; a yell. The editor:

— Least we've got a country of our own. Now get on with your work, you meaningless drone

Now Tony intervenes, trying to regain his friend's attention:

— So you haven't got any advice then?

— Nnn?

Tony imagines Alex sitting in front of his screen, baton-twirling his pencil. Tony coughs; Alex says

— Sorry Tone. 'Bout what?

Tony sighs

— *Elizabeth.* I was saying I was sure she is . . . you know. So . . . Haven't you got some shrink there . . . who might have some ideas of the best way to deal with this? Or at least with . . . heartbreak?

Another musing silence from Soho. The sound of a pencil falling to the floor. Alex swears, and says:

— Er . . .

— Mmm?

— Well, Jane Austen said the best cure for heartbreak was Constantia wine and wanking

— Jane Austen said that?

— Made up the bit about the wanking

Sliding the mug against the grain of the kitchen table, Tony shakes his head, though no-one is there to see it

— You don't have to tell me about wanking. I've been masturbating myself to death. Elizabeth thinks I'm on drugs because I'm up half the night and I'm always pale in the mornings

— Satellite porn?

— Yeah . . .

— Ben Dover?

— Ben Dover

Alex laughs:

— D'you see last night's, that babe in the girl guide's uniform? Lolita and chips or what?

— Right up your street, I suppose

— Right up my street and right down my drive and right up my stairs and righteously sucking my woodlow yesterday afternoon

Panged, Tony says

— You're still seeing that . . . schoolgirl, then

Unabashed:

— Yep

— What is it with you and adolescents?

— You mean my taste for chicken?

— Yes

The sound of Alex thinking:

— That's a good question, man . . . Don't know

— Haven't you thought

Alex interrupts:

— Actually, you know, I reckon it's cause I went to a mixed sex school – Tony can picture Alex grinning as he seizes on this idea, this explanation – Yeah, I blame co-education

— What?

— Think about it – Alex's voice gets louder – At the most crucial stage in my pubescence, when I was thirteen or fourteen, I was exposed to lots of sexy little teenage girls in gymslips and gingham dresses, no wonder I've got them imprinted on my libido

— So

— So that's just as pervy and bad as being buggered in the bikesheds by some Etonian thug, man. Fucks you up for life

— But you ought, really – Tony adopts a concerned-patronising tone – Aren't you ever going to date someone within a decade of your age?

— Don't fancy them

— But you can *talk* to them

— Give me thirty-year-olds, O Lord, but not yet

Unable to help, Tony chuckles

— You're sticking with the schoolgirl, then

— When she sucks her thumb and looks at me with those . . . you should try it . . .

— I think you're in love with her

— Hey. No way, dude. No sodding way

A hint of irritation in Alex's voice; Tony hears what sounds like the *FHM* editorial staff playing an impromptu game of basketball with the office rubbish bin. Alex goes on

— You know my scene, Tone. I have been in love once. I'm still in love once. I will always be in love once

— Ah yes. Very funny. Always like that one

— What

Tony says, staying calm

— You're still claiming you're holding a torch for . . . *Elizabeth*

— Your wife. Yep.

— You've been winding me up about this for *nearly ten years*, Alex

— That's cause it's true

Now Tony detects, thinks he detects, believes and trusts he detects, the undertone of levity in Alex's voice: just as he always believes and hopes, whenever Alex trots out this hoary joke about loving his wife, that he detects the *undertone* of *levity*.

Change of subject; Tony says to his old friend:
— You know what I think?
— No. What do you think . . .
— I think you've convinced yourself you can never love anybody as a kind of defence . . .

A defiant murmur of dissent; then Tony hears Alex talking to someone in the office. Phone in hand, Tony stands and then strolls across the kitchen and stares down the hall of his house at the detritus of early parenthood: at the mess of kiddy books, teddy bears, small plastic tricycles, chunky plastic toys the same colour and texture as the green and yellow peppers they sell in Sainsburys. Suddenly Alex comes back, out of nowhere
— Y'know man I blame the past. If we hadn't all got so weirdy . . . at Lyonshall . . . we might have been OK . . .
— Lyonshall House?
— Eddie, you, me . . . – Alex sighs – All adds up

Now the topic has been broached, Tony says:
— I must admit I've always wondered, do you ever feel guilty? About what you did?
— The night I sorted him, you mean . . . The first time . . . ?
— Course. You might . . . be seen as responsible, in some people's eyes. How does that make you feel?
— Satisifed with my revenge – Alex clicks – What do you want me to say? How d'you think we're gonna do in the footy?
— Seriously
— But it's looking good. Now he's dropped that fat Newky bastard
— The World Cup? Are you really that interested?
— Oh, sorry, you'll be watching the hurling or spewing or whatever it is, the Gaelic Dung-Eating
— Thanks. Would you ever say you're a bit over the top?
— Just cause I'm not afraid to call a spade a spade . . . to his face?
— OK, I'm going

— Me too

Their phones go down. For a moment Tony fears that this is a conversation they will both regret; then he remembers he and Alex have had worse, that their friendship has been strong enough to survive far worse spats than this. Ergo, his mouth full of a last cold gulp of coffee, Tony chucks the remaining dregs of coffee in the sink, and wanders down the corridor. He is suddenly decided: Tony has suddenly determined to find evidence: evidence for his wife's putative infidelity, if only to scratch the itch of doubt. Stiff and purposeful Tony goes upstairs into his and Elizabeth's bedroom. And begins. Opening her wardrobe he is assailed by the scents and smells of her, of his wife. All and each associated with some aspect of their relationship. Even the smell of fabric conditioner on Lizzie's tee shirts is enough to make Tony stop, and remember the first time he took Elizabeth's tee shirt off. By the river Arrow, by the silver Arrow, in Lyonshall . . .

Fighting tears, teargassed by these nostalgic smells, Tony suppresses the feelings and goes for the pockets of Elizabeth's coats, skirts, jeans. He is not ashamed; he is driven. He is a man with a meaning. All he wants is proof, a hotel receipt for two, a whiff of manly cologne, the wifely equivalent of a lipstick-stained collar.

Methodic, Tony sifts, sorts. Diligent and thorough he spends an hour rifling Elizabeth's old handbags, her underwear drawer, her jewellery box, where he finds: a pair of man's cufflinks. A pair of man's cufflinks? . . . No, just a strange earring. Nothing else. Moving back down into the kitchen again, Tony tries another tactic: he goes through the Council fliers, tax demands, itemised phone bills, stacked behind the phone. For another hour he checks the list of numbers. Salisbury? Could be relatives. Glasgow? Could be work. America? Could be *him*, her lover. Her American lover. Her hunky New York editor with the racquetball-player's physique and the Donna Karan suits and the

Upper East Side orthodontistry and the more-than-a-mouthful *cojones*.

But of course, Tony posits, as ever in awe of his wife: she wouldn't be stupid enough to ring her lover on their home phone, the landline. She'd use her mobile. *Her mobile*. But where does she keep her mobile phone bills? Didn't she throw them out with a lot of stuff yesterday?

Outside the back door of the kitchen Tony finds the dustbin; tilting and rolling the dustbin inside he hefts the black bin bag out of the bin, unknots its yellow plastic tie-ribbon; deliberately upends the contents of the open bin bag all over the parquet kitchen floor. Wilted radicchio, soft shards of carrot, crushed Evian bottles, copies of the *Evening Standard* stained with coffee grounds, lots of smells. Scrabbling in the crud and mank, Tony looks, lifts, examines; under a pile of sickly-sweet-smelling pale orange nappysacks Tony locates a magazine which he flaps for anything inside and is about to discard until Tony realises with a start that the little mag is a copy of *Forum*. The pornmag Alex bought last week. Alex must have left it behind and Tony must have thrown it away without him, Tony, even knowing.

Diverted from his cause Tony flicks the glossy damp pages of the little magazine: a porn magazine the like of which he has never seen before. It appears to be a contact magazine. It is full of pictures of people, ordinary people, surprisingly young, pretty people, some with their eyes blanked out by black rectangles, some not. All of them are in various states of undress, or kinky dress. Beneath the pictures are little paragraph-captions:

> Susan. W. Midlands. 33. Into Bondage and SM. WLTM lesbian of similar age. Box no. 87129
> David. 25. North London. Into hosing and sprinkling, keen to meet other men with same desires. Box no. 63207

Lifting and turning the pornmag Tony examines bushes, peruses nipples, is revolted by scrotal jewellery. After a few more pages he comes across a fat section at the back devoted to couples, to swinging couples keen on threesomes, or foursomes, or 'moresomes'. At the bottom of almost every advert is the legend:

> Man would like to watch his wife with other man.
> COLOUREDS ESPECIALLY WELCOME

Squatted down amongst the crushed brown eggshells and dented packets of Special K and the clammy slips of potato peel Tony thinks about this. He thinks about men that want to watch their wives being shagged by other men. About why they do it. Head shaking, Tony wonders why they all, seemingly, want to watch their wives being shagged by *black* men. Why do they want to watch their wives being shagged by black men? As Tony wonders why so many white husbands want to watch their wives being shagged by black men Tony imagines his own wife being shagged by a black man, in front of him, in front of Tony. Surrounded by the trash, the rubbish, the garbage of his marriage and family, Tony thinks about a black man taking his elegant blonde wife in front of Tony: the way he would lift up her dress with his big black muscly arms and throw her over the breakfast table and tear down her spotless white knickers; the way she would squeal with delight and submission as she looked straight at Tony at the other side of the breakfast table; the way Tony would watch his wife smile and moan right in front of Tony; the way Tony would stand there impotently and watch the big black bastard tear away his wife's panties and part her fat soft beautiful white buttocks and shove his huge, his monstrously huge, his zoologically massive black cock hard in his wife's cunt and make her cunt go wider than it has ever been before, pumping her like a cow, pumping her so hard and so vigorously Tony's breakfast bowl of All-Bran would jump along the table and go clattering onto the kitchen floor while Tony's wife would moan and groan and scream, about how big the black man was, how much bigger than Tony, how much thicker and harder and . . .

Godhelpme.

Tony has an erection. Sitting down amidst the contents of the dustbin Tony looks down at his groin and sees that he has an erection.

But so what? Sardonic, cynical, dryly laughing, Tony comes to his feet and his senses, and starts loading the crap back in the bin bag. Walkers, Kellogs, Volvic, Jordans, Harpers, Hovis, McVities. Picking up tiny used torn red condoms of old tomato skin, and soft jade spears of darkly rotting asparagus, Tony concludes that white men want black men to fuck their wives because black men are notoriously bigger and lustier, also more animal: therefore doubly humiliating. But, Tony ponders, do other ethnic groups have similar tastes? Do Indians also want to see their wives being fucked by black men? Or are they into Arabs? And what about the Japs, Tony thinks, they've got tiny penises and whites are much bigger: do Japanese and Chinese masochistically get off on the idea of big strapping Scotsmen shagging their petite little wives? Because Scotsmen are like big ginger-haired cavemen? Or do they want American Footballers? And – Tony ties the bin bag with a final vehement flourish – what *about* blacks? Do they have a taste for ritual troilistic marital humiliation? Do they like to see white men shagging their funky little hos because whites are cleverer and smarter and superior and the traditional oppressor? If so what do black men do who want to see men with bigger dicks shagging their wives? Do their adverts say HORSES ESPECIALLY WELCOME?

Tutting at his foray into complete and utter political incorrectitude, simultaneously congratulating himself on his rather cool and philosophical way of dealing with something that is fundamentally shocking, strange, disturbing and nasty, Tony hoists the bin bag like a coal sack and heaves it into the dustbin and kicks the dustbin outside, before whumping the rubber dustbin lid back into place. As Tony claps his hands he turns to go back inside: and spots that he has left something on the floor. It is a letter. A letter that must have slipped under the bin bag as the bin bag was opened.

The letter is in Spanish. It is damp and tea-stained and corrected so much it looks like a first draft, but still legible. With tweezer-fingers Tony carries it through to the sitting room. Spreading the moist letter paper out on the coffee table Tony begins reading. Even though he cannot read Spanish he has to read the letter: the reason he has to read it is because Elizabeth has been having lessons to brush up her Spanish for a year, and this letter is in her handwriting.

But he cannot understand it. Try as he might Tony cannot understand a word. *Tarde, revelar, cansada, cine, usted, falda*. The word love keeps appearing but that is all he recognises. Love. Love. Love.

Cussing his ignorance, cursing his monolingualism, Tony reads the two page letter again. And again. He thumps his fist on the table and bites his knuckle, and strains. What's that: kiss you? *Abrazarte*? Or just 'embrace you'? Is she expressing affection and greeting: or something . . . something . . . And this? Blood? I am bleeding? *I am red?*

Dictionary?

Dictionary.

By the hallway bookshelves Tony searches the place where his wife stores her Spanish Evening Class stuff. The dictionary; the exercise book; the homework; the parallel text novels.

All are gone, all are not there.

Elizabeth.

Striding back into the sitting room Tony picks up the letter, puts it down, picks it up, puts it down. Subsequently he sits down and takes a pen and goes through the letter for the seventh time, underlining key phrases: phrases where words that he thinks he recognises, words that he thinks mean certain things, words that his heart tells him he does not want to understand, crop up. This done, Tony picks up the phone and rings Eddie. It rings about fifteen times and as Tony is about to hang up it clicks. He can hear breathing.

— Hi, Eddie, it's Tony . . . Eddie?

His voice thick with phlegm, Eddie coughs; coughs again; mumbles something sleepy about having just woken up. Tony swiftly

— You speak Spanish Eddie of course

— Nnnmmm . . . so . . .

— Well I need to pick your brains, Ed. Won't take long . . . It's just that I'm reading this book on our list but the author has left some passages in Spanish with no translation, don't you hate it when they do that?

— . . . Sorry?

— Just a couple of lines. I'm dying to know what they mean only I don't speak Spanish and they seem pretty crucial could you help?

Eddie yawns

— Ssssssure . . . fire away

— Thanks very much

Fumbling with the damp letter Tony goes to the first pencil-ringed phrase:

— OK OK OK. What does . . . er . . . *No tengo mi . . . formulario . . . puedes . . . esperar* . . . – He slows then goes on – *hasta el final de la . . . semana* mean?

A pause. Tony hears Eddie writing; then Eddie's oscitate, languid reply:

— That means . . . 'I haven't got my . . . application form . . . can you wait until the end of the week.' – Eddie chuckles – Fascinating, what's the book?

— Oh, it's nothing, nothing. OK – Another fumble, another pencil ring – What about *perdoname los vaqueros. Puedo . . .* –

Struggling with the words – *pedirle . . . algo . . . mejor . . . de un amiga si . . .* – Stops, goes on – *prefieres . . .* ?

In the distance a river boat hoots on the river; near home a window cleaner carries his ladder down Tony's street; Eddie replies:

— That means . . . mmmm . . . I think . . . the language isn't very good . . . but I would say that means . . . 'I am sorry about the jeans. I can borrow something . . . better . . . from a friend if you want.' Something like that. This book sounds like a real *bestseller*, Tony

Maybe, Tony thinks, *maybe I was imagining. Maybe I was imagining it all. Maybe this letter is just an exercise, just a scribble, just a draft of a note to a friend in the evening class or a teacher or* . . . As Tony scans the damp letter paper Eddie makes an I-would-now-like-my-breakfast noise:

— Is that it? Can I go now?

— Just a couple more, Ed, sorry, I've lost my bookmarks – Down the second page, Tony plumps:

— OK, this one. *Me encanta chupar tu polla . . .* – The letter trembling in his hand – *hinchada hasta que me duele la boca. Me gusta ir a mi . . . mirado a casa con tu . . .* – Slowly – *semen en mi cara*?

Long pause. Tony hears the river boat again. The window cleaner is setting up his ladder against the bay window of a house opposite. A man in a suit is walking down the road doing up his tie as he goes. Suddenly Eddie laughs, a long, languorous, relaxed, raunchy laugh.

— What? – Tony panics – What? What does it mean?

Eddie is still laughing.

— Ed, what on earth does it mean? Please?

— Well – Eddie controls himself – It's slangy, it's colloquial, but I think that means 'I love to suck your hard cock till my mouth hurts. I like to go home to my husband with your seed on my face' . . .

Elizabeth. Elizabeth. Elizabeth Elizabeth Elizabeth Elizabeth Elizabeth Elizabeth Elizabeth Elizabeth Elizabeth Elizabeth Elizabeth.
— Rafferty?
— n
— Is that *all?* – Eddie yawns again – I'm due for my coffee like *half an hour* ago
— Oh. Mm. Yes – Tony stills himself, goes to the bottom of the letter, picks another random line – This is the last one, Eddie. *Es tan aburrido. Le voy a dejar. Le odio . . . Si no fuera por los hijos le hubiera dejado ya* – Pause, breath – *Solo te . . . quiero a ti.*

Eddie goes quiet, Tony can hear Eddie's scribbling pencil, Tony can hear his own heart beating, beating, beating; Eddie concludes, at the last:
— Hold on . . . I think, I'm just working it through . . . mm . . . Yah . . . I *believe* that means, 'He is so boring, I am going to leave him. I hate him. If it wasn't for the children I would have left him already. I only want you.'

Pause. Heartbeat. Sunshine. Windowcleaner.
— Eddie
— yes?
— Thanks
— De nada

Later Tony is doing the rounds for his publishers; later that day Tony is hawking his publisher's books around the bookshops of north London, when he remembers the girl in Waterstone's in Hampstead, the one who gave him the eye, the one Alex recommended he seduce.

Crossing the softcarpeted portals of Waterstone's in Hampstead Tony crosses the soft carpet, through the soft muzak, through the soft focus of his near tears; crossing to the fiction desk he says to the girl, to her pretty face, to any face, to any girl, to anyone, Tony says:

— Julia

The girl, fresh in a summer dress, her eyes April and sparkly, puts down her fashionable, discounted modern novel and she says

— Anthony, we were wondering

Tony raises a hand

— Julia I just want to say – Deep breath, deep breath – Would you like to go for a drink, sometime, anytime, soon?

A happy expression crosses Julia's sweet pretty face:

— Love to

9

the herb

Apricot. Satsuma. Avocado. Sat on an uncomfortably small chair Eddie is counting the different kinds of obscure, pastel fruit-and-veg colours employed in the painting and decorating of the Brady Clinic, London's most fashionable private drug-detoxification-and-rehabilitation centre. The floor is pale-olive. The ceiling is lychee. On the dill-green walls is a selection of studiedly neutral watercolours; on the glass topped table in the centre is a scatter of magazines: *Opera Now, The Spectator, The Tatler, Investors Weekly, The Catholic Herald.*

Eddie vaguely wonders why they should keep *The Catholic Herald* and *The Tatler* and the rest of these mags in the Brady Clinic waiting room. How many moneyed, cultured, upper-class, Roman Catholic heroin addicts can there be? Eddie starts counting the ones he knows personally but before he gets to thirty he is interrupted by a voice that floats across the waiting room

— Doctor Feavis will see you in a minute

In dirty jeans and old corduroy jacket Eddie obediently rises; as he crosses to the Doctor's door the voice from the reception desk chirrups again

— Er, Mr Foster

— mM?

Behind the desk is a louche looking boy with thick lips, and a newish tan, who looks like he should be starring in his first pop video rather than serving behind the desk at the Brady Clinic. The boy:

— Erm, uh

— *Sorry?*

— Ahh, the . . .

— *What?*

The boy looks uncomfortable:

— The . . .

Eddie helps out

— The *money*! You want me to pay up front?

Relieved, the boy flicks back a modish lock of hair and says

— Yes. The money. It's two hundred and fifty pounds for the first consultation. We prefer cash . . .

Undeterred by the fact that an outraged voice inside is saying *two hundred and fifty quid for half an hour with some society quack with a methadone concession*? Eddie takes out a wallet from the back pocket of his jeans and unpeels a sheaf of tens; then turns on the heels of his ten-year-old trainers, slopes loftily across the lobby to the door marked Doctor Feavis, who says *come in* at Eddie's knock. When Eddie enters he is pleased to see that yes, Doctor Feavis is wearing a ridiculous bow tie. As Eddie has gleaned from long experience you can always trust a doctor who wears a bow tie to be totally mercenary as well as completely pompous and therefore largely uninterested in the actualities of his patients: therefore perfectly easy to deceive.

Taking a bentwood chair Eddie tells the doctor the necessary lies. That he is Mark Andrew Foster, that he comes from Kent, that he had a reasonably happy childhood, that he has never been tested for HIV, that yes he would say his physical health is fair, that he has not been immunised against Hepatitis B, that blah, that blah, that blah. At each answer the doctor lifts his shaggy fifty-year-old eyebrows and then Biros a scrawly note on a sheet of headed Brady Clinic notepaper. After the usual questions (usual to Eddie, who has been through this a million times as a supposed drunkard, schizophrenic or deviant), the doctor moves on to Mark Foster's particular problem. The date of first consumption, the method of consumption, the amount of consumption per day, week, month. As he does this Eddie gets a strange urge to *tell the truth,* at least as regards the mechanics and minutiae of his heroin addiction. *If I tell the truth,* Eddie decides, *I might actually get some good advice on my addiction given that it is at least conceivable that I do have something of a problem. And besides,* Eddie tells himself, *if I tell the truth my lies will be more convincing.*

So when Doctor Feavis leans back and pyramids his fingers and says

— What are your feelings about your addiction, your real feelings? – Eddie looks across the doctor's shiny big desk out the window into a blazing June morning in Bayswater, at the sun sparkling off the sash windows and the sun making butter of the stucco and it all begins to spill:

— I often think, I often think . . .

It is an effort; a true effort. Eddie runs his hand through his lank hair; continues avoiding Doctor Feavis's eyes; and admits

— It's weird but I sometimes find myself thinking that I would like to *die* on heroin. That when I am old I would like to go off to Pakistan to Rawalpindi or somewhere where you can score easily and I would die on heroin. Most people die on morphine anyway so I would just be *formalising* the process, accelerating it, underlining it, because, you see, all the *reasons* that heroin is inadmissable in earlier life, that it destroys your ambition, that it negates your libido, that it makes you ugly and poor and lazy and seemingly grouchy, *none* of those apply when you're old indeed some of them are part and parcel of being old

Doctor Feavis separates his fingertips; Eddie does not allow him to interrupt.

— And so when you are old and crap all the *bad* aspects of heroin would disappear and all you would have left is the sweet oblivion, the purposeless pleasure, the terrific analgesia to gently nurse you towards death so I figure why not go out on a warm tide why not open your wrists in a warm bath why not

— Yes – Doctor Feavis interrupts anyway – But you are not old Mr Foster, you are – He checks his notes – Thirty-three. And you accept that heroin is destroying your life as it is now, correct?

Eddie rubs a dirty mark on his jeans, mumbles

— Well . . . Heroin, heroin . . . you see. It. It. When you *start* taking it it seems alright, rather pleasant. When you begin doing gear it's rather like living in a jolly little town full of like-minded people, it's all *fun* and there's quite a few of you doing it and it's all rather social . . . but then people start dropping out they start dying or going to prison or going on year-long safaris to get away from their habits and then . . . then it becomes like a small tiresome village just you and a couple of the same old friends and a couple of dealers and after that it . . . it's just . . . it becomes a house just one house in the middle of nowhere and it's just you and your habit and you are utterly *alone*

— You feel lonely?

— I guess. I presume. I mean

The sensation of truth, of sincerity, of real heartfelt truth coming out of Eddie's mouth is unpleasant. It hurts. It stings like stomach acid, like something not meant to emerge this way. In his chair Eddie squirms and rubs the knees of his jeans and blurts at the patch of wallpaper to the left of Doctor Feavis's grey hair

— *fucking* lonely. Sometimes I feel like the loneliest person in the world, like I've already *died*

The doctor nods, sombrely

— Are you . . . religious?

— No. Absolutely *not*. I despise religion
— Despise?
— I'm sure of course that's some love hate thing with my father, some Oedipal rejection?

Eddie glances at Doctor Feavis: no reaction; Eddie goes on
— I *despise* it all. I hate Christianity, I hate Catholicism. It's the way we are viewed. The way it says we humans are just, like, livestock bred to die, like we are some kind of *cattle* . . . designed to be slaughtered . . . so the sad pathetic meat of our lives can be turned into the hamburgers of glory, the Big Macs of our souls, the burgers of glory God eats in heaven

Doctor Feavis mmms; glances at Eddie; and moves on
— Shall I tell you about the treatments we offer here?

Eddie shrugs; glances meaningfully at Doctor Feavis: thinks how much he hates doctors, *What are they but experts in death, deathologists*? and shrugs
— Please

With a practised, efficient manner Doctor Feavis outlines the Brady Clinic range
— We can offer rapid in-patient detox under general anaesthesia. Essentially that means you book into a private hospital, probably in London, where you will be pre-medicated with anti-withdrawal drugs and sedatives. Then we give you the opiate antagonist Naltrexone, that's a drug that acts to block heroin . . . it sort of pushes heroin off the body's receptors so that instead of taking two to four days to withdraw the patient withdraws in a few hours. During those few hours however we put you under with a general anaesthetic so the suffering is nugatory. The patient usually leaves hospital the next day
— How much?

Eyebrow, bow tie, notebook.
— Rapid in-patient detox under a general costs three thousand five hundred pounds
— What other treatments are there?

Sighing, ever-so-slightly, Doctor Feavis turns a page in his notes and says
— I think if money is a . . . bother . . . you might like to consider a five to seven day home detoxification with Naltrexone, which costs about three hundred pounds. That's where you administer your own oral sedatives, such as Temazepam and Valium, and then when you are completely clean you take Naltrexone as an antagonist thereafter. As I said Naltrexone blocks the heroin receptors, so when you are on Naltrexone taking heroin is pointless. Indeed if you took Naltrexone while you were actually on heroin the results would be – The bow tie is adjusted – Extremely unpleasant.

Eddie says nothing. He is wondering if what he said about drugs, loneliness and God was the truth; he wonders whether truth exists; he is wondering how quickly he can get his chit signed and get out and get smacked up in the Brady Clinic toilets.

Feavis fills the silence by finishing his spiel
— We can also do a Naltrexone implant. That's a disc of Naltrexone we insert into your abdomen or upper arm after making an inch long split

OK, I want to get stoned . . .

Standing up Eddie says he'll take at-home detox. Feavis's eyes gleam like a bad poker player with a royal flush as Eddie takes a thick wad of cash from his back pocket.

Now things are expedited: over the next five minutes Eddie is fully kitted out for at-home detox: he gets a prescription for Valium, a prescription for Temazepam, a prescription for Pemoline, a prescription for Dexedrine, a prescription for Naltrexone. He also gets a leaflet about methadone, presumably in case the Naltrexone fails. Then he gets his chit for being a registered heroin addict named Mark Foster who because of his addiction is officially unable to seek work even though he is a claimant of income support. Finally Eddie gets an over-firm handshake and a pat on the back and Eddie leaves Doctor Feavis's room and goes into the gherkin and mango Brady Clinic lavatories and gets smacked out of his head.

Outside in the warm Bayswater lunchtime air the sun is sparkling on the bumpers of recently washed cars. It is hot; Eddie unsweats his brow with a forearm. Across Westbourne Terrace Eddie heads vaguely and hazily towards the Tube at Paddington but his progress is diverted when he sees a green and white cross on a plastic shop-fascia: a chemist.

Inside the pharmacy Eddie steps around the racks of combs and hairbrushes and goes up to the Asian in a white coat at the Prescriptions counter and hands over his sheaf of thick yellow expensive-looking watermarked Brady Clinic scripts. The chemist does not even flinch at the number, type and unusuality of the scripts: evidently used to Brady Clinic customers. Nodding sagely to himself the chemist retreats into the pharmacologist's chancel at the rear. Sounds of rattling, shaking and then label-printing emanate. Eddie stares at the round tins of travel sweets under the glass of the counter. Eddie is stoned. Monged. Skulled. Ten minutes later the chemist comes out and hands over a big white sellotaped paper bag full of pillbottles and Eddie takes the bag and pays. Yet another hundred pounds lighter Eddie exits into the summer sun and through the vaselined lens of his smacked-upness he notices that the streets surrounding Paddington Station are oddly full of Scotsmen. Full of tartan scarves, red-dragons-on-yellow, men in kilts, and the sound of Glaswegians yodelling their happiness at being drunk-in-the-sun. Through the swaddling of opiates a sudden fact pierces Eddie's consciousness

Scotland versus Brazil. The Match. Alex

Mortified by his selfishness Eddie checks his watch and shakes his head and curses himself for being so late to meet Alex at the pub; again Eddie checks his watch and shakes his head and exhales air at how terribly late he is; for the third time he checks his watch and decides he's got just enough time to nip into McDonald's and do some more gear. As he does this, as he skips down the slippy white burger bar steps to the basement toilets, he considers how strange it is that there's always enough time to do some more gear. It is almost as if gear dilates time, like being on gear is like flying through the cosmos at infinite speed, *everything else slows down, everything else has more time, everything else can go* ***hang***.

Through the crowd of kilted, tam-o-shantered, warbling fans Alex leans and orders another bottle of Czech beer from the cute Czech bargirl of this trendy Clerkenwell sports bar; then resets himself on his bar stool. Above and beyond the ranks of bobbing ginger nylon Afrowigs Alex can just about see the TV screen whereon a tartan-bow tied Scottish football pundit is discussing the upcoming match, the opening match of the World Cup, Scotland versus Brazil; Alex looks at his watch

Eddie

Straight from the bottle Alex drinks, shrugs, swallows, listens to the raucous laughter: and feels the pang of wistfulness any man feels when alone in a pub full of other men who know each other and are having a good time. And boy are they having a good time. Some of the lads around him have even begun a rendition of Flower of Scotland, that so-called song, that morbid threnody, the National Dirge. That they are all singing this forces Alex, in the absence of a friend, namely Eddie, to distract him, to wonder. Conjecture. About his socio-ethnic apostasy. Why? Why, here, of all places: surrounded by Scotland fans singing Scottish songs drinking Scottish beer watching Scotland play football, does he not feel so very Scottish? Is it because he was brought up in England? Or because he hated his father?

The bar goes a bit quieter as the French TV relay scans across the parade of brave, plug-ugly, bound-to-lose faces that comprise the Scotland team, ranked up before kick-off. Then it bursts into dirge again

Ooh flooooer of Scoootlaaaand, when will you Alex wishes, sometimes, he could feel like this: this Scottishness, this small country solidarity, this fashionable Riverdancing Celticness. But he can't. Not even right here, right now. Inside, as a mongrel pseudo-Englishman, Alex can't help actually despising certain aspects of the Celts *qua* Celts. Their tendency to whinge about and diss the English, for a start. Why won't they stop complaining? Fisting beer nuts from the bowl on the bar, Alex takes a bigger gulp of bottle-beer, admires the Brazilian team's girlie fans picked out by the French TV producer, and decides that one of the reasons he has a certain contempt for the Celts *qua* Celts is that the Celts are simply the girlies of the world. With their plaints, their self-hating inadequacy, their moods, their neverending national PMT . . .

But he is, still, a Celt himself; at least partly. So where does that leave him? British? Here we go again. Gargling beer Alex abandons himself to the pointless quest, again. What is it? British? Why? Who still wants to be British? Is he, Alex, the last person in the world who feels remotely British? And what is feeling British anyway? Is it something that can only be seen as what it is not: i.e. not European, not Catholic, not as good as America? Is it just a negative, a transparency that can only be viewed against the lightdesk of French-ness, German-ness, other-ness? *Transparency* . . . Shifting between nuts and beer Alex concludes, helplessly, that there is something intrinsically *transparent, evanescent,* about the whole concept of patriotism and nationality: as soon as you try to grasp its essence it disappears; as soon as you ignore it it forces itself on you. But, still: he does feel a certain Britishness. Yet what is it that Britishness consists of: now? A warrior nation with no wars to fight? A quite good broadcasting company and a decrepit fucking Health Service? What is Britishness but an empty cathedral where the tourists wander, rudely laughing, taking pictures, crassly interrupting the few pathetic believers still praying in the pews?

The match is in swing, the guys in the pub roar too loud, sing raw and hoarse and happy.

— And sent him homeward, Tae think again, Tae think again . . .

— Should hae picked McCoist

— C'mon Scotlaaaand!!

Alex clocks his watch, swears inside, orders another bottle of Star. The Scotland team surges forward and the hordes of Scotsmen around him, his brothers, his cousins, these drunken, happy, sad, historical losers: the Scottish contingent: which for some reason is the entire population of the sports bar: they gurgle and cheer the Scottish team, and then jeer and trash the English. Even though they're not playing the English.

Hugely annoyed, Alex tries not to applaud as the Brazilians nearly score; vastly irritated, he forces himself to clap as the Scottish nearly get the ball across the halfway line. Lifting his bottle mechanically he drinks and gazes at the TV screens suspended by black metal talons over the bleached-plywood modernity of the bar-room and his eyes start to glaze. He drinks. He gazes; drinks. Half-time comes, he takes a leak and drinks some more; just as he is beginning to forget about Eddie, just as he is sucking the hard glass bottletop of his eighth Staropramen

— Who are you supporting then?

Startled, Alex takes a second to realise that Eddie is standing next to him in trainers, jeans, and corduroy jacket. Ed's jeans are as soiled as his *face*.

— Lyonshall, you're pinned

Eddie raises himself majestically to his full six-foot-three and says in tones of horror and disdain

— Yup

— I thought we were just going to have a few pints and watch the match Eddie shrugs:
— Well . . .
— Not watch you get puggled
— So I'm an *homme moyen sensuel*
— *Plus ça* sodding change – Alex tsks, relents, smiles – I'll get you an OJ
— That's kind of you . . .
As he attempts to articulate this small statement Eddie sways, disturbingly. Alex checks
— Seriously, you alright?
Eddie gestures
— Absol . . . Total . . . – Winking at his shorter, younger, possibly smarter, definitely lower-class friend – I'm *fine*. I'll be *fine* – Eddie flicks a semi-interested look at the TV screens, at the football
— Who *are* you supporting, anyway
Alex hisses
— England, who d'you think
— Well, seeing as you are by *birthplace* a Scotsman, that you carry a Scottish name, that your father is Scottish, and that it is *Scotland* who are at the moment playing I thought it remotely possible you might be supporting
— Yeah, well, *not*. But keep your voice down
— Sorry . . .
— And my mum was from Ulster. And I was brought up in England
— So you're more of an octoroon. As I think we established
Alex tuts
— And you are an effete English fuckwit
— British by birth, English by the grace of God
— British by birth, English *bisexual*
A roar full of Scottish vowels that never end makes Alex glance anxiously at the TV screens
— Nearly

— Nearly – Eddie repeats, his eyes misting over again; then Eddie says – Er . . . I'm just going out for a second, I may be some time

— Sorry?

Looking oddly at Alex, Eddie leans to the bar, reels back, leans sideways, and rests a hand on the bar as he throws up all over the floor. Alongside Eddie a Scotland fan whose saltired tee shirt is covered in blood or red salsa or both, steps back: to let Eddie do his business. When Eddie looks up he sees Alex looking over. Alex says

— Do you think you might have taken a bit too much this time?

Wiping puke from his mouth Eddie attempts to be nonchalant as the bargirl comes over carrying a mop, as the Scottish fans cheer

— Why, Eddie?

— Do not go sober into that good night?

Alex gestures at the angry bargirl

— We oughta go

Eddie waves the idea away, irritatedly refusing the wrong vintage of port

— No, I'm absolutely fine, I just need to *micturate*

Stepping aside the pool of his own vomit, Eddie stiffens, girds, and weaves between the football fans towards the Toilets. Inside the Gents Eddie finds and locks a cubicle and wipes his face with tissue. Then he takes out the crumpled paper pharmacy bag from his brown corduroy pocket.

Dexedrine, Pemoline, Valium?

Dexedrine . . .

With some difficulty Eddie unchildsecurescrews the pillbottle, pops a white Dexedrine tablet: just to give him some pep; to see him through the game; before he goes back to the flat to get even more stoned. The pillbottle-bag scrunched back in his pocket Eddie waits a few moments, then walks tall out the cubicle, returns down the corridor, and discovers Alex standing where his vomit was. It has all been cleared up. Eddie relaxes at this: together he and Alex lean matily against the bar and look at the football; they clap and cheer in the right places; soon Eddie finds he is feeling better all round, he is gaining a pleasant sense of comradeliness, of male bonding, from the whole procedure, even though he is not overly interested in the soccer.

And then the pill kicks in.

Eddie stops. Alex

— What

Eddie looks, glares. Alex

— Ed, whassup?

— Noth . . . ing

— You look awful

— S'nothing

But Eddie knows it *is* something: his guts: *jesuschrist my guts*

He feels like some Aztec priest has punched through his chest and smashed apart his ribs and is rummaging for his spleen

— Uh, don't feel too bright . . . Just . . .

Despite his friend's protests Eddie turns, and walks very quickly outside into the warm June air of London. Up the street, down St John Street, Eddie lurches: ignoring the frightened stares of people making way on the way. Inside him the pain is doubling, trebling, tightening

That's it, he thinks, *I've done it, I've really done it this time*

Pavement, death, kerbstone, death, small brown dog turd, death; Eddie lifts his eyes from the asphalt and aches and writhes and screaming helpmeJesusnohelpme he turns left, right, and the wails inside are like his body is trying to burst open, trying to burst open to show the hot plasma throbbing inside; desperate Eddie keys his door and clambers the rotten steps: all his body is shrieking, is being bastinado'd, is being cattle-prodded and horse-whipped and internally flayed

I am going to die I am going to die I am going to die I am going to . . .

Shit my trousers?

Over the threshold of his flat Eddie looks straight ahead like a clown being filmed in close-up as someone custard pies his testicles; then it happens. He starts to shit himself. His bowels heave, his sphincter yawns, his arsehole pukes a torrent of dysenteric slurry down his trouser legs. Now Eddie gasps and crashes forward to the floor, at the same time he coughs and spits a small yellow salad onto the carpet and he thinks *this is it.*

What a pathetic goal. What a crap goal. What an own goal. Trying not to laugh, trying not to gloat, Alex watches as the Scots around him go in to instant national mourning over the Brazilians' taking a one–nil lead: with an own goal. Doing this, Alex is reminded of the last Scotland game he watched: the last time he saw Scotland lose: the time when England won. Euro '96. When Gascoigne scored *that goal*. That *much better goal*. Ring ring. When Gascoigne grabbed the ball, trapped it, snared it, flicked it, ringringring, dribbled it, and kicked it with an almighty rush of heaven-sent talent into the billowing glory of the Scottish net. Ringringringringringring.

His mobile phone is ringing.

— Yes

— Alex

It is Eddie, sounding very weird.

— Eddie what happened to you

— Nothing . . . Took . . .

Eddie's voice fades in and out

— Took the wrong pill, Alex would you mind, I'm . . . ill, at the flat

— Coming

The mobile in his pocket Alex exits the pub into the fresh veils of virginal sunlight laid across his cooling face; quickly Alex steps the street to Eddie's door, finds the way up into Eddie's flat and as Alex pushes the unlatched door he finds Eddie lying on the sofa with his trousers off and a towel around him. Eddie is moaning, clutching his stomach, and sighing: Alex immediately knows by this that Eddie is not going to die, so instead Alex looks at the piles of empty sweetwrappers, the emptied silver Indian takeaway boxes, and the empty orange grease-stained Keema nan paper bags on top of the television; and remarks

— Nice place you got here

Eddie laments; Alex, again

— You haven't heard of hoovering then

Eddie groans, manages to look up:

— Nature abhors a vacuum

Alex shakes his head

— Too much gear?

— No . . . Took . . . – Eddie holds his stomach like his chitterlings are about to spill out – I took the wrong *fucking pill*, didn't I? I thought I was going to lose it

Alex sits down on the end of the sofa and laughs and says

— Which pill?

— Naltrexone. I think I took Naltrexone. I thought it was Dexedrine. I *think* I went into accelerated detoxification

— You mean you did cold turkey in two hours rather than two days?

— In two fucking *minutes*, oh

— You're not going to croak

Eddie lays a limp hand across his brow, like a rich Victorian consumptive.

— No. I'm not. But for a moment . . . Jesus, I am an absolute *arse*

— You are an arse, what do you want me for?

The brow unhanded, Eddie eyes his friend

— I rather thought . . . *Solidarity*

— Hah . . .

And so they sit there, the two of them. Alex turns on the telly and watches the postmortem on the Brazilian victory in the football with the sound down; Eddie moans but slowly gets better. As the afternoon wears on Alex makes some tea and they drink it from mugs and they light a couple of spliffs; Eddie sits up and announces his recovery and then they chat about stuff and drink more tea. Alex tries to describe the beauty of football, the validity, the excitement of the World Cup and the possibility of David Beckham's being selected; Eddie pretends to listen and then decides he would quite like to go to sleep: half out of bed Eddie reaches for his Valium bottle, and for his Evian bottle. Unscrewing both he pops a couple of small yellow pills, and chases them with water.

From the sofa he sees Alex looking with a sceptical expression at his pill-popping; shrugging, almost smiling, Eddie says

— All life death doth end, and each day dies with Diazepam

10

jerusalem cowslip

— How about a feature on crustie fashion?
— What?
— Yeah. We could do a spread on those road protesters on the news last night . . . you know . . . the one with the tunnellers and the tree people, wossname, Boggy . . . and Garlic Pete . . . and . . . Dave.

His gaze aimed at his stylist the editor says, flat
— Crustie fashion? I take it you are referring to those awful people with dogs on strings?

The stylist tilts a defiant nose
— Actually they are quite innovative, some of their hairstyles and their clothes, mixture of ethnic and Mad Max and
— Bin liners – The editor says – Still, I suppose, they are very much *de nos jours* – He taps his Mont Blanc against his capped teeth – Perhaps we *ought* to do something

Directing his queenly gaze to another corner of the grey plastic table the editor fronts Alex, who has hitherto been cleaning his nails with the corner of a Tube ticket
— Alex.
— Alex

— *Alex*

Looking up, Alex is unnerved to find the entire editorial staff of the Weekend Magazine of Britain's Biggest Selling Regional Daily Newspaper staring at him with pitiful contempt.

Panic

— *Sorry?*

— Not with us, Alexander?

— *Errr*

The editor pops a mint. Alex wonders if his editor is thinking of sacking him. The editor chews and sucks and says

— I was saying, don't you hail from those environs . . . isn't that your little corner of the world?

— Errrr, sorry?

Leaning to his side Alex's friend Bernadino whispers

— Roads, roads . . .

But Alex is forced to confess

— Apologies, John. Half-asleep

John rolls the mint around his mouth, levels a gaze at Alex's moderately boyish grin and his considerably dark hair. Smiles

— Well. I'm thinking of offering you a human interest story. The road they're building through that village, Lyonshall, isn't it? Lion something . . . all those delightful youngsters living in trees and not having any lavatories, I thought it might be . . .

Lyonshall? ***Lyonshall?***

His attention more than gained, Alex stares at the editor. Did he hear right?

Lyonshall?

His sadism evidently rekindled, John shakes his head

— But seeing as you are obviously more concerned with matters closer to hand I think . . . – John consults the large black-and-steel notebook in front of him – I'd like you to do the fetish club explosion

Alex, gutted, flailing

— The . . . what? The fetish club what?

— Yes. Explosion . . . Apparently they're quite the thing. Pain is the new black, isn't that right? – The stylist, who has been doodling, nods, vigorously; John sucks at the last of his mint – And I expect you to dress up for the task. Let's have some nice shots of you in leather, hanging out with the boys
— . . . really?
— Yes. Really. And while you're at it we need someone to interview that awful Australian film star flying in next month . . . Davina Something. Whatever her name is . . . – Slapping the notebook shut – Shall we say two thousand words, usual form?

The door clicks behind.
— Great, just great – Alex mutters to himself, as he loosens his large floppy Thierry Mugler tie with tiny bicyclists printed thereupon, as he undoes the top button of his white sea island cotton – I could strangle that screamer

He and his colleague Bernardino Paganuzzi are striding across the hushed, open-plan, hi-tech expanse of the newsroom. Bernadino is humming; Alex isn't. Halfway to the far doorway, Alex revolves on his Italian colleague
— Bernardino, do *you* think I'm a twat?
— Mnn – Bernadino considers – No . . .
— Then why does everybody else? Why don't I get to do a decent serious news story?
— Because
— Why don't I get asked to write about the absurdity of European Monetary Union without an overarching political authority?
— Alexi?
— Why do I always get asked to interview the Aussie bimbos?

His reflection checked in the glass door that Alex is swinging open, Bernadino says
— I think perhaps the reason you don't get to write news is because you don't work for the news sections of newspapers.

They stroll. Alex mmms

— Good point

Matching each other stride for stride now they traverse the startlingly all-glass lift-well and enter into another large open-plan office. This office is virtually deserted, it being lunchtime: a few stalwarts, and a few people worried about their jobs, remain hunched around their computer terminals. Some of the terminals are showing personalised screensavers: nude starlets, flying condoms, football club insignia floating in space. One girl is absent-mindedly munching from a bag of Marks & Spencer crisps as she plays bridge on her PC: her screen is a serene lawn of Wimbledon green. As one Alex and Bernardino sit down at their desks and Bernardino leans across to finger Alex's lapel

— Nice suit. Very nice cut

Flattered, Alex curses himself for being flattered, and replies

— Paul Smith, actually

— But of course!

With a contented expression Bernardino turns to his screen and boots up his terminal and begins writing his piece on the new season's menswear. For half a convivial hour they work together; Bernardino knowledgeably and electronically discoursing on the virtues of Borsalinos, Alex ringing up various contacts in Soho to get the number of the Torture Garden, and the Red Stripe Club, and the Virginia Bottomley Society.

His work nearly done Alex takes a call from Rachel at *Cosmopolitan*, arranging their date for the evening; enlivened by this small evidence of his sexual success Alex drops the phone and turns to Bernardino and says

— Did you see the game?

— Mmm? – Bernadino looks like he is thinking of subtly tweeded English gentlemen decanting themselves from shooting breaks

— The match. Italy. D'you see it?

Bernardino shakes his head

— I told you, yesterday, I am not interested in soccer
— But you're a dago?
— I am sorry?
— You're a pasta-eating narcissistic eyetie twat, right? So you must be into it. The Azzuri? AC Milan? Del Piero? Roberto Baggio played pretty well I thought?
— Unlike you – Bernardino smiles, smooth and unruffled by Alex's customary racial insults – I am not obsessed with macho posturing. Nor am I interested in a very ordinary game which has recently been elevated out of all proportion to its importance in this thing you call . . . a culture
— No, sorry, instead you're interested in *handbags for men*

Bernadino merely half-smiles, and then glances downwards, at Alex's loafers
— Patrick Cox?
— Natch
— In the sale?
— What do you think. Why *did* you come to England, anyway, Bernardino?

Bernardino does an almost-French shrug
— I had a strange desire to see for myself at first hand that paragon of understated elegance that we in Italy know as *il stile Inglese*
— Not because Italian newspapers suck?
— You must imagine my surprise when I walked the streets of London and saw that those people who weren't wearing multicoloured plastic overalls were wearing light brown ankle socks . . . with *sandals* – Bernardino shudders – It was quite a . . . how do you say it . . . fucking bummer?

Patrick Coxed foot dangling over Paul Smithed knee Alex leans back and says
— You think we dress crap?
— *Si.* And yet with some of you . . . there is still something . . . – The Italian shrugs fatalistically – Only an Englishman can

wear a frayed collar and get away with it. Only a certain type of Englishman. Not you, of course

— Thanks. But if clothes are so important

— Not clothes, as such: *la bella figura*

— If togs are so important why are the Italians so keen to get involved in Europe then? You'll end up being bossed around by Germans in multicoloured jumpers

Clicking out of his file, Bernadino offers a weary but compassionate face to Alex, like a good teacher explaining a relatively easy equation for the umpteenth time.

— As I think I have told you the Italians see Europe as a way of giving up what we do not want, anyway. What was our currency? The Lira. What is our political culture? Corruption. For us Brussels is a chance to escape the less pleasant sides of . . . Italian-ness, if you will – Alex nods; Bernardino nods – But of course you understand we will still keep all the things that make us proud to be Italian, our style, our food, our beautiful cities, our beautiful women, none of those will be taken away by European integration. Our virtuous Italian-ness will still be there, unaffected

Alex muses, tries

— Whereas you think with us, with us . . . with the British . . . ??

– But he dries up, confused by a too-wide choice of thoughts.

— Exactly – Bernardino finishes, shooting a pristine white cuff – All the things that make you proud to be English

— British

— British

— Well, English

— All the things that make you proud to be British, like your laws and the Houses of Parliament and your democracy and your Protestant political culture and indeed the very fact of your fiercely defended independence . . . these things will all be threatened if not destroyed by European integration

The office is filling up again; workers returning from lunch.

Alex punches the buttons on his phone, pointlessly. Bernadino looks across the desk at his newly disconsolate colleague, and says

— But you must cheer up, it may never happen

Alex tosses a pencil in the air, catches it, snaps it, chucks the two pieces on to his desk, and says

— How many racists does it take to change a lightbulb?

— Sorry?

— None. Let the nigger do the fucking work

— That is not . . .

With a tone of inscrutable sadness, inscrutable to Alex himself, Alex says

— I know, Bernie, I know . . .

Rachel has arranged to meet Alex at a bar-cum-restaurant called Cape; a huge newish place at the bottom of Kingsway. The evening is damp; the plane trees of Holborn look sad and wet. Wandering down the boulevard Alex dodges some drunken England soccer fans sporting Three Lions tee shirts, presumably on their way to France via Waterloo station. Many of the fans have had their faces painted with the cross of St George; as Alex considers how the Union Jack is so much cooler, prettier, more aesthetic a flag than either the Scottish saltire or St George's cross, the cavorting England fans get horn-honks of support from several passing taxis with red-and-white ribbons ribboning from their aerials.

He is here. The place. Alex knows he is here, at Cape, because all the people inside are standing around in that slightly smug yet also self-conscious way that people have when they first go to a glamorous new drinking hole.

Within the large dark plate glass-windowed mega-restaurant Alex spots Rachel perched on a bar stool sipping from a something-and-tonic. She is in a short black dress and she is looking good: even the fan above her head is flirting with her, pushing her dark hair back from her fine north London face. She is also browner than Alex remembers: her sunbed-tanned bare legs are crossed at the knee and she is swinging a black shoe on the end of an equally suntanned foot. From his vantage point by the hatcheck Alex gets a glimpse of a hint of black knicker; as he goes over to Rachel Alex realises that this hint of black knicker is giving him a profound erection; consequently Alex is forced to conceal it by approaching Rachel side on; persisting in this pose he sidles up and mouths an awkward hello over his own shoulder.

— Alex? Are you OK?

His erection subsides

— Sorry Rachel . . .

— You look . . . uh . . .

— You look very lovely, nice dress

Rachel eyes him: his just-cut hair; his expensive jacket. She says

— Sink a few drinks before you came?

— I'd like a gin and tonic. Tanqueray

Turned from the black waistcoated barman Alex pulls the bar stool under himself and sits down . . . and they start talking. And talking. They talk. And talk. Without even one embarrassing hiatus or awkward conversational caesura they chat and flirt and talk. This delights Alex: he and Rachel are, for all his fears, good together. They flow. It is as if the lights are green. As if the city is empty. While he talks to Rachel Alex gets the immediate and wonderful feeling that this is going to be one of those nights. Tonight, Alex thinks, tonight he will get in his car and drive straight across the dusklit city, tonight he will shoot the Westway and peel off to Shepherd's Bush and swing into Princedale where his dealer will be standing there already, holding a half-G of the purest Colombian . . .

They talk and laugh. They drink and talk. They laugh and

drink. At one point Alex's hand touches her calf as he reaches for his deliberately jettisoned Zippo, *and she does not flinch.* Trying to control his excitement, Alex fails; Alex is excited; Alex is suave; Alex's heart is a Spitfire doing a victory roll.

Tonight?

The evening darkens; the leaves of the plane trees occlude and soft-focus the streetlamps. Inside the bustly restaurant they talk and drink. They drink and laugh. They laugh and talk. Then they go into the restaurant proper and eat rocket, duck breast, osso bucco and figs, and they discuss Rachel's Jewishness. Deftly they dance the conversational dance; him gently leading, her elegantly following. In turn they talk about her faint respect for kosherisms, about her nonetheless tenacious attachment to Israel. With Alex's hand metaphorically placed in the small of her back Rachel smiles and confesses her mixed feelings about her identity: how she can feel British to a certain respect but not English, because English is a racial term. At this Alex smiles inside and smiles outside and pours her some more wine and returns by saying that Jewishness is by definition a religious thing, surely? Hmming, Rachel takes her glass and chugs some more wine, which gives Alex the chance to show some of his own steps. Eyes fixed on her wide eyes Alex explains his misgivings about the sacrifice of nationhood and identity he feels is entailed by European federalism. As she sips the white wine he describes how he sees the drive for European Union as a kind of socio-historical fondue, a fondue in which Germany wishes to disguise the overstrong flavour of her nationality, the rancid meat of her recent history, by masking it in the blandly blended, cheaply melted cheese of Euro-ness . . .

The sound of cutlery. The sound of other people's chatter. As Alex wipes his mouth on a thick white napkin, Rachel sits there, toying with a pudding fork. Then she widens further her honest dark eyes and restates her theory about Alex: that he is surprising, that he is not quite what one expects, that he is a peculiar and unexpected mixture of laddishness and seriousness, that although he presents a front of being frivolously boorish and hedonistic he is surprisingly thoughtful, even intellectual; and when she says this . . .

Alex deliberately lightens the conversation: leaning across the remains of a decent fruit *brûlée* and two empty espresso cups he smoothly torches her cigarette and shifts the conversation to gossipy things, to fashion, sex, the crap weather, England's World Cup victories over Tunisia and Colombia; after that Alex mentions his house in Hoxton and then they pay the bill and go outside and wait by the street and climb into a cab.

In his house his flatmates are asleep or out; thus undisturbed Alex makes a cafetiere of Java; before they can drink it his fingers are sliding under the tiny black straps of her little black dress and he is sowing kisses on the slope of her lovely neck.

As he does this Rachel moans. And sighs. Closing her eyes Rachel kisses him, opening her eyes she kisses him again, and decides. At once she takes his hand and leads him downstairs into his bedroom where they kiss more, and kiss again, and kiss more, more. At the last she steps back and lets drop her little black dress, letting her dress descend to her hips, from where she hula-hoops her dress to the floor. Now she is black bra, black panties, a brown suntan, and standing in a crumpled pool of silk. Alex is excited and drunk; seeing her semi-naked he is thinking about how she will look naked; as he thinks this he knows he has to see Rachel's pubic hair, her tender swatch of fur, and so he pushes her topply body onto the bed and when she stretches out drunkenly Alex looks up between her soft tan thighs and he can see the hairs of her pubes spidering out from under the gusset of her black silky knickers, sweet black hairs so excitingly indicative of the proximity of her cunt and her arsehole.

The sight of this makes Alex's stomach go cold and empty and sad and he nuzzles the fabric stretched across her buttock as she lies there all quiet and hushed for a moment; then she leans back up and grabs him by his neck and pulls him close and fives her fingers through his thick dark hair and swallows his mouth with her mouth, and he thinks, and he is thinking

O you creamy, O you creamy jewish slut.

Rachel is looking up at him, her eyes are as big as her body is small, her shoulders are as narrow as his are wide, she is a hard professional neo-feminist *Cosmopolitan* editrix saying in a tiny little girly voice

— Go on come inside me

— Inside you?

— Yes inside me, inside me *now*

Alex kisses, he dives, he licks. Slow, patient, he moves to enter. Inside her he stoops to lick the sweat from her breast, and then he starts driving, driving them. They are fucking and he is driving them across town. They are fucking and he is driving too fast, much too fast. She is biting, scratching, looking up at him

— Yes yesyesye

But he ignores her; his eyes on the road he drives on: caning her, thraping them, he is driving them both: to that dangerous place, that rough estate, the barrios, he is shooting the Westway and peeling down to Shepherd's Bush and caning up Princedale: he is taking them both to a place he knows, that place where you can always score.

Later that early morning he looks at her as she dresses; the streetlights and the dawnlight filter through the thin curtains and he can see by her silhouette that she is attiring herself in the dark.

The parallels of her dress adjusted around her thighs, Rachel looks over

— Who's Katy?
— Sorry?
— You called me Katy. When we were fucking
— Women should only swear in bed
— Fuck that, Alex, who the fuck is Katy?

Disturbed, Alex pitches onto his side and slips his left hand under the coolness of the pillow's underside. From there he looks sideways at Rachel, as she stands there: proud, haughty, insulted. She is standing the way dancers do: with one heel tucked into the instep of the other foot. She must have been a dancer, Alex thinks; explains the suppleness.

Katy?

He is very confused. Lying there, he says, halting
— You mean, I called you . . . I didn't call you Elizabeth?

Rachel looks at him like he is an imbecile
— *Who the fuck is Elizabeth?*
— Well, she's . . . – He rummages, urgently. Up in the attic of old lies he searches. In the garage of old stories he ransacks. No dice. With a falling feeling inside, Alex admits, despairing
— She's an old girlfriend
— And Katy?

Before he can come up with another lame bit of truth Rachel is gone. Downstairs he hears the door slam. Outside in the quiet streets of Hoxton he hears her high voice, hailing a cab.

Turning the pillow over to cool his cheek Alex shuts his eyes and sighs and thinks: *relief.*

11

love-in-a-mist

Fat? Cuddly? Fat? Cuddly? Fat? Fat fat fat fat fat fat? er, Cuddly?

His stomach sucked in and his cheeks Sting'd into hollowness Tony has one last go at self-deception. Then sags, defeated. Not only is he fat, he is *fat*. Obese. Overweight, ugly, balding, prematurely middle-aged, and possessed of a tiny penis.

And fat.

Punch-drunk from this encounter with the vicious thug who seems to be residing in the section of his brain where most people have an ego and a modicum of self-esteem, Tony lunges a hand so as to tilt the full-length bathroom mirror so it uselessly reflects the full-length of the bathroom ceiling; then he sits on the yellow varnished pinewood lavatory seat in his Disney-character boxer shorts, kneels his balding head in his hands, and he exhales, long and deep and again.

Why should she fancy me?

Why indeed. He is lunching the sweet pretty girl from Waterstone's this Sunday afternoon: he is wondering what to wear, how to wear, why to wear . . .

For no particular reason Tony rises from the lavatory seat and goes into the children's bedroom where the cheaply carpeted floor is half obscured by toys: wooden cars, a plastic Taiwanese Harley Davidson, a floppy woollen doll, a large amount of Lego spilled from a white-and-red plastic bucket. Laboriously shovelling the toys and bricks into their proper containers, Tony feels the chill of his children's absence: the shock of the cold. Blue plastic spade in hand Tony's love for his children gulfs him in waves, waves given added force by the looming prospect, the mooted futurity, a sincere possibility that Tony will lose his children in the courts if he loses his wife as a cuckold . . . If he loses her. If he loses *Elizabeth*.

But how can he be sure Elizabeth is cheating on him? Granted, the *letter*, but . . . Can he truly be so sure? Why is he preparing to be possibly unfaithful to the mother of his children, without final, definitive proof? Venting another heartfelt sigh this Sunday morning Tony wanders downstairs to get a drink from the kitchen. Halfway there he is distracted: in the hall he stops to look at the rows of photos of his and Eliza's wedding. Confronted by the gallery of happy sunlit wedding photos . . . Tony remembers why he hates photos. If you are happy in old photos you feel sad because you are no longer that happy; if you are sad in old photos you get sad because you are reminded of that sadness . . . Tony hates photos but he cannot stop looking at them: at this series of later photos, photo studies of Elizabeth, alone. Alone in his nostalgia and love, Tony lingers, over the framed photos of his wife, the ones he insisted they hang here: the photo of her holding a kitten to her chin, as a girl; with a pretty schoolfriend in a photo booth, girning; on a nameless beach in a bikini with some bastard's yacht in the background, moored.

Scrutinising the most recent picture of his wife, taken last summer, Tony sees the marks of her at-last ageing, the first lines of her late twenties, the delicate crinkles near her eyes. Stood in his shorts in the narrowness of the hall he feels these signs of beauty's departure from his wife's beautiful face as somehow loveable: the fact that she is ageing, that his wife is becoming very slightly less lovely, it only makes him love her more. Moving back into the kitchen, waiting for the kettle, Tony finds himself almost accepting her need to sleep with other men, with another *man*. Knowing and loving his beautiful wife as he does he feels he knows and even loves *her* need: her need to be beautiful again, to be properly kissed and caressed, to be found lovely in the looking glass of a new lover's gaze.

But is she with him *now*? He can only wonder. Speculate. She is in town with the kids but Tony knows that she isn't. Or isn't she? Or is she introducing the kids to her Spanish-American publisher right now? To her big Latino buck? To her Coloured who was so Especially Welcome?

Get out. Get dressed.

Back upstairs in their shared bedroom, sipping from a mug of instant, Tony scopes the scene: her knickers on the floor, her bra hung on the bedstead; the unstained sheets of their bed. How long has it been since they had sex? Four weeks? Four months? For years? How long has he been sneaking off to his secret stash of porn behind the Hoover in the cupboard under the stairs? How long has he been having to move the Hoover so he can furtively climax? And why, why, why *hasn't* she noticed that he seems to be doing an awful lot of late-night hoovering?

Chucking the bra in a drawer full of her cotton and silk, her pinks and blues, her breast things, her cunt things, her sweet feminine underwear things, he tries not to dwell too pleasurably on images of her groaning, grunting, sweating; on images of her blonde fringe damped down by her sweat, of her black pubic hair clogged with someone else's *spittle*.

Godhelp. Tony shuts the drawer with a slam. Erects himself. *Get a hold*. Wardrobe door open he chooses a boldly checked shirt, tucks the shirt into a pair of worn brown cords; chooses his old brown brogues and his favourite second-hand Harris tweed jacket. Thus attired Anthony Jonathan Rafferty exits the bedroom, takes the stairs, and slams the front door of his small Putney house, looking every inch the bookish, donnish, young-but-already old minor public school Englishman; born as he was in Sligo.

The day is breezy, yet muggy. Girls are walking down Disraeli Road in their summer kit. Tony notes, with curiosity, as the novelist he wanted to be and still would like to be but is beginning to suspect he probably never will be, that one ugly girl in particular is wearing, as a result of her ugliness, the Skirt of Compensating Shortness.

Keyturning, foot on the pedal, Tony deals with the gears and pulls out into the traffic and heads north-east; up the High Street, over the river, into town; unto his assignation. Shooting the Embankment he slides the car around the dolphin lamp stands by Westminster Bridge and slides down to the roundabout by County Hall. Making a left he spends an hour trying to find a place to park round the back of Waterloo Station. Finally successful, he suppresses his temper, bribes the parking meter, and walks hurriedly round the corner to the Fire Station, to the nearby fashionable bar wherein they have arranged to assignate.

She is not there. Tony panics; checks his watch. *Has he missed her?* Surveying the high-ceilinged new restaurant and the deliberately beaten-up brown-wood bar he begins to think it was all a misunder . . . but when he turns to check the wobbly pint-stained wooden tables on his left he sees her: framed by the large Fire Station doorway. She is waving; wearing a flowery dress. Tony's mood improves on seeing this: tied around her flowery dressed waist is a jumper. Tony knows what that jumper is. It is an Arse Jumper. The classic Arse Jumper. From long experience, most of it experienced vicariously through Alex, Tony knows that girls with a jumper tied around their waist are almost always hiding a Considerable Arse.

But as Tony cogitates on this, as he greets Julia with a mwah-kiss, and a shy smile which they share, he is cheered. Because, if she's wearing an Arse Jumper, i.e. if she has a Fat Arse, he, Tony, is OK. She's not too attractive for him. Not too hot. They can do a deal; come to an arrangement. Tony can swap his fat stomach for her fat backside.

But that still leaves her prettiness.

As the two of them head towards the bar Tony sidelong examines the nice white teeth, the nice blonde hair. *What about her prettiness? What about that?* **What have I got to offer in exchange for that?** Tony frowns, then notices that her ears are a bit big, and that she is deliberately wearing her hair long at the side to cover them. This isn't much; perhaps it is enough. Tony's mood roller coasters upwards again. *I can swap my balding hair for her big ears; we can barter her slight squint for my lack of a tan; I am happy to overlook her shortness if she forgives my small penis.*

Yes. Tony thinks. *That should do it. Everything else should be OK. She might be well bred and kind, sweet and well read, but I am funny, intelligent and charming. And I probably earn more than her . . .*

The mental contract thus drawn up, Tony smiles at Julia who has been making stilted small talk the while; opposite each other they sit on their bar stools, sip their drinks, and Tony beams and talks about poetry, thinking as he does so, yes, *maybe this is the girl of my dreams; maybe this is the girl who will save my life, maybe we could do it just the once.*

But then it unravels. When they finish their drinks, and go through into the main bustly ex-fire station restaurant, there to eat prosciutto and summer-fruits, the whole delicate balance that Tony has striven to achieve is upended. Once Julia relaxes into her wine and the lunchdate she begins to open up, to expand, to enjoy. And it turns out she is more intelligent than Tony expected. Genuinely smart. To Tony's surprise and chagrin it quickly becomes apparent that they do *not* equate. Julia isn't just some flowery sweet English bookshop girl with a smallish brain and a good background: she is serious. Intellectual. *Political.* Dunking a chunk of ciabatta bread in a dish of olive oil and balsamic vinegar Julia munches the bread and enthusiastically begins a discussion of the upcoming marching season in Ulster, the annual Loyalist agitations at Drumcree. Clearly and fairly she tells Tony she sympathises with Catholic anger, with the underlying tensions of the Irish experience. She tells him how much she understands the Republican cause, even though she in no way espouses their pursuit of an armed struggle. Then she tells Tony how the government and its ministers is dedicated to keeping the Nationalists on board in the new devolved government, unlike the previous administration which was unhappily beholden to the Unionists because of a wafer-thin Commons majority . . .

— Mm – Says Tony – Er. Yes.

He is not quite following, not quite interested: few things bore him more than politics, one of those is Northern Irish politics. So Tony is not following her conversation. He is thinking about how fat he is, whether his baldness is showing, whether if he skips a main course he will be noticeably thinner by this afternoon. Not noticing the uninterest in Tony's demeanour Julia goes on: banging on about how exciting it is to be working for Blair and New Labour and how they are changing everything and how most people don't realise . . .

Tony interrupts

— I thought – He mumbles into his glass of the third cheapest house white – I thought you . . . worked in a bookshop

Julia laughs, waves the hand that isn't holding a glass

— Oh, no, God, do you think I'd be working there if being a student paid any money? *Please*

She laughs, shows her neat teeth, and explains her background, her history, her ambitions; while she elaborates Tony's hopes skulk further into a darkened corner. Not only is Julia not just some dean's-daughter-in-muslin, not just some sweet

English bimbo with a 2:2 from Oxford Brookes time-serving her way through the lower echelons of publishing until she meets the right tall handsome bespoke-suited art dealer from Sotheby's, not only is Julia not just this: she is in actuality about as bright as they get. Muttering questions and half-listening to her eloquent answers Tony gulps more and more wine in an effort to blunt the truths he is hearing: that Julia has got a First in PPE from Oxford *University*, that she is following that with a doctorate at Birkbeck, that she intends to go into political research full time. Julia also by the by explains that she does charity work, that her brother is a well-known West End theatre director, and that her previous boyfriend was a famously good-looking actor met via her brilliantly sickening brother.

And I'm fat with a tiny penis. Literally tiny. Minuscule. Inch High Private Eye. I actually have the smallest penis in the European Union.

The final blow comes when Julia puts down her glass and stops talking about how nice Cherie Blair is, mentions that she's got to go to the loo: and as she gets up and turns and walks to the lavatory minus her Arse Jumper Tony watches her retreating figure samba between the Fire Station tables and he learns and accepts the final awful terrible fact, the fact that acts as a *coup de grâce* on any hope-of-a-tumble he may have entertained. *She hasn't even got a fat arse. Her arse is OK. Her arse is actually rather nice . . .*

Hapless, Tony slumps over his empty plate of carpaccio and parmesan, ordered in an unsuccessful attempt to appear cool and sophis. He feels like swearing at the menu: because she's so out of his league. She's intelligent, pretty, rich, cultured, kind, concerned, and she's got a rather decent little arse. And what is he? A rep. A **rep**. A balding, fat, micro-penised publishing rep with a wife who is screwing some hunksome trillionaire Puerto Rican.

Momentarily, Tony considers the possibility of making a

break for it. Of leaving Julia a pile of cash and an apologetic note:

Sorry, had to dash, my penis is too small

even as he reaches for his pen he hears her speak
— Hi – Says Julia – Split the bill and go?
— Sure

Out of their seats they quit the restaurant; in the cloudy sunshine they walk towards the Hayward Gallery and the river. It is warmer now. Tony unjackets himself and he suddenly thinks *to hell with it*: while they dodge the roadworks and the station taxis he starts telling Julia: everything. He has decided he has nothing to lose, he has decided he had nothing to win, thus Tony stops pretending to be urbane and successful. He just tells Julia the lot. They tango between buses and taxis and as they do he outlines his life: his happy marriage (lack of), his happy sex life (lack of), his happiness (lack of). All through this Julia listens intently, mutely, and so he presses on: in a fit of drunken frankness he tells her about the cache of porn he keeps under the Hoover and how he has to keep hoovering to cover up his masturbation.

Julia laughs. Instead of appalling her, this amuses her; in turn this makes him laugh back. And when they pass under Waterloo Bridge, past the tableau of dereliction: the shouting winos and panhandling junkies and piles of British Sherry bottles Tony gets a rush of bravado and gestures at the underbridge squalor and he says:
— Earth hath plenty things to show more fair, Dull is he of spirit, who could pass by, a sight so touching in its tragedy

The noise of buses thundering across the bridge overhead fills the moment Julia takes to get the nearly-quote; when she does she looks at him with a newly appreciative glance, and then she grins
— Wasn't that Westminster Bridge?

Ignoring this point Tony gets serious again: hardly drawing breath he tells her more, the rest. He tells her how he thinks Elizabeth is having an affair, he tells her about the letter, he tells how it all hurts him, how he loves his children so much the very idea . . .

Julia says nothing. The two of them take the steps up to the South Bank plaza. Crossing towards the Hayward she looks at him and smiles white and neat and, then, suddenly, she reaches out a hand and squeezes his hand.

His hand squeezed, Tony errmms, startled. He squints at her; she looks at him; then she loses his gaze and gazes over his shoulder. But she keeps hold of his hand.

The outreach, the erotic empathy entailed by this gesture, makes Tony wonder. It makes him wonder what such a nice well-educated not-Arse-Jumper-needing sweetheart *is* doing with a married man with two children. Perhaps . . . perhaps she *isn't* so sweet, he thinks. Perhaps she isn't so good. Perhaps she's a devious little dirty-minded homebreaker who secretly wants him to take her savagely from behind as she smears her pussyjuice over his wedding photos

— Erm . . .

Disturbed by himself Tony gestures as if to guide Julia's lower back into the Hayward Gallery. She obeys. Inside the concrete lobby of the Gallery Tony is struck by a thought, a thought that has been banging on the door of his consciousness for about twenty minutes.

Perhaps she just fancies me.

Yes! Considering the remarkable but truly felicitous notion that she might actually simply just *fancy* him, Tony stands in the Hayward lobby and exults; then he confidently scans the concrete walls, covered with posters and noticeboards. A puzzle creases his brow

— That's annoying, the exhibition I thought was on . . . isn't . . .

She shrugs:

— Never mind, we can
— Hold on, what about this Maple . . .
— Mapple
— Mapplethorpe – He repeats, corrected – What about this . . . Robert . . . Mapplethorpe exhibition? – A vague thought troubles, then disappears – He's a famous photographer, isn't he?

Julia equivocates
— Yeah. But . . .

Feeling a need to be decisive, Tony decides
— Come on

Her reluctance outbid, they go to the ticket desk. Together they pay ten pounds for two big rectangular tickets which gain them entry into the hushed interior of the building, where a series of large black-and-white photographs are hanging on the white walls. The first photographs are of anonymous New Yorkers; elegant, monochrome, huge, understated.

They move from photograph to photograph, Tony and Julia converse quietly and disjointedly about Tony again, about his background
— My father was an architect
— In Ireland . . . ?

Julia is eyeing the photographs suspiciously. Tony smiles:
— Yes. In Ireland
— . . . so . . . you came over when?
— Mid-seventies. There wasn't a lot of call in Sligo for neo-Brutalism. My father moved us all to Dublin, then Bracknell
— That's . . . in Berkshire?
— Er, yeah. In. Berkshire. Then we moved on. Yes. Uhm . . . We . . .

Tony has stopped. He has stopped talking because he has just noticed that he and Julia are now standing in front of a large monochrome photograph of a man pissing deliberately into the open mouth of another man.

— I love Berkshire – Julia says, staring defiantly at the extraordinary photograph – A lot of people knock it, loads of people think it's just Reading and railways, they forget the Downs . . .
— Yes – Tony says – Uhm. And the Chilterns, of course. And there's loads of good pubs . . .

The two of them move on. Shuffling dutifully, they position themselves in front of an even larger photograph. A picture of a . . .

Making his own attempt to appear suave and at-ease-with-modern-art Tony leans to the label pinned to the wall by the artwork, and recites:
— Man in Polyester Suit. Unique Silver Gelatin Print. Nineteen eighty-five, hm.

He steps back so as to properly appraise the photo. It is a picture of the middle torso and upper thighs of a man in a polyester suit. The fly of the suit is open, and through it protrudes a frankly enormous black penis.
— nnn
— Yyyyes

He coughs.

She coughs. He says
— So you went to school . . . in Sussex?
— Yes – Says Julia, staring with impressive impassivity at the massive eight-inch-long semi-erect black cock – It was a small private school, a bit too small . . . I liked some of the teachers, though . . . they were very . . . you know . . . enthusiastic . . .
— What did you do for your A levels?

They both gaze intently at a man with the handle of a leather bull-whip inserted about half a metre into his gaping anus.
— English. Modern History . . . Business Studies
— Really . . . – Tony says – I did English too
— I know, you told me you did at Uni, as well, right?
— Er, yep – Says Tony, trying to look interested, but not too interested, in a large black guy with a fantastically distended scrotum.

— So do you . . . – Julia leans forward, manically examining the man's swollen glans penis – Do you miss Sligo?
— A bit, like most émigrés I always think I'll go back there one day, but, you know . . .
— Sisters and brothers?
— One sister, one brother . . . both . . . – A man with a fist and a forearm halfway up his own arsehole – Both older . . .
— What do they do?
A penis laid out along a butcher's slab.
— Civil engineer. Yes
A testicle pierced by spikes.
— Julia
A nipple being bitten off.
— Mmm?
A bleeding anus.
— Shall we go?
— *Let's*

A light breeze is feathering the leaves of the riverside plane trees of the National Theatre esplanade; making an eighteenth century Chelsea watercolour of the scene. Side by side Julia and Tony lean on the bronze rails and watch the Thames roll historically by. They are quiet, together. Languidly they turn and lean back on the rails; cruise-shippishly; appreciating the staggered jetties of the National Theatre building. Between them and the shuttered concrete a man is juggling glittery purple sticks. A crowd of Japanese tourists are queueing up to have their photo taken with. All the time couples walk past, arm in arm.
— This is where they shot that clip . . .
Tony looks at Julia, she is closing her eyes and enjoying the sun on her face as she speaks. He says
— Sorry?

— That scene – She is still smiling – From *Truly Madly Deeply*, where the man hops along . . . I really loved that movie
— Nn? I hated it

Julia opens her eyes and turns and laughs
— You know, it is possible to be a bit *too* honest . . .

Tony chuckles; so does she. The warm breeze kicks back Julia's hair; the yellow-and-ochre barked plane trees shiver. Seized by the moment, Tony broaches the unspoken subject: the appalling unsuitability of the exhibition, the fact that they couldn't have chosen a worse place to have their first date, the absurdity of it all. Relieved to have this aired, engaged by Tony's honesty, Julia giggles, agrees, and then they talk about the photos and then they stare at each other. The sun is shining. The day is warm. Idle, relaxed, happy, they wander up and down the Embankment. The sun beats down and the old river sparkles and Tony starts to get an irresistible urge. To kiss Julia. Standing a few yards from the rails of the riverside his face is turned to hers. He wonders if he should lift her chin at this juncture but she does it for him: she lifts and looks up at him and just as Tony leans, just as he is about to kiss this girl for the very first time, the first time of so many . . . *he sees in her eyes the hint of a blueness, an azurite light, and in her cheek the red of a certain rose, the roses that grew along the chains in the gardens of Lyonshall House, and then the shimmer of the river behind Julia's face is like the shimmering Arrow on a May morning, with the mist rising from the water, clearing mist revealing the uncut green Lammasland beyond* – and then Tony is gone. He walks away. He detaches himself from Julia's bemused arms and walks, and then runs. Away. Back. Away.

12

vinegar leaves

— Where's Eddie?

Alex strolls through the front door into Tony and Elizabeth's house carrying a four-pack of beer over his shoulder; the central plastic membrane slung on a nonchalant forefinger; Tony shrugs

— Well, he's not here yet . . .

— Not awake yet – Alex shakes his head and stands defiantly in the hall, as if he expects children and wives to pop out of the wallpaper and chastise him for something, for everything; a chastisement he is perfectly willing to resist with outright violence.

— Don't worry – Tony says – She's at a launch, she'll be out till late

— Good – Alex belches, scans the house again – Y'know this is the third time I've been here in eight years. Guess I should feel . . . privileged . . . – Glancing at the dining room door – By the way whatever happened to that dinner party? – Sarcastic, smiling – It was meant to be this year . . . wasn't it?

Tony, discomfited:

— Sometime . . . we keep having to postpone because . . . because . . .

Giving the look to Tony's lameness Alex hands the beer over. Obedient, Tony takes the beer and his white-shirted, tipsy, effervescing friend, through the hall to the kitchen, where Tony fridges the four-pack and takes out one of a six-pack he chilled earlier. Cold can in hand, Alex pulls, pfffts, and swigs at the socket:

— Been down the pub

— *No*

— You should feel the atmos. We're gonna hammer 'em

— Really

— Yep. *Rilly*

The can already finished, Alex opens the fridge for himself and finds another

— So who're you supporting?

Pouring his own beer into a tilted glass, Tony shrugs

— I suppose it'll have to be England

— Ta mate

— Well . . . you know it's not my scene

— Dung-eater

Enjoying the savour of cold Bohemian Star, Tony asks about the game: what time it kicks off, who's in the team . . . Before Tony gets an answer Alex has whistled at his wristwatch, cussed, and scooted down the hall to the sitting room; there to squat on the floor in front of the TV. Following on behind Tony stands at the back of the room and listens to Alex talking about football and Katy and football.

Then Tony remembers: his duties. Businesslike he shifts to the kitchen, where he assembles bags of pistachios, crisps, peanuts, and tortilla chips; setting these by two ashtrays and more beers on a tray, he ferries the lot back into the sitting room, sets them on the floor beside his furiously smoking friend. Tony wonders whether to chastise his friend for smoking; decides not. Instead Tony sits in an armchair behind Alex and the TV and watches Alex as Alex cheers, sings, curses, smokes, and does a somehow racist belch. Out loud Tony wonders how Alex can get *quite* so worked up. Executing a breakdancer's swivel on the carpet, Alex:

— Get worked up? **Get worked up?** This is the Argies, man . . . Think about it

— What, the Falklands?

— That. And

— And what?

— Hand of God. *Maradona* – The reference evidently fazing his friend, Alex tries to explain – It's all the history . . . It's got *form*, this fixture – Tony remains bemused, Alex does his best – Imagine we were playing you, imagine we were playing Ireland – Tony's friend puts on a special Hollywood trailer voice – 'We tried to wipe them out in the Famine, they tried to bomb us all to bits, tonight it's England versus Ireland, round three . . .'

Tony sips . . .

— You ever worry you care a bit *too* much?

Fistful of peanuts, mouthful of peanuts, Alex chuckles, sardonic, and returns his attention to the screen; then he says sidelong over his shoulder

— You know what . . . Orwell said: Football is war minus the guns . . . or something . . .

— Well . . . – Tony gazes at the screen, at a replay of some ancient match – In your case I'd stick to war, you Brits are probably better at that – But Alex hasn't heard, Alex is transfixed by the sight of the two teams coming onto the pitch. Alex seems appalled by the stadium's predominance of blue-and-white flags and favours

— Look at them all, how'd they get tickets?

— Probably bought them

— All that support, we're going to lose, know it, *know* it

Alex is rocking backwards and forwards; repeating autistically

— I know it, we're gonna lose, I know it

— Funny, I thought you said that

Alex:

— Gotta remember – Alex slaps his own cheek – They're only *Spics*. Just a bunch of *tapas waiters* – Alex makes a wanking gesture at the parade of handsome Argentinian faces lined up for their national anthem – *Patatas bravas, por favor* . . .

Looking at the televised ranks of the singing Argentinians, Tony can't help pointing out

— They're still considerably better looking than your lot

Alex

— What, better looking than Shearer? Lusher than Ince?

— Which one is Ince?

— Bet *their* wives wouldn't mind some of *Incey's* cable

— Ince is the black one isn't he?

— Dirty little hos: right up the old *honeybadger*

This does it. The reference, the allusion, to cuckoldry, does it. Tony winces, breathes, breathes in too quickly, and despite himself can't help suddenly and unhappily thinking of Elizabeth: the letter, the *letter*. As the football teams disperse around the ground, as the teams kick off, Tony tries to watch, tries to listen. Meantime Alex shouts, claps, bites his beer can, and sings. Until Tony interrupts

— Calm down they've only been playing two minutes

— PENALTY!?? Seamanyoutwat!!

Alex is rolling on the floor. Tony moves the ashtray as Alex laments:

— Jesus . . . Please . . . How could he?!

Ashtray repositioned, Tony looks to the TV. Intrigued by this turn of events, by the penalty award, intrigued by the fact that he is himself obscurely pleased that England have hit a serious problem, Tony watches as the Argentinian player ambles to the spot and slots the ball past the flailing English goalkeeper.

— Noooooooooooo . . . one nil . . . one-nil . . . onenilllll . . .

Tony's friend is moaning, is then quiet. From the armchair

Tony observes as Alex squats, rigid, staring at the early evening sky outside the window: until suddenly Alex bursts

— INGERLUND INGERLUND INGERLUND

Shelling his own pistachio, nutshell chucked in the ashtray, Tony attempts to get involved as his friend, to engage Alex vis-à-vis the game. He tries to discuss wingbacks and mid-field and *offside* . . . but the sight of so many Spanish-speaking players and spectators gets Tony thinking, again, despite himself, about the letter, the letter in Spanish, *Elizabeth*. He tries not to but he can't help: his mind is filled with images of Elizabeth's – what did Alex call it? – Elizabeth's *honeybadger*, her honeybadger filled with some thick Spanish *chorizo*, some red Argentinian banger. Sunk in masochistic misery Tony imagines the entire Argentine team going down on his wife at the end of the match, the wails of her orgasm broadcast on Eurosport: 'Yes certainly those well-hung Latin lads do seem to bring out the best in the English lass, better than that fat balding loser of a husb'

— YES! OWEN! You BEAUtee!

Another penalty. This time for England? Glad to be diverted, Tony watches as Alex can't watch, as Alex turns his head and puts his hands over his ears and sings *Jerusalem* and opens his bright drunk glistening eyes at Tony and mouths the words

— Did they? Did they?

— What?

— Did they do it, did he score?

— Sorry Alex what dyou say?

— Did they sodding score?

— Well, *yes* . . .

— YO!!

Alex tosses a shelled nut in the air and catches it in his mouth and winks at Tony and sits down again. The room goes quiet, gets smokier, smells more of beer. Within a few more minutes Alex is sitting up, edging closer to the screen

— Owen, go on, go ooonn . . . ing HELLLL! YesyesYES, he's going to . . . !!!

An England player has scored. Even Tony has to admit it was sweet: the way the young player, Owen, seemed to waltz through three players and with an almost casual arrogance, a youthful *superbitas*, flick-drive the ball into the top left corner of the net.

When Alex's celebrations have subsided, Tony sits back on his sofa and gazes at his friend. Once more. For some reason, perhaps because Alex is looking particularly boyish and young, in his exuberance, this evening, Tony finds himself remembering when Alex really *was* very young: the day they first met, at University. Tasting some beer Tony recalls that winter afternoon a decade ago when they first ran into each other in a dimlit room in Bloomsbury: when the two of them, Alex in rave-top and weird hair, Tony in cheap brogues and college scarf, when Alex and Tony and their middle-aged tutor spent an earnest two hours discussing Alex's essay on Gerard Manley Hopkins's use of alliteration and assonance, and Tony's minor dissertation on the poet's over-reliance on the Welsh prosodical system of *cynghanedd*

— INGERLUND INGERLUND INGERLUND, INGERLUND INGER-*LUND* INGER-*LUU-UUND*

The next twenty minutes of the match are, Tony is grateful to discover, not quite so fraught, so action-packed. A player called Scholes misses what seems to be an easy chance and Alex pretends to vomit down the back of the sofa; an Argentinian player tests the English defence and Alex finishes a packet of cigarettes. Half-time is approaching, the game is nearly half over; then the Argentinians get a free kick at the edge of the English penalty area. Alex groans

— They're going to score, they're going to score, they're going to . . .

— Uh, they've scored

Alex gazes blankly, saying

— How the fuck did they do that?

Again Alex is quietened. The unarguable ingenuity and skill of the Argentine goal has muted him. Beer, new cigarette, referee's whistle: Alex sits back on his haunches and finally manages . . .
— You can only admire a goal like that. *Grebos*

For most of the half-time interval Alex seems keen to talk about things other than football. Probably because the tension is too much to bear, Alex happily trots alongside Tony as Tony waxes nostalgic about Uni: about Eddie's acid trips, about Alex's acid trips, about the days they spent tripping, in Lyonshall, when they would trip and get drunk and dance by the starlight, in the midsummer moonlight.

Outside the house a humid, damp evening steals quietly over Putney. Disraeli Road is deserted; the quietness means Putney High Street is probably deserted, too. London has been made empty by the match, and the silence of the city wafts through the open window along with the warmish summer evening air as the two old University pals start chatting again: about University days: about Tony's assiduous attendance of lectures, and Alex's assiduous avoidance of lectures. Hiccuping, holding his breath, hiccuping again, Alex confesses
— Tell you what I really dug: Anglo Saxon

Genuinely surprised, Tony:
— Really?
— Yeh. All that fighting. Beowulf. An twa thray feorfan, brill . . .
— I thought it was a bit dull
— Probably cause you're a Gael
— Naturally

Alex looks like he's having an idea; says
— I mean, don't you ever resent having to use English?
— Sorry, don't . . .
— I mean it's not your language . . . don't you feel . . . as an Irishman - Alex half-burps, thumps his chest with a fist - You know, oppressed by the English language sometimes
— Don't we all?

— The English language is the ghost of the British Empire, sitting crowned upon the grave thereof

Alex sits back, waiting for Tony to be impressed by his allusion; Tony isn't:

— *You're* basically a Celt, you should be speaking Scots-Irish by that theory

Visibly irked, Alex takes a crisp from the packet he has just opened; he snaps it in two and waves the remaining half at Tony, the other half being in his mouth

— Had an idea the other day, want to run it by you as a publisher

Sipping his third glass of beer, Tony nods

— Go on

— Updating the Anglo Saxon chronicle. I want to update *The Anglo-Saxon Chronicle*

— mmmm. *Big* seller

— No, I'm serious - Alex makes his serious face - Seeing as England's . . . - He grimaces - Coming to an end, we could do a sort of last chronicle, in the same style, you know: 'In this year did the government sign away our ancient rights in the heathen citadel of Maastricht, in this year did the queen of hearts die because of foul and wicked plots by the Frankish bastards', you know, keep the tenor but update it . . .

The phone is ringing; leaving Alex to his bizarre but-then-again-he's-drunk fantasy Tony decides to take the call in the kitchen; he steps past the wedding photos into the kitchen and picks up the phone and it is Elizabeth.

She says she is going to be late; Tony understands. She asks about the children; Tony says they are safe with his mother, as ever. His wife goes to say something else, but, emboldened by the drink, emboldened by Alex's strangely enlivening presence, Tony asks her. Straight out, his chin firm, gazing at the armoury of Sabatier knives magnetised to their kitchen-wall-holder, Tony asks his wife what exactly *the letter* meant.

A numbing pause. And then: an explanation. Convincing, sincere, believable, Elizabeth's sweet voice explains to her husband that the letter was part of a creative writing course. That is it was pure invention. That it was a test of her own skills, to see if she could still write, creatively, erotically, poetically. Tony lets her go on: she deftly alludes to the old days when they all aspired to be writers, poets. She mentions Lyonshall House, she alludes, she quotes, she mentions; she waffles about Stuart silver fingerbowls . . . full of rose-scented rainwater . . . Tony nods, keen to believe; again, again. He is happy she has not attempted to obscure the issue by getting angry at Tony for stealing her mail or reading her fiction or whatever. She has just explained, calmly. And Tony is won; he wants to believe; he gratefully receives her clever explanation. At once he feels a huge sense of something lift, the clouds part, winter departs . . .

After this they just chat; they have a long heartfelt talk about their marriage, and the children; as they talk long into the evening the conversation is punctuated by various yelps from the sitting room of

BECKHAMJESUS

and

BAST

and

TOILET!

and

YOU STUPID DANISH OPEN SANDWICH EATING NONCE

and by the time Tony returns to the sitting room, after his hour-long sort-out-the-marriage chat, he is in such a good mood he almost wants England to win; he is therefore disappointed to find that England have not won, despite the fact that Alex was cheering a great deal.

— Why were you cheering if it's a draw

Alex's face is white; twitching; strained. Not looking at Tony Alex gazes at the window, his face that of a Vietnam vet returning

from a particularly traumatic tour in-country. Pistachio nut in hand Alex shakes his head
— What a game, like Rourke's drift, Jeez
— So what's going on now?
Alex, gloomy:
— Penalties
— What, a penalty shoot out?
— Uh . . . huh . . .
— So . . . that's . . . good . . . isn't it?

Tony is treading carefully; not carefully enough. Chucking a tortilla chip at his friend Alex sighs an enormous sigh and says
— No. We always lose. Germany in Euro '96. Germany in bloody '90 . . .

The two of them turn to the TV. And watch. The first Argentinian scores. Alex groans. The first Englishman scores. Alex cheers. The second Argentinian misses, Alex cheers; the second Englishman misses, Alex hisses:
— Ince, you . . . **coco-pop**

The third Argentinian, third Englishman, fourth Argentinian, fourth Englishman and fifth Argentinian all score; Alex groans, cheers, groans, cheers, and groans.

The very last Englishman approaches the ball. Alex puts his hands over his eyes
— I know, I know, I just . . .

The last Englishman misses.

The sitting room is quiet. Alex is muttering
— Shit . . . shit . . . Why do we always have to lose, why us . . . why do we . . . every time . . . every bloody time . . . just once. Why can't we win just *once*. It's not too much to ask is it? Just one major overwhelming triumphal victory. Just one, that's all I want, that's all . . .

Gentle, soft, aware of the sensitivity of the moment, Tony says to his friend on the floor
— I thought you always said men should only weep during war

A final nut. A final slug of Star

— Like I said – Alex says, wiping his thumb and forefinger across his embarrassed eyes – Football *is* . . . – He grinds his cigarette into the Argentinian's eyeball of the ashtray – Anyway. Anyway . . . – Again Alex raises his ruined visage – Got any more beers? You murdering Irish mother?

— There's a few more in the fridge – Tony chuckles quietly, stands up – I'll just go and get them, shall I?

— Yes. Yes please. You do that . . . – Alex pulls yet another cigarette from the packet on the carpet – Hey. Maybe we'll win the cricket

13

arse smart

— Driller killer
— Hangover?
— Too right.
— Any particular reason?
— Out with little Katy, I forgot how much she likes to drink, Sea Breezes all night
Eddie chuckles
— Price you pay, of course
— I know – Alex sighs – I know
— So . . . why?
— Er . . . Why what?
— Why do you pay it?
Alex makes a don't-be-stupid voice
— The sex man, what do you think?
— But she's only . . . what . . . eighteen . . . hardly expert
— Hardly expert? *Hardly expert?* I tell you man . . . I tell you, the sex . . . it's . . . it's . . . it's . . .

Alex is pausing to find the right word; Eddie ascertains it is probably important to Alex he do so. Taking the moment, Eddie carries the phone to the window, and stares out at the Smithfield scene: at a couple of striding-to-work City-kids, in matching purple shirts and matching yellow ties, carrying matching Styrofoam cups of coffee from Costa Coffee to the office . . .

Alex has decided:

— Put it like this. The sex is better than heroin

Incredulous silence.

— Better than skag? *Please*

— I'm serious, it's better than beige – Alex laughs down the line – Imagine the best rush you ever had and multiply it by a thousand times and you still wouldn't be near

— OK OK – Eddie is starting to feel morose. He doesn't want to hear about Alex's relatively successful love life: it only reminds him of his absolutely unsuccessful love life. What he wants to do is get Alex off this subject. After all, Eddie muses, it's alright for Alex to talk: he isn't an addict, he is no longer an addict, he perhaps never was an addict. Whereas, Eddie broods, *whereas* . . .

From the window, Eddie shifts across the flat to the kitchenette. Fridge door open, he takes out a bottle of juice, from which he glops as he asks

— Why *aren't* you at work anyway

— *Cosmo* rang up, I'm writing at home

Ah, Eddie thinks, *thank you*. This subject change is not what Eddie wants to hear, either. Just after hearing about Alex's superior love life he doesn't want to hear about Alex's superior job, career, lifestyle, etceteras. Eddie doesn't want to start the day thinking *it shoulda been me, it coulda been me, I would have been the writer, the artist, the anything, if only . . . if only . . .*

— Usual bollocks, holiday sex or something

— Presume you'll make a few hundred, though?

Alex shrugs, verbally

— Yeah, well

— Not bad for half-a-morning's work . . . *at home* . . .

— Guess

Alex is drifting. Eddie is wincing. Wincing at the slightly fizzy taste of the about-to-go-off apple-and-cranberry, wincing at a lot of things. Setting the juice bottle on the kitchen table Eddie slopes back into the sitting room and tries again: desperate to to find some hiding place in the conversation, something that doesn't hurt, doesn't pain, doesn't remind. Football?

— Good result last night

— What, the Holland game?

— Yah, least they beat them. Argies

— Thank God – Alex exhales with feeling – I couldn't have coped if the cheating bastards'd gone on to win – Eddie can sense Alex debating with himself, as he says – Frankly I don't think I can cope if *anybody* wins it: the Frogs, the Huns. Hope they *all* lose

Eddie nods at the wall

— *I* still can't work out *how*, how'd they beat *us*? We were so much better even when we were down to *ten* men, weren't we?

— I know, I know, it's horrible – Over the phone Eddie can hear Alex making a mysterious tapping noise: after a second he works out this is Alex tapping at his laptop while he talks – Still – Alex changes tone – Gotta keep your chin up mate, just cause we're out the World Cup doesn't mean this country isn't going places

— Yah?

— Never forget the UK still publishes more literary magazines per head than any country except Iceland – Eddie chuckles at this; Alex says – And Great Britain's *still* the world's seventh largest island

— And Birmingham has more miles of canal than Venice

— And – Alex thinks – And Tony Blair's haircuts cost more than those of any other G7 premier

Eddie chuckles again

— That true?

— Probably – Alex is making gagging sounds – Probably. Tony Bleaargghhhh, what a suckbag

— You really dislike him that much?
— What do you think?
— . . . I think . . . he's not so terrible. No worse, anyway
— Fuck off – Alex spits – He's totally *bogus*. Did you see him on the telly the other night? Jesus: all those glottal stops, like we're really gonna like him more 'cause he can't speak proppah
— It is Margaret you mourn for

Now Alex chuckles

— Least she knew what she wanted. Does he want to take us into a federal Europe or does he not? Where does the man stand? I'm not sure he even knows. How does he even know if he needs a wank? Does he wait until he's consulted his focus groups?

Eddie makes an agreeing noise. Alex goes on, and on. Eddie half-listens to Alex's rant, watching the world out of his window. A meat lorry is wheezing in Long Lane; a taxi is parking outside the hospital. Quietly, Eddie interrupts:

— Did you know Mozart had his tonsils out in Bart's?

Seconds, respiring, Alex

— What?

More seconds, Eddie:

— Do you miss . . . Lyonshall?
— . . . ?
— Do you miss Lyonshall House? The village?

Now Alex comes back:

— Do you mean do I miss the sight of the violet tide in M'Ladies Wood? Do I miss the smell of white clover? Do I miss rolling back the Savonnerie carpet so we could dance to the light of the Rockingham chandeliers?

Eddie laughs

— Well I
— The taste of Winberry tarts? The spears of blue delphinium? Rose petal sandwiches on the lawns?
— I guess . . . I guess . . .
— C'mon? What d'you think?

Eddie chuckles again, then stops
— I must admit I've been . . . thinking about it myself rather a lot . . . just recently . . . – Using the window from a different angle Eddie watches a group of tourists head for St Bartholomew's Church; the group is being escorted by a guide who is holding aloft an umbrella, like a hussar with a sabre – Maybe it's an age thing. It just seems in retrospect it was so easy then . . . so . . . *pure* . . .
— Tell me
— *I mean* – Says Eddie, suddenly – We were so *stupidly young.* Weren't we?
— Sure – Alex's laughter is strained, sour – 'Snot like I've forgotten – Alex's voice drifts off, comes back – 'What was that wine you gave me in the Spring? Whose adolescent lips have tasted May?'
Eddie
— Ah, the shandygaff they served on silver trays
Alex
— The cherrylogs burning in the grate . . .
A man is carrying sandwiches towards Jacomo's Café. Eddie observes, this, says
— Have you spoken to my sister?
— Nah. You?
— No. You think she's serious about the dinner party?
— Don't know, mate, don't know . . .
Silence. Long silence. Once more Eddie moves from the windowsill, this time to his smoked glass coffee table, his coffee table in the Arab taste. On top of the table is Eddie's old Cohiba box, lifting the cigarbox lid Eddie seeks out his foil, lighter, twentywrap. As Eddie does this Alex starts to say something about having to go; before he has finished Eddie says goodbye and clicks off.

After that Eddie, two-handed now, fiddles in the box properly. Urgent, Eddie takes up and smooths out his sheetlet of foil;

carefully, quickly, Eddie trickles some powder, ignites the powder with the lighter, makes the powder sublime into smoke, then Eddie inhales the smoke through the foil tube. His eyes closed, Eddie smokes the brown powdered poppysap, and forgets.

Forgets.

Hours later Eddie stumbles out into the warm summer air of the London Borough of Finsbury. He is stoned. He is more stoned than he has ever been in his life, or so he assesses: his heart is beating seven to the dozen every minute, his heart is weirdly skipping along like a Dave Brubeck song. Eddie knows he should be staying at home trying not to die, but he has, almost too late, remembered he has to sign on in Islington, in Penton Street. He has a persona to update, an identity to assume, one of his roster of unemployed personae is due to make his fortnightly appearance in the dole office and if Eddie doesn't put in that appearance the claim will be disallowed and Eddie will lose a lot of money. Ergo.

Disguised in an old coat, despite the warm weather, Eddie totters along the curve of Cowcross Street to Farringdon Station and takes the lift and the Circle Line to King's Cross. At King's Cross he doubles back up the hill of Pentonville Road past the car-hire forecourts and converted chapels, turning left up Penton Street into the yellow stockbrick environs of Georgian Barnsbury. Here he takes another left: locates a blistered black door that says Department of Social Security. The door pushed open he finds himself in the signing-on hall, amongst the discards, the jetsam, the shame.

And how many are Celts, Eddie thinks. And how many are blacks. Taking a seat in the corner of the room Eddie tries not to look conspicuous, or conspicuously *in*conspicuous. He also tries not to nod off, tries to stay alert, tries to compose himself so he can remember to assume the right identity when he is called to sign. But it is difficult: he is so out of it. The coat wrapped around his long thin legs Eddie checks out the others in the signing-on hall: the usual lairy Scousers, the usual eructating Glaswegian, the usual down at heel Irish ex-brickies, and the usual scrofulous old wino of uncertain race . . .

But just as Eddie is finding some snobbish racist solace in the fact that the worst of the people in this room are not English, not real English, not (what did Alex call him?), not *Suthangli*, the door to the road noises open and a strutting cockney *untermenschen* walks in with his hideous old slut of a wife; halfway through the door the cockney turns to his downtrodden wife and shouts

— Shut it, just shut it you dull bitch, just shut your fucking fat gob you stupid daft cunt wot did I fucking say to you this fuckin

Eddie can see the words Etc Etc written in a bubble coming out of the man's mouth. Leant forward Eddie stares at the old cigarette butts heeled into the floor, trying not to feel part of this scene, this place, this beaten-up bitch of a town, this helplessly Ethiopian capital, this land of white coons, of helpless black Pakis, of slittyeyed mongoloid Yids

— Trevor Randall?

Eddie doesn't hear.

— Trevor Randall?

Eddie nods and gouches, Eddie dribbles.

— Trevor

His name! His identity! His false persona! Startled from his opiated daze Eddie jumps from the chair and paces over to the desk and nods, and says, and nods at the wide-faced black girl behind the desk.

— Trevor Randall?

— Yeah . . . – Eddie lurches, sways, keeps his eyes open, says – I've got . . . I've got to . . . to *sign* . . . ?

— Erm – The girl looks over Eddie's shoulder; Eddie repeats
— You want me to *sign*, correct?
— Mister Randall . . .
— Yes I've been looking for work, no I'm not working, *is* there a problem?

The girl's face is definitively looking over Eddie's shoulder; then it returns to Eddie.

— Mister . . . Randall . . . there's a bit of a question about your . . . claim

Bile, heartburn, the first hint of panic

— Sorry?

The black girl's large gold earrings jangle as she nods, too vigorously

— You see – She is speaking with painful slowness – Last time you came in, you signed . . . – Leaning to her side she takes out a crumpled signing-on form, and scrutinises it as if to make sure. Lifting it onto the desk she turns it around so Eddie can read the evidence against him, her finger pointing at the bottom line:

— Last time you came in you signed your name . . . Edward Lyonshall

The Glaswegian has stopped coughing. The cockney has stopped swearing. Eddie's heart has stopped beating. Twisting his head Eddie looks behind and sees the signing-on room has suddenly been obscured by two large, besuited men standing right behind him.

The girl stares Eddie in the eyes:

— We'd like to have a word with you. In private. We've got a room . . . prepared.

Coon, Eddie thinks, *coon coon coon coon coon coon coon coon coon coon coon coon coon coon coon coon coon*

14

fuzz

Surrounded by silver, by forks, knives, eyeteeth, waiters, diners, windows, the frenetic skyline of the new-built City visible across the immobile Thames: Alex is doing his best to concentrate, to concentrate on his interview with Davina Ray, the Australian soap star. Sat in the studiedly modern ambience of the Pont de la Tour restaurant, the culinary epitome of resurgent London, of the glinting new capital, Alex tries to focus on her uninteresting answers to his uninspired questions, but all he can think of is what this restaurant represents, a cool new Britain, a Europeanised new Britain: all he can think of is how this compares to the England that was, that he loves: that England that did not have to be modern, that did not have to try, an England that just raped the world and fertilised her, conceiving modernity.

Davina is telling him about when she rollerbladed for Australia in the Queensland championships.

— Y'have to really work at it, y'know, it's kinda difficult and it's kinda simple at the same time

— Right

— And you have to travel all over, Adelaide, Brissie

— Sure. Did you see the match?

The girl looks taken, she glances at the small tape recorder on the white tablecloth; she glances unsurely at Alex, as he lounges on his restaurant banquette, ostentatiously scruffy, ostentatiously unshaven, ostentatiously young and unbesuited amongst the phalanxes of middle-aged pinstripe.

— Y'mean the footie thing?

— Yeah, the Argentina game

— Well, no – She makes an apologetic face – I'm not into . . . soccer . . . so much – Davina looks away, giving him the benefit of her profile she gazes out at the view, at the seagulls wheeling above the Tower, at the Union flags fluttering atop America Square, at the arrays of office microwave aerials that look like Jewish candelabra; turning back Davina says

— Can't believe everybody's so upset over a game of footie, y'know? Just a game of footie? Bloody hell!

Alex shrugs

— It's because it was the Argentinians, there's a lot of history

— Well, I'm Australian, we don't have a lot of history

Alex wonders what it must be like to have no history, to be nationally adolescent, to be a nation still trying to find its style, its clothes sense; Davina beams

— Anyway! I thought we were going to talk about my film!

The twenty-year-old Hollywood film star *manquée* flashes her soap opera smile, again: Alex senses she is trying to be professional, trying too obviously to do what her agent told her to do. Openly Alex yawns and glances between the tablecloth and the girl's chin . . .

The waiter pours far too little wine in their glasses; Alex knocks it back with a contemptuous gargle and wittingly checks out another girl walking down the aisle of the restaurant, a girl wearing a lambswool Arse Cardigan.

Then he turns back and asks questions and doesn't listen as Davina rattles on about pie floaters, Kylie Minogue, Neighbours,

Sydney club-culture, and the Australian film industry . . . and her grandfather the snowdropper
— The . . . What?
— Snowdropper, he stole panties from washing lines
— Like Arnold Layne . . .
— Er, yeah, and that's why he was transported, y'know?
— Right
— All me great great grandparents were crims – She confesses, cheerfully, with that bright neat Australian smile.

Alex
— Funny old gene pool you've got there isn't it?
— No, yeah . . . – The girl looks puzzled, almost hurt – I mean, no, *hey*!

But she is smiling again, smiling as Alex motions at the waiter for the bill:
— Well I think we're done
— That's it?
— That's it – Says Alex, picking up and clicking off the tape recorder, and flashing it at her like a police badge – I can make the rest up
— What?
— Only joking – Alex charms, sidles out of the trap he made for himself – That is unless you . . .

She wipes her lips to remove some Bakewell tart crumbs and smiles happily:
— Unless I want to talk about my film?
— Unless you want to talk about European Interest Rate convergence
— Eh?
— No, 'sOK, got what I want – He taps the bulge in his expensively crumpled linen jacket, the bulge that is his pocketed tape recorder – Can I give you a lift, I'm getting a cab . . . ?

At this sudden end to things, the Australian girl looks crushed, uncheerful: in this big sophisticated European mega-restaurant she looks suddenly forlorn, just what she is: a global provincial in the global capital. The sight of his interviewee's discomfiture makes Alex feel guilty: guilty that he has made this interview such a dismal experience for her . . . but then again he hadn't enjoyed his skate, his truffles and scrambled eggs had been disappointing, even his treacle tart had been as oversweet as it was overpriced, so, Alex thinks: sod it.

Bills paid, receipts kept, they walk out into the Dickensian/hi tech purlieus of Shad Thames, where the gantries and metal walkways slice across the corridor of sky above them; here the girl turns and says to Alex, her small voice lost between the lofty warehouse walls

— Y'know, London's really a cool place . . . I never expected that. I sorta thought it was going to be . . . – She laughs and looks pretty – . . . Fog and beefeaters and . . . pearly kings 'n' things

Alex finds himself puffing with pride, despite

— And?

— Well, it's so exciting, all these great clubs, s'really wild, I mean *really*

— You think so?

Flattered by this Aussie dimbo, this Antipodean skirt, flattered by this girl and her

TITS

Alex and she walk together towards the Design Museum. As they do, workmen and businessmen eye up Alex with evident envy, awestruck by the beautiful blonde leggy Australian he seems to be escorting. The cobbles are tricky; Davina takes Alex's arm; Alex feels good as he looks around, as he sees through her colonial eyes the beauty of Rotherhithe Restored, the elegant stockbrick Piranesi arches of the galleria, the stainless steel footbridge, the black metal balconies, the light that flects and shines from the slap of the oily, wharfside water.

* * *

No handles. The doors have **no handles**. Eddie is sitting in a small white room at the back of Penton Street with three officials from the Department of Social Security and he has just noticed that the doors have *no handles*?

One of the officials is examining a folder of papers; Eddie closes his eyes and girds himself and then opens his eyes to strain and crane and work out the name inscribed upside down on the top of the top sheet of paper in the folder; the name worked out his heart turns to cold grey stone. The name is *Mark Foster*.

His mind spinning, knocked out of orbit, Eddie feels his life unravelling, he actually feels the sense of a thread tugged from the sleeve of his psyche and everything falling away, all his selves, his protection, falling slowly aside.

Inhaling, brave, Eddie looks up at the unsmiling man who is chatting quietly with his colleagues; his colleagues who are scowling contemptuously at Eddie in his miserable trainers and his useless accent and his never-washed blue jeans and his stupid daft coat.

— Mister . . . Lyonshall . . .

Says the man.

It is over, it is done

Eddie croaks

— Yes

— Is this your signature?

The man has revolved and pushed another DSS folder across the table for Eddie's inspection; Eddie looks down at a signature in his handwriting which says . . . *Jimmy Robinson* . . . and Eddie feels the weightlessness, the toppling, the knowledge that the plane really is crashing this time.

But then he fights, bites. *No. Eddie Lyonshall. I am Eddie Lyonshall. Lyonshall of Lyonshall House. Of Lyonshall Park. Of Lyonshall.*

Exhaling, feeling braver, Eddie concentrates on the man's accent, he tries to work out the provenance of the man's accent as the man drones on about fraud, deception, Jeremy Halliday, Mark Foster, Trevor Randall, Jimmy Robinson. Where is that accent from?, Eddie wonders. Surely there is something foreign in there, something inferior, something to get a purchase on, something lowerclass, something *kike, zot, smutt-butt, macaroon, golliwog, kaffir, help me, niggernigger, help me.*

Helpless, Eddie stares at this fucking aborigine who dares to destroy his life and Eddie wants to do some smack and Eddie wants to hate the man, the schvartze, the gibbon, this lower-middle class suburban aboriginal; saying nothing Eddie lifts his head in pride as the handleless door swings open behind him, as a rush of warm air precedes two tall policemen who come in and stand either side of Eddie.

One of the policemen is carrying handcuffs.

— Come and see me?

Alex asks; Katy laughs: so loud Alex holds the mobile phone a foot from his face as he speeds in a cab across a sunny Tower Bridge

— Why should I? – She shouts down her mobile – You come and see ME!

— Oh, c'mon, love-midget

A sarcastic yelp

— Charming old git

— Short-arse, sex-Paki, *micro-Spice*

— Anyway I've homework

— Naked?

— REAL homework

— Just meet me in the pub . . . ?

Her voice fades out, fades in, cuts out

— Where are you anyway – Asks Alex, leaning to open the taxi window and feel the pollution warm across his face.

— Told you you deaf twat

— Women should only
— I'm in FRIGGING South Ken with a friend, shopping
— Shopping?
— For *miniskirts*

Alex smiles and thinks of his teenage lover in her little skirt and his loins enliven and he is forced to swallow saliva, as Katy says too loudly, in her teenage hypersonics
— OH SHIT!
— What? **What?**

Untimely, Alex's cab rattles left into Lower Thames Street and the signal is blocked by Old Billingsgate and when it fades back, Katy is shrieking.
— God I've broken my NAIL!

Alex nods an indulgent nod, he goes to say something paternal and superior but she says
— What have you done to me?! That's so gay! I can't believe you've made me into such a girlie! Broken my nail! What am I saying! You fucking fucking fucking fucking bastard I HATE you!
— So you'll meet me?

Underpass, hydraulics, deceleration, darkness, tunnel, breeze, sunshine,

Katy:
— OK, wrinkles, I'll meet you

Out into Penton Street, cater-corner from the pizzeria, the five of them emerge: two DSS officials in crap suits, two policemen in blue uniform, Eddie with his handcuffs on. En masse they stride towards Pentonville Road; as they do people stop and stare at them, at Eddie; this in turn affords Eddie a strange rush of pride, a rush of agreeable infamy: everyone is looking in awe and slight fear of *him*. All the Chapel Market shoppers, all the Barnsbury housewives and Angel mothers and King's

Cross slappers are stopping to gawk at Eddie: at this prisoner so dangerous he needs an entourage: they are staring at this tall thin scruffy once-good-looking man with the handcuffs cuffed on his wrists in front of him so it looks as if he is being forced to pray. To pray as Eddie is indeed praying, is mumbling:

Oh Merciless God That Made Me. I Know You Don't Exist.

While they dawdle by the road an old woman with a shopping trolley emerges from the end of an alleyway: she also stares open-mouthed at Eddie as he is halted by the kerb of the zebra crossing. Flushed, angry, arrogant, Eddie turns and snarls at the woman and as he snarls she scuttles back, blenching, huddling into the low brick wall behind, using the small blue canvas shopping tolley to protect her from this self-evidently savage beast of a criminal.

— All right – Says the policeman pushing Eddie from the left – Enough of that

— Sorry – Says Eddie, and he almost laughs. He is almost cheery, he is feeling liberated by this experience; he is very nearly happy, it is over, he is free, it is finished: he is beyond the gravitational pull, he feels like a man with his house burned down and his life bombed away: he is feeling the strange elation of disaster, that blissful sense of giving in to greater forces, of acceding to the flood; right now he feels up, he feels good, he feels this mood for almost half a minute: until the five of them go up the stairs into Islington Police Station where the last thing Eddie thinks before they step into the retro yellow-brick building is

God Help Me

Katy and Alex are sitting on wooden pub benches in the flower-thronged front garden of the Lonsdale pub off Edwardes Square. She is showing him the purchases she made, the skirts of quite startling shortness.

— Not short enough, Kate

— Short enough for YOU
— Sit on my lap and say *thigh*

She punches him, slaps his hand, takes a drink; she gets up and sits on his lap, and he says

— Tinkerbell, Pocahontas, John Prescott
— I do NOT look like John Prescott
— Yes you do
— No I DON'T – She is squirming on his lap, deliberately. He says
— Yes you do
— No I don't
— I just love these conversations we have
— Who IS John Prescott?

The sun is shining; the day is hot; the trees in the square are ferny and Jurassic and gold; expensive cars are glinting in the hot lunchtime sun. Katy:

— Don't start wanking on about football again please I don't care, I just don't care
— That's the most words you've ever used in a sentence
— I'll stab you
— Stunted Paki whore

Now she laughs, says

— You're so smooth, maybe that's why I love older men, d'you reckon?
— You like me talking dirty
— Do I?
— You want to don't you?
— Nope

He gestures, hopefully:

— Say nipple
— Say WHAT?
— Say nipple, say nipple, say bite my nipple

She grins – NO!

— If you don't I'll call you . . . *darling*

She makes a face; leg lifted she gets off his lap and sits down on the wooden pub bench and sips her Archers-and-lemonade, says

— Don't be gay

— Explain how your breasts are again?

Half a yard along the bench Katy shakes her black locks; her teeth are white; the sun is sparking off the ice cubes in her glass; the flowers are loud and sweet and aromatic behind; everything is sweet, this afternoon, Alex thinks, this is going to be one of those sweetly perfect London summer afternoons when they've got all afternoon to be happy together.

— Someone at school touched them yesterday

— What?

— My . . . breasts

Her voice is all little and girlie; Alex's voice is all hoarse and phlegmy

— Someone touched your breasts?

She stares at the pavement

— Mmmm, this teacher – She nods at him, seriously, she looks under her eyelashes at her more-than-ten-years-older boyfriend, with an I'm-sorry-but-it's-true face – You see . . . He was a bit of a HUNK and he was giving me extra physics and he asked me to sit on his lap

— He did **what** . . . ?

— Just sort of . . . happened

— What did he

— Well, he touched me . . . you see.

— **If this is a wind up** . . .

Alex is glaring. Hard and long Alex glares at Katy; inside him he has that churning stomachy feeling: he hates the way Katy can do this to him and he also loves the way she can do this to him . . . the way the thought of another man touching her and making her sit on his lap makes him . . . nauseous, aroused. Pointing at something in between them with a finger Alex says

— Ffffffff . . . ssss . . . fffff

— Oh God – She laughs, openly – I'm teasing!

— *Teasing?*

— Yes, CALM DOWN, mister about-to-have-a-heart-attack – Shifting herself nearer to him, Katy puts her little white hand on his thigh, puts her little red mouth to his ear – You know what I think?

— What do you think?

— I think you're so huge you make me bleed every time will you buy me another Archers?

By royal command Alex rises and takes Katy's empty glass, and goes into the darkness of the pub.

— Edward Lyonshall, I am charging you with conspiracy to defraud the Department of Social Secur . . .

Slunked in a chair opposite the white shirt of the police officer, Eddie has his head in his hands: feeling like he is about to dissolve with self-pity.

Meantime, the officer officiates officiously, meantime Eddie despairs, and looks at the window. He looks *at* the window. Eddie hasn't got the energy to look out. He just looks at the glass. At the reflection of photocopiers, desks, sergeants, car-crime posters. Time passes. Eddie wonders how long it will be before he starts coming off heroin, starts withdrawing. Will they give him bail? Will they just shoot him? Which would be preferable? After half an hour Eddie is led somewhere else and the tips of his thumbs are made black with sticky black ink. Detached, Eddie notices the way each inked thumb is rolled clumsily across the paper form by the officer: like an adult showing a child how to do something. Then Eddie's picture is taken; then he is left sitting on a chair in the lobby of the police-station, pathetic in his handcuffs. He is so insignificant he is forgotten. Forgotten, forsaken, a lost kid waiting to be collected, until at the last another different policeman comes along and leads him to another room, where Eddie sits with a duty solicitor in a blue suit and a tie, who matily chats with Eddie; but Eddie does not hear. Eddie is observing the silent shouting of a black man he can see through an internal window, Eddie has noticed the way the handcuffs are making his wrists go white with the pressure.

After a long long time Eddie turns to the solicitor and says
— What time is it?

In Katy's bedroom Katy is step-by-step taking her clothes off and Alex's heart is working so fast he feels endangered, overbuzzed, like a student on too much speed. Stuck with his addiction Alex watches, obsessing, as Katy undoes her jeans, he wants so much to strip the clothes off her quickly, he wants so much to take his time and do it slowly.
— We better be quick my mum will be home soon

Needing no more Alex rips off his strides; his shorts; showing her his erection he motions with a hand; she understands:
— You mean I have to put *all* of that in my mouth?

Oh God. *Oh yes.*

Hopeful, wistful, mouthful of spit, he watches her little hand around his cock and he waits for as long as he can; but then he can't: then he goes: down: to her rose of cunt, where he licks her between, smelling the scent of a St Malo restaurant on a winter's evening, lost in the thick soft furrier's sample; lost in the young Czarina of her cunt. *Oh yes.*

Cunni. Cunniling. Cunnilinguling. Cunnilingulingilinguling.

Gagging, enjoying, gagging; Alex licks, works, and considers the fact that Katy is the only woman he enjoys licking out. He considers this: dismisses it. Dangerous, dangerous. Why should he enjoy cunnilingus with her and no-one else? Scientific, Alex lays off his tongue and considers the taste. It is, he feels, one of those very nearly disgusting lovely tastes that can so easily tip over into complete disgustingness. Like burnt charcoal peppers in oil. Like oysters. Olives. Anchovy butter. Like so much seafood. Like cunt. But because he loves her, Katy, he loves the taste . . . the taste of the blood, from her warwound, from the scartissue, from where she was Islamically mutilated; ohyes he loves it, loves the kowtow, yes he loves the taste.

But not that much. It is time, time to fuck her. Now. Yes. Brupt, he rises, turns her over, flips her white body. Her smallwhite tidy body. She is so small and so compact, and yet she has all the necessary features . . . *Shall I compare thee to a Sony Walkman, thou are more compact and more*

She is his own Toshiba, his dinky little JVC, his sweet Aiwa — Aiwa – She says, as he enters her slimy red-peppers-in-olive-oil cunt – Aiwa, aiwa aiwa aiwa aiwa aiwa aiwa aiwa aiwa aiwa aiwaaaaaaaaaaa*hhhhhhh*

Eddie is alone. Eddie is more alone than he has ever been. Eddie is in a large holding cell in the bowels of Islington Police Station, surrounded by black men and Irishmen and pre-simian Cockneys with spiders' webs tattooed on their foreheads and ACAB tattooed on their fingerknuckles. Where is he? Eddie is in a palaeo-anthropologist's laboratory, surrounded by examplars of the criminous, the racially degraded; Eddie is in a Victorian *Rassensaal* full of Bushmen's skulls and Hottentots' heads; Eddie is trying to stare at the wall as two of the australopithecines in the opposite corner of the cell have a fight, as a couple of hep Yardie gorillas rap about drugdeals, as the cell door swings open and a classically burly sergeant pushes another tiny-headed, dung-worshipping, cave-dwelling, soapdodging, insectivorous golliwog into the already crowded holding cell. Dumb, shit-scared, frightened for his life, Eddie shuts his eyes just as a bloat-faced git who smells of sour beer and bad breath comes along and stares into Eddie's face, his face an inch from Eddie's face. Reeking of himself the git says to Eddie, in a flattened, toneless, nasal, grotesquely Liverpudlian whine:

— Eh mate are you a fraggle. Or what? Eh?

The man is speaking so close to Eddie's face Eddie can taste his saliva. His *saliva.*

— Sorry?

— Or are youse a bacon?

Eddie shakes his head. Says nothing. The man retreats. Eddie shuts his eyes even tighter. Eddie is thinking. Hoping. Praying. He is thinking: no I'm not a . . . fraggle, I'm just one of them, I'm just one of them, I'm just one of you.

I'm just one of us.

15

jump-up-and-kiss-me

Awake into the cauldron of morning Tony leans and looks at the clock, blearily rubbing his eyes, blearily aware of the cool summer air wafting through the window.

5.30 a.m.

Hungover, thirsty, already fretting about how much food he over-ate last night, feeling a slight burning reflux in his lower throat, Tony suppresses a painful burp and lies back down and listens to the birds in the Putney streets. The sound of birds is, at least, sweet, is tranquil; it melds happily with the smell of lime trees and the scent of his wife who is quietly snoring next to him. Tony thinks of his children. He wonders why he always wakes five hours after going to sleep if he has been drinking. He wonders what time the baby will wake. Flat on his back Tony stares at the ceiling like he did when he was ill as a child; then he senses Elizabeth turning over, he senses her stir and he knows her eyes are open too, are also staring dehydrated at the ceiling; and now, he thinks, now we are still and silent and side by side, like those Lord and Lady statues you see in old cathedrals, carved in stone, hand in hand above an Arundel tomb . . .

except . . .

except that we are not like that, Tony decides, swallowing the dryness in his horrible mouth, if we are two supine statues our faces have been erased by Cromwell's troops, sliced away, violently axed of all expression

— God, what time is it?

Elizabeth's voice is as croaky as her husband's

— Five-thirty . . .

— Baby?

— Nothing yet. I'll go look in a minute

Is there anything in the world, Tony wonders, worse than microwaving a bottle of baby-milk, and dealing with a cack-filled nappy, and mopping up probable lots of baby-spew, while also nursing a throbber of a hangover?

— Anthony?

— Nn?

Elizabeth has turned her face so as to look at him; he senses this, as she says

— Why don't you love me any more?

Perhaps there *is* one thing worse than nursing a baby while hungover.

Alarmed, Tony stalls, stammers, wondering why the radio hasn't come on: wasn't it set for five-thirty?

— Bmbmbnb – He says, then – Elizabeth, Is this . . . Is this because of what we talked about last night?

— . . . What did we talk about last night?

— Don't know – He says, hoping the hopelessness of their dialogue will dissuade her; it doesn't; she says

— Is it simply because you don't fancy me any more?

The absurdity of this concept makes Tony even more spastic; unable to articulate, he feels like someone trying to play the guitar that can't

— No, Elizabeth, if you think just because of the problem I don't then . . .

— No, I don't think that, I just – She stifles her own yawn – Are you . . . do you . . . Oh . . . – There is a tone in her voice – Is it because you still think I'm having an affair?

Elizabeth as ever. Customarily straight; so straight he is silenced. Does he need this quite so early in the morning? Does he need anything quite this early in the morning? It is so early Tony can hardly think; but he has to. She wants him to think.

He thinks.

Using the silence of her spouse's thoughts, Tony's wife of eight years reaches over her side of the bed to find a cigarette; match flicked shut Elizabeth Rafferty continues nursing her cigarette, hunching about the ashtray on her bedside table; the smell of her Marlboro mixes with the lime trees, the birdsong, the absence of the radio, the baby not crying yet.

Ashamed of his lack of communication, of their lack of dialogue, Tony leans over to his side of the bed and makes a fetus of himself, as well: and now Tony thinks, now we are like two heraldic symbols, back to back, *addorsed*.

He has to speak. He speaks

— Do you still love *me*, Elizabeth?

— Yes

Larks, thrushes, blackbirds, starlings, a motor scooter thraping down Putney High Street. He says

— So what happened to us?

Instantly she turns over; carefully she spoons her body and bends over his unhappy shoulder and kisses him on the neck; allowing him to smell the whisky still on her breath, which reminds him of how last night they got pointlessly drunk and listened to old records and tried to forget in an orgy of remembrance . . .

— I'll always love you Anthony whatever happens

— *Whatever happens?*

— I'm *not* having an affair, just because you . . . you know . . .

Unrewarded with a reply Elizabeth sighs and her sigh is hot

and sour and scotch-y and smoky in his ear and still sexy, still sexy, Tony thinks, even when she's unwashed and he's hungover, even when she's ugly and he's self-hating, even when the baby is about to cry like the radio about to switch on like his stupid job about to begin like the merciless beauty of the high-summer morning about to be beyond the yellow-and-white stripes of the bedroom curtains, she's still got it for him, somewhere . . .

— But it's not like it was, Lizzie, is it?

Hand cupped beneath her ashy cigarette, Elizabeth shifts sideways to her side of the bed, taps the cigarette. Then she steals a final puff, before fiercely extinguishing the cigarette, before saying:

— Anthony, nothing is like it was, but that doesn't mean we can't make a go of it

— You think?

— I don't know, it depends, doesn't it

— On what?

— On whether *any* love can survive – She sounds thoughtful now, back on her back – When *did* we last have sex, anyway?

Her bluntness, her robustness, her her-ness. Tony loves her for it, tries not to, can't help it

— Just before the Crimean war

— Never. *That* recently?

They laugh. They go quiet. Tony feels the usual panic when they talk about sex, tries to swallow it away, Elizabeth says to the lampshade

— Have you got an erection?

— Enormous

— Do you . . . – She is being sensitive and gentle – Do you want to try again?

— It'll only . . .

— Don't worry – She says too quickly – You mustn't worry. That'll only make it worse

Tony knows his wife is doing her best but her best is the

worst: in her kindness she has tripped the so-easy-to-trip switch; somewhere inside Tony can feel the gorge of panic rising in his throat. He wishes, how he wishes he could just get up and have a shower, how he wishes he could just wank, how he wishes he were divorced, how he wishes he were homosexual and living in Notting Hill with his heavily moustachio'd schoolmaster lover: how he wishes he could nip down to the kitchen and reach for the magnetic knife-rack and open a principal blood vessel in his neck with the Sabatier knife he has often evaluated for the purpose: bleeding in a geyser of beaujolais all over the cafetiere he and his wife bought in IKEA, staggering in a fountain of blood into the copper saucepans they found in France, guttering sticky scarlet onto the bottles of balsamic vinegar they bought on their first holiday in Tuscany last year.

But before Tony can do this the alarm radio comes on and Elizabeth coughs and the suicidal moment has passed; for the moment.

The radio is traffic news, over-bright announcers, the weather. They both lie there, Elizabeth muttering about her hangover, her day ahead, Tony listening to the radio and to her and to the birds outside and for the baby to cry and to anything but himself. He doesn't want to listen to himself right now. He's beginning to piss himself off.

Tony is about to say something to Elizabeth when she turns an alerted face to his and crosses her lips with a finger

— Shh

Dutiful, Tony shuts and cocks his ears and the two listen to the radio report

— A spokesman for the sheriff said they will be trying later today to evict the road protestors from the northern end of the site, at Garway, near Lyonshall Common. Several of the protestors are believed to be barricaded behind steel doors in underground tunnels, which it is believed will take at least three to five days to remove. Fears for the safety of the protestors have grown as . . .

The radio goes on and Elizabeth says

— *Lyonshall . . .*

Tony nods.

— But: *Lyonshall*?

Shrug.

— You mean . . .

Tony nods, again

— Alex told me a couple of weeks ago. Haven't you seen it in the papers?

Elizabeth's quiet, pretty, puzzled face:

— Been so busy . . . but is it true?

— Afraid so

— They're building a bloody *road* across the *common*?

— There's been protestors there for weeks. Alex wants to go down and interview them or something

— Alex?

— Yes

— *My God . . . My . . .*

Elizabeth is mumbling, mute. Elbowed up, Tony stretches and slaps the radio off, like a chess clock.

And then they are both silent. In bed together they lie and stare up, their thoughts and memories unspokenly duetting. They are lying and thinking symmetrically, just like they used to, on the common, or on the banks of the Arrow.

Shaking his head Tony confesses

— I don't know why but . . . It's funny I always remember the curtains

She laughs, sadly

— Utrecht velvet

— Sorry?

— They were Utrecht velvet. The Lyonshall settee, too

— It's a disgrace – Tony says, vehement.

Her voice is just as fierce

— But I mean, my God, how can they build a *road* through it?

— An A Road runs through it

Elizabeth lifts herself from the pillow; looks at her husband and demands:
— What were those things we used to . . . you know . . . those ginger things?
— Carberry ginger hats
— Really?
— Think so
— God yes you're right, and those little apricot jam things, those pastries?
He thinks:
— Kickshaws . . .?
— They were. *They were.* With those finger breads . . . Constance Spry's toffee pudding
— And yellow raspberries . . .
— And Devonshire junket
He laughs and says
— With pussyfoot cup, of course – She looks at Tony questioningly, who explains – That was that stuff like Pimm's we used to have when we played cricket against the village
— Oh God, *yes* . . . – Elizabeth is laughing too, now, laughing like she used when she was even prettier, when she was younger, when they were even innocent. Sharing glances across the duvet they laugh without words: remembering: when they were young and lost, in the lawns and rose gardens of Lyonshall House, when Eliza's arms linked above her head like the pleached plum trees of Lyonshall, when the chains of their kisses were like the chains of Kiftsgate roses, grown along the chains . . .

Remembering, remembering, Tony reaches across the sheets of their bed and now, here, he strokes his wife's soft high-cheekboned cheek, her fair Henrywife white neck, and he feels himself stiffen again and he hears her say
— Anthony . . . fuck me?

And so. *And so.* And so Tony goes, desires, attempts. He can already hear the thundering hooves of his oncoming panic attack but he pretends he doesn't hear. He wants to make love to his wife: what could be simpler than that? He just wants to have sex with his wife as he has had sex with her so many times before. So why not? *So do it.* He does it. He goes to do it. Stirrup, saddle, reins, Tony clutches her still-firm breast in his hand and he kisses her cheek; handing open her thighs he scrys in her vagina, like a Roman emperor fingering entrails so as to foresee the future. The future being: his inability to do it. Of course. He won't be able to do it. *Of course.*

She is saying nothing, significantly; her eyes are shut and she is waiting for him. *So put it in.* Frigging himself until he is hard, frigging himself until he has forgotten for a second that he cannot do this Tony moves on top of her as she opens her legs wider; using two fingers to open her labia he slides himself in and now he is inside her, now he is doing it he is moving in and out he is doing it he is successfully making love to his wife . . . ??

But as soon as he considers what he is about, Tony recalls that he has been so unsuccessful in this in the recent past. Even as he penetrates his wife Tony recalls how the last time he tried to penetrate her he couldn't penetrate her, properly, and as soon as he thinks about this he remembers how the last time he couldn't penetrate because he was remembering how the last time before that he couldn't penetrate, and as Tony spirals down this vortex, as he looks in the mirror of doubt, the doubt multiplies like a mirror turned on itself and now he can feel his penis getting softer, and as it gets softer he knows it will get softer and so it gets softer and now it is soft. Floppy. Gone.

Ashamed of himself: mortified, self-hating, Tony is obliged to withdraw his wet floppy penis, and to gaze masochistically down into his wife's wide open eyes, searching for signs of hatred, of contempt, of loathing, of womanly disdain and derision. Nothing there; but that means nothing. Having to say something, Tony says

— **Jesus**
— It's not a problem
— Oh it is a problem I assure you
— We can try again in a minute – He snorts at this, she goes on – Or tomorrow, anytime . . . really
— Really what's the bloody point, Elizabeth?
Rolled off his wife Tony sinks into the pillows; staring at the ceiling with near tears peppering his eyes he thinks about the knife-rack in the kitchen, and says
— You know, we're never going to be able to do it again, I'm never going to be able to do it ever again
With a tone full of exasperating pity, enraging sympathy, she croons
— Don't worry so. You've simply got to relax
— Oh and that's it is it? Just relax and it'll get better? How long have we been saying that?
— But . . . At least you know it's not . . . mechanical
— Like you understand, Liz. You've just got to lie there and open your legs
— *Tony*
— Yeah – He cracks, spittle glottal-stopping his throat – You've just got to lie there and open your legs haven't you. Eh? To that well-hung boyfriend of yours?
— You'll wake the baby.
— Just open your little legs and take some big guy's . . . thing in you, that's all you've got to do . . . or do you prefer it when he shoves it in your mouth? Breaks your jaw with his big fat erection?
— *Please*, Tony
— You do, don't you? How big is he, darling? How hard? Does it hurt you? Do you squeal when he buggers you? Do you bite the pillow?
For a second Tony reckons she is going to slap him as he deserves: she is rising, her face drawn with shock, hurt, anger,

she is looming over him and as she does he knows more than anything he wants her to

Hit me, please hit me

But instead he hears, above the nauseating whine of his own pathetic pleas, the caterwaul of Polly, crying; immediately Elizabeth is up and down the bed and grabbing a gown; before Tony can begin to think of an apology Elizabeth disappears about the door down the landing to the baby's cot.

Alone, Tony turns over. Alone in their bedroom he turns over and over and over and over and over and over, thinking how he could just slip down to the kitchen and go to the magnetic knife-rack they bought in Habitat . . . and never have to worry about being impotent again.

16

paigle

— In the light of the Accused's drug addiction, Your Honour, I submit that the possibility of reoffence is considerable, given his need for money to support his drug habit. Secondly, such is the seriousness of the charge, the possibility of his absconding cannot either be entirely discounted. For these reasons, Your Honour, the police have therefore objected to bail, and request that the accused be remanded in cust . . .

Caged behind some cheap wooden railings Eddie finds it hard to believe all this, this palaver, all these doings, all these pompous legalistic clichés, are for *him*.

I mean: Eddie thinks. *Wigs. Really*. Stood in the dock Eddie feels like the star in a cheap afternoon made-for-TV courtroom drama. Also Eddie feels like shit. He is coming off heroin very badly now, probably peaking, and he feels shite. In agony. Suffering. Nailed to the cross through the stomach.

The Prosecutor drones on. Eddie detects an accent. A definite accent. From somewhere . . . somewhere . . .

Jewish! The prosecutor is Jewish! Yes! What a stroke of luck! Desperately grateful, pitifully thankful to be superior again, Eddie stands in the dock and gazes disdainfully across the court at this fetzel, the Hebe, the cock-licking kike, die *judensau*, the six million and one-th: the kike so unlike Eddie's hero, the top chap on the side of the court, the defender, Eddie's duty solicitor, his highly skilled advocate, with his nice English suit and his Home Counties manners and his well-brought-up wife and his first class Law Degree and his butter-fed children waiting clean and polite by the Aga for Daddy to

— Mr Greenberg?

From the bench, from the empyrean heights of British justice, the Magistrate has addressed Eddie's duty defence solicitor. Again:

— Mr Greenberg?

Greenberg. Eddie thinks. ***Greenberg?*** *Thank God. He's Jewish too; I've got a Jewish lawyer* ***too*** . . .

Mr Greenberg stands, clears his throat:

— My client is willing to submit to any such bail conditions as the court sees fit to impose, Your Honour. Furthermore he is willing to undergo immediate treatment for his addiction . . .

On cue, Eddie gulps. Gasps. At that moment the stomach cramps kick in. Again. For the seventh time that morning Eddie convulses over as the body-jabs of heroin-withdrawal rain into his midriff. Gaping down his long body Eddie looks at his trainers and wonders if he should tie his laces as the pain comes, an orgasm of pain, the pain of pains, like a fist tightening around his stomach, like a huge screw being driven through his viscera, like all the pain he has avoided in the last five, six, seven smack-addicted years has been saved up to revisit him at this moment.

Eddie groans. Shudders. Feels nauseous. His laces do need tying. Reaching down for his shoes Eddie tries not to think about the state of his guts but as he does it all fades out, the cheaply panelled walls of Bow Street Magistrates Court, the scuffed green leather of the Bow Street Magistrates' thrones, the Bow Street Magistrates clerk in her sensible blue two-piece, the two policemen standing behind him yawning and looking at their watches and thinking about lunch, the public gallery so conspicuously unfilled with Eddie's parents and his missing sister and his absent friends: the whole sad, badly-scripted awfulness of Eddie's predicament fades into the insistence of tears in his eyes: as the grief in his stomach, the mourning in his soul, the hangover in his colon: go on.

— Bail denied. The accused is remanded in custody for seven days.

Behind Eddie the two policemen quit yawning, approach, swivel Eddie round and pull him from the wooden box: and suddenly, at last, the testicular pain in Eddie's guts subsides, and he gains enough lucidity and awareness to hold himself stiff, erect, to gain a semblance of the old pride, to remember the who and the what. **Lyonshall of Lyonshall . . . of Lyon . . . of Ly**

The wood panelling gives way to green paint which becomes flaked paint before it turns into unapologetic concrete. Eddie is being led down the circles of Dantean hell into his holding cell, pending translocation to Tartarus.

The cell is small. But empty. Late summer sunshine from eight foot above comes slanting down, laddered by the window bars. For an energetic moment Eddie stands close to the wall and stares up the window, at the parallel rectangles of blue summer sky, and as he upturns his face he gets a mild kick from the image of himself as the romantic internee, as the oppressed poetic hero, as Mandela, Solzhenitsyn, Václav Havel

a dole scrounger?

More pain. Likewise, sweats. Holding his stomach as if he is fearful that his chitterlings might spill out, Eddie sits on his obscurely damp mattress and stares right through the wall two feet opposite. Eddie blinks. Blinks. Feels the pain, abate, again. Outside he can hear other cell doors banging, drunks singing, policemen shouting down the drunks; and all the time his own mind tumble-drying, incessant.

— Mr Lyonshall?

It is his duty defence solicitor, Greenberg. Being showed in. A policeman with a bristling fist of keys pulls the door to, and the duty solicitor looks at the mattress and Eddie steels and recalls himself

— Gin and tonic?

The lawyer stands uneasy, Eddie sniffs

— Remanded in custody . . . Take it that means I'm *not* walking out this afternoon?

Greenberg shrugs his suited shoulders and sits down at the other end of the mattress.

— Only got your brief this morning, I'm afraid. The other chap . . . the guy you saw last night when the police interviewed you. He had to dash off . . . You have to understand it's very hard with magistrates courts. They're just police courts really

— I saw

— As soon as they see the word drugs, especially heroin, the shutters go up

Eddie makes a so-what face:

— So what *now?*

— Now . . . – The youngish solicitor eyes his brief and eyes the wall, eyes his brief again – Well now they're waiting to get enough of you to fill a van. Probably taking you to Brixton. It could be Scrubs, maybe even the 'Ville. Probably Brixton

— Brixton prison?

Mr Greenberg grimaces

— Well. Yes . . .

Eddie sighs

— And I always vowed I'd *never* live south of the river

Greenberg smiles at this but Eddie doesn't. The famished opiate receptors in Eddie's head are squawking, loudly, again, showing pink, angry, feed-me throats.

— Are you OK?

Eddie doubles forward.

— Mr Lyonshall?

Through gritted teeth Eddie manages

— Oh, dandy. Tip *top*

— I can

Eddie

— Spent all of last night staying awake so I wouldn't be stabbed by an Irish drunk, I'm about to be incarcerated in a Category A prison, I'm looking at . . . what . . . three to five years for serious dole fraud? – Greenberg nods, warily; Eddie carries on – And I'm also coming off a *major* habit – The prisoner lifts his head and glares – So, yes, I'm doing *fine*. Since you *ask*

Greenberg looks like he's thinking of putting an arm round Eddie's shoulders. If he was thinking that, Greenberg thinks better and says

— I can get the police to get a doctor . . .

— Nn

— Methadone . . . aspirin . . . whatever you need?

Eddie ungrits his teeth, the pain going in cycles, again. With a backhand Eddie swipes his brow of sweat, sits back on the clammy mattress, tests the hard brickwork with the softness of his scalp

— Thank you. But I think I'd *rather* . . . get it over and *done* with . . . – Grimacing, sweating – Only wish I had some coke – Now Eddie makes a wan smile – *Où sont les neiges d'antan.* Eh?

Flicking some pages and scanning, the solicitor ignores this. Says instead:

— If you wish me to continue representing you, I believe – The lawyer's face brightens as it reads a paper in the folder – I *believe* it should be possible to get you bail, on the basis that you agree to undergo treatment for your . . . addiction . . . I have done it before with some success – A hint of pride? – But I'd have to have you examined by a doctor, and a psychologist . . .

Eddie looks unswervingly over

— How long before you can spring me?

Greenberg looks frankly back
— Two weeks, maybe three?
— nnn

Eddie's latest grunt ends the conversation. Both of them stare at the painted brick wall, silently reading the graffiti together. Above 'Sod all queers' and 'Sarah is a beef' and 'Police are twats' is written, twice: 'Up the Gunners, kill the Yids'.

Another silence, Eddie says
— Goys will be goys

His solicitor acknowledges:
— Good. It's very important to keep a sense of humour. I'll be in touch

After that Greenberg slaps the door, the policeman comes, the metal door swings to allow Greenberg egress, and Eddie is left alone to gaze at the blank horrible wall, at his blank immediate future.

— Right, you lot, in the back

They are standing in the yard of the magistrates court and Eddie is surrounded by other prisoners pulled from the cells. Some of them are white. Some of them are black. And all, Eddie thinks, are intrinsically Losers. No-hopers. Beaker people. Bell-curvers . . .

As Eddie shuffles in his handcuffs towards the metal prison van being reversed into the sunlit yard, he treads on somebody's ankle: the ankle's face turns around to look up at him, the ankle's face is a face that is so ugly, so downtrodden, so pathetically pinched, pallid, yellow and verminous Eddie feels a kind of sympathy welling up for this . . . this *thing,* this runt, this unabortion, this
— Tossa!

The small white thing is jabbing Eddie in the stomach. *In the stomach.* The pain in Eddie's belly redoubles at the prodding and

Eddie winces, shudders, and looks down at this assailant. At the stringy black hair. At the non-existent shoulders. At the terrifying accent. And Eddie cannot stop himself, even though he knows he shouldn't; should be wary, he blurts

— Fucking ho*minid*

The man blinks:

— Yer what?

— *Schvartze*

The man steps back, Eddie repeats, surprising himself

— Sodding *monkeyman*

And before the man can do something, can react

— OK, get on!!

The policeman cattle-prods them with a stave and they begin to climb the metal ramp; cuffed like slaves they chain gang it into the back of the prison van.

Inside the all-metal truck there are rows of pop-festival metal-urinal type cubicles each individually lockable: in a few efficient moments they are each individually locked into these perpendicular metal coffins. Then the van backs down a ramp and reverses into the street and Eddie rests his head against the thick tiny tinted-glass window pane of his personal steel cubicle; and as they grind and clutch up Drury Lane and along New Oxford Street Eddie watches the tinted streets of London panning by: watching all the normal world going on. All the people who aren't in prison. All the people who aren't screwed for good, forever.

What makes it worse, what makes Eddie flinch and close his eyes, is the *route*. After Marylebone and Paddington they veer north, and west, into Notting Hill, Ladbroke Grove. Into the postcode of Eddie's youth. London W Heaven. This is worse, yes worse there is some. Eddie cannot bear it. Why? Here he is being carted off to the misery of his future and they are driving with an almost calculated cruelty through the purlieus of a happier, freer past: Portobello, Powys Square, Campden

Hill, the Globe, the Ground Floor Bar, the Cobden Club, *oh the Cobden Club . . .*

At last the driver seems to think he's had enough of torturing Eddie and they take it south, down, and across the water: further in, further down, further out. And all Eddie wants to do is lean forward and rest his sweating, weary, surely-about-to-be-beaten-up face against the rattling metal wall of his cubicle.

— Tea and a slice?

Eddie is standing in line in a large shabby room somewhere in the precincts of Brixton prison. He is surrounded by a job lot of other remandees: all similarly tired, similarly vexed, similarly defeated, entirely dissimilar to Eddie in every other way. Eddie can't help wondering at what the warden behind the window has just said. *Tea and a slice?* Something about the inapposite domesticity of this affords Eddie some comfort as he takes the red plastic plate with the slice of bread and butter; along with the red plastic mug of weak milky tea. *Perhaps it will just be like a public school just like everybody says . . .* Hopeful, hopeless, Eddie pushes through the throng of chatting, silent prisoners to a corner of the off-cream-painted brick room where he sits at a formica table and tries not to think. *Best not to think.* Instead of thinking Eddie sips his tea until it is quite cold; he nibbles his buttered bread until it is just crusts; offers thanks that at least the heroin-withdrawal seems to have peaked. Meantime the prisoners around him mutter and chat and curse, and swear, and swear, and swear, ceaselessly swearing, saying cunt and fuck and cunt until it feels to Eddie like the English language has been petrified, mineralised, calcified into the bare Anglo-Saxon, the Jutish, the Beaker speak . . .

— Lyonshall, Eddie?

Jostling past the mob and the motley, carefully avoiding the ankle he trod on earlier, Eddie approaches the desk where two wardens quiz him, eye him, tick off his name, and then hand him a plastic knife and fork, a plastic mug and plate. A third warden loads Eddie with a plastic bucket . . . Eddie gazes bemused at his luggage. A fourth warden comes through a door and gestures: like a nervous nursery school first-timer with his crayons and pencil case, Eddie follows. From the big room he is guided into the future: through a series of clangings, corridors and yards, and under a final jamb, he enters into a vast long hall, a vast great film set very cleverly arranged to look like all the prison wings Eddie has ever seen in newsclips, sitcoms, *The Italian Job*, and bleeding-heart documentaries. Ahead and above Eddie there stretches a wide circus trapeze net, strung between gantries and walkways; above and beyond the net is an atrium filled with shouts and lounging cons and the smell of bad cooking. The noise is deafening; so deafening Eddie cannot hear his warden's commands: so Eddie just nods as he is led up the metal steps to a landing overlooking the net; here they turn smartly but Eddie has just the time to catch a last glimpse of a lurid red sun setting over a south London skyline visible through a huge arched window: a window that entirely fills the end wall of this huge brick Victorian warehouse, this great old warehouse of despair, this East India Wharf of Human Wickedness.

Just as Eddie thinks he is about to lose it, to jump the rail, to throw himself into oblivion, the prison officer revolves and looks directly at Eddie for the first time: the two of them are stopped outside the sixth metal door down the third landing. Twisting a big key the officer pushes the metal door open, snaps out:

— V42685. Your *cell*

Dazed, still freighted with a bucket and soft plastic crockery, Eddie steps inside the cell: which has one window, two bunk-beds, one chair, one table, one screened-off steel lavatory, three Page 3 girls tacked to the wall, and one other occupant. Eddie stops. The cell's occupant is lying in his grey-blanketed top-bunk, his face hidden by yesterday's *Daily Star*. As the door swings shut behind Eddie, the occupant of the top bunk drops the tabloid and stares over and looks at Eddie as Eddie stands there feeling as awkward, frightened, and unhappy as he no doubt appears. The occupant of the top bunk flicks another disdainful glance at Eddie and returns to his paper. Unable to imagine what else to do, Eddie sits quietly on the bottom bunk and watches as the eye-hole flickers shut and the keys of the warden jangle. As the door locks tight shut.

The screams won't stop. Eddie is lying in the twilight, the screams go on. *A riot? What the hell is it?* Outside the tiny window of the cell Eddie has already ascertained there is a yard: from across this yard, from . . . *what? another wing of the prison?*, Eddie can hear horrible wails, weird foreign gibbering. This painfully loud babble and gibber has been going on for hours: ever since lights off, ever since seven

— **Jabbba jabba jabba helll ffflll j'ba**

— **Jabba yaaaa llllll llll IIII**

— **Gyg gnnnnmmmm**

— **Babbab arrrr gonnnnnnar!!!**

— Christ

— Sorry?

Eddie's cell mate has spoken. For the first time since Eddie arrived six hours ago Eddie's cell mate has spoken.

From his position on the bottom bunk, Eddie hears his cell mate's bunksprings squeak; in the semi-darkness Eddie sees a pair of legs dangle over the bunk, white bare feet, white hairy calves. Paused, for a moment, Eddie's mid-twenties-ish cell mate jumps softly and athletically to the floor, pads over to the window, highbars himself up, and shouts out the half-open window at the top of his voice

— *Shut up and do your bird!*

Silence. For a while this shout seems to silence the screamers.

Eddie hears sarcastic laughter from another prisoner down the landing. Then more laughter, then more silence. Distant car lights make vague shadows on the ceiling of the cell and just as Eddie is getting used to the blessed silence the howling starts up again

— Ga ga ga ga ga ga ga ga ga **nnnnnnbbbbbb wyooooo!!**

Sat in his wooden chair, the only wooden chair, Eddie's shirtless, trouserless, blue-boxer-shorted cell mate is crossing his musclebound arms, admiring his own tattoos. Eddie says nothing. The cell mate nods towards the window

— Them's the fraggles

Eddie pauses, wonders, replies

— Sorry?

— F Wing. Fraggle Rock – Eddie's cell mate yawns, sighs – Every fucking night 's' like that. Why they have to bang all the nutters up in Brixton I don't fucking know

Again the cell mate rises, does a chin-up to the rusty sill of the four-barred window:

— **Fraggles, be quiet!**

Ignoring the ensuing cacophany, Eddie's cell mate drops back down and returns to his chair. Serious, he finds a pouch on the table, from which he extracts enough rolling tobacco and a Rizla paper, wherewith he meticulously rolls himself a tiny cigarette. This he then lights with a lengthways-spliced quarter of a match. The flame flares; illuminated eyes stare at Eddie's. The cell mate says

— Name's Dave. Want some salmon?

— Uh . . .

— 'Ere – Dave tosses the pouch of tobacco and the box of slivered matches onto Eddie's grey-scratchy-blanketed stomach; now Eddie sits up and says, extending a hand

— Hi. I'm Eddie, Eddie Lyonshall

In the dark David ignores the hand; in the dark David tokes, respires smoke, says

— Where do you get a fucking accent like that then? Oxford?
— I . . . er
— Betcha didn't get it in Peckham
— No, I
— Tell you what, Oxford – David sits back and blows a perfect smoke-ring at the ceiling – I'd say it was your first time, right?
The smoke ring rises and breaks on the ceiling; Eddie nods
— If you mean have I ever been in *prison* before, yah
David laughs
— Yah, yah, yah
— Sorry?
— Don't go talking like that round here. Get yourself jukked
Eddie shakes his head, reminding himself of his surname . . .
— Well, they could just . . . try . . . pond scum
Eddie is attempting to sound hard. Dave laughs
— Scum, yeah. Murdering fucking bastards, I agree. But a decent bunch of lads all the same. You could have done a lot worse
— Meaning?
— Brixton's OK. Apart from the fraggles it's better than most. Not so banged up – Another smoke ring; Dave goes on – Watch out for the geezer in cell five though. Filipino mass murderer. Keeps winning at chess. Can't think why
Now, at last, at this touch of humour, Eddie relaxes, a tiny bit, in a very small way. Lighting his own cigarette, Eddie inhales, exhales, remembers where he is, panics, says quickly:
— So, erm . . . what are *you* in for?
Dave shakes his head, says nothing; Eddie repeats
— I mean, what did they accuse you of?
This time David hisses
— There are two things you should never say in prison, Oxford
Eddie flinches:
— . . . What?
— The first one is, 'What are you in for?'
— The second?

Dave's face glows as he puffs
— 'Get out of my way you great big fucking black bastard.'
Silence. Dave laughs. Eddie does a weak smile. The screams go on, and on. All the time Eddie tries to casually smoke his roll-up, pinching the odd bit of rolling tobacco from his lip; at the same time Dave blows another smoke ring at the light fitting. The two of them watch the smoke ring's ascent: the smoke ring is even more perfect than the last, so perfect Eddie is impelled to remark
— Impressive
— Wha?
— The smoke ring: impressive
Dave shrugs
— Yeah, well. You know what they say
— What?
— You can always tell someone who's been banged up 'cause they can juggle and blow smoke rings. That's what you learn in bang up. How to blow fucking smoke rings, and how to fucking juggle
More screams from the fraggles. Silence otherwise. Eddie brushes tiny embers of burning tobacco from his blanket as Dave suddenly slumps forward, a dark white figure in the half light
— Christ this place does my head in

17

spinkie

Alex buttons his jacket and makes a brr-it's-cold noise, as he and Tony walk through Covent Garden, en route to the Tube, en route to Brixton.

— Cold for August

— It's September

Alex considers:

— God I hate Autumn

Stepping into the road to avoid a *Big Issue* seller Tony replies

— But if Autumn is here, can Winter be far behind?

No response. They continue, not really talking, until they reach Garrick Street, where Alex glances up the side street at the inviting sign of the Lamb and Flag.

— Pint?

Tony, checking his watch

— We're due at the prison in about twenty minutes. We're already going to be late

Inside the comfortable, smoky confines of the crowded pub Alex waits for Tony to get the round. To pass the minute Alex looks at a guy in a beautiful dove-grey suit and cool blue shirt, with a beautiful yellow tie and overdeep tan and razorcut blond hair. Satisfied the man is gay Alex turns to his pint and his friend and they commence a discussion of Eddie's predicament: concluding in turn that Eddie is (a) probably guilty, (b) probably going to go down, (c) probably being sodomised as they speak. Alex drinks, Tony drinks, Alex drinks, Tony mentions that he has just received a letter from a cousin describing how the cousins used to torment the Raffertys' cleaner as a child.

— Her name was Titmuss

— . . . So?

— . . . So we used to run around the kitchen table shouting 'titgonk, titgonk!' and she used to run after us with a wooden spoon

Silence; slot machine; Alex

— Thanks for that

— Anyway. *Eddie*

— Yeah

— I reckon he could be in for quite a while, I mean if he doesn't get bail

— Poor sod

They nod, drink, agree. Tony says something about lawyers and Alex shrugs, checking out a pretty red haired girl across the bar talking animatedly to two kids wearing khaki Gap strides. Careful, thoughtful, Alex notices the girl's breasts beneath her skinny-rib jumper; surprised by joy, Alex notes for the sixty-eight-thousandth time in his life how girls' breasts bounce as they move. Reminded, now, Alex mentions

— Got laid last night

Making a pained face, Tony returns his empty pint glass to the bar top. Then he exhales, then he says:

— Go on then

— Fat ugly posh bird

— *Really* fat? – Tony cannot disguise the hopeful tone.

— Huge – Alex confirms, tipping the last of his pint down his mouth – I was searching for her clit for about five hours

— Yeah?

— Like looking for a coin down the back of a sofa

Laughter. Paying the barman for another Pedigree and a second Guinness, because Alex claims he is broke, Tony waits for his change while Alex leans between two suits, takes his Pedigree, gulps, and slides his hand across his beer-wet lips:

— Then she gives me a blow job, right? She gives me this blow job and it's OK and I'm getting quite excited because I'm closing my eyes and thinking of Elizabeth but then I open my eyes and I see a photo of the fat ugly posh bird on her bedside table and . . . and so I start to lose wood and I have to lean across as she's sucking me and turn the photo flat on the table

Tony chooses to ignore the reference to his wife. He nods and collects his shamrocked Guinness as Alex admits:

— Then I fucked her. Sort of

— Not a sterling performance?

— Not exactly. She was on

Making his lips white with Guinness froth Tony licks:

— Admiral of the red, eh?

— Went down on her, too

— Jesus

— Yeah, I know, it was dark, I didn't realise at the time, thought she was a bit wet, but . . . – The jukebox comes on but Alex is louder – In the morning I went into the bathroom and looked in the mirror and all my mouth and teeth were red. Like rust . . .

Tony is halfway through his Guinness:

— Why did you do it, anyway?

Alex glances through the pub smoke at his friend as if Tony has just deliberately lacerated his own scrotum in public.

— Er?

— You're in love with Katy, why bother sleeping with some . . . ugly woman . . .

— I'm not in love with Katy. Just fancy her. Only ever loved your wife

Tony scoffs:
— Oh . . . *come on*
— You think it's a load of pants?

Leaving a damp ring on the bar top as he lifts his pint Tony affirms:
— I think it's something . . . you like to wind me up about
— Well, you were there too, *dude*
— Was I? Was I?

Eyeing his not-quite-as-drunk-as-him friend across his uptilted pint glass, Alex chuckles and says
— Ah well . . . Maybe not

For a quarter of a minute they both fall silent, listening to the boy band on the jukebox, the girlish chatter in the bar. While they are silent two young black guys in blue pinstripe suits diffidently approach the bar and order drinks. A mouthful of bitter unswallowed, Alex looks at the black guys ordering drinks and feels a sudden unwonted pang of pity, a painful empathy for their predicament, at how it must be to be a black guy in a white pub, to be a black guy in a white city, to be a black guy in a white world working in a white man's job wearing a white man's clothes using white man's words surrounded by white men, knowing that the only reason you are here in this cold white man's country is because three hundred years ago some white men came to your sunny homeland and bought your great-great-grandfather for 30p. Mid-reverie, Alex is startled to hear the black guys order ale, order Theakston's, a middle class white man's drink. Then Alex is startled by the fact that he is startled. What does he expect them to order? Lager? Red Stripe? A quart of de cane juice?

All through this Tony just keeps thinking *the black ram who tups your white ewe,* and because Tony does not want to think about this he reaches for the loose end of their interrupted conversation:
— Had a dream last night

— Sorry?
— This dream . . . last night
Alex gives a good-natured groan
— Oh good
— We were in this shed. I was in a garden shed, a potting shed, and I was with you and your sister . . . and you were feeding some chicken pieces to your sister – Tony closes his eyes to grasp the details – Yes, that's right . . . and . . . then you asked me to help you by feeding her some of the chicken. And then you lifted up your sister's skirt and . . . and you asked me to shove some of the chicken up your sister's . . . vagina . . .
— And did you?
— No. I think the chicken pieces were too big.
Alex laughs. Tony shrugs, almost smiles. Alex's laughter reminds him he wants to keep in good humour: picking up his third pint Alex begins making headway while Tony gives an emboldened-by-beer expression and says
— Alex I need . . .
— Mmm?
— I need your . . . advice on something
Alex grins encouragingly; Tony says
— It's difficult . . .
— Try me
— It's . . . it's . . .
Tony opens his arms and his heart and his eyes and finally says
— I can't get it up
Slot machine; cash register; Alex:
— What?
— I . . . – Anxiety crosses Tony's chubby face until he seems almost relieved to say – I don't think Elizabeth is having an affair. Well, I'm not sure any more . . . – He sighs – We've had this problem, I might have been transferring my anxiety because . . .
— Cause you're Mister Floppy?

An honest grimace:

— It's . . . *awful*. Every time . . . for months now. Every time I go to put it in I start worrying about whether I'll be able to keep it up and then . . . bang . . . down it goes

Alex, sceptical:

— Man, we've all been there

— Please

— Usually after a night on the Aznavour

— This is serious

— *Being* serious – Alex retorts, affronted – it's just performance anxiety. Standard stuff. You just gotta go out and find some sympathetic bit of poontang and take your time and you'll be fine

Halfway into his third pint Tony makes a distinctly unimpressed face:

— Poontang?

Alex grins. Says nothing.

Tony says:

— You know I sometimes wonder . . . whether it's just a pose

— What?

— Your anti-feminism, your laddishness. You don't really mean it, do you?

Chuckle; drink:

— No, you're right. People don't seem to realise how much I respect and agree with feminists

— Sorry?

— Feminism's *fab*

Ignoring Tony's ever more sceptical face Alex swallows some of his fourth pint, burps exuberantly, laughs, and his eyes shine as he explains:

— I mean, think about it, there's nothing as exciting as meeting some radical lesbian feminazi in a bar and you argue with her and you chat her up and six hours later she's a total naked pussycat lying in your bed gagging for cock. Right? Right? It's better than underage briffit. Wouldn't you like to have Germaine Greer on all fours in your kitchen begging you to take her hard up the arse? Wouldn't you like to have that fat one, Andrea Dworkin, asking you to lose your mess all over her dirty great tits?

Tony is not laughing; Alex is not caring. Alex is leaning to his left and asking the red-headed girl in the acrylic jumper if she wants to hear about the Barbarossa campaign.

The girl looks down her nose at Alex as if he has just obscenely propositioned her; which he hopes he has.

Undaunted Alex continues: moving onto Afro-American albino hairstyles. At last the girl realises Alex is talking about her putatively red pubic hair and she looks as if she is thinking of slapping him but before she can slap him Tony steps between and says

— Come on – A fistful of Alex's collar in his hand.

The two of them, led and propelled by Tony, head for the pub door. Outside Alex whistles:

— Lovely bit of grumble

— I don't think you were getting very far

— She was wetting the seat

— She was going to hit you

— Didn't she remind you of Elizabeth?

— I thought more Katy, actually . . .

Along the little road they walk towards the soot-blackened palazzo walls of the Garrick Club; turning right they pass a travel bookshop and a shoe shop and head into the throng of office workers walking fast and tourists walking slow. As they dawdle behind a gaggle of window-shopping ship-and-tunnel people, of vacationing Continentals, Alex loudly starts talking about foreigners. Tony, weary, irritated:

— Alex, please

But Alex is in full flow

— Fucking French, nation of rude shopkeepers

Tony hisses

— *I think they're German*

— *Ah, die Land ohne Pop musik*

With a skip Alex rounds the busload of foreigners and walks on; turning only to wink at Tony, Alex goes up to a smart-suited City girl who has a trim briefcase under one arm while with the other arm she points out the sky: trying to hail a taxi.

— Hello

The girl turns on her importuner, her blonde hair frizzed by the traffic-breeze:

— I'm sorry, do I know you

Alex smiles

— I was wondering . . .

An empty taxi shoots past and stops for someone down the road; the girl stamps her sensible black shoe in frustration and looks even more impatiently at Alex. Who is still smiling:

— I was wondering . . . are you available?

It takes a moment for the girl to compute this, which gives Tony the chance to intervene. Grabbing Alex for the second time he steers his drunken, chortling friend down the road towards Charing Cross and Leicester Square whence they take the steps down the Tube and feed their tickets and all the way from Leicester Square to Embankment to Brixton Tony keeps marvelling at quite how desperate he is to urinate.

Emerging into the badlands, the desert that is Alex's perception of south London, they start walking in the wrong direction, then they nip into a pub to take a leak and ask for directions, then they have another pint to gird themselves for the ordeal, then they have a second pint because the first one gave them a taste and as they finally emerge from the scuzzy old-fashioned south London Irish pub Alex gestures at Tony and stumbles and laughs and says

— OK softboy

— ??
— How late *are* we?
Tony suppresses a hiccup; says to his wristwatch:
— Uh, three hours
— Ai . . . Not too bad then

Seated on plastic chairs in the Brixton Prison visiting hall Alex is wondering inebriately at the beauty of the women visiting their villainous partners.
— But look at them
Tony hushes him, unsuccessfully. Alex clucks
— Fucking incredible. Off the dial
Glancing around at the rows of tables peopled by gangsters' molls and burglars' babes and Sikh terrorists' squeezes, Tony is constrained to admit that yes, the amount of good-looking women in the room is out of all proportion to the attractiveness of the prisoners the women are visiting
— I mean – Alex gestures at one shaven-headed crim in blue jeans and white tee, who is having his finger sucked by his visiting spouse, a tarty but schoolgirlish blonde – Look at *him*. You wouldn't call him Leonardo da Caprio wouldya?
— *Shhh*
— Every girl loves a bad 'un
— Here we go
Alerted by a bell, the two of them look up and see: the door at the end of the hall has opened and another busload of convicts and remandees is shuffling between the tables to where their wives, children, friends, girlfriends are already sitting. From twenty yards away Alex checks to see if his friend is amongst them, and if he is, if he is looking better, or worse, or *non ano intacta*. Forced to the front of the group Eddie lifts an eyebrow at Alex and Tony and as he does he gestures at his wrist where his watch should be. Then, attaining his friends'

fake-wood formica table Eddie pulls out a seat and sits down and says

— *Four hours?*

— Er sorry

Alex grins

— Yeah, sorry mate

Eddie reels back from the fug of beery breath

— You're *pissed*, aren't you?

— Might be

Mournful, Eddie shakes his head:

— I'm in prison, and you're drunk?

Tony looks uncomfortable; Alex says

— Had a couple of sharpeners. We didn't think you were going anywhere

— Thanks

— Hey, at least we made it over the river

— Right. Fine – Eddie clicks his teeth – S'pose I should be grateful for tiny mercies . . . It's just . . . – He shakes his head – It's just a little weird to know you two were having a social while I was being . . . *raped*

Alex and Tony start. Eddie chuckles:

— Er, I'm *joking*

— Y'sure? We did wonder

— Well don't. They're not *animals* in here

— No?

— No. They're actually rather charming in their own way

— Yeah?

— Yah . . . if a bit bonkers – Eddie gestures at an older con three tables down – See him?

— The black guy with the scar on his head?

— The Mars Bar. Yah. That's Jimmy. From Trinidad. He think he's Simon de Montfort . . .

— Simon de Montfort?

— Yep – Eddie laughs, points out another convict sat opposite his wife and kids, at the other end of the hall – And *that's* Liam the Lion Bar . . . keeps giving away chocolate because he reckons he's won the Irish lottery

— Right – Alex looks at his friend – Right – Alex says again, gazing at Eddie. Alex can see that Eddie is trying to be brave; trying to be tough. Attempting to see through his own selfishness, his own drunkenness, Alex tries to empathise, to relate, to reach out to his friend. Making a real effort Alex says

— So you stupid old cunt, what the fuck were you thinking of? I mean: *dole fraud*? What happened to the Trust Fund?

Pause. Eddie glances at Tony, who glances at Alex. Tony glances at Eddie who glances at Alex: who glances around the cheerless prison hall, taking in the glaze-eyed prison wardens, the screaming black kiddies, the shaven-headed crim who is now shoving his hand openly up his girlfriend's skirt. Inexplicably, Alex starts laughing; this in turn gets them all laughing: as one they burst into strange-but-genuine laughter, laughing so loud they get wary looks from the wardens, laughing so loud Eddie has to wipe tears from his haunted eyes.

When they stop laughing a slightly awkward silence fills the space between the three University chums. Then Tony coughs and says:

— We got you some biscuits

18

apple virgin

— What are you doing?

Alex is slumped over his laptop; moaning, pretending to be dead. At his girlfriend's words he lifts his head and looks at his girlfriend in her short skirt, black tights, bright eyes, dark hair. Replies

— I'm *trying* to write a piece for *Cosmo*. What Men Think About Nose Rings . . .

— Nose rings?

— Well, nose rings, nipple rings, body jewellery in general

Katy gazes at him

— Jesus, who CARES – She is crossing and uncrossing her little black legs, the tights that make her clever knees shine through the denier.

Alex wonders

— Shouldn't you be at school?

— COLLEGE! I'm at *SIXTH-FORM COLLEGE!*

— I know. But school sounds sexier

At this she squeals and smiles. His gaze cast across his room, locked on the sight of his nineteen-year-old schoolgirlfriend, Alex's mind reverts to type. He tries not to think about sex but he can't help. What else is there to think about, what else is there to do? His brain is, Alex has long realised, essentially a one industry town, a Newfoundland fishing village. And in the one industry town that is his brain the miners are clacking down the cobbled roads, the weavers are shuffling to the mill.

She is whining

— College is *boring*

— But you've got to get your A levels, you've already missed a year and you don't

— And I DON'T care

— But you want to go to university – Alex makes a serious face, turning from his blank grey screen – Don't you?

Girlish shrug:

— GOD you sound like my dad when you talk like that

— Like who?

— Like my . . . daddy

Alex urges:

— Say it again

Katy shakes her head

— Don't be a PERV

— Just being myself

— I don't know why I go out with you . . . You're old and crap

— Go on, say daddy

— Ooh Daddy will you fuck me

— *And now take your clothes off*

Katy laughs

— Nooo . . .

Her schoolbag lifted from the floor she pretends to look inside, as if she is thinking about something else; then she says idly

— I met some guys on the bus this morning, when I was meant to be going to college

Taking the bait

— What? What guys?

— Some guys, they were lush

The sweet bile of jealousy:

— Did you measure their penises?

— Yeah – Katy lifts a big A level textbook from her schoolbag and lays it on her lap and opens it, pretending to read

— It was lucky I had my ruler in my bag, they were really big

— Really big?

She looks up, nods her cute chin:

— HUGE, REALLY BIG

Alex looks over, croaks something; she repeats

— So big they hurt

He is slumped again, groaning; she asks

— What's wrong NOW

— Dunno . . . – He sighs – Do you think I need help?

Rising to her five-foot-three, Katy comes across the bedroom, pushes Alex's laptop away across his desk, sits herself on his lap:

— Yes you need help and anyway you KNOW you're the biggest

— Am I? Honest?

— Sometimes I'm scared I'll POP when you SLAM it inside me

— Shall we have a go in front of the mirror?

— Nope – She says, laughing and moving her hips on his lap so he can feel quite how light she is: her fifty-one kilos – No, first you gotta do some work, you've got to earn some money so you can buy me EXPENSIVE PRESENTS

— I can't – Alex looks around her body atop his lap to his idle laptop – It's just so . . . mindless. How many times can I write the same piece?

— Write something else then . . . – Katy tucks her head in the crook of his neck and toys with his top button and murmurs – Write something SERIOUS . . . you keep saying . . .

— Yyyeah . . . I guess . . . I sort of started something but it . . . it wasn't . . . *you know* – His thoughts wandering, vaguely, Alex drops his gaze to his desk drawer. Surprised, Alex sees the bottom drawer is half-open. This is peculiar. Did he open it? Or did *she* open it? *Could she??*

Dismissing the thought he discreetly shuts the drawer with his shoe, while at the same time he sinks his mouth into Katy's blouse and says

— Mnnbbnnmmmnnn

Tilting herself away from him, Katy runs her fingers through his thick dark hair; adopts a pitying tone

— You REALLY want to do it in front of the mirror?

Later they lie in his bed; her smoking, him thinking. The TV is doing the lunchtime thing: crap quiz shows, Australian soaps, local weather. Her head softly haloed by white pillows Katy blows her smoke straight upwards to the ceiling and says

— Do you remember counting the ceiling cracks when you were ill as a kid?

Alex thinks about the sex they have just had:

— Yeah

— What did you read?

— What?

— When you were ill what books did you READ?

He muses

— *Malory Towers* . . . Enid Blyton's schoolgirl books

— Enid Blyton?

— Yeah

— But those are girlie books

— That's why I read them – Alex confesses, blindly searching for the remote on the duvet; finding it; changing channels – I fancied all the girls, I always wanted to give Darrel Rivers one, during a Midnight Feast, and as for Alicia

— With the sharp tongue

— Gagging

Her laughter full of cigarette smoke Katy says:
— Gwendoline?
— Nah, didn't fancy her, what about you?
Shaking her head, finishing her cigarette, saying *oh sure,* Katy moves from her pillow and uses Alex's chest. The way she rests her sweet little head on his big manly chest means Alex can see her head slightly moving up and down in time with his big Burundi post-coital heartbeat. She admits
— I used to read Jennings books, and football things
— You're such a *bloke*
— You're such a GIT
Stroking the soft feminine hair that curls around her little fragile white ear Alex dreams, drifts . . .
Katy says from his chest: says in a way that makes her voice resonate in his chest
— Alex . . . you'd never be unfaithful to me . . . would you?
— Course not
And she smiles, he can feel her smiling as she says
— Thought so
Evidently satisfied she takes the remote from his hand and presses the volume button to do him a favour and make the News get louder. Northern Ireland. Russia. Diana's Anniversary. The road protest at Lyonshall. Alerted, Alex lifts Katy away so he can sit up to hear the report: to hear the TV hack describe the way the protestors have been evicted from one tunnel but are now busy digging themselves into another.
Katy thinks aloud
— Didn't you used to live near there?
Trying to be unconcerned, Alex replies, his eyes fixed on the TV
— Yeah, I grew up near there
the scent of her bare skin after we swam in the Arrow, the coltsfoot tobacco we smoked on the wheelbarrow seat
— How near?

He looks at his girlfriend, at her cheeks: *the colour of the Lancaster rose*?

— Near enough

Acceptant, Katy leans across for the bottle of Evian on Alex's side of the bed: glugging water so it dribbles down her bare breasts as well as her chin, she wipes her mouth, re-tops the waterbottle, and motions at the TV pictures of eco-warriors chained to trees

— I should be there

— What?

Naked, Katy explains

— I should just chuck college, I should be doing something like that . . .

— What: tunnelling under a field for several months so you end up in court and the road gets built anyway?

— Cynic – She keeps looking at the TV, goes on – At least they're doing something to help save the planet, to save the . . . environment

Intrigued by this, this unpredicted idealism, Alex looks at her profile

— I didn't know you were so concerned?

Her eyes meet his

— Last time I mentioned that I was worried about whaling you said – She makes a now-I-am-quoting-you face – 'What's so fucking special about whales they're just fish with tits' – Her expression reverts – After that I thought it best not to say anything

Alex, griefstricken

— *Fish with tits.* I said that?

— Yep

— Oh well

Katy chuckles, runs four fingers through his chest hair

— It doesn't matter anyway . . . Daddy . . .

— . . . What did you say?

— I said that's all right . . . DADDY

Alex tries; he tries hard.

The remote falls from the bed as he dives between his girlfriend's laughing breasts.

19

gallant soldier

— V42685?

The prison warden is rapping smartly on the half-open steel door of Eddie's cell; Eddie looks over from his bunk, his book

— That's *Mister* V42685 to you

— Yeah? . . . Shower time, Lyonshall

The warden has wandered off down the landing to alert other prisoners. For a second Eddie sighs and stares at the wire under-mesh of the bunk above him. Then, energised, Eddie swings his feet out into the empty cell, picks up a towel and a change of shorts, steps out of the cell. Outside on the landing some guys are lounging over the railings, staring down at the trapeze net thirty feet below. As Eddie passes down the landing he catches through the half-open doors glimpses of other prison lives: sad-faced remands listening to the radio, murderers in white paper jump-suits playing chess, recently intaken inmates lying on their bunks smoking roll-ups in the clothes they were arrested in. From one of the cells a man in pinstripes and collar looks up at Eddie and Eddie moves quickly on. Past a black guy in green-and-yellow checked dungarees, past the doorless toilets, Eddie finds his way to the metal stairwell.

Clattering down the grille'd stairs and the next stairs, Eddie raises his towel and his eyebrows to another warden who opens a big steel door and lets Eddie into a further part of the wing: the showers, kitchens, chapel, ancillary areas. Two big tattooed wardens with long staves stand at the end of this corridor next to an alarm button but Eddie (even as he does this marvelling at the ordinariness of it, marvelling inside at how quickly this nightmare has become routine) ignores them: ducking through a door he enters a room on the right where guys are stripping down to their underwear, then to nothing.

Their clothes hung on pegs the prisoners are stepping one by one through another door into the big communal shower: where about thirty prisoners are simultaneously abluting. Where all the black guys are standing under their shower-roses facing into the middle, into the communal gaze, with their huge penises sticking out like fresh blood puddings in a butcher's shop. Eddie winces. *The usual gauntlet.* Taking one unused shower head Eddie twists the metal tap, the pipe burps, hot water spurts, and now Eddie has to decide how to stand: not being as big as the black guys he does not want to face directly into the middle of the communal shower; not being as badly-endowed as the Orientals or Asians he does not want to stare at the wall with his blushing arse all-too-obviously facing his fellow prisoners. Accordingly Eddie adopts a kind of casual, side-on stance: this delicate manoeuvre accomplished Eddie is soon soaping his face and his arms, closing his eyes in momentary bliss; as the shower floods endless warm jets over his face.

Opening his eyes after washing the shampoo away Eddie sees with interest that his bollocks are bigger than the IRA terrorist's at the other end of the shower; and with concern that his cock is quite considerably smaller than the disgraced Tory MP's. As he rinses the last of the endless prison grime from his armpits and shoulders Eddie also notes the spindliness of the calves of the Nigerian drug smugglers from the third landing. Just as he is doing this a Nigerian turns and catches Eddie's eye; Eddie gives a weak smile.

Ten minutes later, his shower over and his time-out-of-cell expired, Eddie retreats into the changing room and towels himself down and slips on new underwear and old clothes: then he retraces his steps, up and along and through the noise and smell of this place, this weird place that is now his home, this unabolished monastery, this anti-Crusader castle, this place full of celibates, Hospitallers of Hate.

Eddie slows: realising that when he gets back to his cell it will almost certainly be bang-up time, the cell door will be locked for the next twenty-three hours out of the next twenty-four: so he slows his walk to a dawdle. Savouring each step. Each step a tiny freedom. *How good it is to walk.* Even along a hard metal landing, up hard metal stairs. *It is good to walk in a straight line.*

Eddie has almost halted, to take in the scene: the arched windows at the end of the wing, affording a view of the chapel and exercise yard, and beyond that Beirut and Fraggle Wing, searchlights and razor wire. And beyond that, the slates and stockbricks of South London. Then England. Still on the stairs between second landing and third Eddie gazes down the nave of the wing, at the unstained glass window, at the sun casting a square of light onto the flagstoned floor of *the Great Hall, that morning, that morning when he came downstairs with Elizabeth and they found the door open and a fawn standing, trembling, in the slanting sunlight in the middle of the*

— Fuck you you cunt

Startled, Eddie looks down: a fight. Two guys are fighting: at the end of his very own landing, his very own neighbourhood. Panicked, curious, Eddie stands, watches: the new black guy in the green-and-yellow has got a white guy by the throat: the white guy is struggling to escape but he seems hypnotised by something in the black guy's hand, poised an inch from his neck.

Hands anxiously pulling down the towel around his neck, Eddie strains to see: what is it? A flash, a flash of glass: the black guy moves his hand so the glass catches the light and Eddie sees: the black guy is holding a broken piece of light-bulb glass to the white guy's throat.

— Take it back, slag

— Fuck y

— *Better take it back*

The noise of the alarm bells is bouncing down the landing, and down the wing, and around the prison, echoed by the shouts of other prisoners: come from their cells to spectate. Black boots ring and clang against the steel, wardens barge past Eddie and Eddie stoops towards his cell where he finds Dave, watching, slouched against the jamb of their cell door. Dave winks at Eddie, says

— Nice shower?

— Er – Eddie says, both hands twisting the towel around his neck. Gazing at the life-and-death struggle taking place at the end of the landing Eddie nervously angles his head

— Er. What's going on?

— White guy called the black guy a cunt

— Yes?

Dave shrugs

— So the black cunt took a bit of exception, seeing as the white cunt is also a cunt

— *Right*

Side by side, Eddie and Dave watch as the black guy with the yellow-and-green dungarees presses the broken light bulb into the white guy's neck. The first beads of blood have begun to spot the white guy's off-white tee shirt. The shouts of the other prisoners are getting louder; the wardens are circling the embracing couple: some coming at the twosome from behind, some from in front, all of them crooning and cooing at the black guy, like they are cornering a dangerous animal

— OK, Solo, let him go
— *Why?*
— 'Cause if you don't you know what'll happen
— *Like you're not going to kick shit outa me already?*
— Just drop him

The black guy looks very unimpressed; the white prisoner of the prisoner looks even more unimpressed; his head in the arm lock, his neck bleeding down his chest he struggles to say:

— Get this bastard offffff me

But before it's over, it's finished. Just as the white guy goes to push his head free, just as the black guy goes to react, one of the wardens leaps on the black guy's back, puts a knee in his back. The black con bellows: instantly two others jump him, pin him down; in the same manner they turn on the white man, and despite his yells, subdue him too. Yards away Eddie gulps; next to him Dave shouts some encouragement; moments later ten wardens are dragging the two plastic-handcuffed brawlers down the stairs by the legs, making sure their heads bounce blood on each step, dragging a sticky red stripe down each step.

— Fancy a spliff?

Dave is talking to the ceiling, talking to Eddie.

Eddie puts down his Dostoevsky and says, to the bunk above

— Girlfriend came to see you, I take it
— Yeah – Eddie's cellie chuckles – Sweetheart got me a quarter
— It hasn't been up your *arse*, has it?

Mock-insulted, Dave returns

— And what's wrong with my arse, you've had enough gear out of my arsehole
— It's just the *thought* . . .
— Anyway no it hasn't – Dave reaches for his tin – She gave me a kiss, nearly choked on the fucking thing
— No search then?

— Nah . . . Screws in 'ere got shit for brains
— Perhaps they're turning a blind eye
— Shagging Yorkshire miners

Eddie can hear Dave making reefer-rolling noises. Sounds of cigarette-paper licking, sounds of roach tearing; Dave says, as he finishes the spliff

— Tell you what Oxford, I miss that tart
— Your girlfriend?
— Randy little witch
— It must be difficult for you
— Could say that . . .

Dave is smoking the spliff; clouds of blue heady smoke are rolling up to the ceiling and across. For a while there is silence; apart from the sounds of the fraggles; the distant Brixton traffic.

Then Dave says

— Being here makes you realise
— What?
— 'bout, y'know . . . *birds* . . .

His voice already sounds stoned, Eddie thinks, listening to Dave smoking and the spliff popping and the flick of ash into an ashtray. At the last a blind hand reaches down and proffers; Eddie takes, draws and inhales: feels his mind swim; meantime Dave is already rolling another, and explaining:

— It's like you only realise how much you need birds when they're gone . . . this place is so . . . blokey
— What do you expect?
— But . . . – Dave smokes, tries again – It's like something's been taken away, it's all . . . there's no . . .
— Softness
— Yeah. I s'pose – Dave thinks – There's certainly no tits. I miss tits. Don't you miss tits?

Eddie laughs.

— *Absolutely*

— But no I mean really tits are so great, don'tchathink, birds are so amazing, their bodies. Fuck me

Smoking the second spliff Eddie gets a rush of blood, a swim, a rush of articulacy. His words a volume of smoke Eddie replies:

— It's all down to evolution. Women are the product of billions of sexual choices made by men. Women have been designed by men to be attractive, they've been engineered and built by what men want in a woman's body

Silence. The night. Dave laughs

— Lot of award-winning design work went on my girlfriend's arse, I can tell you

— Yeah?

— Fucking nectarine, mate, fucking nectarine

— Right . . .

— And her pubes, they should win a few prizes – Stops, thinks – Mind you, her fanny should win . . . whatchacallit

— *Sorry?*

— Fuckin' UEFA Cup, amount of times she plays away . . .

Eddie thinks, interrupts

— I must say

— Whassat?

— I'm *very stoned*

— Moody gear isn't it?

— Telling me

— Ha . . .

Perception dulled, perception warped, Eddie tries to remember where he is; then tries to forget. Cool September blows through the small cell window, ruffles the Page 3 girl blu-tacked to the wall. The sound of the night warden's television percolates up the landings. With nothing else to do in the dark the two continue talking, and smoking. With nothing else to do but be friends they talk about Eddie's sister, they talk about Dave's dad, they talk about how Dave's dad tried to knife him when he was a kid, they talk about how Eddie loved his mother, his real mother who died. And all the time the spliffs pass between them, a small red glow in the dark, passing between: as the endless conversation riffs, rebounds: like they are guitarists jamming in a blues bar after hours.

At the end, right at the edge of consciousness, at about three in the morning, when the prison is dead, when the traffic has stopped, when even the fraggles are quiet, Eddie thinks about how hungry he is, about the munchies. Eddie thinks, into the blackness

What . . . would he have?

Silence

Baked hayneck pudding?

Silence

The Elva plums we used to have?

Wardonys pears?

And that day we went swimming?

When she was frightened, when she got up in the morning to kiss the dew, when she was in that high-wheeled yellow dogcart –

When we went up Harepit Hill –

When she was wearing chains and carcanets of primroses –

And violets from M'Ladies Wood –

And that was the day we went swimming when we were naked but the sun was so hot we dove straight off the great big lugger into the bay and when we swam back to the beach someone had folded our clothes and when we'd put our clothes on we rode those Dartmoor ponies back up the dunes and over the hills to Lyonshall Park and then we went into the house and in the Hall in the Great Hall on the elm table there were plates of lobsters and great dishes of honey and piles of Devonshire cream and someone had chilled the glasses and filled them with cold pussyfoot cup and the ice cubes contained tiny blue sprigs of borage and England oh England you are a green cunt and I love you

20

forebitten more

— So this is it then?
— What?

Face raised from his portfolio of book covers, proof copies, sheets of sales figures, and PR handouts, Tony repeats to the eager young face of the Waterstone's Bookshop buyer:
— Wasn't with you. Sorry?
— How long you been doing this job?

Tony looks at Andy Falloway and thinks: *got to be at the clinic in an hour. Then I've got to fetch Toby*. Half-awake, Tony looks at the picture of Constable's Haywain on the mock-up cover of *The Encyclopedia of English Painters* and thinks of

Elizabeth in that high-wheeled yellow dogcart, spanking along the drive lined with wild Canterbury bells . . .

Tony:
— Seven years

Sifting through the same mock-up covers Andy expels air
— We'd better have ten of those *Painters* jobs – And then he says – Seven years, eh?

Warily
— Yess . . .

— You know what they're beginning to call you round here?
— Tell me
— Old-timer

Tony is prepared to be angered by this . . . but isn't. Standing here in the whispering quiet of the bookshop he finds that he simply doesn't care: he doesn't care if he drops dead, or if he is the butt of everybody's satirical pity. What he cares about is Julia. Permitting himself a sly glance over to Non-fiction Tony sees Julia looking slyly back at him, unmistakeable reproach on her face. Andy clocks

— You always fancied her, didn't you

Sad nod. Andy nods too:

— She's leaving next month. Going on to better things

In her high-wheeled yellow dogcart

— Mmm?
— She's got a better job
— Really
— Look, Tony, what I'm trying to say is – Andy searches the rack of Booker Prize winners behind Tony's head for the rest of his sentence; finds it – Is this really what you envisaged doing all your life when you graduated? – Pause, another shot – I mean, we all love seeing you round here Tony . . . but . . . but . . . Are you happy?

Tony eyebrows:

— *Happy?*
— Yeah, happy. Are you happy?
— . . . I don't really know . . . – Tony delays, says – I suppose I go by what Freud said. The only things you need to be happy are work, love . . . and a Mercedes convertible – Silence. Tony shrugs – No I'm not happy but it could be worse
— Meaning
— At least I've got my job. Rafferty's Regular Routes
— Ouch

Tony goes on

— Look. It's reliable. If I drop dead from lugging three million Harry Potters round London the wife gets fifty thousand

Andy persists:

— Must get a bit tedious, though?

Tony changes subject:

— So how many of the Rackhams are you going to take?

— The new illustrated one?

— Yes – Tony reaches into his briefcase and extracts a big shiny new paperback which falls open on a picture of a tree

The dodderel paks in the Park, the stag-headed oaks . . .

— So?

— Well I reckon – Andy gets equally professional. – *Yep*. Yep. I think . . . five of those. And those. And . . . and we'll have eight of the Julian Barnes, he always sells – Andy pulls out the author photo from the publicity guff – Mind you he is one ugly fucker, no wonder his wife went off with that clam jouster

— Want any of these?

— Bridget Jones Mark II?

— Sort of thing, have a look

Andy accepts the proffered proof copy, shakes his head in what looks like suicidal despair. Tony

— Not interested?

— Yeah, go on – Andy flaps a hand – Gizza dozen . . . What else you got?

— Ermm . . .

— Any new pop science?

— We're bringing out another Stephen Hawking

A professional glint in Andy's eyes:

— Really?

— Next year. I've . . . got some bumf here somewhere . . . – As Tony rifles through his portfolio for the laminated sheet of blurbs he mutters to Andy – I never really could work out why that *Brief History* book was so popular

— Cause he's a spaz, innit?

— Perhaps – Tony muses – But why don't people just go for the real thing? You know: religion?

— Like believe in God, you mean?

— Yes, God, the thinking man's Stephen Hawking. Ah here we are

Pulling out the sheet Tony lets Andy be impressed, allows him to make a sizeable order; as they are doing this Tony glances across at Julia again. She is leaning under her desk for a book: where her figure should be is the poster behind, a poster advertising a new printing of some new *Book Of British Flowers*, with a photograph of raspberry brick walls, *old sunlit walls thick with clove pink, and marjoram, and thyme, and in the middle a roundel of grass and a wheelbarrow seat where they kissed.*

— Tony? Hello? Tony?

Ignoring the hand Andy is waving in front of his eyes Tony takes up his briefcase and strolls across the thick carpet of the bookshop to the Non-fiction Pay Here desk. Where Julia is sitting with a new paperback collection of Housman's poems on her lap: where Julia is saying

— Hello

Her voice is more clipped, more English, more estranged, more cool, than he recalls. Or maybe that's just her mood.

But her cheeks are creamy and red, *the double quarter creamy blush rose.*

— Jules – He doesn't know how to say it. She looks at him. He says again – I'm sorry for just dumping you like that. At the Hayward . . .

Nothing.

He repeats, says

— Honestly

Still nothing. Then she says

— Wasn't Housman an old bore? I never realised before. All those piles of dead soldiers

— He called his poetry a morbid secretion

— Did he? – Julia smiles, politely, then says – You could at least have rung

— I know. I *am* sorry

— Just a phone call?

— I know. I know. Would you like to . . .

— What, again?

— Some other time . . . when . . .

— When you're not still obsessed with your wife you mean? When you won't just dump me??

— Well

— Well?

— I think . . . – He stammers – I think . . . – She looks at him; he stammers again – I think maybe I'd better go . . .

— So you inject it straight into your penis about an hour before you plan to have intercourse

Tony is sitting in a too-low armchair in the slightly tacky consulting room of the Belsize Medical Centre, a clinic he chose this morning because in its classified *Time Out* advert it promised it specialised in Male Sexual Problems.

Opposite his armchair, his female sex therapist is outlining one treatment:

— After a couple of stabs at it you soon get the hang

Tony sweats; his groin is aching with imagined pain; he doesn't say anything. The early middle-aged woman crosses her legs at the knee, looks importantly into her lap, into her newly opened file now Biro-headed: **Mark Nicholson. Impotence**

— As I said, Mister Nicholson, your problem is 'spectatoring'. You are too conscious of your own sexual performance to let yourself relax, and thereby achieve a sustainable erection . . .

— . . . So?

— So you need something to give yourself confidence in your erections again. Prostaglandin can do that

Squirming at the mere fact that he is here, discussing his penis, his woodlow, in such detail, Tony returns:
— But I was hoping there might be . . . something else . . . I mean, these injections . . . they sound a bit . . .
The woman nods
— We find that most of our patients get used to them very quickly. As we discussed the important thing is to remember to keep the ampoules cool
Tony mentions:
— Well that's another thing
— Mm?
— The ampoules. What if my wife and I are going out and we want to do it somewhere else?
Rush-hour traffic noise.
— We recommend a Thermos, that keeps the ampoules sufficiently chilled
— So if my wife and I are on holiday and we're getting romantic and we want to make love on the beach at midnight: I just say hold on I have to get me Thermos out?
A Tube train rumbles somewhere.
— Mr Nicholson. We *are* trying to help
— I know, I know
— You refuse to take Viagra, because you're worried about . . . dependency. You don't want to take any other chemical medication – She fixes him with a stare – So I'm trying to offer alternatives. The injections are just one treatment. You could also try a suction pump . . . – She gets a stare in return, goes on quick – But frankly if I were asked to recommend one particular course of action
— Yes?
— Well – She seems to be searching for the right tone of voice – It appears from what you have told me that your impotence is psychosomatic rather than . . . hydraulic . . . therefore . . .
— Sorry?

— We have to ask why have you lost your confidence? Until we answer that I am somewhat working in the dark

— Of course . . . – Tony nods, blushing; the woman smiles sourly, uncrosses her legs, crosses them the other way. Makes a note in her file.

— We do understand how awful impotence can be

Now Tony stares at his knees, at the worn patch in the corrugations of his cords, like a crop circle in corn.

— Perhaps I'd better go away and think about it

The woman eyes him directly

— Perhaps you had, Mister Nicholson, perhaps you had

Outside in Belsize Park it is getting dark. Yellowing leaves are beginning to stick to the windscreens of parked cars like flyers. It has been raining. Walking to the Tube Tony thinks about her. Miss Elizabeth Lyonshall. His Bess. Sweet Beth. Elizabethlehem.

Turning, Tony heads back to the bookshop: *maybe he can just catch her.*

21

mollybobs

Concrete, stockbrick, breezeblocks, barbed wire, searchlights, steel fencing, rain. Head pressed to the rusting black bars of his cell window Eddie stares into the rain and thinks. About food. About food, sex, death, race, his dead mother, and how much Russian Literature he has got through since he arrived here in Brixton prison. What has he read? All of Tolstoy, Pushkin and Turgenev, most of Dostoevsky and Solzhenitsyn, a smattering of Mandelstam. Eddie wonders if he'll run out before he gets bail. *If* he gets bail. He wonders whether he would recommend a short stay inside to someone who really wanted to immerse themselves in nineteenth-century Russian novels: *after all, who else has the time*? Eddie constructs an elaborate fantasy where judges measure sentences by the same tariff as himself: 'How long did he get?' 'Oh, the Cavalier poets and modern Spanish drama . . .'

Then Eddie just stares. At the sea of south London slates, reflecting the colour of the slate-grey sky. Far away Eddie can hear some drummy reggae: the percussive susurrus reminds him of the sound of a boatyard in a Spring breeze, of ropes and lanyards rappling and knocking in the wind.

Dropping down from the bars, Eddie returns from the cell window to his bunk under Dave's bunk; picks up his Dostoevsky, puts it down; takes a cigarette from the packet on the table next. Hears

— Fraggles're quiet tonight

— Eh?

Dave says, again

— Fraggles. Quiet

Eddie blows smoke at the wire-and-mattress of Dave's bunk; and says

— Yeah, they *are* a bit . . .

— Won't last

— Probably

Eddie smokes; Dave doesn't. Dave goes silent, then says

— Oxford

— What

— Are you wanking?

— *Sorry?*

Dave chuckles, repeats

— Bunk's shaking. You having a tug?

— I'm scratching a leg, if you *must* know

Dave laughs

— Go ahead, don't mind me, I only 'ave to put up with you moaning about your mum as you spunk all over the fucking drum

Now Eddie laughs, too, and taps ash into the mini metal tray that once held a forest-fruit pie, a mini forest-fruit pie that was brought by Alex on his last visit. Presently Eddie says

— Talking about your mother

— Yeah?

— When I get bail I'm going to go round and give your mother a proper rogering

— Yeah?

— Just as she asked me to in that dirty letter she sent me

Dave snorts:
— My mother would eat you for breakfast
— Ooh I do hope so
Around Eddie the bunk frame quivers as Dave laughs, and leans down to peer over the bunk
— What about that bail, anyway, what's the news?
— Well – Eddie tries a smoke ring, fails – Well, my brief *said* there's a chance next month, in the High Court
— High Court?
— Yah
Knowledgably, Dave rolls back on to his bunk:
— That'll be your last chance then
— *Sorry?*
Dave, gently:
— If you don't get bail at the High Court that's it, good night, Nigella
Stifling his anger by grinding the cigarette butt into the shiny metal tray, Eddie replies
— Yeah, well
— Tough break
— *Thanks* – Flat on his back Eddie listens to the sound of the distant city; a police siren; a car alarm, a man shouting. And that music, still very faintly carrying across the cool wet dank evening air, across the walls, and the exercise yard. Somewhere a prisoner snores. More quiet. Speaking to the mattress and wire above him Eddie says
— What's your mum like, really?
— Haven't seen her in years
Long pause, Eddie
— *Sorry*
— Don't be
A silence, then
— So . . . – Eddie tries again – What about your dad?
— You what?

— Is he . . . does he . . .

Double pause, Dave says, loudly:

— Yeah?

— I mean . . . Do you blame him in any way for . . .

— For what?

— Well . . . being . . . being . . . you know

David makes an incredulous noise

— You mean do I blame him for me being a crim? For me doing bird?

— Yah . . .

Dave pauses, half laughs, says

— Nah. Course not . . . – Dave pauses again. Eddie can hear Dave thinking, Eddie listens to Dave say – My dad's just ga-ga now, can't get his head round the fact I'm not still in the army

— Yeah?

— Yeah – Dave clicks his teeth – Every time he rings me, when I'm outside, y'know, he says: 'So how's the army?' and I go: 'Dad I left the army four years ago, I'm living in Spain.' – Doing his dad's voice now – 'I didn't know they had an army base in Spain.' 'They didn't, dad. I was dishonourably discharged.' 'Spain eh? Didn't I tell you the army would be the making of you? And wasn't I proved right?' . . . – Dave goes quiet; quietly says – Stupid old twat

Intrigued, Eddie leans out from under his bunk and gazes up at the profile of his cell mate, as his cell mate repeats

— Just a stupid old bastard

— So you *do* blame him then?

— Nope . . . told ya. S'not his fault

— Well . . .

— Anyway – Dave leans over – Why, Oxford? D'you blame yours?

Taking time, Eddie:

— In a way

— What *way*?

— My parents were . . . Certainly my dad and my step mum . . . They were . . . They were rather . . . – A warden coughs down the landing; a radio is switched off, Eddie finds the words – I can't help thinking that their generation squandered the legacy given by their parents. Y'know? Their parents did all the hard work and stuck with their marriages and fought in the war and then their children just thought *fuck* it and they went off and shagged each other's wives and abolished grammar schools and took acid and pulled down whole cities . . .

Dave interrupts

— And that explains why you're a junked-up dole kiting tea leaf?

Eddie ruminates, smiles, says upwards

— I suppose not

Dave swings his legs off the bunk, says

— Anyway, I thought you didn't believe in right and wrong . . .

— Did I say that?

In his white shorts Dave goes and sits on the wooden chair and rubs his face and yawns and looks across the cell at Eddie. Dave says, wearily:

— You said it didn't make any sense . . . I think

Propped on an elbow, Eddie replies

— Well I've been thinking ab

— What's that?

— I

— No – Dave raises a hand, authoritative – That noise

— Uhn?

— It's coming from outside

— Sor

Barefoot Dave crosses to the cell window and presses his face between the bars and looks out and whistles

— Fuck me

— What is it?

— Fuck

— What

— One of the bastard guard dogs has got out

Eddie shakes his head:

— Sorry? Wh?

— He's eating all those kittens

Eddie says, as he shifts

— *What cats*?

— Family of stray cats, lives in the bins by F Wing

Jostling next to Dave Eddie squeezes his own face to the cold iron of the bars and looks out. In the evening dusklight he sees a big Alsatian dog nosing around the bins. Between two of the bins a mother cat is crouched: yowling. Behind the mother cat a pile of kittens are making pitiful noises. The dog is trying to get between the bins, trying to get at the kittens. Eddie

— Shouldn't somebody . . . ?

Nobody does. Eddie can hear the sound of other prisoners, standing to their cell windows. The other cons are talking, muttering, watching. The whole wing watches as the dog growls and pushes further between the bins. In the gloom of the rainy evening Eddie can still see quite clearly the mother cat, lashing out at the dog. The dog retreats for a second but then, with a clatter of bin tops and a squeal from one of the kittens

— *He's got one*

Eddie watches as the dog retreats from between the bins: a kitten in its mouth. Alongside Eddie Dave is saying, pointlessly, through the window

— *Get the fucking dog*

The dog bites. The kitten's head and half of its tiny torso falls to the rain-blackened asphalt. Dave

— Cunt's not even *eating* it

The dog goes back, sticks its head between the bins. Eddie can't see what happens then but he can hear: the noise of the mother cat, the clatter of the bins; the kitten; he can hear the other prisoners yelling out of their cells and banging metal cups on window-bars.

The dog is now aroused, Eddie reckons. Seemingly excited by the squeals and shouts the dog shoves lustily between the bins and scrabbles, and then re-emerges with another kitten in its jaws. The dog bites the back legs off the kitten and eats half of the torso. The mother cat comes out, crouches, hisses. Disgorging the half-chewed kitten, the dog slams hungrily between the bins to find another kitten.

— Get the **dog**

The shout is echoed by a score of other prisoners, the whole wing yelling out its barred windows

— Get the dog

— *Bastards*

In the cell Dave shakes his head

— They're not going to do *anything* . . .

Nobody does anything. The dog is knocking the bins, and knocking bin lids off, in its attempts to get at the remaining kittens. The noise of bin metal clattering on stone echoes around the wings mixed with the shouts of the prisoners. The dog is scrabbling and lunging, seeking one of the kittens; in the semi gloom Eddie sees one of the kittens scamper, squealing, across the asphalt. Paws out, the dog moves towards and pins the kitten, and then playfully bites the kitten's head right off. Then the dog goes back to the bins to find another kitten. Eddie looks away, looks at his hands, goes to say something to Dave; he is pre-empted by a shout from the other spectating prisoners. Simultaneously Eddie and Dave return to the window and they see a shape of white light thrown across the yard and Dave chuckles, and mutters

— It's Fuller

— What?

— Big Fuller. Number one from the bottom landing

Eddie questions

— Yeah?

Dave explains

— He's that nutter. Who topped those cops?

Blinking, Eddie cranes his head and sees that Dave is right. A prisoner, Fuller, has managed to get out of his ground-floor cell and is now outside in the yard: alone in the darkened yard with the dog, the rain, the detritus of dead kittens.

Dave is laughing.

Baffled, Eddie says

— What?

More weird laughter.

— What? What *is* it?

— Dog hasn't got a chance

Together, they turn and watch. Down in the yard Fuller is a blue shape, a figure in tee shirt and jeans: moving slowly towards the bins, towards the dog.

At first the dog doesn't notice. It continues scrabbling between the bins, trying to get at the last kitten. The kitten squeals. The mother cat hisses. The dog barks.

Then the dog hears Fuller. Growling, the dog turns, shows its fangs to Fuller; Fuller seems unconcerned. Fuller just moves, towards; then stops. Bending his big thick back, Fuller squats like a sumo wrestler roughly a yard from the dog. The dog growls. The dog's fangs are white in the prison arclight; its hackles rise; for a moment it looks as if Fuller has misjudged it, looks as if the huge prison guard dog will just spring up at Fuller and rip out the veins from his neck but instead

— *Oh my G*

— Told yuh

Fuller lunges, grabs the dog with one hand, on the dog's foreleg. The dog howls, contorts, tries to bite a piece out of Fuller's arm: but as it goes to sink teeth into Fuller's arm Fuller puts a fist on the fur of the dog's neck. With one movement Fuller lifts the dog up above his head and then Fuller slaps the dog's head down onto the asphalt, banging the dog's head against the floor and instantly the prison erupts

— **Fuller!!!**

Yelling as loud Fuller now picks up the dog by its back legs. Giving himself room Fuller moves left and hoists the dog and swings the dog by the back legs: swinging the dog so that the dog's head smashes against a wall. The dog's head bursts open. Blood and bone and other stuff splatter Fuller's tee shirt and jeans, his face and his hands. For half a second the whole prison is silent. Then a door flies open and three wardens come racing out into the yard.

Pressed so hard against the bars it hurts his face Eddie can hear Fuller cursing the wardens as they run to him, as they jump him, as Fuller drops the dog's body to the ground. Next to Eddie Dave shouts; Eddie shouts something, anything, too. Down in the yard one of the wardens grabs Fuller round the neck and forces him to kneel, in the blood and rain. At the same time another warden boots Fuller in the side, making Fuller slip, making Fuller's prison trainers scrape the wet asphalt. Meantime the third warden cracks Fuller over the head wlth a stave. Eddie gulps. Another crack. Eddie stares. Another hard punch. Through the gathering dark Eddie sees a wide red gash gleaming in Fuller's unshaven cheek: then Fuller is taken. Shouting orders to each other the wardens grab Fuller and drag him off, back over the asphalt, tugging him by the neck and the legs. Handcuffed and manacled by their grasp Fuller struggles but it is no use: almost as quick as they entered the wardens have him away. A door slams; the light goes; the yard is empty; and then and thereafter all any of the dumbstruck prisoners of F and B Wing can hear is an injured tabby cat, skulking, yowling, mewling.

22

sulky ladies

— How about pubic hair
— Pubic hair . . . mnnmnn
The editor of *FHM* puts a square jaw between thumb and crooked finger. His elbow on a knee the editor takes in the *Playboy* poster on the wall, listens to the office tape-player playing Seventies TV themes, and says
— But didn't *Maxim* do a piece on pubes in June?
Frank the deputy ed looks up at Mike the editor, what looks like a flash of hunger for Mike's job on his face; suppressing his appetite, Frank shrugs and says
— How 'bout a piece on thick girls, bimbos
— What, like, the daft remarks they make . . .
— The Things They Say
— I had a girlfriend who once saw me eating salad and she said: 'I didn't know you were a salad person.'
Alex comes in:
— Last night I was talking to my girlfriend about Clinton and Lewinsky, and I asked her what she thought about Al Gore and she said: 'I don't know, what is it?'
Mike laughs; Frank doesn't; Mike says

— Royston?

The features editor stops flicking over pages of his notebook; V-neck sweater striped with sunlight from the half-closed window blinds, he wags his close cropped head, says

— You mean do a piece on exactly how stupid most women are deep down exactly how contemptibly retarded?

Mike mmms

— Perhaps it is a little . . . misogynist

Royston:

— Remember that warning we got

— The thing we did on whether ugly birds were better in the sack?

— Why don't we do something on the Anniversary of the Hong Kong Handover – says Alex – You know, the end of Empire? On what it means for the state of English nationalism, of national self-esteem in God's first-born?

The editor looks at Alex, Alex says

— OK, how about Britain's favourite nipples

Now the editor perks up:

— Go on

Alex:

— We could find out which kind of nipples our readers like best

Frank:

— I really hate those hairy ones, with the elephant hair sticking out

— Yeah, no, me too

Royston:

— Mm. I like brown ones, big brown ones like backgammon pieces

Happy with the argument he has kicked off Alex sets back a little in his chair, feels the warm sunlight on his face, the sunlight intensified by the window glass. Lulled almost into sleep Alex tries not to think about sex, so he thinks about

Elizabeth, instead. *Her neck like a demoiselle crane. Standing in the Arrow. Her hair like yellow flag iri*

— Perhaps we could do something about those road protestors

Alex turns. Thinks. Marvels. *Uncanny.*

Stood up Alex goes to the *FHM* bin and coughs phlegm into the trash.

Mike calls over

— Alex what do you think

Still clearing his throat:

— Whassat?

— We really need a spin on these road protestors, we need to do something

Royston:

— Well I want to know what they do down those tunnels all the time. They've been down there for days and some of the girls are bo*dacious*

Back from the bin Alex panics. Then he says

— You really think they're still going to be around in three months time? I mean, we're talking about the January February issues here, aren't we?

Royston:

— I was watching the news last night and they reckoned they could be there for *years*. As soon as they knock down one camp they put up another, they build *another* set of tunnels, you've got to hand it to them

Mike nods, businesslike:

— That's what I mean, it would be good to get an *FHM* spin on this, this is a serious phenomenon. This is a big thing. So we could, we could . . .

Royston leans in:

— We could get an *FHM* sponsored streaker to run through the protestors' camp with *FHM* stencilled across her tits

Mike slaps his expensively trousered thigh

— Brilliant

From over the chewed plastic brim of his cup of crap coffee, Alex says, quietly

— I was brought up near there

— Pardon?

Again, a little louder:

— Near there's the town where I grew up, near Lyonshall village

Alex's editor slowly scrutinises him. Then says

— Great. So you know the area well. You do, right? You do remember it?

— Well – Alex says, wondering – Well . . . – He is wondering: well, *do* I? Do I remember it? Do I remember anything? Do I remember cedarn alleys and hazelwoods? The reddled whitewash walls of Moortop Farm?

Revolving in his chair Mike says

— Do you wanna do something about

about a young man in a white shirt stained red with ash bark juice, his arms full of wood pigeon eggs?

— Alex

— . . . ?

— Alex, are you OK?

— . . . Yeah . . . – Shaking his head – I'm fine. Can we open a window?

Mike looks at his freelancer. Says

— . . . Feel free

Rising once more from his chair Alex slips between the big cardboard boxes of last month's issue and the similar boxes of next month's featured leather jackets, and he leans up to the window and lets in the cool fresh restorative October air. He tries to breathe this so as to clear his head: to lose the thoughts, to remember less. Alex tries. He breathes. He tries.

As he wanders back to his chair, as he daydreamingly sits down, Alex half-listens to the chat. To the ideas meeting slaloming between absurdity and obscenity.

— So who is the hardest member of the Cabinet in that case?
— Well, I reckon that Chris Smith, he's a bit handy
— Hur
— What about Michael Meacher, nasty piece of work
— But could they handle the Tories? That's the point
— No way
— No chance. That Ann Widdecombe? *Spiteful* . . .
— Yeah, well warm . . . don't you think? Alex? Alex? Alex?

Alex nods, says yes. Says *yes I do*. Then he looks down at his lap, at his notebook. Reading his notebook Alex sees that through the ideas meeting he has made precisely three notes. *Elizabeth*. *Tushy-luckies*. And *Carcanets*. Scribbling over these notes Alex pretends to write something more constructive, but doesn't. So?

Across the grey carpet indented with wheel pressure points Alex looks up, and spies his editor analysing his Tag Heuer watch. The ideas meeting is nearly over, and Alex can't help angsting. Has he contributed anything substantial? Anything at all? Has he just spent half the day in a stupid daze, dreaming of fucking tushy-luckies and fiddleheads and Savonnerie carpets and not doing a stroke towards his future?

— How about something on orgasms

The editor turns

— What?

Royston and Frank openly stare at Alex: pleased that their chief freelancer has so apparently screwed up: offered such a duff, overdone, tired, unspun idea.

— What about them – Frank repeats – What about orgasms?

Obliged to busk it, now, Alex says:

— Well I reckon maybe we could do a piece on whether all orgasms are fake, all female orgasms are fake
— Sorry?
— Well I mean how do we know any of them are real? They

could have been invented by feminists to oppress us, have you ever thought of that?

The theme tune to *Nationwide* chimes with the whirr of the photocopier. A hint of a smile passes over the editor's face. Alex seizes this and continues:

— Haven't *you* ever wondered? Haven't you ever in your heart of hearts wondered whether your girlfriend has faked every one? Cause if they have faked all of them perhaps we should just quit worrying about them and get back to proper decent rough two-minute shags

Royston snorts. Frank stares. The theme tune to *Magpie* echoes around the office. Mike takes up his expensive Biro and slips it in his breast pocket and says, with a chuckle

— Glad I'm not your girlfriend

And that's it. Crisis over. Alex's daft idea was neither derided nor accepted and he is still the chief freelancer for *FHM*. Relieved, Alex stretches and yawns. Animated by the prospect of lunch, Mike commands:

— OK workers, that's it

— Thought I'd drop by

Alex climbs into Tony's car; straps himself in as they drop down the sideroad into the traffic of Oxford Street, thereto illegally mingle with the taxis and buses.

— Thanks for ringing

Says Alex, Tony shrugs

— I was in the area, thought you might like a lift home. Good meeting?

A grimace. Tony says:

— That bad?

— Y'know sometimes I really hate my job

Pained, Tony says

— You should try mine

— At least you get plenty of time off
— So do you
— Too much . . . maybe
— Hnn . . .

Eyes on the bus in front Tony blindly reaches for a tape amongst the mints and maps and invoices and toys that fill the gearstick well of his car. Shoving Vaughan Williams in the tape player as he accelerates them down New Oxford Street towards Holborn and the City, Tony says

— I hate having all this time to myself. I start thinking
— About what

Tony laughs, dryly

— Oh, stuff
— Stuff?
— Yes. Death mainly, of course
— Course – Alex chuckles – Time of life mate

Winding the wheel right:

— You think
— Yeah. You're nearly thirty. That's when the bill arrives. Physically. Spiritually. Morally
— Sorry?
— Late twenties, early thirties. That's when you get the bill for all the fun you've had. S'like you've been drinking and eating and having a laugh and you didn't even know you had to pay for it and then suddenly someone comes up and says, 'The bill, Sir.'

Tony thinks about this, laughs

— *Die Rechnung*, you mean

Curtly nodding Alex turns and looks at black girls in combat trousers gossiping outside a clothes shop. A Japanese girl with an Arse Denim Jacket. Alex murmurs

— Didn't ever think I'd get old . . . Didn't think I'd ever get old*er* . . .

Unreplying to this, Tony drives them on: through the littery wilderness of condemned Paternoster, round the roundabout of

St Paul's Cathedral, stalling at the police anti-terrorist roadblock. Where Alex suddenly says
— He's a big bastard
— What?
— A big black bastard
— Sorry? Where?

Alex says, explainingly
— Death. He's a big black bastard who's been following you home for a while now, right?

Tony rolls his eyes; Alex restates
— Death's, like . . . a big black mugger who's been shadowing you all the way home from the Tube and you know he's going to get you before you get to your door

In the second-hand Harris tweed jacket and yellow waistcoat he is wearing, Tony mmms, nods, says
— You know. It's not just death I've been thinking about . . .
— No?
— No
— So?
— Lyonshall

Staring out the car window at the City, at the green and orange fascia of a 7-Eleven, at the gold and black fascia of an upmarket tobacconist's, Alex sighs
— Me too

— Just here? – Says Tony.
— Just here – Says Alex, alighting on the corner of Hoxton Square, click-shutting Tony's car door.
— Don't fancy a pint then?
— W . . .

Before Alex can be persuaded he sees Katy standing on the corner of the square, near his house. Tony spots Katy, too. Cognisant of what this means Tony says, with a sigh

— I'll leave you to it
— Yeah, gimme a ring or . . .
— 'Bye

Tony's car swings back, three-points, and speeds out the square; meantime Alex heads towards his girlfriend who is standing with a hand on her hip, *contraposto*. Alex is pleased to see Katy is dressed in a cinched black jacket that emphasises the slenderness of her waist.

— What the fuck are you doing here?
— I quit college

Alex opens his mouth:

— You quit school? But you can't
— Shut the fuck
— But sw
— Shut up Alex you're NOT my PARENTS

Alex puts a hand to her cheek; she bats it away

— I just decided I didn't want to go anymore

Alex, baffled

— You don't want to go anymore?
— Yes are you deaf as well as OLD no I don't want to go anyMORE

Alex shakes his head

— But you've gotta go, I mean
— WHY?
— Er
— Well – She makes her are-you-a-moron? face – I'm WAITING . . .
—

She stares at his silence, then says

— I want to do something serious with my life . . .
— Serious?

Her face certainly seems quite serious. Stood here looking at his girlfriend's face Alex finds he wants to bite that serious little face, see those lips peel back in pleasurable pain, *her hair everywhere*.

Katy is saying
— Of course if you can *tell* me what's the fucking POINT in doing business studies
— Well there must be . . .
— Must be what? – She says, then says – Why don't you just SHAG me. You know you will as soon as you get me inside
— Shag you?
— YES, SHAG ME – She shouts at him, laughing – I WANT YOU TO SHAG ME

A man coming out from the minicab office across the square glances over; Katy laughs, says even louder
— COME ON, I WANT IT OLD MAN, YOUR BIG FAT COCK UP MY

His hand over her mouth, as if he is chloroforming her.
— OK, titch

23

eye of the child jesus

Grey wiry prison blanket thrown from his bunk, Eddie stands up and screws his eyes against the morning sun. *Another day.* He thinks. *Another day. God help me another day . . .*

Girded, Eddie looks into the slant October sunlight streaming gaily through the bars, as he buttons the fly-studs of his jeans. *Mustn't think about it. Mustn't think about it. Just another day. Another hour. Another second. Just get through another second . . .*

Plastic plate; plastic knife; plastic fork; these three in hand Eddie steps through the already open cell door into the rush-hour traffic of Brixton Prison at 9 a.m.: arsonists carrying bowls of cornflakes and madmen throwing crusts of bread over the rails and pickpockets shouting unwitty jokes at wart-faced ramraiders and with a nod to the gay murderer who cut up his boyfriend while he was still alive and burned him in his back garden

— Morning!

And a nod to the scarcely sane Filipino serial killer standing at the door of his cell

— Hello!

Ed joins the mass of prisoners descending to Landing One for breakfast, winding down the strangely hi-tech metal grille'd steps: round and down, down and round. Plastic utensils in hand, Eddie gazes along the nave of the Wing at the big window and the blue sky beyond: thinking of . . . of anything else . . . *of milk and brandy drops. Saucers of white Lyonshall raspberries. His sister and her friends in jeans and bare feet running down the lawns of the beech allee to the lake.*

— Get a fucking move on

— Tired of living?

Pressed from behind Eddie moves down the final steps to the bottom landing; following the prisoner in front he crosses the red tiled floor to the metal trolleys behind which three black guys are taking plastic plates, and loading them with a greasy floppage of bony bacon, rusky sausages, gruesomely sweet baked beans; at the end of the queue Eddie adds three slices of thin white bread and margarine to his plate and walks across the floor to the opposite staircase; before he can get there he stares down at his frankly rank meal, at the weight of plastic and grease in his hand, at the symbol of his degradation, and he shudders, and he stops and he halts at the foot of Staircase A and he looks at the grease and the crud and the junk and he sees tables. *Tables set for breakfast. Tables bright with tazzas and toast tracks. White-clothed tables set with poached eggs, ptarmigan, and pots of Indian and China tea, and rolls and tongues and chops in aspic surrounded by concentric rings of minted peas*

— Oxford you alright?

— Wanker

— Brrp brrp

And there would be rows and rows of little spirit lamps, and dishes of Bradenham ham and devilled kidneys, and alongside them plates of little fishy messes in shells and saucers of cold blackbacked gulls' eggs with cayenne pepper and celery and warm brown farmhouse bread and and and.

* * *

— Chapel

Still polishing the tomato sauce from his plastic plate with a crust of crap bread, Eddie looks up. A warden is at his door, looking at him, repeating

— Chapel

A sigh. Eddie puts down his plate. Above him Dave leans from his bunk and drops his own plate on the table. Mouths wiped on blankets the two of them go to the door where they meet Solo the black escaper and Alaric, Solo's cell mate. Together the four of them jostle each other down the landing. Turning a left they push and rag each other as they follow each other along the metal walkway, down the metal stairs, through the metal doors, down the metal corridor and through more metal doors. Into an oasis of Scandinavian wood and warm cream paint. The chapel.

In the Brixton Prison chapel about fifty other cons are already sitting in cheap plywood seats, seats like Eddie remembers from school assembly. These chairs are ranked in files facing the chapel windows: under which stands a cheap plywood pulpit, next to a dilapidated piano. Three wardens are leant against the rear wall of the chapel, yawning openly; meantime a vicar and an assistant vicar are handing out hymn books.

As the congregation begins its drug-dealing, the officiating cleric for the morning's service steps into the room and proceeds up a side aisle to the front. It is a woman of late-middle age; grey-haired; bespectacled; fat. Taking a small bag of grass from the Sikh terrorist on landing B who is sitting directly in front of him, and handing back a tiny roll of banknotes, Dave simultaneously whistles at the old woman

— Getcha saggy old horrible tits out, Luv

Eddie hisses

— You *couldn't*

— Fucking well could, that's the first bird I've seen in six months

— But she's sixty if she's a *day*

— Then she'll be a squirter

Alaric interrupts:
— She could take her teeth out. Ja I'll have a quarter . . .
All around Eddie, as the vicar's assistant starts plonking away on the piano, the drug-dealing goes on
— S'enough for a boot
— Mummy's got the cash
— Bones?
The matronly female vicar has assumed the pulpit; with a mixture of firmness and nervousness she addresses the assembled prisoners:
— Good morning, gentlemen. My name's Mrs Wait. Today we are here to celebrate the harvest
From the seat on Dave's left Solo hoots with sudden laughter; Dave nudges him roughly
— Shut it, Solo
But Solo is convulsed with laughter. Loud laughter. Doing her best to ignore the noise the female vicar goes on:
— You may or may not be aware that at this time of year we celebrate the harvest with a special service – She attempts a smile – A service to give thanks for God's plenty. Now, as you can see, Mr Binnersley has brought in a few items to represent the harvest . . .
Solo is still laughing; Eddie follows Solo's laughing gaze and sees that on a table on the right of the altar someone has stacked a pile of soup tins, biscuit packets and jellymix cartons: a harvest festival offering.
Dave
— What're they going to make us sing, we *didn't* plough the fields and we *didn't* scatter?
— Can we all sing Hymn Three One Four. *We Plough the Fields and Scatter*
The piano, played by the assistant vicar, kicks off into an echoey intro that drowns their laughter. Dutiful, trained, Eddie rises and opens the hymn book and starts warbling.

The song drifts from verse to verse; the wardens yawn; the assistant vicar plinks away; then the vicar stands up and lectures. Vague, vaguely unhappy, Eddie watches the prisoners around him not-so-furtively trafficking, he watches the Harvest Festival of Brixton Prison: little wraps and bags of hashish, grass, heroin, acid, and cocaine being swapped, re-swapped, sibilantly haggled over. He watches the new sex offender from Landing 3, in his paper jump suit, failing to score some poppers. He observes the Filipino mass murderer scoring home-grown. He sees the guy who stabbed a bus driver on Oxford Street with a pocketful of Lopez. He thinks of haymakers in white shirts and waistcoats walking along the hedgerows, searching for brown bumblebee honey . . .

— Edward Lyonshall?

A tap on his shoulder. Eddie opens his eyes and turns his face upwards. It is the female vicar, Mrs Wait. Mrs Wait looks down at Eddie's cheekboned, aristocratic, pale, intelligent face and ventures again

— V42685 Lyonshall?

Eddie blinks

— Er . . . yah?

— You requested a meeting with the chaplain, after the service

Beside him Dave and the others, waiting to file out, hiss encouragement

— *Lucky boy*

— Oxford, you old dog

— Try Swarfegar!

— Would you like to have a chat now?

Belatedly remembering that, yes, he did request such a meeting, inasmuch as he has learned to request anything that allows him time out of his cell, Eddie shrugs, nods, chides his departing friends, and follows the fat-bottomed, grey-skirted figure of Mrs Wait, as she leads him out of a door he's never used, into a side chapel furnished with two chairs, and a table.

On the table is a plate of biscuits, a tartany Thermos of tea, a Bible.

The two of them sit down. Awkward, out of synch with the social niceties, Eddie informs Mrs Wait he takes his tea white and unsugared. Mrs Wait nods, and unscrews the Thermos, and pours. Taking his cup Eddie sips at his grey tea. Her own cup in hand Mrs Wait sips, smiles, and tells Eddie all about herself: and how she sees herself. Hardly pausing for response she tells Eddie what it's like to be a female vicar in a predominantly male environment. About how she tries to 'empathise without condoning'. About those of her criminal congregation who have discovered God. After this strange presentation Mrs Wait fixes her bespectacled gaze on Eddie and says

— So what was it you particularly wanted to discuss with me?

Searching for something, anything, to justify his request for a meeting, Eddie kicks off by mendaciously confessing he has been having a crisis of faith: as a result of all the suffering he has witnessed in prison, not least his own. In reply, Mrs Wait gives him the usual guff about mysterious ways and unknowable purpose; Eddie crosses his legs and uncrosses them; hardly listening. Offering a biscuit Mrs Wait suggests Eddie read the Book of Job. Eddie picks up the Bible and does not open it; finally he admits that he does not like the version. Mrs Wait tells him, in reply, that he should not sneer at the New Revised Version of the Bible as its very accessibility is responsible for the coming-to-faith of several prisoners she knows; in turn Eddie says that as far as he is concerned this debased modern version of the English Bible symbolises what is wrong with the Church of England. The Church of England, Eddie explains, intones, is like the countryside of England, or the governance of England: what was created and developed by men of talent and of genius has been destroyed in a generation by petty-minded mediocrities, by those who could not or would not understand the value of their patrimony.

Mrs Wait looks puzzled, offended, intrigued. Teacup set on the table she leans forward and says that Eddie's statement would seem to indicate that he, Eddie, *has* some faith, that he at least *cares*. Swallowing tea Eddie shakes his head and says that his words merely mean he cares why religion exists, that he reveres its role, its historical role.

— Anyway – Eddie adds – Religion is merely the coinage. God is the gold

Mrs Wait replies that that must indicate he sees value in God.

Eddie replies that gold has no intrinsic value, merely the value men ascribe to it.

Taking her third Rich Tea biscuit Mrs Wait asks how can one doubt the value of a religion that can produce such marvels as Dante, Martin Luther, Michelangelo – not forgetting the thousand years of monks who kept alive the flame of learning

Interrupting, Eddie replies that monks are the fowl of the church: Périgord geese force-fed the corn meal of theology and liturgy to produce the pâté de foie gras of their prayer

The chink of cup and saucer. The door opens. A warden.

— Lyonshall?

Biscuit successfully balanced on the saucer of his teacup, Eddie looks up

— Yes?

— Your lawyer is here

Eddie's heart starts thumping

— My lawyer?

The warden says again, in flat Northern vowels

— That's what I said, get a move on

— My *lawyer* . . . ?

— Yes your sodding lawyer hurry up sorry Mrs Wait but we got a hundred cells to lock up

— My LAWYER!!

Leaping to his feet, Eddie punches air. Then he stops, stoops across the small table, kisses Mrs Wait on the cheek. Mrs Wait jumps, the warden frowns, Eddie just laughs and kisses Mrs Wait again

— Thank you, thank you

Mrs Wait chuckles

— Now now, don't get your hopes up

Ignoring this advice, Eddie claps his hands together and marches to the door: listening to his own heartbeat joyously and anxiously pounding *bail? bail? bail? bail?* At the doorway Eddie stops, pauses, and thinks better: on a heel he turns to say to the prison chaplain, to this middle-aged woman with her doing-my-best clothes and hard-to-really-hate smile and not-such-a-bad-old-stick hair

— Mrs Wait, this has been a most informative and instructive discussion and I hope I *never* have to see you *again*

The warden flinches

— *All right*

But Mrs Wait just says, good-naturedly

— Goodbye, Eddie, and good luck

Down the corridor the two of them walk: Eddie almost leaping ahead of the warden. Evidently irritated, the warden tells Eddie to stay back, back behind the jangle of silver keys hanging from his hip. An impatient Eddie obeys: shifting from foot to foot as they wait at yet another door. Eddie waits. Eyeholes flick. Hinges creak. Eddie counts the seconds. Finally they are through the door and into a room: where Eddie's lawyer Greenberg is sitting on a metal-and-plastic chair in a Sundayish outfit of blue woollen pullover and button-down. The lawyer is smiling.

Eddie sits down. He and the brief are alone. Eddie blurts

— Well??

— Mr Lyon

— Did I?

— Calm down

— But *did* I?

Greenberg opens a file, coughs, consults, looks up
— Yes, I got you bail
– Yes!
The door swings open: the warden pokes his bullet head in:
— Everything OK?
The lawyer nods
— Fine, everything's fine
The warden ajars the door. Across the table Greenberg smiles again, and then elaborates
— There are certain conditions
Controlling his glee; imagining his first beer; feeling all the bottled-up fear, horror, sadness, anguish, terror and weirdness of the last three months beginning to spill out and over; sensing all the psychic tension of all those weeks of determination and bravery and self-control beginning to unwind, to lash and unspool, Eddie tries not to emote. He sits in his seat and shivers. He looks up at his laywer; tries not to kiss him as he kissed Mrs Wait. Then Eddie takes a grip:
— What conditions
Betraying just a hint of lawyerly pride Greenberg pulls a sheet from his file:
— I managed to get you bail on the grounds that you would receive professional treatment for your drug addiction
— Absolutely, of course, no problem, *Jesus*
— That means you can either take methadone under supervision, and live in a rehabilitation centre
— Or?
— Or you can take regular counselling, and live in . . . what are they called . . . – Greenberg frowns – A . . . halfway house for reforming addicts, until your case comes to court
Eddie nods, dittos:
— Or?

— Or . . . – Glancing down – Or . . . you can take something called . . . Naltrexone . . . an antidote . . . no an antagonist . . . to heroin . . . to ensure that you are clean. But then you have to undergo a hair test at a police station for every week or so after that . . . to ensure that you have not relapsed

Prison noise. Distant shouts of bang up, distant barking, distant clatters and alarums. Eddie gazes into his lawyer's eyes:

— And if I agree to any of those I'm free to walk out of here?

Slight smile:

— Sign here and I'll process the paperwork and you'll be out . . .

— When?

— In a couple of days, three at the most

Sitting back: Eddie thinks. Eddie thinks on the things he has seen, has witnessed. He thinks about the fights, the nights, the bodysearches. He remembers the screams of the fraggles, the teeth of the guard dogs, the smell of Dave using the toilet a foot from his face, he remembers the gait of the lifers, the eyes of the rapists, the pitiful defiance of the sad-eyed black twoccers

— They don't let us carry pens

24

badman whotmeal

— So what you gonna do, then, Oxford?
— Sorry?
— When you first get out, what's it gonna be, birds or booze?
— Don't know, haven't really thought about it

Quietly Eddie lays a card on the makeshift card-table. A seven of hearts. Eddie feels weird this morning. In a few hours he is to be released and he feels elated, cheerful, optimistic. But he also feels anxious, ashamed, somehow guilty that his imminent release is making everybody else tense and angry, reminding everybody else of their ongoing incarceration. Filling the silence, the awkward silence, Dave says to Solo

— Hear bout Tommo?
— Who's Tommo?
— Scouser down the landing
— Oh yeah. What?
— Got lifed off, yesterday

Spinning a card on the table, Alaric grimaces and says

— Tss. How much?
— A thirty

Now Solo shakes his head, rubs his hands on his yellow-and-green checked overalls, says
— 'Claaat, what'd 'e do?
— Chucked a bottle of petrol over a jeweller in Hatton Garden
— Yeah, so?
— E was bending over a Bunsen burner at the time
— Nice
Another silence. To distract himself, his friends, Eddie lays a card. Solo lays a card. Alaric lays a card.
— Imagine . . . – Dave is saying – Thirty years. No wonder he looked a bit pissed off at breakfast. Ain't gonna suck a decent pair of tits ever again
— Poor bastard – Says Eddie
Dave says back
— Well he shouldn't have fucking torched a sheenie, should he? Eh? What did he expect? A *medal*?
More silence. Alaric lays a card. Solo lays a card. Fanning out his hand, Eddie lays a card, then takes a tug on the joint just rolled by Dave. As he does so Alaric hisses:
— Kanga!
A warden is standing at the door, peering through into the dope-fugged cell. The warden squints, frowns, looks at the fat spliff in Eddie's hand . . . and decides not to intervene. Without explanation, the warden merely says:
— Get your stuff together Lyonshall – And disappears down the landing.
Taking the wet-ended joint from Eddie's hand Dave sucks and exhales smoke and says to the open cell door
— Least you won't have to see that cunt again
Turned to his bunk, Eddie starts on wrapping his stuff.

— Making love to a new woman is like learning to play a musical instrument

Tony nods with a hint of disinterest; Alex explains, further
— You spend about a year trying to learn to do it until you finally give up and chuck the fucking thing away
— I see
— But after you've chucked it away you still keep taking the thing out of the cupboard, just for the occasional strum
— I think – Tony clucks – I get the point – Expelling air he lifts up his hands behind and jumps youthfully back onto the hip high rustybrick wall that faces the little doorway of Brixton prison, from which they are expecting Eddie to emerge. From his new vantage point Tony says
— How is Katy anyway?
— Pukka
Tony wonders
— So . . . are we ever going to meet her? Properly?
— Why would you want to meet her *properly*?
A forelock of red hair nostalgically dangling over his sad eyes, Tony says
— Because you've been going out with her for two years. It's usual
Silence. Alex is saying:
— So we're unusual
— You do love her, though, don't you?
Alex, mildly impatient:
— I . . . don't know, Tone. Do I? It feels like love, it tastes like love, it smells like love . . . it certainly fucking hurts like love – He sighs – I don't think it's love
— So what is it then?
— A genital reflex
— But isn't that what love is?
Leant backwards against the brick wall, Alex
— Maybe. It's different . . .
— Different to what?
— To what I felt for Elizabeth

— Steady
— *Well* . . .
A little moody himself, now, Alex heaves himself up so he too is sitting on the wall. Now the two of them are sitting on the wall kicking their heels against the bricks and falling-out mortar like a couple of schoolboys waiting for the bus. They both squint at the un-opening little doorway set in the big blue doorway of the unimaginatively Gothic greystone portal of Brixton jail.
— Do you remember her bathroom?
Tony ignores this. Tony scans his paper, his *Independent*. Alex looks back at the jail door and then his eyes rise to the cloud-patched blue October sky.
— Still – He says – Nice morning to get out of prison
And then he blurts
— Look she's too young and it hasn't got a future so what's the point?
Looking up from his paper Tony makes a middle-aged noise of mild sardonic disbelief and Alex shakes his head and says
— What? What?
— Methinks you doth go on a bit too much
— Come again?
— For someone allegedly not in love with the girl you do talk about her an awful lot
Visibly, Alex bridles:
— How's the wife?
— Mn
— And when's that dinner party?
Tony does a pained shrug.
Alex
— If you want to meet Katy *properly* you could just invite her and me to your house. You know. To meet your wife. Elizabeth
Tony is silent; Alex isn't:

— For someone allegedly still in love with the woman you don't talk about her very fucking much

Paper flat on his lap; a slight shiver in the October morning chill; his tweed jacket failing to exclude the cold, unlike Alex's fashionable anorak, Tony gazes at the door of Brixton prison and says

— It's still very difficult

— Whassat?

— With Elizabeth. You know

Alex:

— You still can't get it up?

— I can always rely on you to approach these problems with a certain delicacy and sensitivity

— Or do you reckon she's still getting it from some wop

Sad laughter

— Thanks . . .

— Well, which izzit?

Not really reading the headline to his *Independent*:

— The impotence, thing . . . – Big sigh – I might be getting these things to help

— What to help? Like Viagra? Cool. Can I have some?

— No – Tony pretends to finish a clue in the crossword; Alex presses; Tony exhales and faces into the slightly younger face of his friend, and says

— I decided pills were a bit of a . . . cheat. So they're thinking of giving me . . . Injections

A low whistle

— Wow, man. Like, in your dick type of injections?

Pained nod.

— Fuck – Alex chuckles again – Fuck

Another pained gesture:

— So what do you think I should do?

— Instead of injecting your glans penis you mean?

Wincing, nodding, listening to Alex say

— Well I dunno. How about . . . – Alex moves his face to within three inches of Tony's and says – How about trusting her? How about trusting your wife? That's the psychological hurdle, the psychological dynamic isn't it? You don't think you're worthy of her so you think she must be shagging some other bloke which reinforces your lack of self-esteem so you end up losing it

Tony turns to the door; Alex turns and does the same.

Tony closes his eyes and says

— Do *you* remember her bathroom?

— You mean, Elizabeth's, Lyonshall House . . . ?

— Of course

Closing his eyes too Alex laughs and says

— The gloves scented with frangipane

— The gilded washstand

— The lion-footed bathtub

Tony's voice going dreamy

— The copper kettle on a copper tray, on the rosewood dressing table

— Next to the King James silver hairbrushes

— God and her underclothes, yes!

Alex's laughter more light-hearted than Tony's

— You mean

Traffic noise; Tony's eyes still closed:

— Weren't they hand woven by blind girls in some French school?

— And kept in blue-and-white linen bags . . .

— *The Lyonshall racing colours* . . . of **course**

— Alright Oxford?

Dave is shaking his departing cellie's hands. Eddie goes to embrace him in turn; Dave shies and says

— You old nonce

But then they sort-of-embrace, anyway. For a very brief

moment they hug and slap. As they do Eddie gets a level look into Dave's eyes and discerns an unexpected expression: a mixture of envy, and something else. As if sensing his feelings have been clocked Dave backs off and away. At the same time the warden outside the half-open grey metal door twirls a key-ring impatiently around a finger. Meantime Eddie tries to think of something true, sincere and valedictory to say; failing, he just says

— See you around, then

— Sure. Like in some pub, down Camberwell?

— You never know

Dave tuts, grins

— North Londoner like you, don't think so

Turning to Solo Eddie nearly says, but Solo says

— You know why your mum's asshole is so big?

— No . . .

— Cause she likes taking black dick right up it every night

Solo grins. Eddie slaps Solo on the shoulder; Solo slaps Eddie on the shoulder

— Watch out for the H

Alaric leans in and says

— But I know where you can get some very good stuff

Solo chortles; Eddie turns to the warden; they are gone. Eddie is out of his cell for the last time, with the warden. The two of them walk down the landing, down the stairs, down the hall, down the corridor, down a corridor, down two more corridors: into a white painted room, with a table and a book and a bag. The book contains Eddie's name. The bag contains Eddie's possessions, whereof he was dispossessed all those weeks ago. Behind the table the warden stands and sighs and counts out, methodically, laboriously, sarcastically:

— One Biro, blue

Eddie takes the offered pencil, ticks.

— One book of matches, two matches left

Eddie ticks.

— Assorted loose change. Four pounds thirty seven pence . . .

Eddie leans down and ticks again. In front of him the warden pauses and looks at Eddie and takes out the final item from its clear plastic baglet:

— And one sheet of aluminium foil. Folded.

Another meaningful look.

Eddie looks at the foil, puts the money and matches in his pocket and stares at the foil again. Eddie stops. Listens to himself. Listens. Eddie says, visibly stiffening

— You can keep that

— How much do you drink then?

— Don't know. Too much

Jumping down from the brick wall and spanking the dust off the back of his jeans Alex curses Eddie and coughs in the cold October air and curses Eddie again and looks at a black man walking down the end of Jebb Avenue towards Brixton High Street and Alex says

— I wonder if he'll cope with outside

Tony says, wearily:

— You what?

— I mean. He's probably been institutionalised

— He's only been in three months

Alex raises a hand

— You forget he was a nutter anyway

Tony, even more wearily

— I wouldn't quite go that far

— Drugs, man, why did he do so many drugs?

— Well – Tony makes an obvious face – One reason might just be not entirely unconnected with the fact that you gave him smack all those years ago . . . Or am I wrong?

Alex flaps the idea away, quickly
— No, man, it was his psyche. The love that dare not speak its surname
— You mean – Frowning, Tony gazes at his dark-haired, cheery friend – You mean . . .
— I mean
— Here he is!
— Yo!
The little Oxford-College-after-curfew door of the prison has swung open. Stooping into the bright open dirty Brixton air comes a pale, thin, gaunt, hollow-cheeked figure. Alex, immediately:
— Looking *good*
Eddie gives him a wry glance; Alex says
— I'm serious. You're actually looking better
Tony interrupts
— You presumably have managed to keep off the . . .
Eddie turns his wry look on his other best friend
— I intend to
— . . . good
— Did they bugger you? Did you like it, deep down? You did didn't you you *ginger*
Eddie ignores Alex; Tony steps in again:
— We're under instructions from your lawyer
Taller than both of them, breathing the clean sooty air of freedom with relish, Eddie nods
— You're to take me to a clinic?
Tony touches his friend on the arm, concerned:
— Afraid so. There's some pills you've got to take to keep you on the straight and narrow
Lifting unconcerned shoulders in the refreshing outside air Eddie smiles and says
— I know
Alex guesses

— And after that you wanna get *monged*, right?

But Eddie is gone. Before Alex and Tony have had a chance to divine his mood Eddie has started walking and then jogging and then running and then sprinting. Within a minute he is halfway down Jebb Avenue.

Tony and Alex look at each other. Alex says

— So I win the bet then

— Sorry?

— Told you they shafted him

And then they both start running, too.

— Try this

Alex takes the little paperback proffered by his friend, recites the title

— *Soul on Ice?* Yeah?

Eddie, explaining:

— Black chap gave it me in Brixton

— That right – Alex looks at the author's name – Eldridge Cleaver . . . who's he then?

— Famous black radical

— Black Panther?

— Yah, he was in prison in the Sixties

Perched on the opposite, flipdown seat of the cab, Tony leans to tilt the cover and he asks Eddie what the book's about and Eddie says

— Well . . . Race, I suppose. He . . . used to rape white women on principle

— Delightful

— It was really quite famous at the time, there's a passage at the end you should . . . you really *should* read . . .

Fanning his face with the riffled pages, Alex shuts the covers and pockets the thing and says, as he pulls down the taxi window:

— So we're taking you to the Brady Centre in Bayswater, it's all been arranged, the lawyer, doctor, everything

The cab accelerates, cool air fills the cab, Eddie's face is a picture of amusement

— The Brady Centre?

— Yeah

— The Brady Centre in Bayswater?

Patiently:

— Yes. That's right. 'S a drug clinic

— Ha – Eddie laughs – Ha

Alex doesn't join in

— Hours of amusement, I'm sure . . . whatizzit?

— Ai, nothing, nothing . . .

Eddie goes quiet. Across the cab floor Tony twists his head and swears at the Marble Arch traffic, and says out of the side of his mouth without looking at his two friends

— We should be here soon, it's around here somewhere, I think

— It is – Says Eddie, and as the two of his friends gaze at him slightly puzzled, Eddie knuckle-taps the partitioning glass, the driver makes a grunt, the cab halts, and Eddie swings the door open and alights. Ed's thinner, healthier, smilier face fills the kerbside window as he says to his friends

— No. You go on and have a drink

— You don't want one before . . . ?

— No. Absolutely. I'll be fine

Alex squints at Eddie, suspiciously

— You're not going to nip round the corner and score then, or anything?

Pained, insulted, amused, the collar of his jacket turned up against the breeze, Eddie says

— What do you think I am?

— Er, a junkie . . .

But Eddie has already skipped away towards a nondescript

door in the stuccoed Bayswater terrace, whirled around by wind and perfect yellow fallen planetree leaves. From the cab Alex and Tony watch him press the buzzer on the right of the door; as the taxi pulls away Tony murmurs

— You know, he seems different

— Like?

— More . . . soft . . . Not so . . .

— Completely stoned?

Shifting from the flip seat to the back seat of the taxi Tony makes a don't-quite-know face

— No . . . more thoughtful . . .

And Alex makes a sarcastic face

— Eddie would never be that clichéd

— Sorry

— A liberal is a conservative who's been to prison? Gimme a break

— I didn't quite mean that

But before Tony can make his point felt Alex is staring out of the open taxi window, lost in appreciation of Katy, remembering how she masturbated him that morning, remembering how the come dripped down and thru her fingers like an ice cream melting in an infant's hand on a hot summer day.

Seated in the familiar waiting room of the Brady Centre Eddie notices the Brady's clientele are, this morning, a little less highborn than he recalls. One couple, in particular, seems particularly plebeian. Seated beneath a sign warning against DRUG TALK and a sign offering information about NEEDLE EXCHANGE they are discussing their personal intake of alcohol, unconcerned by Eddie's presence.

The guy (trainers, dirty flared cords, spots)

— So I reads this hand-out and it says like twenty-one units is OK

The girl (trainers, dirty flared cords, spots)
— Yeah
— And that's like OK
— Yeah
— I mean like one unit is like just half a pint right?
— Yeah
— So I reckon I'm doin about that, 'bout twenty units, cause I'm only doin 'bout nine or ten pints or a bottle of Thunderbird and a bottle of sherry in total at most y'know?
— Yeah
— So then I goes and says to the doctor what's the fucking problem, doc, I'm only doin 'bout twenty units so I must be all right, right?
— Yeah
— And he says, straight aht, it's twenty-one units A WEEK, not A DAY

Silence. Eddie's breathing. The girl scratches a crack-addict's spot on her face, one of about thirty weeping sores and pimples. Making a grave effort the girl keeps her eyes open and says
—..........................Yeah
— Mr Lyonshall?

Eddie's familiarly bow-tied quack is waiting in the nicely-carpeted corridor with a file, a mug of coffee, a smile. Rising obediently from his seat Eddie proceeds down the narrow corridor, past the prints of Pisa and Perugia, into a familiar room: huge desk, leather chaise, volumes of De Quincey, gold discs on the wall gifted by grateful ex-addict pop stars. From his attitude and expression Eddie perceives, with relief, that the doctor is not going to mention the previous time the two of them met. Nor the deception involved. Instead the bow tie bends, portentously, to the file and says
— I take it you are clean, Mr Lyonshall?
— Yes
— Definitely?

— Yes – Eddie nods his head – *Squeakers*

— Well then, we can proceed

With a shoot of his cuffs the doctor goes on to describe the effects and side effects of Naltrexone, the opiate inhibitor. As he has already been there, done this bit, Eddie immediately switches off. Looks outside the window at the familiar view of sash windows and expensive bedrooms and cast-iron lampposts. Above the wine merchants across Westbourne Street Eddie sees big baskets of autumn flowers dripping wet after a recent, watering by the Westminster gardeners. Pink flowers, yellow flowers. *And yes.* Eddie thinks. *Yellow flowers. Pink flowers. When the ridges were yellow with buttercups. And the furrows were pink with cuckooflower. When was that?*

— So if you take Naltrexone simultaneously with any opiate you will feel decided discomf

In the Spring. Yes. In the Spring. When the scent of wheatstraw was on the night air. When her hair was the yellow of the flag irises on the lake.

— Of course we can offer you something to combat any unpleasantness caused by the inhibition of your endorphins

Carcanets of primroses. Coot soup and scrambled lapwings' eggs. A few of the family diamonds in her hair

— And we shall conduct tests every four weeks if that's all right with

— During the cotillions Lancelot Rolleston and I

— . . . Sorry?

— Raced through paper hoops for the honour of dancing with Miss Grey . . .

A motor kicks over, outside. The bow tie twitches

— Mr Lyonshall?

Silence. Eddie comes to. Stalls. Says

— Nothing, Doctor Feavis. Something I read . . .

The doctor adjusts the bow tie, lapses into undoctorese

— Are you sure you're quite all right?

— No, yeah, I think I'm in a bit of a daze after . . . *getting out* . . .

— I understand

— Actually I've been having lots of rather disorientating . . . daydreams?

— Entirely natural

— It *is*?

— This is the first time you've been truly clean in years

— Yyyyes

— And you are clean aren't you?

Eddie nods his head again

— Apart from the odd . . . spliff, *yes*

— Well there we are then

Satisfied, the doctor nods and looks at the file and makes an anyway-we're-nearly-finished cough; says

— The one thing I will repeat is that you should really be very very wary of taking any heroin while you're on Naltrexone

— *Yah?*

— That's when disasters occur. We've known – Doctor Feavis half grimaces, half shrugs – You see . . . Naltrexone prevents the heroin having any effect but people keep on taking more and more heroin in the hope that it will get them high despite . . .

— So they . . . OD?

Silence.

— They die

— . . . *Right*

With a brisk and efficient air, as if to elide the impact of what he has just said, the doctor taps some information into his computer terminal; almost as briskly and efficiently his computer printer spools out Eddie's prescriptions. While this happens the doctor picks up a pen and says

— But that shouldn't be any problem with us, should it?

And he flourishingly signs the prescriptions.

Eddie shakes his head

— No, no problem

The doctor gazes over his desk. Mentions

— Not that we can really do anything anyhow. It's really up to you from here on

— I know

— After all, you're a big boy now, Mr Lyonshall

— I know

Car-noise. Bus-noise. Suddenly, unapropos, Eddie says

— Doctor Feavis, have you ever wanted to do anything extraordinary with your life, anything creative, or artistic, in some manner?

The doctor flinches, seemingly insulted by the notion that dealing out downers to uppercrust junkies is anything but Michelangelesque in its import.

— Well I do do carpentry in the evenings

— That's not quite . . . – Eddie scopes the gold discs on the wall, finds the words in the wallpaper – I really always wanted to be – He sighs – I don't know. A writer, or an artist . . .

Half-interested

— Since when?

— Well. Long time ago . . .

— Since you were a boy then?

Eddie nods:

— A little later than that. It was really a college thing, when I went to college I decided I wanted to be an artist and then *just* as I was . . . you know – He sighs again – Just as I was about to write something . . . I got into . . . the dealer from Porlock came by and . . . and ever since then . . . ever since *then*

— Yes?

— I mean I've got this English Lit. degree and I'm not *entirely* retarded and yet I've spent my entire life doing smack and it seems . . .

— Something of a waste?

— Yes – Eddie does a wan smile and takes the prescription with its familiar snake-round-a-poppy hallmark from the doctor's well-manicured hand – Something of a waste . . .

A glance at his old-fashioned wind-up watch. The doctor says

— Afraid I've got some other appointments. Nice meeting you . . . again

On his way out of the building Eddie nods at the junkie in the corridor, the addict in the stairwell, the crackhead in the waiting room, the dope fiend in the vestibule, the pair of mainliners in the reception, and the glue-sniffer at the bottom of the stairs. Outside on the pavement Eddie stops and breathes; sweet damp sour London air: late autumn air, getting colder. Spirals of black cloud are massing over the park; shoppers are running towards the cabs heading for Paddington Station. Eddie breathes: the air. The thoughts that come with it. It is autumn, he thinks: *it is autumn and now the harvest is over. The girls of Moortop Farm will have kissed the sheaves and laughed. The kern doll will have been carried down Drover's Lane to the gates of Lyonshall House and* fuck it fuck it fuck it fuck it fuck it

Hours later, Eddie stands at the window of his flat in Smithfield, surrounded by the dust betokening his weeks of absence; standing at the dusty window, he is surrounded by evidence of his unlived life: unwashed cups, unrinsed plates, unlaundered clothes, unread magazines, unfinished poems, and the numbers of unrung friends and ansaphone messages from unpaid creditors – along with a head full of things he should have said, and women he should have wed, and situations he should have fled.

Disconsolate, maudlin, Eddie stares out across the twi-lit purlieus of Smithfield, of Limeburner Lane and Giltspur Street and Bartholomew Lane, and he sees the unseasonally early soft October snow descending on the roundabout, on the copper-green cupolas of the meatmarket, on the thick-legged trainee nurses, on the black guys shivering in their shortsleeved blue acrylic shirts running into the safety of St Bart's entrance, the snow falling from the overturned tombola of the heavens, the soapflakes always falling falling falling.

He rings the doctor.

— Doctor Feavis

Sigh

— Yes, I'm about to leave, what is it?

— You know you told me to take some Naltrexone as soon as I got back?

— Yes

— And you know you told me to take two if I wanted to remain safe for more than one day

— Yes

— Well I took *four* because I was so scared of weakening, of scoring – Eddie squeezes the phone between chin and neck as he lights a cigarette and as he does this he feels the emptiness and bleakness – Doctor Feavis I just feel terrible, suicidal, what's happening to me? What's going *on*?

Another sigh, perhaps a little less impatient this time. Breathing deep the doctor outlines Eddie's predicament, explaining how all Eddie's natural endorphins are being suppressed, are being prevented from doing their normal job.

— So that – The doctor says – That alone accounts for any dysphoria. It's nothing serious, it'll pass in a few hours, it's not a permanent thing

The doctor is still talking but Eddie has stopped listening. Dysphoria? *Dysphoria?* The phone drops from Eddie's neck and he just stands there: the snow is sweeping everything away. The snow is whitening, blanching, bleaching, erasing. Eddie smokes, thinks, looks, thinks. *Sweet Eve, tonight I am full of evenings. Tonight a dusk of melancholy overcomes* . . . and even as Eddie thinks this the snow comes on, in greater flurries, erasing it all, wiping out all the bollocks, all the waffle all the garbage all the poetry he should have written. And now all Eddie can see in the cruel cold truthful light of early winter is him and his sister and Alex and Tony at a sunlit Glastonbury Festival ten years ago. The three of them are tripping. Eddie is tripping the most. Flat on his back and as young as his friends and numbskulled by mushrooms, Eddie is wittering on about hot cockles and Suck Cream and Lancelot Rolleston and coursing deer across the moors and as he trips out he overhears his slightly more sober friends talking about him and Elizabeth is looking at Alex as he skins up a reefer, as Alex expertly licks the remaining flap of Rizla paper, and Elizabeth is saying to Alex as Tony playfully kisses her slender white neck *God knows I worry about him if he ever got hold of some serious drugs, well, that's it, he'd die. That would be the death of him. His middle name isn't exactly self-control, is it?*

25

itchycoos

On Haverstock Hill Tony is amazed by the fact that everybody and everything he sees is the result of somebody fucking somebody else. As Tony stands and points his key ring at his company car and locks it with a press of his thumb, the car responds with a coquettish flash of her indicators, and Tony looks at the nurses from the Royal Free on the hunt for late-morning sandwiches and a couple of baggy-jeaned Asian boys loitering outside the pub and he marvels at the fact, again: that this, all of this, all these buildings, all the Volvos, all these shoppers and parking meters and Mercury phone booths and book shops, all these book shelves, all these books, all this Shakespeare and Rousseau and Dava Sobel, is the result of some guy pawing a rosy buttock, some girl choking on a cock, some bitch opening her legs and groaning, some hairy-arsed man sliding his cock in and out as the woman sucks cunt from his thick-knuckled fingers

— Hi Tony

Julia is looking her usual best; elegantly bohemian, cashmerely cardiganed. Her bonny smile. Her serious face.

— Julia – Tony makes a fluttery movement with a hand and curses himself; momentarily Tony wonders if he looks gay. *Great.* Politely smiling Tony places his leather briefcase on the thickly carpeted Waterstone's book shop floor. Says

— Are you well?

She smiles

— Fine

— That's good . . . – He thinks of something else to say – . . . it's a bit chilly outside

— I know

— Right

She looks at him. He looks at himself in the mirror behind the till and shudders at his baldness. Almost certainly too late to buy a toupee. What else to do? He looks at his watch, stagily.

She figures:

— We should go?

Relieved:

— Yes, we should

— Well I'm ready right now – She has stepped out from behind her book shop till. Slipping on a raincoat she flicks her hair over the beige raincoat collar: all the time smiling.

Her confidence, her seeming unflusteredness, unnerves Tony. He is so crap at this, at infidelity, at sex, yet she seems so relaxed. Concerned, Tony wonders if she's actually conned the subtext, the unstated purpose of this lunchtime assignation. Surely she knows they are probably going to have sex? Surely she knows that he is married and has children and they are going to have adulterous sex?

— You look a bit tired – She says, as they guide each other to the door and the street. He smiles with a mature, confirming weariness, and mentions the kids and potty training. One arm stiff, he holds the door open. Still chatting she ducks under and exits and they walk down the Hill and talk about the children. Dispensing with the small talk Tony admits; almost pointedly, he tells her how much he loves his children: how when he opens the door to his house and his children at the end of the day it is like stepping off a plane in the tropics, the way the warmth hits you, the love. She nods. More pointedly still Tony mentions how much losing his kids would kill him. If it came to it. If something happened (sidestepping an Arab lady and her yappy lapdog), if something happened between him and . . . Elizabeth. Face framed by the green plastic fascia of a bookmaker's behind, Julia looks at Tony, curiously, distantly. Tony notes that her coat has too many buckles and buttons.

Half a mile up from the Tube Tony spies the trendy bistro he has already mentally chosen for their tryst. Brighter than him Julia intuits

— See you read the restaurant columns then

— Well it sounded OK

And they continue their staccato converstion, so heavy with meaning, so gravid with unspoken doubts and purpose, as they dash across the drizzly street and duck into the doorway.

— Apparently they do these set

— Here let me ope

— Thank

Inside the bistro Tony tries to come over properly masterful. Recalling that Julia is modern enough a woman to be slightly old-fashioned about these things, he raises his voice a few decibels and commands a waiter to find a table. This happens. In turn they get chairs, napkins, menus. Now seated across the cloth from his lunchdate Tony relaxes, and smiles: notes the way Julia's breasts warm the cutlery as she leans forward to light a cigarette from the flame of a candle stuck in a Portugese wine bottle. She is puffing the cigarette amateurishly.

— Just started – She says – Not very good yet

— Really?

Puff of blue, her blue eyes behind

— Well I hate the health fascists, it's enough to make anyone do heroin

Checking down the menu Tony says with his head tilted tablewards:

— Heroin?

She looks at him

— Only a joke

— Right

— Didn't mean it. Irony's the ice I keep my dreams in

His eyes over the menu:

— Sorry?

— Drop some in your whisky, leave it there

— Er . . .

— It's a quote – She leans forward – *Kate Clanchy, poetry*

His face is obviously a bit blank because she asks

— You do *like* poetry? I thought it was one of things we . . . *shared*

Her last remark came with a visible palpable flutter, with a flash of her indicators: as if he has just found her keys, and pressed them. Flustered, now, bamboozled by the coquetry, Tony slugs hard on his second double gin and tonic and munches his third breadstick. Tony is trying not to think about his impotence, about his wife, about his children, about Alex, about the way this girl across this table reminds him of

Elizabeth, walking barefoot through the fernstrewn glades of M'Ladies Wood, Elizabeth, on a summer's day, when the windows of the long room were open and he could see her pelting eggshells filled with rosewater at her brother, Elizabeth, ten years ago, when the cornfields beyond the Arrow were the same sunlit yellow as her hair . . .

Half a mile away, half a metre across the table Julia is check listing the poetry she would keep on a desert island

— I really like Milton

Startled, Tony realises he has been talking to Julia all through this, through his reverie. Judging by her happy demeanour he has even been making sense, doing the right things, choosing wines, cracking jokes, making her laugh. With a glance downwards

Tony is also mildly astonished to see his plate half-covered with food. It is retro food, fashionably Seventies food: boeuf bourguignon. Which is only right, Tony thinks: given that the two of them are about to do this retro thing, this lava-lamp thing, this trendily amoral very Seventies thing.

Finished with her chicken liver risotto Julia goes so far as to light a cigarette between courses. Evaluating her curly blonde hair Tony drops his gaze to her breasts that are now hidden by her folded arms, as with one arm she takes and removes a cigarette from her thick red lipstuck lips. Her sticky red lips. Her soft red lips that might soon be a soprano's O around his stiff upstanding

upstanding?

Interrupting his own thoughts, Tony says two of his favourite modern poets are Simon Armitage and Glyn Maxwell. Nodding brightly Julia agrees on Armitage but demurs at the other. Enthusiastically stubbing out her cigarette she says she hates Glyn Maxwell, finds him too obscure; hates that deliberate opacity. Her eyes bright Julia says in a rush that life is too short to spend several months discovering whether a poem was actually on about anything at all; taking some conversational curves at speed, she also says one of the reasons she dislikes Maxwell is because he doesn't turn her on, and that in fact she's thinking of switching the subject of her PhD to the Erotic in Modern Verse. Pause. Tony knows what to say to this:

— Well you should try Craig Raine

— But isn't he all about comparing things, rivets on a ship to mangetout and all that?

— Yes well but – Emboldened by two gins and half a bottle of *vin de maison* – Tony continues – He also compares cunnilingus to nuzzling ambergris

Enlivened by the risqué nature of the quote, Julia smiles and nods and knocks back some of her wine, lustily, like a stevedore sinking a pint at the end of the day. Curious, Tony wonders whether she is actually a slut, after all: whether many are called, and many are chosen. To cover the tracks of these thoughts he quotes another relevantly erotic bit of Raine:

— Here we stand without our clothes, one enthusiastic watering can, one peculiar rose

And it is a success. Out loud now Julia laughs and says maybe she should try Raine again. So now they are getting along. Now they are talking as good friends, as about-to-be lovers: hardly aware of the waiter they order oranges in Cointreau and cappucinos and a brace of Armagnacs and they compare record collections, films, favourite childhood confectionery: separated only by the table they reminisce, even, recalling all those times when he would come into Waterstone's and flirt with her so successfully she'd end up buying far too many books from him:

— All those awful Aga sagas

— Sorry about that

— Don't be. They all went. What makes them sell so much?

Thoughtful, Tony dangles the Armagnac glass from the lazy claw of his hand and posits

— It's the covers, they always have pictures of flowers and rose-hung country cottages on them

— You think it's that simple?

A swallow of liquor

— Covers sell books, you know that

— But still

— Besides, English people are obsessed with flowers, I sometimes think they love them more than their children

Dammit. Tony remembers he shouldn't have said that. Repeating his early mistake. He shouldn't go on about children, his children, any children, too much. Swiftly Tony finesses the mistake by dissing the English country novel, sarcastically pseudo-quoting, going on about *candlelight on old silver* and *white doves cooing under a cottage window* . . . but even as he says this, even as he tries to be lofty and urbane and parodic and distanced his heart is aching, is rotten, is soft and long-gone like the *crumbly pink heartwood of the Milking Oak . . .*

And now he is lost, again. Wiped out. Drunk on the memory, the mass unconscious; and as Julia and Tony rise, as they go to the door to get her coat, and their exit, Tony is struck at the heart, sent elsewhere, sent blackberrying, sent mitching down the Drover's Road on a hot June afternoon, and yes, Tony thinks, yes yes: if there was one scene that would sum it all up, would sum up what it was to have been him, to have been young and in England and in love it is of the four of them, of he and Elizabeth and Alex and Eddie sat by the Arrow on a summer evening with a bottle of wine cooling in the water, the four of them laid out on the grass, as the English summer dusk stole over, as the owls hooted in the park: the four of them lying there drinking and talking until it was so dark Tony could hardly see his friends, so dark he could hardly see the riverbank distant, so dark he could not see whose lips it was he kissed, so dark the shadow of the carthorse carrying a hayload of cherries down the lane was barely distinguishable from the shadows of the high-banked hedgerows.

— Come on

Julia has spoken.

— Are you sure?

— It's just down here

— What about the shop?

— I'm on flexi

Acceding to her will, her sweet will, Tony permits her to lead him by the hand, to hold his hand, to take his heart in hand and accompany them both down a sideroad to her Belsize Park flat. Cars are everywhere: cars double-parked; cars on pavements; cars slowing for speedbumps: thru the traffic-clogged short cuts of Belsize Village she leads him. Drunk, Tony makes an unsuccessful joke about her *coming-in-handy*; drunk, she teases him back. As they approach the Victorian stucco house wherein she has her one-bedroom flat, she looks him in the eye from about five inches below him and says

— Can you believe it! We're going to commit adultery, in Hampstead!

Alarmed, he laughs; she giggles:

— That's very postmodern, isn't it?

And after this, Tony feels like giving her money. With this remark she has lifted the burden of guilt; with this remark she has made it easy for them both, made light of it all, made a soufflé, made it something frivolous, playful, French filmy: she has even made it easier for him to get it up, he hopes. Maybe, *maybe*.

Inside the flat she turns and with hot, Armagnacky lips she kisses him. He stiffens, moves, embarrassed. Ardent and drunk she reaches down and holds him, holds his hardness: it stays. And so they move. Into the bedroom. Drunk. Both toppling onto the bed, finding it awkward to take off their clothes. It is too light: Tony is embarrassed by his fat stomach and his hairy shoulders but she is too drunk to notice his embarrassment so this makes him less embarrassed. She is taking off her bra and offering her big soft heavy breasts to his mouth: like the gardener offering the best from the melonground, her big soft womanly breasts which he worships with kisses, with servile kisses.

So this is it. At last. Tony's head spins. *This is it. The real thing, this is the real: this girl, here, me, her shaven armpits, her open swollen mouth; her cunt. Cock. Cunt. Cock. Concentrate.* She is kissing him behind the back of his ear, and holding his head and kissing his forehead as he feasts on her breasts: *concentrate on her breasts,* he thinks, *and on her blonde hair.* Face between her breasts he finds this is working too well. He is nearly coming. Disaster.

So think of something else. Flowers. Think of flowers. Think of football. Think of the ridges yellow with buttercup, the furrow pink with cuckooflower . . .

Or no?

Steadied, stalled, Tony moves: moving up he closes his eyes

and tries harder not to be worried about coming or not being hard or anything. As he does this she holds him and frigs him a little too keenly, too ardent; for a moment he thinks he is going to lose it but then he sees her breasts again and he restiffens, even as he thinks: *God I'm crap at this*

— God I'm . . .

— Yes!

— Chri

— Put it inside me

His cock in her hand looks big and ready; as Tony looks down it looks like a man in a hat, the witchfinder general in his Puritan Hat . . .

Don't come!

But he is about to come. He isn't. He is . . . *He is about to come too soon!* His eyes squeezed shut not looking at Julia's nudity Tony just-in-time remembers the one thing guaranteed to make him not prematurely ejaculate. *Of course . . .*

— Jules – his voice a little strangled – Do you want me to wear a condom?

— What?!

— Condom . . .

— Doesn't matter!

— Sure . . . ?

— Yesss!

She is very aroused now. Loving it. Her body is wanting his attention. All his attention. Oh, she says, nearly says. Oh it doesn't matter. Fuck me. Fuck me. Take me hard and take me hard. Say to me: bite pillow, bitch. Take me harder than you've ever

— But

— Oh jeeee

The flowers, don't lose it, the flowers: her hot forehead, her blonde hair. The ridges yellow with buttercup; the furrows pink with cuckooflower. The negus was passed around all evening. Drops

of brandy in the milk. White Lyonshall raspberries plucked by slender fingers from a silver epergne. Flowers, flowers, flowers.

— I love your tits

— Oh God

— They're so amazing

He is ready now, he is too too ready: it has been too long; too long since he did this. He is very hard, harder than he has been in months but he is all-too-desperate not to come, all-too-anxious: and it doesn't exactly help that she is naked and wild and retreating up the bed with a face full of lust like an animal, filthy in her loveliness with his spit on her big nipples shining.

— Are you going to fuck me with your big willy?

He can't believe she has said this. He can't believe that he loves it so much: her I'm-actually-a-filthy-slut voice, those naughty words said in her pure English accent: it is too much, too much; biting his lip Tony holds his erection in his hand and tries to concentrate as he follows her up the bed where she has her legs splayed wide open waiting for him, her cunt lovely dumb, her legs open and waiting, waiting to

Flowers, flowers: huge arching sprays of green cymbidium, laburnum walks of golden rain, the girls from the village making hollyhock fairies, the heather under their beds, the maidenhair fern of her pubes, the may blossom smell of her sex, the chestnut bloom smell of his semen. Tony stares down. *The chestnut bloom smell of his semen. No. Please. Oh God.* Tony swears. Looks down. *Oh God. The chestnut bloom smell of his semen*

He has come all over her. All over her stomach. Her stomach looks like the floor of a Spanish church, spattered with wax. Spattered with his semen. The semen that smells of the yellow flowers of the sweet chestnut tree . . .

Grieved, shattered, Tony closes his eyes; shudders. He has

come; too soon: she was too beautiful and he was too crap and he has come too soon.

— It doesn't matter

— Don't

— But it doesn't

Her hand is on his shoulder, his shoulder is a knot of tension as he turns and sits up and sits naked on the side of the bed and feels like smoking a cigarette, even though he doesn't smoke. Her hand tries to comfort him again; he shakes it off. Tries not to snap, says

— It's never happened before

— I know I know

— Not for a long time

— I know

She says this in a special understanding voice; but it's Tony that *knows*. Swivelling, he looks in her unfucked eyes, at her unfucked body, at her why-didn't-you-fuck-me-hard-from-behind-you-useless-loser breasts, and he *knows*. Her whole body was begging for him, aching for him, wet for him, arched and parched and cock-thirsty for him: and he failed. Again. Tony knows this; with all the bitterness, all the wormwood, all the Japanese Knotweed in the garden of his heart he knows this. *Softboy. Bad in bed. Crap in bed. Can't do it. Tony Rafferty. Can't do it. Wife's shagging some other bloke. Wife's getting serviced by some other bloke, by that visiting basketball team, by all those big black blokes with their cocks as thick and black and hard as Telecom cabling*

— Oh Jesus, Julia

And to her consternation Tony puts his head in between his hands and cries, and doesn't stop, the tears running between his fingers as he cries and cries, as he sits on the side of a strange girl's bed on a drizzly November afternoon in west Belsize Park, and cries.

26

yarroway

A stripe of sunlight moves across the flat and finds Ed's eyes: but brightens eyes already light with thought.

Eddie is awake. Supine, but awake.

Through closed windows, Eddie can hear all the London traffic; morning traffic: splashing through winter slush . . .

Thrusting away his sweat-drenched duvet Eddie leans to the side of his bed and finds a glass of stale water from a couple of days ago.

He swallows, he drains the glass. Eddie flops back in bed and rubs the ache from his eyes and he stares at the ceiling and tries to forget

the pain.

Up and half out of the bed Eddie sits on the side with his arms angled either side and he gazes flatly ahead. Every part of his body, every part of his brain, is crying out for heroin, to take away the pain of being without heroin.

But he knows he must be strong; knows that he is getting better; knows that it is these pills, the Naltrexone, that are making him suicidal, making him weird, making him have bad dreams, making him *dysphoric*. Eddie also knows the selfsame pills are his best and maybe only hope: he wants to live; more than he wants to die on smack, Eddie wants to live without smack. That much he learnt in prison. So he has to carry on.

Valiant and determined Eddie unscrews the bottle of Naltrexone pills; pill nestled in his palm he walks to the window where he finds a bottle of Evian on the sill. He drinks the mineral water and the pill; tastes the pill. Shakes his head.

The horrible taste.

Eddie swallows, grimaces, swallows. Eyes dull, brain duller, he leans on the sill and gazes. But as Eddie gazes and tries to stay sane he finds that a gulp of something is rising from his stomach, surging up his gullet, coming out of his mouth and nose; as he stands here all the thoughts and hurts he suppressed for so long, that he opiated away, for so many years, all the griefs and regrets are gulping and yulping from his sobbing mouth as he doubles over and cries like a child, crying into a cold empty flat, crying about his poor

mother

his

p o o r dead mother

his

fucking mother

stone cold

dead

in her **grave**

Pill swallowed, eyes swabbed, nose Kleenexed, Eddie leans on his window sill and looks at the Smithfield traffic, the slush-dirted taxis parked ouside the car park. The sun has gone on; clouds have moved in; the first spots of wintry rain are chasing the blue-shirted ambulance workers under the hospital archway.

27

goodbye

— Think I know her
— What?
— I'm sure, I'm sure I know her

Her eyes rolling, Katy watches her boyfriend as he watches a girl's lamentably beautiful arse disappear down the cold pre-Christmas pavements of Hoxton, of Charlotte Road. Burdened by two big purple Liberty plastic bags full of Christmas shopping, looking cold despite her denim jacket, thick dark denim jeans, and long platform boots, Katy says

— You always say that
— Nnn
— ALEX

He doesn't hear. Freighted by his own Xmas purchases: a Hamleys bag full of toys and another bag with rolls of cheap wrapping paper sticking out like baguettes, he is still looking, still craning his neck to the left so as to enable him to see the arse as it disappears behind a bus stop.

— Hello? Hello? – Katy is rapping the side of her boyfriend's head with her knuckles – Hello?

At last he flinches

— Ouch
— Well
— Well what?
She shakes her head
— Why do you ALWAYS say that don't you think I REALISE
— What
— EVERY time you see some pretty girl on the street you have a good old look and then you say OH I think I know her or I can't believe what she's wearing or I'm sure she's on telly to cover up the fact that you are totally STARING

They stop. They were on their way to the Canteloupe Bar for an early evening drink. Now the two of them stop on the sidewalk and look at each other. Stood still Alex considers the undefinable grey-green-blue of her multi-racial eyes, the rainbow coalition. Their beauty makes him feel weird, nauseous, they make him feel like he does not know what to say. To hide this confusion he pretends to be distracted by some youthful trio pushing past them along the pavement: some model and a couple of artists in ludicrously self-conscious Hoxton attire: polyester flares, platformed trainers, National Health glasses circa 1974, the boys with special tufty little beards like a Spanish *grandee* gone to seed, the girl not evidently wearing any underwear under her tight green stretchy golfing strides.

Quietly, Alex mutters
— Look at that, I can't *believe* what she's wearing
— Jesus – Katy half pushes half punches his overcoated chest with her small hand – Shut up you OLD TWAT
— Girls should only sw
— You do it deliberately, don't you?

Behind them a taxi slowly negotiates its way down the narrow street; above them the throb of drum-n-bass reverberates from a long loft-conversion window. Alex thinks *fuck it* and says
— Look, honey
— Don't call me tha

— Sex-Paki?
— Thank you
— You don't seem to understand – Alex patronisingly cups her chilly chin with his hand, a hand she immediately bats away. He goes on – You don't seem to realise that I'm working, when I look at a woman and eye her up I'm working, doing my job
— Come aGAIN
— I'm a breeder – Alex takes her hand and holds it and it is cold and the dusk is growing and her eyes are wider than he has ever seen them before, strangely shiny – That's my job, as a bloke, to select and breed with the best, that's why I'm so attuned and obsessed, why I'm distracted by a decent arse at a hundred yards, you know me, I can tell a fake pair of baps through eight sheets of lead in a snowst

She is stalking down the road, toward his flat off the Square, away from the Canteloupe Bar. She has left him with all their shopping bags, giftwrapped boxes, and Xmas kit dumped on the damp kerb. Quietly, he says to her retreating figure
— Kate

She is ten yards away, he repeats
— Katy . . .

Twenty yards, strange panic
— KATY!!

She turns
— What
— Where you going, I thought . . .

Not waiting for him to finish:
— Alex. I'm tired. I'm cold, I'm bored, I'm going back to your place for a shower, I'm . . .

She is stopped outside the other pub: the Bricklayer's Arms. Her face is as defiant as her persona. Even from this far down the dusky lamplit road Alex is grieved by her good looks: he notes how the top photographer that is her youth and the top make-up artist that is her youth and the top stylist that is her youth have got together to make her look rather youthful, and very very beautiful. At this moment. And the sight of it makes a strange sweet ache in Alex's heart: he knows it is a trick of the genes, an evolutionary swiz, but he can't help feeling the pain already, the pain *manqué* that is love, all love.

Alex swallows saliva, a strangled tone giving away his weird inexplicable feeling

— Katy, I only want to have a drink

— Well - She says - You have eighty drinks, I'll be back at the flat

And she goes away.

She goes away.

His heart is pounding; his mouth is dry; the air is cold, damp and streetlit, and Alex finds himself fighting a rising sense of panic, that she really might go, properly, that she really might go and leave him, that she might leave him alone, alone and feeling like his friends have left the party without even warning him.

Strained, confused, puzzled, cold, pissed off by the shopping she has left to him to carry, Alex decides to go into the pub. *When in doubt go to a pub. When in doubt go to a pub and get pissed and chat up women and go home with waitresses and end up living in a bus stop in Poplar stealing car stereos to support your £3000 a day crack habit.*

Along the street Alex hoists his bags. Twenty metres later he turns and kicks the bar door open and enters. Inside the just-beginning-to-fill pub Alex approaches the bar and orders some obscure East Anglian ale, scans the chalked-up blackboards of groovy Anglo-Italian food, scopes the tables half-full of suits and Westminster Uni students and circus trainees and the odd muddy-fingered sculptress and dozens of hepcat workers from AcidJazz Records in their mock crocodile loafers, and *perhaps not,* Alex thinks. Instead he opts for a bar stool.

Atop the stool Alex sips his cellar-cold Anglo beer from a tall glass; wiping his lips with a hand Alex smells perfume and twists and finds he is sitting next to a pretty pretty girl who is sitting next to him.

Sip, look, sip, look. Gazing at the blackboard Alex reads about polenta and rocket for the seventh time and tries not to look; he looks. Alongside, the girl stares at the blackboard and sips her neon-pink alcopop straight from the bottle. Braved by his beer Alex turns properly and sizes her: her nice face, her nice-ish legs, her cropped dirty blonde hair, roots showing.

Mmm, a **slut**.

Sinking his drink and wafting a twenty at a tremendously bored looking barman Alex comes over even more confident and nihilist and he says to the girl's thrice-pierced ear:

— Can I get you a beer?

Silence. Returning to his own just-bought second beer Alex shrugs and remembers he's got a girlfriend soaping her firm defiant breasts right at that moment in his flat a quarter of a mile away; thinking this obviously gives Alex a pheromoney air of self-confidence because the girl unexpectedly turns and says

— No, but you can get me a Hooch

— A Hooch?

Her OK face, her nose ring, her not-quite-placeable socio-ethnic provenance, appeals: Alex buys her the Hooch, they talk. At first it is small, about the bar, about the menu, about Hoxton as a place to live and work: an elaborate take on do-you-come-here-often. All the time the Crufts breeder, the pinstriped pedigree assessor in Alex's brain is scoping the girl's credentials, her fitness-for-purpose, her

OK tits

After a few minutes the conversation warms: she starts talking about the hundreds of artists and artistic types who have moved to Hoxton. This gives Alex the chance to be fashionably scurrilous and dissy about the area, about its over-exposed trendiness (thus allowing Alex to surreptitiously reveal that he, of course, was one of those real trendy movers and makers who knew Hoxton when it was truly cool).

In response the girl nods, agrees and talks about BritArt and her opinion of it. Specifically she describes how her suspicions of the phoneyness of the movement were summed up for her when an allegedly homosexual BritArt dealer came on to her at a Damien Hirst private view (thus allowing her to subtly reveal that she knows lots of famous bohos and that she is attractive enough to be chatted up by millionaire faggots).

In response Alex nods, smiles and thinks

Decent arse as well.

But just as he is decided that they are getting on famously and she is well-worth-a-seeing-to, just as he is about to make a pitch to buy her dinner she goes and blurts

— The worst thing about it was that he came on to me right in front of my boyfriend

Alex swallows his beer, hmms, nods

— . . . Your . . . *boyfriend?*

Pretending not to notice, pretending not to be aware of what has just happened, she yeahs

— Yeah, he's an artist . . . works around the corner

— . . . Around the corner?

The girl smiles, her nose ring twinkles, her eye teeth shine

— I'm waiting for him

Courageously stifling the almost overwhelming urge to shout in the girl's face So Give Me Back The Fucking Money I Paid For Your Beer You Duplicitous Tart, Alex nods, smiles wanly, thinks about Katy, feels guilty. As Ms Boyfriend goes on about her boyfriend's work and her boyfriend's upcoming exhibition Alex wrestles, internally, with the Philanderer's Dilemma: how long do you keep talking to a girl once you've discovered that it's pointless talking to her? At what point is it polite to quit a conversation with a woman you have been chatting up, once you have established she is spoken for?

The girl is still chattering

— He does all this conceptual stuff, we were hoping that Charles Saatchi was going to come to hi

Jumped off his stool Alex picks up the bags and heads for the door. He can almost hear the girl opening and closing her mouth in shocked silence, behind him.

Outside, cold air. Overcoat buttoned up Alex quickens his pace across Old Street, into the uninviting expanse of Hoxton Square where he hangs a right and climbs a stoop; dropping two bags on his left and holding another bag awkwardly under his right arm he filches in his deep overcoat pocket for his keys and remembers that he gave them to Katy. Cussing, he buzzes. Her voice is crackly over the been-meaning-to-replace-it-for-ages intercom

— Hello

— It's me, Katy

— Hello? - Crackle - Hello?

— Kate, you daft canary, open the fucking door

— Oh Romeo - Katy's sarcasm is resonant even over Alex's intercom - Wherefore art thou

— It's starting to snow Katy

His voice is urgent: she mellows

— *OK*

The battered door buzzes open; Alex enters. Up the stairs and past the scented, just-used bathroom and the cold, unused kitchen he dumps the shopping under a Museum of Modern Art poster, by the telephone table, and pushes the ajar door of his room and finds his girlfriend saronged about the chest by a bath-towel, and turbaned around her head by a bath-towel. He also finds his girlfriend hastily closing the bottom drawer to his desk. To his desk? He hangs his overcoat over a chair:

— K?

Her reply is way too calm

— Yes?

— What are you doing?
— Drying myself off after a bath what do you think you spac?
— No, I mean, in my drawer

She looks at the drawer, he looks at the drawer; they look at each other. She says, shrugging
— I was looking at some of your manuscripts
— What – He is taken aback, the reply is so unexpected – Why?

She stalls
— Why what?

He looks at her
— Why the obvious? Why would you want to read that old bollocks? *Katy?*

No answer. Instead Katy vigorously rubs the towel-turban on her head to dry her wet hair, which expertly causes the towel saronged about her breasts to fall to the bare floorboards. She is now standing there naked. Alex's mouth goes dry; he gazes at his naked little girlfriend. Her thighs rosy and warm as a Tuscan sunset. Her cunt demure in its muff; a Gestapo Officer's mistress. Oh, her cunt. His stomach opens up in agonies of desire to have her, to have her right now: he wants to consume her, use her, to smoke her, inject her, to chase her across foil and inhale her and flop back on the bed elated and happy.

And so he does. He goes over and gathers his naked girlfriend, wet and shampoo-scented, in his much stronger arms: wondering as he does what she saw, in the manuscript. He kisses her too-tonguishly and he wonders if she read about the broken winged heronshaws *staked out on the grass*. His mouth compressed to hers, their breath suffocating each other, he thinks of the typescript, the hunting scene, when *all the lords and ladies mounted their horses and spurred away into the champaign landscape, a sparrowhawk on each noble wrist.*

Alex kisses her better, harder. He is kissing her and he is not kissing her: he is burying his face in her hair, her wet cold fragrant hair, his hand on her left buttock, clenched. Thinking of the dogs panting after the horses, the *running dogs in decorated collars and silver gilt muzzles and leashes of golden thread.*

Two, three, four fingers: forced between her legs, up and inside her; one finger flicking her clitoris painfully, she gasps. Her breath comes hotter, faster; he feels the wet inside begin; he pushes her back on to the bed and falls on top of her still clothed, clumsy.

— Kate

— Go onnn

— There is that

One moment he is hot against her thigh, like a hot blade, the next he is inside her; so deep inside her she stiffens, circuited, touched on the live rail. She grabs his arse and makes him fuck her deeper, deeper; choking on his own spit he responds, letting her hear the oncoming cavalry, the oncoming hunt, the horses hoofbeats, the panting dogs, *the panting dogs in leather armour, the blowing the mort on the horn*, he fucks her and fucks her, until *the huntsman feeds the testicles to the foaming alaunts.*

Katy is staring at the ceiling. Staring.

Her heart is pounding, so loud he can feel it.

Alex:

— Kate?

— Katy . . . ?

— K?

She sits up. Sitting up Katy pushes the wet hair from her eyes and stares at his bookshelves: history titles, philosophy, pop science, politics. She turns to him and says

— Alex

He is lying on the bed half-clothed, half aware

— Yeah?

— Alex I've met someone else

Heartbeat

— What?

— I've met a guy

— What the hell're you talking about?

Katy says it again. She says it for a third time. Katy closes her eyes, as if she is unsure if she means it, or whether she can say it even if she does mean it. Closing her eyes even tighter she says

— Alex I want to break *up*

Putting on his I-can-deal-with-this face, Alex says

— Yeah right

Silence, the silence of the snow falling outside; Katy

— I think I love him

— That's cool - He grins - Another barman?

His patronising flippancy gives him away, seems to give her courage. Up now, putting her clothes on, she says

— OK he may be a barman but he also happens to be BIGGER than you, and YOUNGER

— Finished?

— No . . .

— So?

— OK - She shakes her head - OK. He also makes me COME more than you

— Really

— Yes. Really - She stares, bravely - And . . . and there's other reasons too

— Other reasons what?

— Why I'm *leaving* you - She looks at him.

He snaps

— I said go on

Taking a breath

— OK, Alex, OK, APART from the fact that you're a selfish patronising bastard, that you are TOTALLY fucking inconsiderate, that you *never* introduce me to your friends, and that I know you've been sleeping around all the time you've been seeing me . . .

His face hardens; through set teeth:
— Yes, apart from *that*, what real reason do you have for finishing with me?

She does not laugh. She points to the drawer she closed when he entered the room. He says, perplexed:
— What? The *drawer*?
— The book

This time genuinely perplexed
— What *are* you on about?
— I mean – She finishes putting on her clothes; she does up her denim jacket and checks herself in the mirror and turns back to him – Who is Elizabeth?

His face dumbed, mouthing
— Who is . . . ?
— Yes – Her chin is jutting, not wobbling – You wrote a whole crappy book about her, I've been reading it for months – Chin still firm – You're obviously totally in love with her, aren't you? With this girl? So you know if it's not too *much* of me to ask could you, like, tell me who she is?
— She's . . . – Beginning to think he can see what has happened, Alex sits up in the bed and reaches for his girlfriend's wrist – She's no-one, Katy, she's no-one, she's . . .
— No-one?
— No, she's . . . just . . . she's . . . you see . . .
— Yeah YEAH – Pulling her wrist away.
— . . . What?
— Don't *bother*
— But you don't understand

Marching to the door; her jacket buttoned for the cold outside, she says nothing.
— K – He is still trying to be flip, to be cool – Katy, get a grip. It's just a stupid typescript

From the door she looks over, as if thinking. Then she says
— Goodbye . . .

— Where you going?
— What does it matter to you
— The barman?
Level gaze
— 'Bye . . .

The door slams. Alex sits there, alone in his bed. He hears the stairs. He hears her go. The door to his flat slams. He hears the house stairs, he hears her take these two at a time. And now the street door: the street door slams.

For a moment Alex thinks he can hear her feet in the street outside; but the snow muffles it, the snow muffles it all. It muffles everything but the pounding grinding shearing pain of incipient heartbreak: as if tiercel falcons are eating out the marrow of his wingbones, as if noble ladies are bending to his corpse to wash and whiten their skin in his guttering blood.

28

jinny nettle

— So she's left you?
— Yep. Dumped me for a barman
— She told you that?
— In spades
— How do you know she's telling the truth?
— Don't. Sure she is tho
— Yes?
— I . . . asked the Nick Hornby questions
— Was he better in bed, did he make her come?
— Yeah
— Jesus. And was he?
— What do you think

Tony wonders what he thinks, Tony tries to say what he thinks: says nothing because he is distracted. He is at home, in his bedroom, listening to Elizabeth bathe the kids. Even from here, the other side of the house, Tony can sense the faint smell of bubble bath, baby soap, laundered towels, the heat from the bathroom coming down the wintry landing. Doing his best to follow Alex's dissertation on his ex-girlfriend's cruelty and immaturity and sit-up-and-beg breasts, Tony imagines how it would be to be in this house and know the children were never coming back

— Tony?

— . . . m . . .

— Lost in space?

— Sorry

— *Need* your advice here

— Er – Tony tries to remember what his advice was going to be – Yes . . . Just . . . so . . .

— I'll ring back

— No, no – Tony quickens – I was going to ask why else she left you. Apart from the fact that you are a misogynistic bastard

— Did I not mention I was heartbroken?

— Oh come on

— I am – Alex repeats – Unexpectedly. Actually

— OK, OK. So – Tony engages – *Were* there any other reasons?

Evasive cough; evasive sigh; then

— Manuscript

— . . . What?

In reply, Alex exhales. Six miles across London Tony can almost smell the smoke and the beer and the whisky and whatever else his friend has been using to dilute the sorrow. Tony

— Alex?

— Said – Alex makes a *tsch* noise – The sodding manuscript . . . she pulled it out my drawer and read it and she thought, well, you can guess . . .

Tony sits on his bed wondering if he should turn the central heating up as the kids will soon be getting out of the bath.

— I can't

— You can – Alex insists – All the wank about . . . Lyonshall House, she went fucking nuts

— I see

Now Alex starts explaining the means of Katy's attaining possession of the manuscript; now Tony starts staring at the duvet. Just detectable, after all this time, is a faint red stain in the duvet cover. Tony pangs, looking at this. The stain is an old Rorschach of blood, made by his wife a long time ago when they used to make love so much they didn't care if she was on. Grieved, heartstruck, Tony thinks how their marriage has changed so much they actually welcome her periods as indicative of the one week they don't need an excuse not to have sex.

Alex

— I guess the fact that I am a cunt might have had something to do with it

— I did try to warn you

— But I *am* a cunt. That's *me*

— You could change

— Why? I thought we were meant to be true to ourselves. They're always saying men have got to learn to let their feelings out. So I did. I let Katy see the inner me

— Mm . . .

— I told her what I was really feeling

— Uh-huh

— I said I really feel like taking her from behind and coming in her hair and then sodding off down town for a Ruby

Silence, Tony

— Tad insensitive?

— Never – Alex sighs – Never work with actresses or teenagers

— *Thanks* . . . As if I'm going to get the bloody chance . . .

Alex:

— Things are still pretty bad then . . . ?

— Yes – Smoothing the duvet – Pretty bad

— You've really gotta try shagging somebody else

— Tried it

The phone goes so dead Tony thinks Alex might have put the phone down in unlikely moral disgust, but then Alex says

— Way to go!

— Yes . . . well . . .
— You old *dog*. Well *done*
— Thank you
— 'Owd it go then?
— What?

Alex almost stumbling over his words:

— Did you do it *per ano*
— Sorry?
— Use the bus or the Tube? Eh, eh eh?
— If you have to know
— I do, I do
— It wasn't exactly the longes
— DAddy daDDY DADDY daddy *DADDY*

As Tony goes to explain what happened twixt him and Julia he is engulfed by his son, followed by his wife with a tired smile carrying Polly. Before Tony can say goodbye to Alex his damp, pyjama'd son starts climbing the climbing frame of Tony's legs and arms.

— Gottago, Alex
— OK I'll
— Daddy tell me dat song, tell m

The phone set down, Tony looks up at Elizabeth, at his wife's it's-your-turn-now shrug, at her fading jeans, at her white shirt still damp with a bit of bathfoam on the breast. Weary, Elizabeth says

— Just sing it once and then I'll put them to bed
— YespleaseDaddy
— *Quickly* for God's sake
— OK, OK . . .

UnVelcroing his son from his hair and his shoulders Tony puts him down on the floor where Toby sits like a perfect Victorian child: gazing up at Tony with proper filial adoration. Alongside Toby Elizabeth has set Polly down, too: Tony's baby daughter sits and gravely contemplates the carpet. Fatherhood-struck, Tony recapitulates in his head the pristine beauty of his childrens' faces: like cover versions of the sweet sad song that is their mother's *haute* English loveliness.

His own brown Celtic eyes wide open, Tony sings

— The mayor of Bayswater

Instant applause from his audience of two; Tony sings

— The mayor of Bayswater, he had a pretty daughter, and the hairs on her dicky-die-doe, hung down to her knees . . . – Toby smiles, claps, Tony sings on

— One red one, one white one, and one ba ba ba ba ba ba, and one with a fairy light on to show you the way . . .

More applause. Tony sits back and rubs the day from his eyes and yawns and says to his smiley-sleepy children

— OK, that's it

— Da

— No come on

— Listen to your mother

— Buh

— But nothing

Obedient, Toby nods; doing a cute smile Toby gets up and demurely follows his mother, Indian file, as his mother carries Polly before. Down the hall the three progress, into the bunk bedded bedroom. From along the landing Tony listens to the tucking up noises, the whispered kisses. *There there. Daddy'll be in in a minute. Shhh. Goodnight goodni* . . . Sad, wan, confused, Tony sighs. Leant back on the bed in his shoeless socks he looks at the dressing table and make-up thereupon. Tony remembers how he used to help cleanse the make-up from his wife's face, once. *Long time ago.*

Lifting his head a little Tony stares at the mirror on the dressing table, at himself. But the sight of his conscience staring back at him from the mirror reminds Tony of Julia and even though Tony doesn't want to, he starts to wonder, again: why he did it, why he did*n't*. Tony tilts his head and thinks about his love for his wife: *is it really going? Their love? Has it gone already? They made so much you'd think some might still be lying around somewhere . . .*

Bang on time, his wife walks back in the bedroom, sits at the dressing table, and starts doing stuff to her face. As if he is averagely calm Tony says nothing; his wife looks at him in the mirror and says:

— Who was that on the phone?

— Mmm?

— While I was doing the kids?

— Oh – Tony admits – It was Alex

— Did you invite him?

— Yes

The monosyllable infers her next question

— And that was it?

— Well . . . – Tony spectates as Elizabeth scrapes a cotton wool swab across her face, smearing the cotton with beige make-up, white cream. Attentive as ever to all things feminine, all things Elizabeth, Tony observes as his wife drops the swab in the bin, there to join the solenoids of her hair and the tissues kissed with lipstick and the tweezered clippings of her eyebrows. Considering these details Tony realises with a stomach-acidy feeling that he loves even this: that this is where the love went: inside him, it is locked inside him. His wife's beautiful body is inside: locked in the glacier of his heart, in the glacier of memory: only to be disgorged in years to come, *perfectly preserved in its youthful beauty*.

— He's just been dumped by Katy

A little too quickly his wife turns from the mirror

— Katy?

— Yes

— The schoolgirl?

Curious about his wife's over-curiosity, Tony:

— Yes. What's so amazing about that?

Elizabeth shrugs, again, in her singlet: in the singlet that shows her dimpled womanly shoulders, the cello-waist of her waist. Dismissive, Elizabeth torsions back to the mirror, to herself. She carries on swabbing; Tony carries on watching. Tony watches, and agonises. The sweet sadness of his wife's fading beauty being slowly revealed by the disappearing make-up makes Tony ache with desire, still: to kiss the sweetness while it lasts, to kiss the lines around her eyes, the brightness falling from her hair.

Vague, Elizabeth says

— Is he going to come then?

— What?

— Alex, the dinner party, next month

— Oh. Yes – Tony tries not to think about his wife's buttocks.

— And . . . Eddie?

— Yes. Of course. He's your brother

Tony can almost hear his wife's lips pursing; Tony tries to de-ice the room

— You did invite him

— I know

— He needs a break, Eliza

— Hn. I just hope . . . – Sudden, unexpected, Elizabeth slumps forward and catches her face in the palms of her hands, then rests her elbows on the dressing table – I just hope he doesn't disgrace himself . . . I just hope, I love him, you know that, he's my brother, I just hope . . . you know

Tony knows

— He's been off it for quite a while now

Bitterness muffled by her hands

— So he says

Tony, defensive

— No, it's true. I've seen him. He's changed. Prison really . . . shook him up . . .

A sigh, slightly less muffled

— You told me – She breathes – But after everything . . . and with Alex coming too . . .

— It was a long time ago
— Ten years?
— Ten years . . .

Her face unhanded Elizabeth stares in the mirror: at her husband sitting on the bed behind her. Then she says, quietly

— Carberry ginger hats

And he smiles and says

— Rose-petal sandwiches, in the Mary garden
— Devonshire junket
— A slice of Mrs Sleightholme's delicious seedcake

And now the two of them are looking at each other via the mirror and they are lost, now, lost in the memory they mean to each other. Laughing, smiling, recalling, they talk about the times they used to swim naked in the lake, about sunny afternoons of laughing tennis, about drunken games of croquet with flagons of icy cup. And about the day they went down to the sea. When the four of them, when Alex and Eddie and Tony and Elizabeth, stood young and laughing and suntanned on the strand by the silent sea and they watched the fishermen pulling net after net of glittering mackerel into the red-sailed fishing boats.

Later, his wife in bed, Tony potters about the house, clearing up plastic Star Wars swords with flashing lights, putting away bottle-blonde Barbie tarts. Careful, Tony locks the back door, the window of which is rimed and dabbed with frozen kiddie fingerprints. Now Tony moves into the living room: onto a floor awash with Sunday newspapers and supplements, and an empty bottle of wine and a half eaten four-year-old's cheese sandwich and lots of glossy inserted adverts that have fallen out the newspapers. Sighing, twice, Tony goes back into the kitchen, rips off a bin liner from the soft plastic baton, returns to the living room; bags all the crap. Tying up the yellow-handles of the bin liner he returns to the kitchen and unlocks the back door again and decides he should not be an ergonomicist as he dumps the bin liner of Sunday's crap in the overfull dustbin, the lid of which perches precariously on top of too many bulging bin liners like a cartoon beret.

Back door locked, again, Tony attends to the lights: flicking his way around the house he darkens his way to the stairs and then he climbs the stairs and takes a leak; all this done with effortful quietness, so as not to wake the children.

His protective instincts gratified, Tony pauses on the landing to catch the sound of his children breathing . . . but instead he catches the sound of his wife.

Tiptoeing to the door Tony peers silently around and sees his wife, naked, on the bed. She is masturbating. Elizabeth is sitting on the side of the bed with her hands draped down between her thighs and one finger moving up and down and her eyes are closed; she is swaying; her tongue is slightly protruding from her mouth. Her bare toes are clenching the pile of the carpet as she drapes her hand between her soft white thighs. For some oblique unhappy cynical reason he cannot place, Tony is reminded of all those eighteenth century portraits of English court ladies fondling their pet monkeys.

— Ah

Elizabeth is murmuring

— Ahhh ah a a ahnn

Tony feels embarrassed, embarrassed that he's turned-on.

— Ah!

Her hand is moving quicker, expert, pizzicato; her hand is flicking upwards, between her legs, between her thighs, her head tilting further back all the time

— Siempre *siempre*

She is speaking Spanish to herself: whispering Spanish. Tony's wife often does this but this time it unsettles Tony more than it has ever done before. Because it reminds him. As Tony stands hidden by the door, as he spies on his wife's private devotion, he is reminded of the time he stumbled into a church in a Mexican village on holiday years ago and inside the nave the swart handsome filthy barefoot dwarvish natives were wafting incense and offering fruit to plaster saints and laying down palm leaves and singing in a hushed, strained, hypnotic Spanish polyphony in pagan worship of a god who was half Christian saviour and half Mayan idol.

And just as he did then, in Mexico: Tony feels revulsion at his own voyeurism, ashamed of his pallid inadequcy, mortified by his physical and spiritual etiolation. Getting a grip, Tony prepares to slip quietly away. But as he does he hears Elizabeth speaking, to herself, again in Spanish.

Spanish.

Standing on the cheap carpet of the landing Tony sees the entire conspiracy plain and apparent: at last. *Of course. The love that dare not speak its surname.* In Spanish. The **surname**. *In* **Spanish**.

29

jew guts

— Drinking a lot?
— Nn
— That's your third and we haven't even ordered yet
Alex lifts his shoulders
— I'm on retox, I'm heartbroken
— Retox?
— Retoxification
Now Rachel smiles
— And dehabilitation, I suppose?

Nodding, and draining his beer with a flourish, Alex catches the waitress's eye, and simultaneously looks at the orange menu. The menu is bordered with orange, and written in orange print. Setting down the orange menu next to an orange box of orange-headed matches, Alex looks at the orange chairs and the orange cornice, and the orange piping on the waitresses' basically orange uniform.

— Do you think they'll do me a glass of orange?
Sitting back on her soft orange banquette, Rachel admits
— It is a bit *themed*
— And they don't even do mash

— Sorry?

Alex tilts a flat hand at the gatefold menu

— Well it's called Mash so you think they'd do *mash*, right?

She shrugs, opposite. Still happy trashing the menu Alex says

— It's all girlie food, little bits of pizza and salad and feta and fiddly bits of dingle dangle

— You want something a little more butch? – Rachel eyes him – There's a proper restaurant upstairs that I'm sure would do you a . . . cow's head . . . if you really want . . .

Remembering that she is buying him lunch, that this is on *her* and that, therefore, certain rules apply, Alex upholds both his palms in mock-surrender, says

— Only whingeing, I'll have the salad. With Sea Bass

— And some more beer?

— Yeah

Minutes later Alex is chugging another wheat beer; and gazing across the buzz of tables and girls and lunchers and Christmas office-parties. Happy to be drinking, and thus forgetting

Katy

he barely listens as Rachel discourses, as she talks about the magazine, gossips about the editor, evaluates the competition, and moans about her Picture Editor. Halfway through Rachel's monologue Alex unexpectedly recalls that time when he and Rachel went to bed. Try as he might, as he does, Alex can't help finding it somewhat odd that the two of them, that he and Rachel, he and the *Cosmo* features editor, should be sitting here having an almost normal lunchtime ideas-meeting when six months ago he went to bed with her. When six months ago he pulled her little black knickers down her creamy white thighs and plunged his feasting mouth into her tangled snatch.

— So Wendy thinks we ought to have a few more *Marie Clairey* things, some interviews with weirdy couples and the like

When six months ago he took her head and rammed it down on his thick fat cock until her lipstick *flaked*.

— The publishing director is a bit worried we might get too ... you know ... tabloidy ... but I think we ... we ... Alex? *Alex?*

Filthy jewish slut

— **Alex**?

— Yep?

— You're not really listening, are you?

Drunk, Alex does a nod and shrug at the same time, then takes up a fork and attends to his plate of just-placed food. Half hungry, Alex shovels a forkful of green and fish in his mouth and says with his mouth open

— I just need crimson, Rache

— *What?*

— Nothing ... – Quickly he amends – I was just thinking ... just wondering ... – Head up – Doesn't it ever, like, amaze you, Rache – Fixing his drunken gaze beyond Rachel's hair, affixing his eyes on the huge, glittering aluminium beerstills set up behind glass at the end of the restaurant – Doesn't it ever like *amaze* you that you and me ... that we ... that ... we ...

— Yes?

— That we ... you know?

— You know *what*, Alex?

— That we *did it*. That we made love – He burps, into his fisted hand – That we boffed, shagged, swived, that I once kissed your nipples and shoved my hand down your panties and licked your

— All right, Alex

— But you know whatImean it is pretty freaked when you consider it, that I did all these weird massively intimate things to your body and now here we are pretending nothing ever happened like this is all normal, like it was perfectly normal for me to shove my hand into your *vagina*

Rachel says nothing. She glances at a waitress. The waitress who was about to put another beer on their table hesitates: professionally sensing a certain scene. As the waitress hovers Alex narrows his eyes and thinks about vaginas. Specifically K's vagina. Her little swatch of miniver. Slumped ever lower and angrier in the soft orange banquette with the orange piping Alex burps and yearns and lusts for Katy, *Katy*, **KATY**

Evidently decided that the best way to deal with her drunken freelancer is to employ him, thereby distract him, Rachel Levy reaches into her bag and pulls out a big matt plastic notebook with an integral matt plastic pen. Eyes on him, pen poised

— So. Let's get to work

He hiccups. She frowns

— You do *have* some ideas, don't you?

— Uhh

— Or is this a waste of time and money?

— No . . .

— So . . . ?

Behind his lofted glass, holding open his own notebook with the other hand, Alex says:

— I kinda thought we could do a piece on sex and race

Flinch. Squint. Scowl

— Sex . . . And *race*?

— Yeah

— Sex – Another scowl – . . . and race . . . ?

— Like I said – He hiccups again – For instance we could do something about different kinds of pubic hair different races have. You know black girls have brillo pads down there, and Orientals have this downy stuff

— Alex

— Or, or, we could do something about miscegenation. You know? I know loads of white blokes who fancy black girls, like to get their black wings

— And you *really* think that we

— You must have heard the saying: 'You ain't a man 'till you've had your tan'?

Rachel stares frostily at him, saying nothing. Then she says

— And this is your big idea, is it?

— Yeah – Alex's eyes glisten – This is my big idea

He thinks about Katy: her vagina, the little Zairean she keeps between her legs.

Rachel:

— You know I *don't* think that's really *us* **somehow**

— You don't? . . . – Alex knocks down the weissbier, sets down the glass, scans down his scrawly notebook – Well, if you don't like that, we could always do it from another angle . . . like . . . we could run a piece 'bout how black guys fancy white women, how they get jungle fever – Looking over at Rachel, not really looking over, Alex goes on – I thought about *that* 'cause I found this passage in this book – Alex goes to his jacket side pocket and takes out a paperback; lifting and opening the book he stares close at a bookmarked page as if he has just become shortsighted – It's by Eldridge Cleaver you ever heard of him?

— No

— Black guy in the Sixties?

— *No*

Alex, burping

— You see he wrote this book and there's this passage and he says – Alex lifts the paperback to within an inch of his boozed, myopic gaze – I can't do the accent, but, here goes, this is what he says: 'There is no love left between a black man and a black woman. Take me for instance. I love white women and hate black women. It's just in me, so deep that I don't even try to get it out of me any more. I'd jump over ten nigger bitches just to get to one white woman. Ain't no such thing as an ugly white woman. A white woman is beautiful even if she's bald headed and has only one tooth. It's not just the fact that she's a woman that I love; I love her skin, her soft, smooth white skin. I like to just lick her white skin as if sweet fresh honey flows from her pores, and just to touch her long, soft, silky hair. Ain't nothing more beautiful than a white woman's hair being blown by the wind.'

Rachel is silent. Alex can only hear the deafening clatter and buzz of about fifteen Christmas office lunch parties. Across from Alex Rachel closes her notebook, slips the notebook into her bag, and sits back. Then she looks squarely at Alex

— Anything *else*?

Not needing the prompt Alex nods, vigorously; scanning the Eldridge Cleaver book he locates another biro-ticked passage:

— And there's this bit, get this, there's this bit Rachel where he goes – Alex's eyes adjust once more to the page – yeah, here we are, 'In my dreams I see white women jumping over a fence like dainty little lambs, and every time one of them jumps over, her hair just catches the breeze and splays out behind her like a mane on a Palomino stallion: blondes, redheads, brunettes, strawberry blondes, dirty blondes, drugstore blondes, platinum blondes – all of them. They are the things in my nightmares.'

Leaning over to the side of the table, Rachel takes up her bag. Bag open, money found, Rachel puts three twenty-pound notes on top of the bill, in a saucer. But even though his lunch-partner is evidently on the verge of leaving Alex is still quoting

— One more bit. This is a good bit. Get this: 'When I off a nigger bitch, I close my eyes and concentrate real hard, and pretty soon I get to believing that I'm riding one of them bucking blondes. I tell you the truth, that's the only way I can bust my nuts with a black bitch, to close my eyes and pretend that she is Jezebel. If I was to look down and see a black bitch underneath me or if my hand happened to feel her nappy hair . . .'

The table has moved. Alex drops the book and looks up. Rachel is standing, saying

— Did you see my last piece in *Cosmo*?

Letting the book shut, Alex

— No

— Squelch And A Belch: What To Do If He's Crap In Bed?

— Er . . .
— It was about you, Alex
— Was it?
— Yes. It was – Rachel picks up her bag, clasps it shut – You were the worst shag I've ever had. Did you know that? You didn't even touch the sides – A Parthian shot as she turns and leaves – It was like going to bed with a hamster
— A hamster? – He opens his mouth, repeats – A hamster? Rachel? Rache? A hamster? *How would you know?*

But she has gone. The banquette opposite is empty. Avoiding Alex's eyes, the waitress collects the saucer of money. Alone on his orange banquette next to the orange trimmed table, Alex slaps his notebook shut. Spearing a quarter-circle of cucumber from Rachel's uneaten Greek salad, adding to the tined cucumber an olive half and a chunk of oily feta cheese, Alex lifts, mouths and swallows, and sluices with a fresh slug of weissbier. The beer still tastes good. He takes another big gulp. He sits back and listens to the Christmassy chitchat: the conversational effervescence that is the Media Futures dealing floor that is Mash Restaurant, Great Portland Street. Straining to hear the words spoken, to decipher the babble, Alex is not surprised to find that all he can hear is

— Katy Katy KatyatyKatyKatyKatyKatyKatyKatyatyKKKKKKKK

30

ranting widow

New Year's Eve and Alex stands in the middle of a kitchen in a party somewhere in Docklands listening to chatter, gossip, banter, verysmalltalk. Bleakly drunk, he looks at the other women, the late twenties, thirty-something women, and he feels the lack of Katy's youth and beauty like an ache. Everything here reminds him of her absence: the fact that he isn't in north London reminds Alex of Katy's house in north London. The lack of a pool table in the kitchen reminds Alex of how Katy liked to play pool. The fact that none of the women hovering around the kitchen remind Alex of Katy reminds Alex of Katy.

And what reminders, what memories of Katy. Alex stands and chugs and swallows and thinks. The mythographers have been hard at work in his head ever since she nixed him. Very hard at work. Where Katy once had a decent little arse, to Alex her arse is now superb, peerless, a traffic hazard. Where her breasts were pert and playfully small, now they are frighteningly big, scarily glorious. All and everything Katyish is being sourced by the team of scribes who are busy in the scriptorium of Alex's heart: everything is material to their mythmaking: the shortness of her skirts, the smallness of her shoes, the dimpledness of her half-smile, the adorable ludicrousness of her speech patterns. Everything is limned in cinnabar, vermillion and albumen, gilded and silvered in the manuscript of Alex's memory, the *Lindisfarne Gospels*, the *Book of Kells* dedicated to his love for her. His love.

And so this is what Faith must be like, Alex thinks, as he nibbles a tortilla chip half hidden by chivey cream. *When everything in the world is charged with the grandeur of God; when every five spotted flower signifies the wounds of Christ's Passion.*

— You *must* come and meet

— Fancy another mulled wi?

— How is that girlfriend of yours

— βςαχη Γδκσ βγχ ηφμ Ψαι

Maudlin, lonely, still drinking, still Katyless, Alex dips his wineglass into the washing-up bowl of hot, steaming, clove-scented, toothachey mulled wine; drinks; drinks; stares into the New Year, into the gloom of the future. A girl passes before his drunken gaze as he leans against the fridge, as he tries to talk to an economist. A girl. A woman. NotKaty. Alex tries to muster up the desire to chat up NotKaty: to chat up this girl who is so obviously interested in him; he fails. He feels too detached from all this: from the people talking and chattering and drinking and going about their social business. He feels exiled, sexually exiled: feels like a football hooligan excluded from his home team's ground. He can attend the odd away match but from the place where his heart truly resides he is barred.

Or is that too fanciful? Alex lurches to the pine kitchen table and stares out the window at the darkness and the distant red and orange lights of the Millennium Dome.

— Nice piece in *FHM*

— You do look a bit buggered

— Obviously not drinking enough

— Happy New Year Alex you old bastard

* * *

Four miles across London Eddie sits alone in front of his television. The television is full of happy people counting down the seconds to the end of the year and Eddie feels so dysphoric he wants to die. He feels trapped by drugs, the medicational maze. He thinks he ought to do himself in, because he can't think of anything else to do. If he comes off Naltrexone he will surely go back on heroin and then his life will be so pointless and horrible he will kill himself. If he stays on Naltrexone so as to stay off heroin this horrible Naltrexoney *dysphoria* will continue and he will kill himself. And over it all the looming prospect of his trial, for dole fraud, promises a return to prison, where he will surely kill himself.

So he might as well kill himself? What's so wrong with that? *It is,* Eddie thinks, *only the bad press that Death gets that puts us all off. Why do we always see Death as a horrid skeletal figure in a black hood carrying an evil scythe? Who does that help? We all have to face Death at some point so how much better if we saw Death as a kindly matronly figure. As sweet Mrs Death from the Village. With her pinny and her rosy cheeks and her wicker basket, waving through the kitchen window as she comes up the path to sell us her home baked cottage loaves, her cottage loaves of personal annihilation. Her scones of eternal desolation.*

31

what's-your-sweetheart-grass

Damped by vinegary London drizzle, watched by wet dole-queues of pigeons, chilled by the cold estuarine wind coming upriver, Eddie and Alex continue up the incline of Putney Bridge; away from where Alex has parked his car. Away from where they met.

A train, a boat, a bus, the whining wind. Eddie shivers and wishes he had a proper coat and looks at Alex, who is quieter than usual. Eddie says

— You OK?

— What?

— You seem . . . rather . . .

Buttoning his proper coat Alex admits

— Katy

— Yes?

Glancing at his taller friend, Alex:

— Y'know me man, I always try to stand upwind, emotionally; I guess I hadn't really expected . . .

A taxi scoots past, slashing puddle water onto the pavement; they both pause to avoid; Eddie

— She screwed you up?

— . . . Yyyeah. Swhy I want to walk a bit. Need some air

They are stopped in the middle of the bridge. Alex turns and gazes down the river, to Trinidad and Hurlingham Wharves, to Wandsworth Bridge, to the unseeable blackness where barges with red lights come and go, come and go

— I guess I *must* have loved her

— Presumably

— But what's the fucking point in an emotion you can only confirm when the reason you have the emotion has gone?

— Sorry?

— Nothing . . .

Eddie touches his old, oldest friend on the slightly padded shoulder of his expensive cashmere coat, says

— You'll get over it

— I'll get over it

— 'Sjust hurt pride

— Yeah . . . – Alex looks at a taxi shooting past, at a blonde-haired girl in the back who does not look remotely like Katy who therefore reminds him of Katy – It's just . . . y'know . . . I spent so long fighting it, and now . . . – Now Alex leans over the granite battlement and spits, teenagerishly; watching the molten pewter blob of spittle whip under the bridge in the wind he sighs, and expands – She was my little girl . . .

Eddie:

— Why exactly . . . *did* she go, then?

Hand backhanding his lips, Alex says

— Load of reasons. Met someone even nicer than me

— Goodness

— Exactly. And she found the manuscript . . .

— What?

— The manuscript

— Yah . . . ?

— Yeah

— That one?

— Yep. All that stuff with . . . you know who – Giving Eddie a Can-you-believe-this? face, Alex combs a young lock of hair from his eyes and half-closes his eyes as he does so – Fancy believing all that crap . . .

Confronted by something he cannot quite fathom, Eddie decides the only thing is to tilt his shoulders southwards, to encourage them both on; Alex responds: pushing himself off the parapet he follows Eddie's damp and muddy old trainers over the bridge to Putney village. Attaining the southern bank Alex changes the subject in an attempt not to think about Elizabeth, or Katy, or Lyonshall, or Katy. Or Katy. Gesturing across he says

— You know that place?

— Hn? – Eddie was staring up at the sky, trying to see the stars – Miles away. What?

— That place. You know what it is?

Alex is pointing to a low slung, ugly, dark, Kentish ragstone church at the end of the bridge, tucked in its lamplit churchyard in the armpit formed by the Putney strand and the bridge. Eddie

— Ah. A church

His brown mongrel eyes given pitifully to his friend Alex shakes his head and says

— Not just a sodding church, dude

— No?

A sceptical eyebrow:

— You're telling me you've never heard of *Putney Church*?

Eddie, with an air of defeat

— I suppose I should?

Dragging his friend by the lapel of his denim jacket Alex leads him to the gate, which is surprisingly open, and then down the wet black asphalt squidged with last autumn's leaves. At the pinewood-and-glass door of the church, which is also surprisingly unlocked, Alex pushes against the brass hinges and pulls Eddie inside; inside Eddie grimaces at the comprehensively restored interior

— Christ. What happened?
— It was burned down in the Sixties or something – Alex looks distracted – I think it was restored in the Seventies . . . by . . . Grand Funk Railroad. Anyway that doesn't matter, it's this bit at the end that matters

At the further wall of the church they stand in front of a simple slate plaque which simply states:

> In this place, Oliver Cromwell, the General Council of the Army, and elected soldiers of the regiments held the Putney Debates, the first recorded public discussion of democratic principles.
>
> 28 October – 9 November 1647

Alex is gazing at the plaque as if it is his mother's gravestone, Eddie is simultaneously perplexed and uninterested; Alex is marvelling
— This is it, the cradle of democracy, man, the navel, the fucking birthplace of England's greatness, the, the, the
— You know – Eddie murmurs – We ought to get some wine

Alex
— Oh Lords and Commons of England, consider what nation it is whereof ye are

Eddie sighs:
— *Wine?*

Virtual silence. They both stand alone. In the musty, cold midwinter church it is so quiet Eddie can see himself breathing; meantime Alex can hear himself thinking, thinking too much, about Katy and England and Elizabeth and Katy and what it all means. What if it means nothing? Any of it? Any more? What if it meant nothing, ever?

Alex:
— Guess we *should* get some booze

As they walk up the path, as they latch shut the iron gate of the church, as they continue down the road towards Elizabeth and Tony's house Alex turns to Eddie and says, blurting

— Doesn't it matter to you at all?

Eddie's mind is hardly there, it is half an hour ahead, it is ten years ago

— Wha?

— English history, you used to at least pretend

— *Did I?*

— Prison's changed you, man, it's fucked you up – Alex clucks. They are standing in the doorway of Fullers the off-licence with its bright enticing windows painted with holly boughs, snowdrifts and Santas, all faintly ludicrous now, given that Christmas was fifteen days ago. Alex repeats, as they go in – You used to be a fascist bastard, a right old Nazi, what did they do to you in there?

— I think – Eddie is moving to the racks of New World White – I just realised . . . we're all, you know . . . the same

Alex wonders what to say to this; says nothing for the moment. Next to him Eddie is half-heartedly debating whether, if he *does* buy white for a change, Chardonnay is simply too passé; Alex is debating whether German Riesling will be seen for the correctly trendsetting selection it is, or, unfairly, as a ghastly error.

Both their choices made, they meet at the till; Alex presses the point and Eddie explains

— When you're banged up you start to see . . . we're *all* coons – Face to face with Alex – We are. We're all white trash, Alex. All anyone does is drink and brawl and fornicate and throw up. It's just that some of us do it in rather more agreeable houses than others

— So? – Alex hands over a tenner to the obviously listening-in off-licence employee, Eddie goes on

— So . . . *so*. There it is

— Don't under

— Countries . . . what are they for? It's all something of a delusion when you see humanity . . . close-up – He sighs – . . . What exactly is the point in favouring one bunch of . . . *nignogs* . . . over *another*? Mm?

Alex looks quizzically at Eddie. Eddie decides to ignore this; he accepts his change and his brown-paper wrapped bottle; then the two of them exit the off-licence and make their way across the rainy street to the corner of Disraeli Road. Alex, unable to respond to Eddie's latest remarks, such is his profusion of conflicting thoughts, mentions instead

— You're looking way better, you know – Their eyes meet – Being clean takes years off you. Could pass for forty . . .

Under a Wandsworth Council streetlamp that makes millions of tiny silver flecks of the drizzle, Eddie shakes his head

— Well. I wish I could say I was *feeling* better – His long face is longer – The stuff they're giving me is a bit of a mare, frankly

— The . . . Naltrexone . . . ?

— The opiate inhibitor

— Bad scene?

— Yah. The doctor called it . . . – Eddie manages to smile again at the scientific precision – Dysphoria . . .

— Feeling shite, you mean?

— I feel fucking *awful*. It's like I stopped believing in God

— You never believed in God, Eddie

— I am the apostate of love

Alex's turn to slap Eddie on the back

— C'mon dude. You'll be OK – Theatrically glancing at his watch – We better get a move on. First time your sister's invited either of us to the gaff for half a century. Don't want to be late

— What time did they say?

— About half an hour ago

Eddie breathes, looks down the drizzly street; Alex

— You nervous about meeting Elizabeth?

Eddie checks his friend's face for sarcasm

— Of course

— It'll be fine, man
— N
— *Will*
— It's . . . just . . .
— Come on – Alex takes his friend's lapel, again – If you got to worry about meeting anyone you should worry about meeting Tone.
— m?
— He sounded like he was wigging out on the phone. Weird
— Probably stressed about his pheasant stuffing
— Hah. Probably

Thus they step down the road, down Disraeli Road, to the Raffertys' front door: with its hoop of green holly, red berries and scarlet bows. Stood together like carol singers they press the buzzer, and wait for a second. The door opens, and there she is: Elizabeth Rafferty, nee Lyonshall. Elizabeth Lyonshall. Elizabethabethabethabeth. Elizabethlehem. Sweet Bess. Beth.

Their sweet Eliza, sitting beneath the oak at Hatfield in all her teenage loveliness . . .

— Hello Elizabeth
— Hello Alex

He, Alex, is searching for something in her face, for what, for what, for forgiveness . . .

But Elizabeth's attention is elsewhere. On her brother: her face is a portrait of love and astonishment, an astonishment that makes her finely plucked eyebrows arch high above her deep blue eyes that stare into deep blue eyes that exactly and genetically mirror her own. So enrapt is Elizabeth she hardly acknowledges Alex; instead she reaches up and holds her taller brother's head between her two hands, and kisses him on the cheek near his mouth.

Eddie:

— *Ola . . .*

And now there is a pause, as Alex push-click-shuts the front door, a pause that ends with Elizabeth saying:

— *Ola . . . Eduardo*

His moment chosen, Tony, in a crap new Christmas black brocade waistcoat, and black corduroys, is approaching from behind; staring hard and fixedly at his wife Tony says nothing as Elizabeth says, close to her brother's ear

— You look so much . . . better . . .

His face hung low, Eddie says

— Yah . . . I know

Now Eddie nears and kisses his sister, too, on the cheek he used to kiss as a boy; Eddie leans, the kiss lingers, Tony abruptly coughs and says

— Come on, Alex, let's leave them to it

Almost brusquely, Tony guides Alex down the hall and through a doorway with mistletoe Sellotaped to the lintel. Now they are in the dining room and Tony introduces the rest of the guests to Alex. The rest of the guests are a Jewish-American publishing couple, Tamara and David, and an English girl too unattractive for Alex to remember her name.

— Alex, this is Laura

As one the four of them sit down to a table set with saucers of post-Christmas nibbles: obscure nuts, weird crisps, pimento-esque olives. They talk about the weather, the season, parents-as-children, and as Tony, the chef, disappears into the kitchen and as Eddie and Elizabeth fail to emerge from their dialogue in the hall Alex is forced to join in. A few minutes are enough to convince Alex that The Girl Whose Name He Has Already Forgotten is one of those *desperate* thirty-somethings: she keeps looking at him, hoping to catch his eye. Giving off the pheromones of sexual failure. Alex knows this type: he could confess to alcoholism and arson and attempted rape but as long as he was at least occasionally hetero she'd marry him after the pudding.

As soon as he thinks it is polite, probably before it is polite but *who cares?* Alex makes his excuses and dashes into the hall unto the kitchen. On the way he catches some of Eddie's and Elizabeth's impassioned, by-the-coat-rack conversation. It reminds Alex of something. He mentions this to Tony, in the kitchen, Tony who is attacking some mangetout on a bread-board, topping and tailing them with his trusty Sabatier. Alex:

— Those two. Sounds like a Lorca play

— Yes

— In there

— Yes

— Eddie and Eliz, I mean . . .

— n

— Anyway, man – Alex wonders what's up, what he can say next – Who's that desperate old slapper in the dining room?

Tony says nothing. Alex tries again

— What about the Americans? Who are they?

— *Americans*

— Right . . .

Alex watches as Tony slaps the blade, decapitating his mangetout with a vicious *tchock;* leaning around Tony's back Alex thieves a green olive from a bowl; spitting the stone into his palm and dropping the stone in the sink Alex says

— Why d'you invite them, you know I hate having dinner with Americans

His face elsewhere, Tony mutters:

— Pardon? What?

Alex thinks about another olive, chooses not, says:

— They're such a wind-up

Tony continues working

— *Yes . . .*

Changing his mind, Alex reaches around and takes another olive and says through a mouth of salty, slightly cunnilingual savouriness

— 'Slike, every time, you have dinner with Americans or go to a party with Americans you know, you're all British and funny and witty and cleverer than them, and then at the end of the party the Americans go off and run the fucking world and the Brits are just left there with their irony and their wit and their sodding cigars

— Perhaps – Tony says, uninterested – You're meeting the wrong Americans

— Yeah . . . Perhaps . . .

The two of them go quiet. The two of them are quiet. Alex contemplates the way Tony is working too hard; thwapping the blade, cutting into the chopping board every time he sorts a mangetout. More silence. Chop chop, chop. Chop, chop CHOP. Just as the silence is about to get weird, Tony says, surveying his works

— So perish all traitors

Chop, chop, chop. Chop chop chop chop CHOP CHOP.

— What?

Tony lifts the as-yet-unblooded knife; it glitters in the kitchen striplight. Alex feels like he wants to leave; he can't leave. Alex says

— Tony, whassup man?

Dropping his balding head, Tony wipes his eyes with a sleeve and he says, as he blindly continues to attack the mangetout

— D'I tell you I had another dream?

Hoping this is by way of light relief, Alex shakes a No and Tony extrapolates

— This dream. I had to go into a Kwik-Fit to get my car exhaust fixed, but they'd made a mess of everything, so – Tony stares down at the chopping board, notices he is now chopping air; grabbing another fistful of greenery, he starts again – So I asked to be taken to the manager, so they led me into the manager's office – Scraping a load of headless, bottomless mangetout into a bowl, Tony pauses and says –

And when I get into the manager's office the manager denies that they've made a mistake and we have an argument – For the first time Alex notices that Tony is evidently drunk, he is swaying over the chopping board; as if to confirm this Tony reaches for a big tumbler full of ice and lemon and, presumably, gin, and takes a big swig and barely grimaces as he tilts the chopping board to dump the bits of unwanted mangetout into the sink and now Tony says – Where was I, no, yes, the manager, the Kwik-Fit manager he leads me out into the forecourt but as he does this we're crossing the yard he gets his dick out and it's hard and he starts poking it against my thigh saying ooh yes you know you want it you dirty sod and when I turn around the Kwik-Fit manager is Eddie, it's Eddie . . .

Unable to stop himself, Alex bursts out laughing; Tony glares at Alex with his knife still in hand; Alex stops laughing as Tony stares at him, the knife upraised in his hand.

— Tony are you OK?

— Yes

— Is it something to do with

— Go in. Go in there and talk to them. *Talk*

— Not until you tell me what's wrong

As if not able to trust himself, Tony lays the Sabatier flat on the metal draining board, shudders, reaches for his glass; before he drinks more gin he makes plain

— Elizabeth and . . . And Eddie. They're . . . having an affair

Dumbed, mute, silenced, Alex stares at his erstwhile best friend. Tony stares at his knife.

Mangetout. Knife. Chopping board. Tony. Alex. Tony.

Alex says

— Are you fucking mad?

— No, I'm not mad, Alex

— You dropped your clock? He's her *brother* for Christ's sake . . .

Tony, bitter:

— You've seen them, you saw them just then

A thousand explanations in Alex's mind, Alex gabbles the obvious:

— Tony, she hasn't *seen* him for about five years, he's been in prison, she *is* his fucking sister

Tony's face is unchanging, unrelenting; his eyes rise and accept Alex's incredulity and do not flinch.

— I realised just before Christmas

— You . . . realised . . . that . . . ?

Glugging more gin Tony nods and makes another go-into-the-dining-room gesture. Alex bridles, leans nearer, says

— *Not until you tell me this is a joke*

The strangest expression on Tony's face

— Yes it's a joke, yes it's a big big joke. Go on

— *Tony*

— Go in . . . I'm OK

Dumbed, again, but unable to think of what else to do, Alex carries a plate of canapés past Elizabeth and Eddie, still huddled in a Spanish dialogue, into the dining room, where the American couple and Other Guest, are talking crap, talking politics. Taking a seat Alex proceeds to pour himself a very large glass of red wine. Alex wasn't going to drink, as he was driving; now he has decided: if he has to spend the next three hours at what is obviously going to be the world's worst dinner party he might as well do it drunk. Very drunk.

Thus Alex spends the next half hour working through an Australian Shiraz and half a Californian Grenache-Cabernet. Blithely unaware of the tension around them the American couple and the Other Guest chatter about politics and related affairs . . .

— So. What do you think?

Stirred, physically nudged by Other Guest, Alex lifts his eyes from his wineglass and sees he is being directly questioned by the American guy, David. Alex knows he cannot hide any more.

As noises of Tony swearing come from the kitchen Alex replies, drunk, slurring:
— Sorry? What were you talking about?

Unfazed by the rudeness, too eager to talk, David the Jewish-American publisher repeats
— We were just wondering, you're a journalist, whether you see any difference between US papers and English ones

And that is enough. Minded, now, that he is not going to avoid conversation: Alex decides the best option is to go into rant-mode. So he starts to talk about politics, and Eurofederalism. *Anything to take his mind off*. Barely allowing the American couple, let alone Other Guest, a word in: Alex says he sees a lot of differences between US culture and British culture nevertheless he would rather be overtaken by US culture than submerged by Euroculture. Apropos of very little that has been discussed before, and with a leer at David's wife, Alex slugs more wine and says that he thinks England faces a future between joining America or joining Europe, and that the choice, as he sees it, is like that faced by an old woman: whether to move in with the kids, i.e. America, or be forced into an old people's home, i.e. Europe, an old people's home smelling of wee and cold sick and full of dribbling old gits angrily waving sticks at each other. And I know which one I'd choose, says Alex.

This trope, although a conversational non sequitur, goes down well and sets off a debate which makes headway towards diverting Alex's attention from the fact that Tony and Eddie and Elizabeth have still not appeared in the dining room. The American talks about the euro, about the dollar, his wife talks about the differences between Europe and the States as evinced by the differences in publishing mores; bored of this debate now Alex knocks back another glass of whatever and turns to race. Bluntly interrupting Other Guest before she can speak Alex starts on blacks, he starts talking about how he pities them yet how he resents them for causing him to pity them, how they are probably less intelligent than whites, as affirmed by the Bell Curve, but how this should be seen as an argument for miscegenation rather than discrimination. Affronted, as Alex intended, by the racism of this, the Jewish-American publisher loudly retorts that Alex is obviously a man insecure in his own place, probably a lower-class provincial if not a working-class outsider, just like most nationalist bigots, like Hitler, like Mao, like Stalin. Instead of acknowledging how effectively this skewers him Alex makes a who-gives-a-fuck shrug and goes straight for the guy's jugular: his Jewishness: lips black with Shiraz-tannin Alex states that what he really hates about Jewish liberalism, about soft Left PC liberals, about guys like David, is their support for affirmative action.

— I mean – Belches Alex – What was the fucking Holocaust but affirmative action for Germans? The Jews had all the jobs and all the cash because they were cleverer and harder working so Hitler started affirmative action for Germans, by killing all the Jews, so as to guarantee the Germans got their fair share

The American is balling his napkin angrily but Alex goes on

— Course Hitler was a homicidal git but it doesn't detract from the argument, still shows how fucking stupid affirmative action is, just like all that women-only shortlist bollocks in the Labour Party why don't they have fucking special shortlists in the Labour Party for stupid people, why don't they have quotas for spastics or morons or anti-social bastards or people who aren't very clever at all oh yes sorry they have haven't they they've got **women only shortlists**

— *Take your hands off my wife*

Setting his glass on the already wine-stained tablecloth Alex flattens his fingers either side of the glass-stem and gazes quietly into the rubescence of the wine as he listens to the noise of an argument in the hall. It sounds like Tony is confronting Eddie. It sounds like Eddie is arguing back: Eddie's voice is shocked, angry, confused. Tony rants. Says something about the love that dare not speak its surname.

Alex winces: *my line. I meant his mother. You stupid Irish twat.*

More shouts. American couple and Other Guest are exchanging uncomfortable glances. Alex sits back and regards his wine. Tony is still shouting in the hall; Alex hears a scuffle. Something knocked over.

Then Elizabeth screams. In the dining room Other Guest and American Couple pick up their jackets and head out the door. Alex hears them try to say something calming in the hall: this merely seems to provoke another drunken shout from Tony. All the time Alex stays, statue-like, in his chair, gazing at the now-deserted table. The front door slams once and twice as the guests presumably flee for the street and then Alex raises his head at the noise of Elizabeth screaming abuse at Tony and rushing upstairs.

For the kids?

Another indefinable breaking noise. Finally Alex half rises: his adrenalin obliging him to do something, anything. Alex doesn't want to see, to know: but these are his friends and he is obliged. At last getting out of his chair Alex pushes open the door to find Tony standing in the hall with his Sabatier knife in his hand. Tony's face is puckered, mad, nearly crying. Across the hall Eddie is staring at the knife in Tony's hand. Alex stares at Eddie. Eddie does an angry shrug. Alex says

— Jesus, what do you look like

— Alex

— You stupid *cunt,* Rafferty

Tony is now pointing at Alex

— He says it was *you*

— *What?*

— With Elizabeth

Now Alex is looking incredulously at Eddie who is still looking at Tony's knife. Tony:

— He says that's why Katy left you

— *What??*

— What the?
— Why did she leave you, Alex? Why?
— Tone. It wasn't fucking me
— So it – Tony looks desperate, confused, tears on his fat cheek
– So it was Eddie, with Eliza . . .
— It wasn't fucking *anybody*, Tone

Tony looks like he is about to collapse.

Eddie exhales, vehemently:

— I'm getting out of here

Eddie turns. He turns to the door and pulls it open to the cold night air. He departs. Alex looks at Tony and says again:

— You stupid arse
— But . . .
— He's right on the edge as it is you idiot

And then Alex turns too, and goes to the open door and disappears into the rain. For half a minute Tony stands there, knife still half-heartedly upraised in hand. Then his wife comes down the stairs with two weeping infants and his wife does not even look at him as she too goes to the door and opens the door and departs into the silvery drizzle.

And then Tony just looks from where his wife was to where his brother-in-law was to where his best friend was. Then he drops the knife on a phone book, goes into the dining room, and starts clearing plates away.

32

winter crack

The silver Romer epergne; the crespell silver achett; drinking sack from the Bettiscombe skull and shooting dabchicks by the lake and wolfhounds snoring in the Hall and serving girls practising the Versailles curtsey and

And sitting on the Tube.

Eddie sits distractedly on the Tube, heading home. The armpit-prickles of his adrenalin rush are taking time to subside; the scenario of the scuffle with Tony is still replaying. What did he do? *Elizabeth's face. Lancaster roses. Crixies.* What should he do now? *His sister's beautiful face; so like his mother's . . .*

Sitting on the Central Line heading east Eddie looks out into the blackness. He hears the rattly, sooty, Londony sound of the Tube. Feels the sooty, ammoniac, warm, acrid, Londony smell of the Tube. How comforting it is: anonymous, nostalgic, amniotic, opiating . . .

His face reflected, Eddie tries to see the platform of Museum Tube. *The lost Tube station? Isn't that here?* Perhaps he should get out here. Where should he get out . . . ?

Sat on the Tube, Eddie wonders. Wonders how long he's been on the Tube. Sometimes, Eddie thinks, sometimes it feels like he's been on the Tube all his life. Like he's been riding the Tube all his life; like he's been riding the Tube so long he's started to think the Tube is all there is, all there is is crowds, boredom, grime, rats, mice, dirt, tedium, but what should happen if he should finally get off? Finally find the Way Out sign? What would happen? What if he should step from the carriage and ride the escalator, what if he should ticket the gates and climb the stairs what should he find? What would he see? Would he emerge into the dazzling cold beauty of the City at night, see the splendour that was always there, always above him: the glory, the floodlit condominiums, the financial cathedrals, the soaring blue and silver skyscrapers?

Stepped from the carriage, Eddie changes at Holborn, takes the Piccadilly Line; north.

— Hello, hello?

Nothing. Sat in his car, Alex checks the mobile read-out to ascertain that he's through. He's through. But

— Hello? Is there some?

Nothing. Again.

— . . . I know it's late bu

Finally

— Yes hello. Who is that?

It is *Katy's mother. Katy's mother*. This is not what Alex wanted. What can he do? Apologise for ringing so late? Apologise for the last twelve months? Apologise for getting Katy to bleach his toilet in a netball skirt?

— It's me. Mrs Jarrett

— Who?

— Alex

A second silence; Alex

— Yes, it's Alex, Katy's

— You

— Yes . . . I just wan

Before he can explain Mrs Jarrett interjects. With force. Mrs Jarrett's rant is so loud Alex is able to drop the mobile on his lap so as to light a cigarette and still get a pretty good picture of his failings, inadequacies, deficiencies, perversities, and felonies.
— OK, Mrs Jarrett – At last, Alex gets a word in; what word? – Look Mrs J . . . I'm sorry and all that and I'll get off the phone but all I want to know is is Katy there?

Breathing. Over the phone Alex can hear Mrs Jarrett's slightly asthmatic respiration, that and a TV in the background. In his head Alex fondly pictures Katy stood behind her mother reaching imploringly for the receiver wanting to speak to him, to *Alex*, her lover, her truelove, after all this time, after all this time Alex can see Katy wanting to speak to him because she *still* loves him and it's going to be *all right*, it's *going* to be all right.
— I'm afraid she's not here
— Oh . . . – Alex pauses – OK . . . Is she due home soon?
— I don't think you understand. We haven't seen her for weeks

Heartbeat. *Heartbeat.*
— Sorry?
— She left sixth-form college about a month ago. She ran away

She. *She*
— *She ran away?*
— Yes. We haven't seen her for weeks, not since . . . – Alex is starting to taste panic; Mrs Jarret's voice is going flatter – We simply don't know where she is. She's run away with some . . . barman. Are you satisfied now? Satisfied with what you've done to us?

Clack.

Katy's mother has slammed the phone down: so hard she's missed the cradle. Alex can hear her swearing and fumbling for the receiver as she swings it up and drops it again with a second, quieter *click.*

His hands hanging on the bottom of the steering wheel, Alex gazes ahead of him. Rain drumming impatiently on the car roof.

Run away?

Too late Alex realises he hasn't figured on this. He hasn't factored this in, emotionally. All the time he's been sort of expecting that if he left it long enough Katy'd start missing Alex even more than he missed her and she'd get bored of this boring kid, this barman, and when Alex finally deigned to ring she'd be totally overjoyed and

Gone. We don't know where. Barman.

Anyway winding down the window for some air Alex leans out of the window and blinks into the spattering night rain and gazes up at the dark grey blinds of Eddie's Smithfield flat. Where is Eddie? He evidently hasn't been home since fleeing Tony's dinner party. Where is Eddie? Where is everybody?

Squatted on the filthy floor of Dee's flat Eddie looks about him at the stuff, bits, gobbets, blobs, gubbins, wotsits, the repulsive chunks of yuk, and the endless copies of the *Daily Star* half-heartedly wrapped around dreck. Eddie wonders if he dare sit down, properly. On *that*? He feels if he so much as touches a surface, any surface, it will be tacky and brown stuff will get on his hands and he will contract typhoid.

But so what if he does?

Letting himself descend the last few inches to the carpet Eddie stretches out and gazes across at Dee, who is sitting on the edge of her bed, her thin cream legs sticking out from her extremely off-white pyjamas, her holed socks the colour of Hoover dust, her limp hair lank. With a tiny set of scales centred on her lap Dee is scrutinising her dusty pile of heroin with an obsessive, Dickensian, fingerless-glove-ish-ness.

— So, Dee – Eddie bleats, wound up by the time-she-is-taking – You can *definitely* do me a half-gee?

Pretending not to hear.

— Dee, you *can* do me a half, right?

Still pretending not to hear.
— Dee, DEE, *DEE*??

Slow as a lizard Dee turns and looks at Eddie with her pickled, preserved, kippered, leathery, eight-centuries-in-the-peatbog-of-smack-addiction face. Without saying anything Dee gives Eddie a glance that says shut the fuck up *or*.

Eddie shuts the fuck up. He knows too well he has no choice: if he continues to pester Dee, the longer she'll take to sort him. But . . . *Christ*. To distract himself Eddie reaches across the variously burnt carpet and picks up a clear plastic egg that looks like the clear kind of plastic eggs that come in a Kinder surprise chocolate egg; soon as he's done so he regrets: the small clear plastic egg is *slimy*.

Dee has noticed Eddie disgustedly dropping the egg. She cackles, takes a break from her smack-weighing
— Wouldn touch that
— Sorry?
— That's where I keep the gear
— You mean – Eddie shudders – When you pick it up you put it in your mouth so the police don't . . . ?
— Nah – Dee cackles, returning her attention to her scales – Not in my mouth

Oh. Christ. The bile rises, Eddie feels as if: he shudders and shivers and his flesh goes clammy. *JesusGodhelp*. What is he doing? What has he done? Where is he going? What has he said? *Tony?*

The table polished, the walls wiped, the bins overfull, the dishwasher buzzing and humming, Tony searches the house for more things to do, more things to take his mind off

He sits in an armchair in the sitting room and despite the fact that it is 3 a.m. he flicks casually through a property freesheet. Perhaps they should trade-up, him and Elizabeth. Him and . . .

Don't

Perhaps they should buy somewhere a little bigger, for the children

The children. *The children.*

Pained, agonised, Tony sees the children: as they were: small in the hall, Toby clutching eyeless teddy bears and asking yawny-weepy questions as Elizabeth fitted him and Polly into C&A raincoats and carrycots, bustling them into the Astra.

Elizabeth?

Eddie is trying to get stoned. Trying very hard. But every time Eddie takes a toke nothing happens; he chases, he pursues, he follows endless serpentine trails of treacly heroin around vast acres of silver Alcan and he feels exactly the same, only worse. He is on Naltrexone, he knows there is an inhibitor at work, but *surely*, he didn't *really*, and anyway he took the last pill over twenty four hours ago. *Right?*

What he needs is more, *more*.

— Dee, could you do me another bag?

For the first time in Eddie's experience, Dee demurs. From her vantage point on the bed where she is burning her lips black on a crack-pipe, Dee looks over, at Eddie, and says

— Yer sure? You've already done a load, Ed

— No. Yes – Eddie snaps – I'm fine, it's just . . . I've got a . . . *tolerance*

— OK . . . – Pipe set down, rocks safely wrapped, Dee unsquats and stretches for the little plastic bag that contains lots of very much smaller plastic bags – How muchya wan then?

It is three or four or five in Putney. Tony knows it is the hour because he has turned the television on and it is the news: yesterday's news.

What makes this old news interesting to Tony, what makes Tony lean forward, is that it is from *Lyonshall*. From the road protest. A naff local TV News reporter is standing in a swampy clearing in a wood, quizzing a well-spoken dreadlocked eyebrow-pierced road protestor about how they are intending to camp through the winter, and through the summer and the next winter and the next summer if necessary. The road protestor talks straight to camera; to Tony. Tony looks semi-interestedly back, trying to recognise the clump of trees behind the interviewer/ee. *Pickering Lyth? M'Ladies Wood? Carcanets? Rumfustian? Pippin tarts? Panjotheram? Arzy-garzies? Dover House Chutney? Harvest cakes on sycamore leaves? The nuttery where the cowslips bloom in Spring? An old timber-jim standing in a field? A lovely cottage with a palfrey in its pightle?*

— Ed

Eddie can't hear properly; he wonders, vaguely: why is Dee slapping him?

— Eddie

— Dee . . . plee . . .

Dee . . . ?

— Eddie for Christ's sake wake up yer

— Mmmm

— Eddie, Eddie, God I bloody knew it

— Call a cab, Mum, we don't want the warlords all over the drum

— Eddie

— Eddie

Eddie nods, he nods twice, his eyes shut, he thinks

Perhaps if I fall asleep she'll stop

— Eddie!

Reaching for the phone Tony dials Eddie's number. His flat in Smithfield. It rings. The phone rings and rings and rings, rings, rings, rings and rings

No answer.

The phone rings

No answer.

Tony keeps ringing all the same. Looks out the window at the rain as he cradles the phone on his shoulder. Tony looks at the rain, the rain. The rain that feeds the wheat that grows to feed mankind that he may sing the praise of God.

Tony puts the phone down. Looks out the window. The rain.

In Tufnell Park Eddie sits, trying to smoke more. His eyes are shut, at least he thinks they are shut, he still can't much hear, he can hear Dee saying something, can hear somebody shouting his name down a long long tunnel, full of mice, a long Tube tunnel full of little mice, those Tube mice what do they live on Eddie wonders? Down here, in the Tube? The Tube. A Tube in his mouth. The Tube. How he always loved the Tube. The rattling Londony sound of the Tube. Down here. Down there?

Down here?

Eddie feels his ears going blind, his sense of smell going deaf, it is nice and dark

But

But he wishes they'd stop shouting for him. Shouting down the emergency stairwellllllll

Sto

Stopped

But, but, bu

Like Wilde, [Beau] Brummell pleased himself by giving unexpected answers to commonplace questions. Asked his favourite vegetable, he professed disapproval of that unassuming article, while denying that he had ever eaten any. 'No, that is not quite correct: I once ate a pea.'

Peter Vansittart, *In Memory of England*

Passing over the hills one winter's day, when the Downs looked all alike, being covered with snow, I came across a 'gip' family sitting on the ground in a lane exposed to the blast. In that there was nothing remarkable, but I recollect it because the young mother, handsome in the style of her race, had her neck and brown bust quite bare, and the white snowflakes drove thickly aslant upon her.

Richard Jefferies, *The Amateur Poacher*

33

mutton rose

The funeral day is inaptly sunny; January with a lying hint of Spring. Parking his car at the distant end of a country lane full of other parked cars Alex joins a procession of people he doesn't recognise: the men in naff black woolly ties, the women in dowdy black dresses: all of them traipsing down the country lane like a misplaced busload of Stoke Newington Jews. In his own conspicuously superior suit, in his tastefully understated Milanese tie, Alex can't help, in comparison, feeling a puff of sartorial vanity. *Not here,* he thinks. *Please.*

Onwards they all walk, past the little shop where he and Eddie and Elizabeth and Tony would buy drinks, past the path that leads off to the Park, on into Lyonshall village.

Lyonshall. Lyonshall. *Lyonshall.* Alex stifles the memories that come unbidden with the name, the sights, the place, the memories that might flashflood his psyche, carrying all before . . .

Elizabeth?

Elizabeth Lyonshall is standing, head turned, at the end of the lane where it forks. Stood a few yards from the Lyonshall daughter, Alex remembers despite himself, the last time he saw her here, between the pub and the church. Bright and ten years younger and carrying something significant, he had hopped happily off the bus and walked around the corner and come across Elizabeth and her brother. In a car. Sort of . . . holding each other. Sort of . . . embracing . . . *Or was it?*

He never knew then; he doesn't know now. Befuddled, still, after all this time, Alex murmurs

— Elizabeth?

At Alex's words Elizabeth turns and looks at him and looks as if she only just recognises him.

— Elizabeth. I'm so sorry

She gives him the winter sunshine of her hair, the wasteland shore of her smile. She says

— Go away Alex

On a low black heel she turns and Alex is left. Alone. Alone with the unwanted truth: with the burden of guilt he so wants Elizabeth to lift from his blue-suited shoulders. But she is gone, gone on.

To allay, to distract, Alex surveys the rest of the black-tied mourners still walking past him, walking whisperingly, churchwards. Alex notices there is a weird feeling about this gathering, a weird atmosphere: the presence of so many young or youngish people gives the crowd an almost-gaiety which everybody is trying to suppress. Like they are attending a shameful-but-exciting wedding, the wedding of youth and death.

Up the damp churchyard path under the Norman tympanum into Lyonshall church they go. Not recognising anybody, any of the old school friends or distant cousins or military-looking uncles, Alex ushers himself into the church-smelling church. Inside, an organ is humming, a cleric bustling. Seating himself alone in the pew nearest the door Alex scans the scene: checks out the vicar, his helpers, the trendy cassocks, the hideous tablecloth on the altar, and as he does he feels strangely but strongly let-down: it is all so middle class, middle brow, so middling, mediocre . . .

— Alex

It is Tony. Puffed, damply bald, badly suited, incredibly welcome, Tony puffs some more:

— Sorry. Bit late – Flicking his red hair back – Had trouble leaving the kids . . .

Remarkably, Tony has sat himself down right next to Alex: as if this is normal, as if they are at a concert, or the theatre, as if this is not a funeral, as if the last time they met Alex was not accused of cuckolding Tony, as if the last time they met Eddie did not run off and kill himself. Not knowing what else to say, Alex says:

— How are you?

Tony puffs

— Not so bad. Not so bad . . .

— I saw Elizabeth. I tried to speak to her, but . . .

Skimming the order of service pamphlet Tony shrugs again.

— She's very upset . . .

— But she, d'you think . . .

— Oh – Tony exhales – I wouldn't be so sure

The two of them fall silent. Alex has the feeling their friendship will survive, survive it all: *perhaps*.

The service drones into life. A vicar whines. Alex wonders where vicars get that special nasal C of E voice. *The creeping jesus*. Next comes a choir, then a weedy singalong from the congregation, then Eddie's father strides up to the lectern. Alert now Alex lifts his eyes and studies Eddie's father: his red socks, his vulgar winter tan, his double-breasted suit. At once Alex feels he knows this man: the kind of Englishman who thinks humour and wit are a matter of talking too loudly, and wearing red socks. Poised at the lectern, Eddie's father looks to his Spanish wife, Eddie's tarty-looking stepmother, who has situated herself in the middle of the front pew. From eight pews back Alex can smell Eddie's stepmother's perfume.

Eddie's father talks, Eddie's father asserts, Eddie's father concludes his drear, unconvincing, inapposite eulogy. Alex subsides. The vicar returns: they kneel and pray. Alex brings his fingertips together and stares down at the Norman flagstones, and remembers, again, the time he came here. The time he came to the village for the last time, when he stepped off the bus and walked to the pub, to the Love Pool, carrying a pocketful of something, of nothing, for Eddie, for Eddie, for his best friend . . .

Up and out of the church they parade. Eddie's coffin is being borne out of the church to a corner of the churchyard, to the corner of the churchyard where they find the just-dug grave. The pityhole.

At the sight of the soily grave, someone stumbles, someone weeps. Eddie's father puts his arm around his daughter; Tony helps five others to carry the coffin through the crowd. Stood at the edge of things, Alex observes as the box that contains Eddie is clumsily lowered, to the grass, thence into the new trench dug alongside Eddie's mother's grave. Once Eddie's coffin is below ground people come forward and throw sprigs of something – box? – onto the lid. Adrift, unanchored, Alex wants to be one of the ones to throw the sprigs of whatever it is onto the coffin-lid, but no-one asks, no-one has asked.

The pale winter sunshine is reddening the trees across the churchyard: otherwise: black trees, white faces, black clothes, white sky. Whiter than most, Elizabeth moves forward past her mother's gravestone and throws a single green sprig onto the coffin.

The vicar intones.

Wind in the poplars.

Rooks.

In near silence the troupes of mourners move from the churchyard along the frosty village road to the Love Pool, the pub. Alex follows a middle-aged lady and her husband as they push the door and go into the pub. The pub where they used to trip; the pub where they used to take mushrooms and play pool and get drunk and.

Inside the saloon bar of the pub there are rows of tables, decked with tureens of soup, plates of bread rolls, bottles of beer and wine.

As if they have been starved for a month the mourners set to: they eat, drink, talk. To Alex, however, the talk is painfully meaningless: mild chat about the weather, whispered gossip about the shame of drugs, considered whingeing about the nearby road protest. No-one will talk to Alex about the thing that matters – That is: Alex's guilt – and Alex can't cope with talking to anyone, even Tony, because of all the guilt he feels. Eager to fuddle his thoughts and fuel his sociability Alex glugs the cheap nasty wine but it does not help; hungrily he spoons the warm tinned soup; it warms only his stomach.

All the time, between weather and drugshame and nearby-roadprotest, Alex shoots looks across the pub at Elizabeth; looks that seek forgiveness; that seek a signal, a hint, a word, a glance. Nothing doing. Nothing. What makes this all the worse for Alex is that as he gazes he can't but help admitting that his gaze is, still, sharpened by desire. He just can't help. Elizabeth looks fine: slim, well-bred, sombrely nubile in her clinging black dress. In her black tights. Or are they stockings? And what about her poor bereaved arse? And her tragedy-struck snatch? And her sad brotherless grief-stricken alone-in-the-world tits?

Alex winces at himself. *No*. Soup dumped, spoon dropped, Alex quits the bar and his unwonted thoughts, and opens the pub door to the cold outside world. Pensive, frowning, he paces the frosty road, the black tarmac broderie anglaised with rime. His footfalls scrunch in the midwinter silence and he listens to the near silence as he walks. Wind. Trees. Redwings? Rooks. Given the cold freshening wind Alex is grateful to up-handle the door and get in his car and drive away. Left, left, right; he remembers. Londonbound he remembers a traffic jam he suffered on the way down, and decides to take a different route home: veering left Alex third-gears a couple of country miles and suddenly he is brought up short. Everywhere: stuck traffic. Pick-up trucks carrying muddy-booted men. Other men in yellow hard hats. Big black cars knee deep in mud. Pissed-off looking policemen in wellingtons.

The road protest. What else?

Interest aroused, *professional* interest, Alex parks badly and climbs out the car and walks up to a policeman and asks him if he can get past the cordon to have a look at the site: of the road protest.

The policeman looks down at Alex in his elegant blue suit and Italian tie. Says

— What are you?

— I'm a journalist

— Have you got accreditation?

— Well . . . no . . . I was just . . . passing

— Sorry, you need accreditation

— Oh go on, what's the hassle, I only

— No

— But

— No. I said no. Which part of that word isn't totally clear?

— Fine – Alex makes a sarcastically grateful gesture – Thank you so much

Walking back up the road, conscious of the policeman's eyes on him, Alex gets to his car and makes as if to get in but then, seized with rebelliousness engendered by the policeman's attitude, Alex ducks right and jumps a farm gate and starts scrunching his way across the hard-frosted field, the furrows of icy mud. Scrunches. Walks. Tops the field. Comes slap bang into an angry farmer, a farmer with a face as red as his rugby shirt.

Oh, *forchri*

The farmer, presumably disenchanted by the country's media and the nation's hippies trespassing his property for the last six months, makes no effort to be polite. Unselfconscious of the cliché, he steps right up to Alex and blurts

— Get orf my land

Momentarily: Alex halts. But only for a moment. Alex feels he has had too much today; more than enough. Half a foot from the farmer's weatherbeaten face Alex says

— This isn't *your* land. This is *Eng*land

And with that Alex just walks around the farmer and carries on up over the top of the hill and strides the side of a field of winter wheat; then he leaps a second gate and walks down a lane that opens out onto a view of the road protest. Two miles in the distance is a huge great milk-chocolate brown gash in the rolling green landscape: a half built new motorway buzzing with JCBs, workmen, concrete mixers, lorries full of landfill. One mile away is a buffer-zone of police, bailiffs and men-with-wire-cutters, sharing the swamp with more police cars and council Land Rovers. Half a mile nearer is the road protest camp itself: a sad, Third World hamlet of tents, tarps, and the odd rickety tree house. The tree houses are linked by dodgy rope walkways. The tents are decked with pennants and bedraggled banners. In the middle of the tented settlement a miserable looking wood fire is sending defeated Red Indian signals into the dank winter air.

Alex tries. At the crest of the hill, chilled by the hilltop wind, he tries to make some sense of the scene: some sense he can turn into an article maybe, a proper serious article, an article in a broadsheet newspaper, perhaps; an article not necessarily about Britain's Bounciest Tits or Why Men Like Burping. Alex tries. He thinks of the allegory: of the way they are raping his country with this motorway, striping her. He considers the scene, the countryside, the scarred green heart of England: God's first-born, the Israel of Liberty, the Holy Island of Democracy –

But fuck it. What of it? What, frankly, the fuck of it? How can he possibly relate all of what he feels, all his confused feelings of self, of disappearing selfness, of compromised identity, to this: a mere road protest? A bunch of eco-yippies? Standing here, on this chilled and windy hilltop, Alex is downcast and defeated by the very incoherence, the very complexity, the pure intractable bombast of his thoughts. All he knows is that those idiots down there, those wet, pathetic hippies, those tented dongas of the road protest have not a hope in heaven of stopping that unstoppable thing: the motorway: those grinding lorries, those wailing mixers, those gear-shrieking JCBs, that First World War army of sappers, diggers and explosives experts coming so inexorably and wickedly their way.

Alex turns, internally shrugging. He walks back down the way he came: towards his car. As he turns he does not see first one wet hippy, then another, emerge tentatively from their tents. Alex is not there, Alex has gone home, Alex does not see. He is not there to see as the two hippies unfurl another home-made banner, another damp white cotton sheet which they stretch and pin between two leafless saplings.

In scrawled red paint and dodgy majuscules, the banner says SAVE ENGLAND FROM THE ENGLISH

Seventeen Months Later

34

lily of the valley

— Tony
— Alex

They sit down simultaneously. They pick up the menus; they sip their just-collected pints: Tony's Guinness, Alex's Pedigree.

They are in an Islington pub which does decent food and very good beer: just as Alex phrased it over the phone. Scanning the menu Tony is pleased to see that gravy is called gravy and not *jus*. As he gets older, he notices he notices these things more; he mentions it approvingly to Alex but Alex makes a couldn't-care-less gesture: which is slightly deceptive: one of the few things Alex still cares about is food. And beer.

Awkward, at first; they soon slide into a kind-of groove. Tony asks Alex about Janine, his girlfriend of six months. Tony chooses not to ask why he has never met her, instead asks

— So what's she got that the others didn't?

Wet-mouthed by the beer, Alex muses, drinks, says

— Decent wombats

— Nice breasts?

— Yeah
— That's it?
— And cool ankles
— And
— And she's got . . .
Tony guesses:
— A marvellous honeybadger? Wicked marmosets?
— Money
— Ah
— You know – Taking another slug of pint, Alex grins, ruefully – That's the one useful thing my dad taught me
— What, marry a girl with nice ankles?
— Nah. Marry cash. At's what he said. 'Marry money, son. Because you're no gonna earn any o' your own yer useless gobshite'

The impression is good enough; Tony laughs affably and lets Alex continue
— Drunken old bastard
— Perhaps . . . – Handing a stray lock of red hair back into place Tony starts to say something about Alex being too cynical; Alex ignores this, starts rhapsodising about the joys of first-class flights and first round Wimbledon tickets; Tony is silent for a bit but then unable to keep silent, after all this time, all these months of meetings and drinkings he wants to ask the question he has not dared to ask for a long time
— I've always wondered . . . Alex . . . how . . .
— How's me woodlow?
— No
— So?
— Er . . . Katy
— *Katy* . . .
— Yeah . . .
— Why should you want to know about . . . Katy?

— Well, I've always meant to ask, I know she buggered off but . . . you never really talked about it
— *Surprising*
Tony checks Alex's contemptuous expression, changes tack
— Alex I . . . don't want to drag up anything, I . . . just . . .
— Spit it out
— I . . . just
Alex:
— Did I mention my new job?
Tony gets the courage:
— What I'm trying to say is, you were very in love with her, right? And she just walked out on you. So: have you just forgotten about her completely or what?
— Steady
— Well I'm curious . . . – Tony thinks about telling Alex what he knows; decides *not yet, not yet* – What do you think now? After all this time?
Alex raises a hand. Seated on the pub banquette Alex looks at Tony and wonders whether to tell Tony what he really thinks. About what it's really been like, the last seventeen months. About how on the Tube sometimes he thinks about something funny and he looks at all the glum rush hour faces and Katy's isn't amongst them and then he feels ill. Should he tell Tony that? Perhaps, but maybe he should tell Tony about the time Katy wasn't in the back of a taxi that pulled up beside his car in Piccadilly one rainy Spring morning and he nearly crashed or maybe he should tell Tony about the time she wasn't in the group of backpackers he saw from a bus while on holiday in Burma the next Summer and he couldn't sleep properly for a week. Sitting in this packed, smoky, convivial Islington pub Alex drinks and drinks and says
— Nah, don't really think about her that much
— Really
— Really

They sit there. They sit and talk about cricket, football, architecture, Tony's vague Labour tendencies, tits. They talk about an old drug story. They listen to songs on the jukebox that neither of them selected, that neither of them recognise. Then Alex says

— How's the job anyway?

Now it's Tony's turn to procrastinate, to vacillate, to consider lying. Tony watches Alex lean back to accept his plate of food, a puddle of red Thai curry in a snowheap of fragrant rice; gazing hungrily and enviously at Alex's order Tony says

— It's OK

— Truly

— Sure . . .

— But – Alex seems to be wondering whether to be a bastard – You're still doing the same thing, man

— Yes, so . . .

— So you've given up all ambition, like, totally? – Alex chews food and coughs and says – So that's it, is it? You're just going to listen to Radio Four and watch gardening programmes and just fucking accept middle age and that's it? Finito?

Alex's words are being mumbled through lemongrass flavours and clods of rice, and then a napkin he uses to wipe the curryjuice from his chin. Tony takes the time to consider what to admit, how much to admit. Some of Tony feels like admitting it all: the appalling truth. How he actually likes middle age, how he welcomes the menopause of youth, the mysterious climacteric of the early thirties, as a kind of manumission from the indignities of staying young. As emancipation from the need to pretend to enjoy disagreeable nightclubs, from the obligation of having to try and experiment unsuccessfully with unpleasant drugs.

Leaning back to let the Thai bargirl plonk a plate of his own food, Tony looks at Alex looking at him, waiting for a reply. What *should* he say? Should he admit how he actually likes shocking his desperate-to-stay-young contemporaries with his honestly expanding waistline and unabashed penchant for gardening? Should he tell Alex how he likes hanging out in the flannelette pyjama department of Marks & Spencer, like a nervous but proud first-time skinhead in a speedmetalbar?

Most of all, Tony frets about whether he should confess the true beauty of middle age as he sees it: the chance to accept he no longer has ambition: the chance to jettison all that baggage of duty and responsibility – the duty to succeed; the responsibility of having a decent brain and a good degree . . . Should he tell Alex all of that?

Eating his first forkful of Thai curry Tony says

— Maybe

— Maybe?

— Maybe

The conversation is about to dwindle into not-getting-on: into Alex eating, and Tony eating, and both of them not saying what they think, and both of them questioning why they still bother meeting after all this time. Then Tony's other dish of *pad thai* arrives and he starts concentrating on his food: the taste of excellent food lends Tony renewed vigour: and so he starts telling Alex about the children. As the good friend he still is Alex makes a fist of being interested, and they chat about the kids, and kids, for a while. Then Alex asks about the wife, a sensitive subject which, as the friends they are, they both expertly touch on without properly discussing. Tony mentions how Elizabeth's and his love life is now much better, how they are making love unassisted, unViagra'd, sans obscure injections. Lastly, Tony remembers

— You got a new job?

Alex rolls his eyes, wets his mouth

— Yeah. Porn mag

— Porn?

— I'm the political editor
— *Political editor?*
— Yyyeah – Alex shrugs – They're trying to take it up-market, take it off the top shelf
— Are you absolutely sure that's a good move? – Tony makes a genuinely concerned face – It might not do much good for your literary reputation

Alex does a terminal laugh
— Literary reputation, ha
— Serious

Alex stops laughing
— I did think about writing under a pseudonym, but what the hell, who cares . . .
— You do
— Do I? Do I?

Another pause. A pause while Alex self-analyses. Alex is contemplating whether to go into all his thought processes of the last year. Alex eats, napkins, drinks, burps, napkins . . .

No, Alex decides, he doesn't care to tell Tony any of this, because he doesn't really care about any of this.

So Alex says nothing. Instead they sit there; they drink; they eat their meal; they wipe their lips and talk about bras and sit back and drink another pint. The evening drifts by and it looks like neither of them is actually going to say anything of real significance so Alex says
— Had a weird dream last night

Tony chuckles
— *You* had a dream
— Yep
— Go on then

His curry nearly done Alex napkins his mouth; sluices a bit of pint: says
— I had this squirrel, this pet squirrel, I really loved this dinky little pet squirrel

Behind his pint Tony makes a nodding, I-can-interpret-this-face; Alex goes on

— But I lost it. The fucking thing ran up a tree and I couldn't coax it down

Tony waits. And waits. Alex drinks. Tony waits. Tony says

— And that's it?

Mouthful of cool beer, Alex nods; Tony shakes his head

— That's the single most boring dream I've ever heard

— I know, man – Alex laughs, dryly – I know

They drink on; they talk about girls' arses; they talk about restaurants. Tony asks Alex if he is going to marry this girl, Janine; Alex nips to the lavatory then comes back and says *maybe*. Tony

— But you don't love her

— I know

Slightly fake horror from Tony

— But you can't do that to the poor girl. Not if you don't love her . . .

— Can't I? – Alex eyes his old friend, says – I feel like the last man left on the *Titanic*, Tony. Like everyone else has died, drowned. It's lonely. I want to be miserable and married like the rest of you

— But me and Elizabeth . . .

— Yes yes you're OK you rub along, I know, well that's what I want – Alex is making a loud point, emphasised by a vigorous nod of the head – I don't care any more. I want the fucking boredom, the rubbing along, the oh-it's-OK, the crap sex, the kids, the horror, the tedious dinner parties, the trips to Glyndebourne, the Sloaney wife with thick ankles, the conversations about pelmets

— I thought you said she had nice ankles

— You know what I mean. I want to use the word pelmet without laughing. I want to give up. Love is just bollocks anyway

They are both silent. From the end of the pub comes the clack of poolballs; pop muzak; other conversations. Fat, bald, married, mortgaged, Tony looks at his friend and says

— Are you happy, Alex?

Alex clicks his tongue. Gives Tony a sharp, almost hostile glance.

Undeterred, Tony takes a deep breath and looks straight at his oldest friend, and decides that yes, after all, this *is* the right time and place.

Pause. Tony says

— Did you see the stuff about the road protest?

Finishing his pint Alex thinks he's mis-heard

— The come again?

— The road protest. Near Lyonshall

— Kidding me – Alex picks up his empty pint glass, weighs it – They're still at it down there? That was, like, *years* ago . . . wasn't it?

Tony shakes his head

— You didn't see the News then

Alex shrugs:

— Don't watch much News these days . . .

Tony pushes his own empty glass towards Alex, says

— Well. You should. Because they . . . they won

Alex takes Tony's empty glass, weighs that one too

— What do you mean they *won*?

— I mean they've won, some court order, it looks like they're going to stop building the road, and go for a tunnel. After all this time, it's quite a victory, considering . . .

— Well, good for them – Alex makes like he doesn't care about this either, he makes like he is going to the bar by saying

— 'nother Guinness?

But before he can completely leave his chair Tony says, firmly, urgently

— I think I saw Katy, on the news, at the road protest

Pub noise, pub jokes, pub laughter. Alex's face trying not to express anything.
— Who?
— Katy?
— *What?*
— I saw Katy
— Katy? My Katy? *Katy Jarrett?*
— Katy Jarrett – Tony smiles – That was her name, right?
— But you've . . . only seen her from a distance . . .
Tony says, factually
— How many Katy Jarretts can there be?
— Bu
— Anyway I recognised her
— *But*
— I'm convinced it was her. About twenty years old? Unusual looks? Mixed race? *Very pretty?*

Alex is sat back in his chair, breathing hard, breathing very hard, looking urgently into Tony's eyes, as Tony explains
— They were interviewing all these people about their victory, over the Department of Transport, or whoever it was, and one of them gave her name as Katy Jarrett. I'm sure . . . I know it was Katy. Your ex. Your – Tony smiles, again – Your little love squirrel

Pub noise. Pub smoke. Pub smells. Disturbed, confused, angry, at a loss, Alex sits in his chair and shakes his head. Then he whistles and sighs, and laughs for some reason he does not quite understand; then he tilts his head to one side and stares vacantly out the window of the pub at the warm Spring evening, at the apple blossom of the trees on Hemingford Road. Pub chatter. Pub people. Pub windows. Alex keeps staring out of the window because he does not want to show to Tony that he is biting his lip. Stifling, manfully gulping back the embarrassing rush of emotion Alex keeps looking out of the window at the starry sky,

the jasmined, purpled sky; then he turns back to the pub and he says to no-one, to God, to the barman, to Tony, to the dry roasted peanut packet in the ashtray
— *Katy* . . .

35

bastard killer

Englandwards, deep into the sunlit dales of *l'Angleterre profonde,* Alex drives. Fast. The sun is spangles through the moving and occluding branches of the roadside trees, the sun is octagons on the windscreen of his car. It was raining this morning but now it is sunny, gloriously sunny. Alex's heart lifts. In front he is forerun by pigeons and songbirds scaping from the slades and hedgerows, up and away into the summer coming, icumen in.

So much sun. Morning sun, late May sun, oak apple sun, English sun. Alex looks at the blue barely-clouded sky, a San Franciscan bay with a few white windsurfer sails scudding against the heart-aching blue. Car-window down Alex holds his arm out and up and feels the cool late Spring wind buffet his palm, like he is holding up a waterfall.

Violets on a southern bank. Trees of green and yellow light. Birds, breeze, gearchange, corner: skidding the still-wet road that leads to the road that leads to the road for Lyonshall Alex thinks of Katy, Kat, K, and as the sun shines down he drives faster and sleeker and he slips into a blue thought in this green place: he turns and accelerates and allows himself erotic reverie: a carnal daydream: how he shall kiss her sweet white thighs like a Crusader kissing the blade of his sword before a battle; how he shall take her; how he shall go on the gamewalk of love, spotting the honeybadgers in the forest, scaring the serval in the rowetty, spying the bluethroated iridescent birds of her bright bright blue-and-green-and-violet eyes.

Katy, Katy, Katzenjammer, Pocahontas, John Prescott Junior, Titch; the way she grasped pints with two hands; the way she didn't know what an Al Gore was; the way she held his thing like it was the biggest thing in all the world: *you mean I have to put all of that in my mouth?*

It is Spring, late Spring, the meadows are full of water-avens, the oaks are full of kings. Abrupt Alex turns a hazely, cow-parsleyish corner and finds himself behind a large lorry busily driving down a road too narrow for it. The lorry is knocking twigs from every maple, every ash, every small leaved lime. Sitting back in his car listening to the radio Alex finds his sexual reverie for Katy segueing into thoughts about love. How similarly pointless all love is, he thinks: how ludicrous and incomprehensible: how sweet. Gazing out of his wound-down car window across the sweet fractal complexity of green and golden England Alex thinks it is all so painful, so true, such a dream.

The lorry brakes, the lorry hisses, the lorry grunts: a fat man squeezing down an airplane aisle. Alex turns up the radio, and glances at his watch. He swears. His hand back on the wheel, Alex swears at the time he is taking, and swears at the lorry as he overtakes the lorry on a wider stretch. Now he is making time: pushing the pedal to the floor he accelerates gloriously and wildly down the Lyonshall road, towards the watermeadows of the young Arrow, towards the future and his past. Third gear, fourth, fifty miles per hour, Alex races: until he has to brake suddenly because he is about to drive straight into a TV outside broadcast van.

— Sorry

Alex leans out of his window and waves, saying again

— Sorry about that

The driver in the van barely acknowledges: continues flicking through his newspaper and munching on a garage pasty with half the wrapper still on. Negotiating around the van Alex finds his way is still blocked, this time by police tape: finding a wider space by a hedge he parks and steps out of the car and steps from road to mud to track. Halfway along the track he spies a turquoise feather stuck in a watery rut. Over a stile and up a lane Alex walks; after about a quarter of a mile he looks across and sees: the site of the road protest itself. He is here. He is within a hundred yards of a huge great camp of tents and campfires.

The site itself is bigger than Alex remembers. Much larger, more populous. Everywhere there are protesters: pretty skinhead girls in ankle-length coffeebrown cardigans, unpretty skinhead boys with leather waistcoats and darkbrown suntans and silver nipple-rings. Eco-hippies are proudly photographing each other in front of their teepees; other hippies are singing strange songs and playing flutes and being interviewed by American TV hacks with overlarge microphones. On one tussock Alex sees a discarded violin case; on another a collection of khaki bags, rolls of bin-liner, and a sign saying PEACE being guarded by an ugly lesbian eating a prawn sandwich.

Tribal drums come from one of the treehouses; seated on the fattest bough of the tallest tree, another eco warrior is ostentatiously playing a didgeridoo expressly for the benefit of still another TV camera which is filming out of the sunroof of a Toyota jeep. And where is Katy?

Heart beating faster, Alex wanders amongst the victorious eco generals and tambourine-shivering students and spectating local countryfolk; inhaling clouds of patchouli scent, slipping on unwanted tarpaulins, ignoring plastic cider bottles full of urine and the gaggles of never-washed children and the sunlit pools of rainbowy motor oil and the St George's flags and the CND flags and leadless dogs fighting on the path that leads down to the village, to Lyonshall village, Alex searches, and seeks, and looks, and does not find. He starts to panic, tries not.

The place has an air of victory, but also of departure. Alex sees that tents are being folded; rope bridges cut and burnt. The war is over; the army is going home; so has he missed her? Where is she? Katy. Katy?

Deceived by a topknot of black hair and a cute combat-trousered arse Alex approaches one girl from behind and taps her arm and has to apologise more than profusely

— Sorry so sorry I'm sorry . . .

It wasn't Katy; it looked like Alex imagined Katy'd appear after a year and a half; wasn't her. So where is she? Has she gone home? Gone away? Gone on? Left him again before he even found her again?

Katy?

The sun is hot; Alex strips off his V-neck jumper and strides the camp in his tee shirt, still seeking, still looking: but there is not a sign of her; there are nose rings, puppies, old aluminium loud hailers, council bailiffs in luminous yellow tabards, but there is no Katy; there are minstrels and pilgrims and ululating earth mothers and incomprehensibly stilleto'd London-girl newscasters getting their heels irritatedly stuck in the soggy turf and there is no sign, not a hint, not a glimpse.

Disconsolate, maddened, maddened by the fact that he is feeling so bleak and disappointed, Alex does a final circuit of the battlefield, the Somme that was won.

No good. No K.

So.

So what . . .

So back to the future. Back to the humdrum. Back to the stupid. Back, back, back, back.

Perhaps a pint . . .

Perhaps a pint first.

Taking the path he knows so well Alex jumps another stile

and follows a field edge and find himself on the old-stone Spring-flowered lane that leads into Lyonshall village. Left, a right, past the old post office, warm and mellow and eminently postcardable in the noontime sunshine, Alex passes the gate of the churchyard, where he pauses.

Up the churchyard path Alex does a widdershin around the grey-gold stone of the church and approaches the twin graves: Eddie's grave, Eddie's mother's grave. The sun is high, sweet, the air is sweet with the smell of Spring flowers. The churchyard is green and blue and yellow with forget-me-nots, saxifrage, iris, alexanders. Plucking a clutch of sweetsmelling lily of the valley bells, Alex lays the tiny white bells on Eddie's grave and senses the quiet of the sun, the lilies, the grave, the countryside. And then the feeling, the pang, an old panic.

Katy

That pint . . .

Down the churchyard path and through the wooden gate Alex walks along the sunhot road to the door of the Love Pool where he barely glances at the white plastic table situated underneath the swinging pub sign. Sitting on a white plastic chair by the white plastic table is his ex-girlfriend.

Katy.

It is Katy: alone in front of an empty pint glass reading a book in a slightly muddy red dress with big muddy Doc Marten boots laced up to the calves of her dark bare honey-brown legs. Alex gazes upon her beautiful legs; drinks in her beautiful face: older, cleverer, wry, amused, maturer. Katy has not seen him. She has put the book down and now she is staring out at the sun-shady road with that unconscious half-smile, that dimpled half-smile he loved, so much; he loves, so much

— Katy?

She turns: her face

— *Alex??*

Her voice has got older. Instantly Alex is conscious of how he

must have got older; how he must have aged too; and given that he is already ten years older . . .
— How . . . are . . . YOU – She lays the book flat on the table. Alex sees it is poetry: Keats.
— . . . I'm . . .
— What the F
— I came to see you
— Scary . . .
— How are you? – He looks at her; she looks back
— Fine. You got wrinkly
This hurts. Alex feels his face grimace; Katy sees his pains and says
— I'm joking Alex . . .
— Katy I
— Alex?
— Katy you don't . . . you . . .
— Alex what ARE you doing here? You idiot
She has stood up to kiss him. She kisses him. Alex feels the kiss dry on his cheek as she sits back down on the pub garden chair. He mumbles. One hand on his hip, other palm flat against the black-painted sunwarmed doorjamb of the pub doorway, Alex mumbles while his heart carries on thumping, and he says
— . . . Someone saw you on telly
— Oh – Katy makes a face – That stupid interview, knew I shouldn't have
— Well apparently you were great
Another face from Katy; Alex tilts his head at the pub table, her pint glass
— Would you like another drink?
Looking up, into the sun, looking at him
— I'm not going to say *thigh*
— You never did
— You look OK you know
— That drink?

She smiles, nods

— Pint of lager, export

— Good to see you're still

— QUICKLY or I'll bugger off

In the dark, cool, varnish-scented pub Alex buys the two pints and takes them out into the momentarily dazzling sunshine. Undilating, adjusting, remembering, he carries the pints and sets them down on the table, then sits next to his ex-girlfriend. All the time trying not to remember her, all the time remembering the smell of her, all the time smelling her.

Seated half a foot from each other Katy and Alex look at each other: and then they start. They do the catching up: she tells him how she joined the road protest. He tells her how he's still doing what he was always doing. She tells him how happy and fulfilled she is to be doing something significant for the first time in her life, Alex tells her how he is doing pretty much the same as he was always doing. Holding her pint glass with two hands and burping between slurps, Katy laughs, smiles, looks momentarily too young to be drinking, and then she tells Alex about boyfriends and bonding and living in tree houses and reading love poetry by moonlight and making magic mushroom stew with fifty Dongas by the Arrow; in turn Alex mentions how he's doing pretty much the same as he was always doing.

The only thing Alex is still doing which he has always been doing which he does not mention to Katy is *loving her*, every word he speaks to his beautiful suntanned young-yet-grown-up muddy-booted much-changed-but-still-somehow-the-same ex-girlfriend he wants to be about the love he now realises he's always had for her: instead he tells her crap about newspapers, magazines, his flat. Then Alex runs out of crap to say and he just looks into her enormous Anglo-Portuguese-Pakistani eyes; and she replies:

— You're still in love with me, aren't you

— Katy

— You are, my GOD – Katy sets down her already empty beer glass on the white plastic table, she wipes some sweat from her forehead with a forearm – STILL?

Alex does not know what to say. Katy says

— You know . . . Alex . . .

But then Alex decides, he interrupts:

— Fancy a stroll?

— *What?*

— I want to show you something . . .

Sidelong, she smiles

— I can guess . . . Lyonshall House?

A car swerves by the pub, heat rises from the road, Alex:

— You've been there?

She shrugs in her red summer dress

— Believe it or not, no . . . The police kept it . . . you know . . . pretty much off limits . . . – Frown, pause, confession – Actually, that's not the whole reason – A youthful shrug – After your book . . . after I read all that crap . . . I didn't really *want* to see it. Anyway

— But you still came down here to do the protest?

Katy adopts a wise, pitying expression, an expression Alex has never seen before, then she says

— Completely different . . .

Feeling suddenly alone, Alex gazes over the two empty pint glasses at the road that leads to another country at the end of the village and he sighs

— So . . . ?

At last her hand settles on his hand, her small lovely hand with its badly painted nails; he looks down and says

— When did you start painting your nails?

— Come on, if you really want to show me

Together they rise, as one they follow each other down the lane, down the lane that leads to the Drover's Lane, that leads to Lyonshall Park.

The sky is high. As they walk the lane they both sweat; not minding her sweat Alex takes Katy's hand as he stops and pushes open an old iron gate, hinged on two mouldering stone piers. Surmounting each pier is a crumbly stone lion. Still holding Katy's hand Alex guides her across the meadows, across a shallow stream, following the Queen Anne's Laced lane that leads out onto the lawns that lead up to the House, to the ruins of Lyonshall House. To the shattered grey stone ruins that look monastic against the blue summer sky.

Katy stops. Halted. In her red dress she drops his hand, her jaw drops, she gazes at the ruined mansion. Alex looks at a smudge of grey mud on Katy's nut-brown calf, wants to lick this mud from her calf. Next to him Katy looks at the puzzling shell that was a house; then she turns to Alex and says

— But this house hasn't been lived in for, like, *centuries*

— I know

— But what about

He shrugs; she says:

— You mean it was BOLLOCKS?

— Yep

— The whole thing? All of it?

— Yep.

Soughing in the wind: the wych elms. White stock is swaying and nodding under the burnt-out Jacobean windows of the long-gutted building. The two of them have walked up the weedy lane between untidy trees to the rear of the ruined house; side-by-side they peer inside one of the glassless windows at a room, they scope the fungified plaster on the walls. Her eyes bright, Katy sees the rosebaywillowherb growing through a floor. Beside her Alex sees the rose in her cheeks, roses of Lancaster . . .

Her voice stiff, Katy is saying:

— But what about . . . your friend Eddie, wasn't he a . . . ?

— You mean his name?

She nods; Alex confirms:
— He was a Lyonshall, sure – A shrug – I think there was some connection with the village, otherwise they wouldn't be buried here, all his ancient granddads, but the house . . .
— So all that poetic stuff – Katy steps back from the window and claps the brick dust from her hands; her boots crunch the grass and rubble as they walk away – I mean, I knew you'd overdone it but . . . I didn't think it was TOTAL wank
— Women should only swear in bed
— Ah. Thank you
Alex stares; she stares. Emboldened by her beauty, her tan, the mud, the moment, Alex takes her hand again; irritatedly Katy shakes it free; Alex says again
— Katy I tried to explain it wasn't but you just ran out on me . . .
— Hnn
— To that barman
— *Please*
— So what happened
— ?
— *To the barman*
She pouts, distant
— He was a bit boring, tell you the truth
Alex's heart beats faster; she says in turn
— So what's with that girl, Elizabeth?
— There's nothing to explain . . .
— But you still wrote about her? All those lines?
Alex fumbles a reply. Katy shakes her head and starts walking away from the house down to the riverside; Alex follows her, explaining
— Look. It was crap, just a laugh, druggy crap, that we wrote down. You know? – She is still walking, still ignoring him. His arms outstretched, he keeps trying – We just used to pick mushrooms round here and . . . have a laugh and tell stories –

His eyes widen; he looks at the back of her retreating neck – I mean, it was partly Elizabeth, and Eddie, they had this childhood thing, you see, this fantasy about the house being theirs. And like maybe it was, centuries ago – He gains on her, still gabbling – But we made it up when we were wankered. Tripping. All that dancing cotillions stuff, I mean: *really*. I'm not even sure what a fritillary *is* – Now he shrugs, wistfully – And as for an onyx-topped table . . .

He has run out of things to say, things to explain. The two of them are almost at the river, the banks of the silver Arrow. In a still-huffy way Katy sits down on the grass and starts pulling off her muddy boots; pained by her silence Alex feels he has to go on because he doesn't know what else to do. He wants closure and release, an end; he wants to close with her and never release her. He burbles

— Did you really think that they'd allow them to build a bloody great motorway if there was a real old country house here? Even the Department of Transport wouldn't do *that*

Boots off, Katy sits forward and drops her silver heels into the silver Arrow. Wincing at the coldness of the water, she leans back on straight arms and enjoys the sun on her face, saying nothing. Alex

— It's actually kinda ironic, really, isn't it? You left me because of some trippy load of rubbish we just made up

The sound of a car a long way off. At last Katy speaks, eyes closed at the sun

— Alex I left you cause you were a selfish twat

— But you said

— Yes well, I SAID quite a lot

Lifting her feet from the water, her wet feet on the grass, Katy squeezes her bare knees to her mouth; she pauses, she sniffs her own skin, she mumbles something into her knees. Then she turns from her knees and looks at him and repeats

— I suppose you want to shag me then?

Water, trees, breeze, a heron.

— *Yep*

They make love. Beside the river, they make love; Alex lifts up her dress and pulls down her knickers and he kisses her thighs like a Crusader kissing the blade of his sword before battle and then he penetrates her; her hands twist the timothy grass beside her head; her lovely mouth bites air; dampness stains her summer dress; the herons flap overhead and the kingfishers of her eyes flash in the water; the water of the Arrow of the river, the Arrow of their river that will always flow into the sea.

After they have made love Katy picks bits of England from her dress, from her arms and thighs and between her toes; she pulls on her boots and laces the boots up and then they walk slowly back to the pub, this time via the uphill lane that goes via Moortop Farm.

— So – Katy says – Is this Moortop Farm?

— No, at least, don't think so

Her finger points down the hill they have already championed to a small wood by the river

— Mm . . . Ladies Wood?

— Nope

— Drover's Road?

— Probably not. Think Tony lifted the name from somewhere

— The gardeners? The harvest-thingy?

— All crap, all sampled – Alex shrugs an honest shrug – All tosh. Everything was made up or ripped off. We all . . . sort of . . . you know . . .

They have stopped. They have stopped because Katy is laughing. She is laughing out loud and laughing at the sky and laughing at Alex. Between her giggles Katy says *onyx-topped tables, onyx-topped tables,* and shakes her head. Alex waits, resisting the urge to thump her.

Finally, Katy goes quiet; she smiles, makes a sarcastic face.

Silently they start walking the final uphill yards, until they are standing at the top of the hill: looking down on the village. Stood sturdy and young, like a Soviet World War II heroine in a Stalinist poster, with her fucked up Doc Marten boots, with her ragged but fetching red dress, with the smudge of grey mud on her firm nut-brown calves, Katy Jarrett reaches out a small hand to her older, sadder ex-lover and says

— It wasn't ALL crap you know

His face already burnt by the sun, already hurting, Alex says, half-distracted by the view

— What? The relationship?

His ex-girlfriend, patient

— No. The book, it wasn't all bad. I wouldn't have remembered so much if I hadn't liked . . . bits of it – Eyeing him – You shouldn't give up *totally*

A tractor, a car, Alex

— You really . . .

— Yes, I really

— Really?

— REALLY. Spac

The two of them stand on the lip of the hill that overlooks the village. They stand and gaze and Katy says

— You know I'm not going to go out with you again – She pauses – You know that don't you?

In front of them, out of the hedge, a hare leaps out; trembling, taut, it stops and stares at them, then lopes speedily away. *Like a rabbit by Giacometti*, Alex thinks; *like a rabbit by Giacometti*

Alex says

— I know

And so the two of them stand there; for a moment, for a moment together, they stand and stare, hand in hand, looking out over the landscape, the place where the road stopped. The place where it finally stopped. Beyond and below them the vista stretches, like a tapestry of green and gold, threaded with the silver Arrow; a landscape explained at last, unravelled; a country glinting, minted, fresh with summer rain; an England dewed with Jordan water.

36

welcome-home-husband-though-never-so-drunk

— She's teething, I think

Tony nods, and grunts. Without moving from his pillow he turns over the page of his TV Guide, and smiles: happy to find another reason to stay in for another night. He has found another gardening programme in tomorrow night's schedules. Putting down the TV Guide and picking up his newspaper Tony starts reading the news he should have read that morning.

Across the pillows his as-ever-determined wife props her cheek on a fist and looks across at him and says

— So how was your day

Tony grunts, turns to the Arts pages. Elizabeth repeats her question, louder. Paper laid flat on his lap, Tony sighs, and says

— It was OK. Met up with John . . .

His wife nods. For a moment she seems to think about this answer and then she says

— And the other evening, how was that?

— Sorry? – Tony is stalling, hoping she'll give up; he knows she will not give up; not giving up Elizabeth repeats

— The other night when you went to that work do, how was that?
— Work do?
— Yes, the other night, you know

Tony knows. He knows she knows, or suspects, probably. Fingering his paper he thinks about lying and then he decides on the truth; face to face his wife, he looks into her blue eyes
— I saw Alex

Downstairs the dishwasher completes a cycle, rattles loudly; Elizabeth does not flinch, she says
— I know
— You knew?
— I always know when you've seen him
— Yeah?
— You're always drunk, for a start, you always smell of pubs

Shrugging, unflustered, thinking *what-the-hell* Tony picks up the paper again and starts trying to finish the crossword he started that morning; Elizabeth:
— So
— ?
— How *is* he?

Stuck already on a clue Tony says
— Fine. Ish
— Just that?
— N

More dishwasher noises; Elizabeth reaches over and takes the paper from Tony's grasp and chucks it behind her head onto the floor; he laughs; she says
— Come on. I want to know. Is he OK? Is he still seeing that . . . Janine character?
— Think so

Elizabeth kicks her husband under the duvet
— Ow
— Talk to me, Anthony, you might like it

— What do you want to know? He's seeing some girl, that Janine, he's got a bit older, I think he's receding, he's working for a porn mag, he's still quite amusing . . .

Elizabeth, slowly

— Does he still think I blame him?

— Yes

Elizabeth, decidedly

— Good. Let him stew. Just a bit more

Now Tony chuckles

— You are so kind

— Well

— Well?

She starts

— If you think about it he was still somewhat responsible if Ed . . .

She stops; pretends to listen to the sounds of the house. Tony knows she finds it still difficult to say her brother's name; he knows to stay silent. Bright and determined Elizabeth gets up out of the bed and goes to the bedroom light-switch; from his pillow Tony watches Elizabeth's body filling out her silkthings as she leans as she stretches, he listens to the sss of silk on her thighs as she darkens her way back to bed.

— We've got to get that lamp fixed

Tony nods, reaches out for his wife, in the dark, under the duvet. For a second he considers the sad fact that, at thirty-one years old, he has already made love to the most beautiful woman he is ever likely to make love to: then, as ever, he reassures himself that that was the woman he is about to make love to now, his **wife**, *when she was a dozen years younger; when together they walked the fern strewn glades of M'Ladies Wood, when they ran barefoot down the lawns . . .*

But now to do the trick; Elizabeth is kissing him: waiting. He knows he has to do the trick, to trick the demon of doubt; any minute now

— Shall we?

Elizabeth murmurs, hot murmurs, her pulse visible in the pit of her neck

— Yyyyyess

They kiss, they kiss, he kisses her shoulder; he thinks she is probably not on the pill but what the hell, what the hell if they *do* have another baby, what does it matter, what does it matter what happened, what happened in the past, when the bluebells were a low flame of blue, when the lawns were dappled with deer, when the rooms were bright with silver and candlelight, what does it matter? Tony moves, thinks, *now*. Now for the trick; the psychosexual manoeuvre he knows will arouse him, will gird him; the trick they have come to rely on. On top of his wife Tony leans to her face, her beautiful uplooking eyes, her azurite Lyonshall eyes; he whispers into the curlicues of his wife's small, wifely, aristocratic ear

— Did you?

— Wha

— Did you do it elizabeth?

— Whatdidwhat?

— Didyoufuck him, did you ever fuck Alex?

— Ohhhh

— You diddidn't you

— Ohyyyyyeessssss

— You fucked him

— *Yes he fucked me*

— Didheputitinside you

— Yyyess

— Was he big and hard

— Harder yes harder

— Lizzie

— Harder go *onnn*

— What did he do

— He took me from behind and I . . .

— frombehind?
— Yes he did and he was so
— Did he do it like thi
— So *hard* and so big ohmy
— Jesus I lov
— Tony myG
— Eliza he did oh my sw
— Oh he f o tony my darl oh he oh y oh f oh y